Into the Mindsai

A Region of Significance
Beyond the Veil

A novel

By Nathaniel J. Ratcliff

©2019

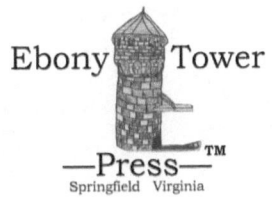

Ebony Tower

—Press—™
Springfield Virginia

Published by Ebony Tower Press™

ebonytowerpress.wixsite.com/ebonytowerpress

ISBN-13: 978-1-7339239-0-3 (Hardcover Edition)
ISBN-13: 978-1-7339239-1-0 (Paperback Edition)
ISBN-13: 978-1-7339239-2-7 (Ebook Edition)

Printed in the United States of America
Library of Congress Control Number: 2019904303

This is a work of fiction. Characters, places, corporations, institutions, and organizations in this novel are either the product of the author's imagination or, if real, used fictitiously without any intent to describe their actual conduct.

Lil' Red Riding Hood
Words and Music by Ronald Blackwell
Copyright © 1966 Sony/ATV Music Publishing LLC
Copyright Renewed
All Rights Administered by Sony/ATV Music Publishing LLC, 424 Church Street, Suite 1200, Nashville, TN 37219
International Copyright Secured All Rights Reserved
Reprinted by Permission of Hal Leonard LLC

Interior designs by Nathaniel J. Ratcliff
Book cover design by Haddy Kreie

10 9 8 7 6 5 4 3 2 1
First Edition

Dedicated to my parents whom keep me focused on the future and not the past.

Dedicated to my loving and ever supportive muse, Shana, who mutually treasures all the memories we have built with one another—and who graciously ignores the ones that should remain in the alleyways of our minds.

CONTENTS

Into the Mindsai

A Region of Significance
Beyond the Veil

Prologue
The Korah Chasm Dig Site
Thirty years B.R.D.

Dark was the night that draped over the scarred desert landscape. The air still had not cooled from the day's sun, whose dying light slipped past the horizon a few hours ago. Gregory surveyed the landscape upon a high outcropping. Before him, a giant fissure split the arid earth, emanating a blackness that swallowed the earthly and heavenly light. In some places, he estimated the chasm to be nearly fifty meters wide. How far down it went was difficult to determine. He would need to wait until the morning light to better assess the lay of the dig site.

Standing there, the paleontologist reflected on the day's journey. It had been just six days since the seismic calamity that shook the Middle East. Estimates had come in that the earthquake registered a 9.6 on the moment magnitude scale which had led some to name it the earthquake of the millennium; the tremors from the quake were felt as far away as Paris and New Delhi.

According to the reports he read, it was believed that the earthquake had been triggered when a meteorite composed of primarily iron and about one hundred meters in diameter struck directly on the Dead Sea Fault. Scientists speculated that the odds of such co-occurrences were astronomically small. Working in an academic field with similar odds to find a fossil on a given dig, he was inclined to agree.

The images that he saw of the aftermath were remarkable. The meteorite left an impact crater two kilometers wide and 500 meters deep. People looked like small ants standing in the bottom of it. From aerial shots, the fissure that scarred the earth was perhaps more astonishing. Extending for dozens of kilometers in northerly and southerly directions, a great crack had split the surface of the earth along the main fault line. It was wider than a car in most places and went to depths that were difficult to determine from the footage.

Striking in the mostly rural and uninhabited area of Mitzpe Ramon in southern Israel, the impact did not cause much direct damage.

The indirect effect of the quake, however, did deal substantial damage to the surrounding areas. In particular, the city of Jerusalem, located 130 kilometers away from the epicenter suffered tremendous shaking. He had seen it firsthand once he stepped out of the airport. Many parts of the holy city had been completely leveled. Perhaps most tragically was the complete destruction of the Islamic holy site, The Dome of the Rock. The shrine had stood the test of time, surviving environmental, political, and religious strife since the first century C.E. When the earthquake shook Old Jerusalem, people reported that the golden dome split in half before crumbling down to its foundations. In the aftermath, only rubble and scattered mosaic tiles remained of the revered site. By contrast, the foundation on which the Islamic shrine stood, the Temple Mount, remained relatively unaffected save for scattered cracks that were added to the others in the long-standing stone walls.

The destruction of the Islamic holy site had inauspicious timing for the perpetually unstable region. Tensions had already been high since a series of remote-controlled drone bombings had killed nearly a dozen Israeli school children in previous month. Now with the ruin of the holy shrine, tensions were flaring between Muslims who wanted to rebuild the shrine just as it was and Jews who viewed the destruction as divine providence, and an opportunity, to finally restore their own holy temple. After seeing a large protest of activists on both sides throwing rocks at one another, he was glad to get out of Jerusalem as soon as he could.

Overall, the earthquake damaged or destroyed many homes and businesses in the region, killing about 1,500 people. In its wake, the quake left many pronounced seismic fault lines that etched through the regional landscape. Even the timeless Dead Sea and Sea of Galilee were affected; the seismic activity had nearly drained the Dead Sea and the Sea of Galilee had become a turbid black color with the smell of sulphur and a bitter taste that killed all of the fish and animals that drank its waters.

The region was in turmoil, but with great change, there can be great opportunity, and that's what brought him here. When word reached him after the earthquake event, of strange reports by Bedouin shepherds of dinosaur bones and early human artifacts being found in the remote southern desert of Israel, he was eager to see what had been unearthed—despite the dangers of potential aftershocks. If the stories he was being told by an old archaeological colleague were true, then he had hope that the earthquake might have brought forth a priceless new paleontological discovery.

After arriving in Jerusalem, it would be a long two-day journey through Israel's scorching Negev Desert. He was accustomed to the heat, having grown up in a rural town in the outback of Australia. After obtaining his doctoral degree in paleontology at the University of Chicago in the United States, he returned to his homeland to search for prehistoric fossils in the Australian deserts.

They had set out on the expedition with a host of Bedouin guides, his archeological colleague Dr. Byran, an undergraduate research assistant, and nearly a dozen Israeli laborers to help with any potential excavation. It was small expedition, but it was what he could put together in such short notice. He could not let this discovery go to waste.

The earthquake had damaged many roads so the expedition had to go forth on camelback to reach the intended location about eight kilometers northeast of the small village of Shitim. During the journey, he had mused that it was amazing how quickly a calamity can reduce human beings to such primitive states; only a thin sheet of ice exists between civilization and falling into barbarism.

The caravan had reached the site of their dig a few hours before sunset on the second day. At first sight of the trench that had opened up in the ground, he was in awe to see it up close. Many of the Israeli laborers were uneasy around it and had begun to refer to the great gulf in the earth as the 'Korah Chasm' after the family in the Hebrew Bible that had been engulfed by the earth for disobeying their God. Some of the more superstitious workers even noted they could hear whispering sounds emanating from the black pit, but he had dismissed these concerns outright. These phenomena could be explained by the natural reverberating of the ground as it settled from the quake.

What was truly remarkable was the dinosaur bone that their elder Bedouin guide had showed him and the team upon arrival. Protruding from a rock outcropping, on a recessed ledge about twenty-five meters down into the chasm, was a well-preserved ilium of a predatory dinosaur.

"It was a beaut," he had commended to the guides.

Upon closer inspection it looked like a small fissure had set in the dorsal half of the fossilized bone. With a closer look, his heart nearly stopped when he recognized something lodged in the crack, something that had no rightful place in the Cretaceous Period. There, embedded tightly in the fossilized bone was a twenty-centimeter bronze spearhead, dull and jagged.

There was no doubt that the spearhead was authentic. Dr. Bryan had confirmed it himself. As an archeologist who specialized in Bronze Age civilizations—and who had a flair for the obscure—he was one of the world authorities who could confirm its authenticity.

Despite the verification, the past rumors, and the sight that had been before his very eyes, he had questioned the Bedouin guides relentlessly about whether they had planted the artifact in the dinosaur bone. *It just couldn't be possible*, he had thought to himself finally coming to terms that, despite the questionable antics of the Bedouin guides, they had led him to a magnificent dinosaur specimen that he was ready to excavate immediately. He needed time to reflect on it, which is what had brought him to his vantage point that evening.

He had been standing there for probably an hour. The darkness drew in upon his vantage point requiring him to squint to see the terrain. He stood stoically, lost in his thoughts, overlooking the camp that was now abuzz with productivity. A small band of laborers had already begun the meticulous process of removing the overburden from the fossilized skeleton. It was good to start at night to avoid the harsh desert sun that would come with the day and he did not want to risk aftershocks potentially upending his find that laid precariously close to the mouth of the chasm. The journey had been too long and arduous for that.

Down the embankment, he heard footsteps rolling over rocks. His young undergraduate assistant, Henry, came to join him on the outstretched crag that overlooked the camp and the chasm.

"G'day, Professor Allen, I hope I am not disturbing you," Henry said as he approached him, watching his feet as not to stumble on the coarse boulders at the hill's summit.

He kept his gaze transfixed on the black gulf before the two of them, giving Henry only a passing glance. It was enough to see that Henry's blue cotton shirt was still covered in a fine grey dust from the day's journey.

"No, not at all," he replied curtly in his thick Australian accent.

"Is everything coming together all right? The camp, I mean?" Henry asked, his eyes darting to search for the response in the low light.

"I think she'll be all right, if I do say so myself. We're making excellent time and should have a good portion of the skeleton uncovered come sunny side up."

A period of silence fell over the two overlooking the camp until Henry broke it, "Do you mind me asking you a question?"

"Oh yes, you're quite fine to do so," he responded without moving his eyes from the landscape before him.

"Well, I've been thinking a lot on our journey down here…a lot about what some of the Bedouin tribesmen have been telling us about our digging site, especially in light of what we found today."

"Now, Henry…" He started, as he turned to finally look at his undergraduate assistant. He could see the zeal on the young lad's face which was partly obscured by the mop of dirty-blonde hair that was blowing in the evening breeze. "…you've got to know that these nomadic herders still cling to very old beliefs and superstitions and do not have the trained eye to discern the scientific realm from the impossible."

Henry kicked a few stones over the rocky outcropping with his brown hiking boots before looking like he had mustered up the courage to push forward with his inquiry.

"I know the stories of fossils in this area was a driving force to bring us out here. Some of the tales were pretty fantastic alluding to human artifacts being found near the same layers of bones that should predate them by millions of yea—"

He interrupted abruptly, "That can easily be explained by geological disconformities when layers of rock are upended and appear to mix with other layers. This would especially not be surprising given the amount of seismic activity in the area. And besides, these nomads might have planted that spearhead to increase their pay for such a bizarre and priceless find. Once you have more experience working with these sorts of blokes, you'll soon learn their sly trickeries."

"I know, I know, but hearing these stories directly from some of our guides and seeing the sincerity on their faces really makes you think about the possibility, doesn't it?"

"For me, no. The science has provided evidence for many centuries that the co-existence of animals in the Cretaceous Period and the Quaternary period to be highly, I mean *highly*, unlikely."

"I don't know, I guess that tribesman with the unusual gold and dark blue head scarf who I spoke to on our way down here got into my head," Henry replied with a half shrug.

He looked ponderously at his assistant for a moment, "Hmm...I don't recall seeing that individual in our party, what did he tell you?"

"For a rural Bedouin, the man was strangely knowledgeable about our science. I guessed he had once lived a life with good education before moving to this rural environment—he must have learned fast because he could be no older than in his mid-thirties. He spoke so quickly that my life nexus device could barely keep up with the translation on-the-fly. He told me, and I'll read it from my nexus' transcription,

> The popular sense of time occurring over the course of millions of years seems to be in contradiction to what we can see and what has been passed down through legend and myth which are all rooted in an original truth. Every ancient civilization has some depiction of great beasts that resemble dinosaurs; the Chinese have their dragons, the Sirrush of Babylon adorn the Ishtar Gate in Persia, the Roman St. George is painted slaying a dragon, and the temples of Cambodia are carved with large beasts with the spines of which could only resemble plant-eating dinosaurs. Given that humans on record had not begun to fully-assemble ancient fossils until the near-end of the nineteenth century, it's hard to fathom how cultures pre-dating paleontology by hundreds and thousands of years were able to

provide accurate depictions of the creatures that had been buried in the ground…and merely stumbling across a lone bone or two would not account for that level of accuracy.

And that's what he told me," Henry said looking back at Dr. Allen.

"Did you try to educate the man on the current consensus of scientific thinking on the geologic record and our use of advanced radiometric dating?" he inquired, half with curiosity and half to test the knowledge of his young pupil.

"I did indeed. But he had a clever retort for that as well. He pointed out to me that most evidence seems to point to the fact that animal fossils were deposited rapidly due to some cataclysmic event, like a flood perhaps. He said that the discovery of fossils where dinosaurs were found in mid-birth or in a final death grapple suggest that their burial wasn't due to chance conditions that allowed for a slow preservation of the animals.

"To radiometric dating point, he strongly questioned it as our basis of time. He suggested that radiometric dating is fallible due to its fundamental assumptions of decay rate; decay might vary across the same elements and, being in an open system, decay rate could be affected by other environmental forces like cosmic radiation. Even our observations of decay are over a relatively small time period—maybe a couple hundred years—and then extrapolated to be occurring similarly over millions of years. It could be quite possible that decay is not linear but logarithmic; like how the rate of water flow changes from when a gallon jug is full to almost empty, if we're just measuring at the near-empty point then our measurement will be off for the larger timescale."

"That is indeed an interesting way of putting it," he said chuckling, "Although it is true that we can't go back to the beginning and observe elements across time, and therefore, don't have the complete picture, we do have countless studies that replicate the same pattern of findings that provide inarguable evidence for the use of radiometric dating. It's basically settled science at this point."

"That's exactly what I told him, Professor! And, for his part, he was very gracious in listening to me without trying to interrupt. After I finished, he smiled at me and tilted his head before telling me,

> I know I am but a man of the earth, but I tell you true, man of science, you only study nature in a man-made room and come out into it when required; we live with the earth, we were born in it, shaped by it, and our every sense is connected to it. We might not have the words to describe it, but in our own naïve way, we have our earthly science of how things work and what might be possible, that you would never see in your laboratory surrounded by your own fallible man-made devices. You might never discover something if your very assumptions are wrong, and don't seek it out. Perhaps the present is not the key to the past, as you claim, but the past is the key to our present; I think you'd be amazed at how quickly man forgets truth with the passing of time and human memory.

That was the last thing he said to me before going off to set up camp."

He shrugged, "He sounds like an interesting fellow, I think I would like to speak with him, maybe provide him a bit more insight on why we are here and what we do…And maybe ask him why we haven't found a dinosaur and a man holding hands," He added, chuckling.

Henry's eyes turned away quickly, "That might be difficult, Professor. I have asked all around and no one has seen the man with the gold headscarf with sapphire eyes since we went to look at the dinosaur bone. I asked the Bedouin elder's son and he told me that he found a note in the man's tent with an old proverb that he could make little sense of."

"What did the note say?" he asked softly, slightly intrigued.

"The son told me that it said 'Seven signs, seven veils; in the land of the blind, the one-eyed man is king' which meant nothing to him. However, he repeatedly told me not to worry, the man with the gold headscarf only joined his group the day of our arrival. He believed him to be a vagabond and not too reliable. But he has plenty of hands to do the work that is required."

He considered the strange behavior for a few moments before shaking off any concern for a man that didn't understand their purpose.

He stared back down at the camp. The bright work lights were now at full intensity.

"We've been absent from the action too long, my boy. We should return to the dig. There will be time enough to ponder philosophies in our drafty old lab after all. We must relish the thrill of the dig while we can!"

He grabbed his upturned bush hat he had laid on a large rock and trudged down from the cliffs overlooking the camp to head back to the dig site. It was a moonless night, making every lantern in the camp a lonely light in the darkness.

As he walked, he reflected on the conversation he shared with his assistant. The conversation had been somewhat unsettling to the excitement that he expected to feel the night of a big dig. However, he found himself lost in thought about the arguments that had been brought forth by the strange Bedouin man. It would have been easy to dismiss everything the man said out of hand based on his scientific training, but for some strange reason, the points that were raised dug deep within him.

He recalled past debates that had shaken the fundamental thinking of his field. In the late twentieth century the evidence had mounted to move past the long-standing idea of uniformitarianism and gradualism, or the idea that the geologic record reflects a slow, continuous account of the past, to the idea that the geologic record reflects episodic events laid down due to catastrophes such as volcanic eruptions, asteroids, and earthquakes. Once more, at the turn of the century, the field almost succumbed to a schism in thought when soft tissue was found in the bones of a Tyrannosaurus rex from the Cretaceous Period.

Many began to wonder if perhaps the entire field's accuracy of dating might be in question with the discovery of intact red blood cell proteins that were previously thought to be impossible to be preserved on timescales longer than a few thousand years, let alone, sixty-seven million. However, the field retrenched itself and dismissed the episode as an outlier when no fossilized bones since had shown any similar levels of preservation. Some even suggested the original finding to be a fraud and not much more was discussed or investigated further, to what many established experts, including himself, had felt to be a distraction and a pox on the scientific integrity of the field as a whole.

The dig site was abuzz as he approached. In the glow of cold blue lanterns, about a dozen laborers were painstakingly removing the gravelly overburden from the exposed bone. It had only been a few hours, and the workers had exposed most of the fossilized pelvis and the beginnings of the dinosaur's rib cage. He was now assured that it belonged to a predatory animal in the genus tyrannosaurid, perhaps a Tarbosaurus.

He was impressed by the progress and was about to return to his tent for a coldie when a bulbous shape caught his eye between one of the exposed ribs.

"Oi! Henry! Grab me a brush and the geo hammer," he said urgently as he moved carefully across the make-shift wooden walkway that was scaffolded near the edge of the obsidian-colored chasm.

Henry acted with haste and brought him the tools he had requested. He slowly brushed away the grains of sand from the smooth, rounded object that began to take shape.

The more debris that he removed the more his hand began to tremor; at first, he thought it might have been an aftershock but soon realized that his nerves were beginning to fray.

"What is it?" asked Henry curiously.

"I'm not quite sure…" he replied, grabbing his geological hammer to knock away some loose overburden.

A chance hit from the hammer splintered much of the remaining rock, revealing the mysterious shape he had been so feverishly pursuing.

"It's…just not possible…I mean how could it be? No one could have planted this here, I cracked through the rock myself, but how…" His voice lost itself in the light breeze that had just began to whistle through the chasm.

He and Henry stood in silent astonishment for a few minutes as they attempted to process the scene. Before them, in between the two ribs, was a round human skull. The mouth was agape and a tiny crack permeated up from the right eye socket.

"That's unequivocally human, Professor!" Henry exclaimed.

"But it can't be, how over the course of almost some hundred-fifty years has no other person uncovered something like this? I just can't fathom it," he said in utter disbelief.

"That's true, Professor, you'd think someone would have stumbled upon some evidence like this," Henry paused and just shook his head trying to mouth out words for half a minute until something came out again. "But I guess when you think about it, not too many complete dinosaur skeletons are found, and the number of ancient human skeletons found to date could fit on a pool table, so I guess the odds have been infinitesimally small to find both in the same place in a way that could be directly connected." Henry finished, trying to grasp at some reason in the sight of the impossible.

Dr. Allen continued to stare and cock his head.

"If we can verify the veracity of this find, this could change everything, I can't even process this right now. Could we really have deceived ourselves so long in our own murky assumptions? I can't believe that. Entire history books would need to be rewritten, our field would fail to be paleontology anymore but would becom—"

"Archeology," Dr. Bryan said, cutting Dr. Allen off. "This is quite remarkable. All the rumors, artwork, and sculptures from antiquity must have been true. We thought they were but myths, but myth is staring in the face of reality."

All he could do was shake his head in disbelief at the new truth that now befell him. He did not want to believe; to believe would mean he would have to uproot everything he knew to be true. His training and education were as fossilized as the bones before him, but now it all was beginning to erode away into the wind.

In fact, the wind had noticeably picked up around the dig site. It was noticeably chilly for this time of year. And with the wind, a silence fell across the desertscape. He felt that something was not right. Looking at Dr. Bryan, his research assistant, and the laborers, he saw the excitement of the find wash from their faces, turning to a fearful, vigilant stare.

Reverberations from below began to tremor up the walls of the chasm. Tiny rocks began to rattle on wooden planks on which he stood.

Bugger me, an aftershock! His mind cried out.

The ground began to shake violently.

Falling to the side of the cliff, he desperately crawled up the embankment trying to hang on with all his might. Chaos ensued around him; laborers scattered up the cliff face to try to get to safety. A man ran too carelessly amidst the turmoil and lost his footing. He flailed his arms trying to grab for the ladder out of the dig site but it too was torn from the cliffside and all fell into the black depths of the chasm.

A growling sound pierced his ears and the smell of sulphur strangled his nose. Cursing his luck, he reached to grab a small pickaxe to help secure him in place.

And then something caught his eye. At first it looked like a passing, darting shadow of one of the many tumbling rocks that were falling all around him. Peeling his eyes, he knew it wasn't something rolling down—no, it was something was crawling out of the fissure!

Its shape was hard to make out, almost as if it was blurry. He could tell the thing was long and slender with elongated fingers slowly grasping the rocks towards him. Its eyes, could be made out clearly, however, and they were terrifying. They were the glowing red embers of a dying fire, hot and unmoving. And there was more than one shadow figure creeping towards him and the rest of the digging party. Some shadow figures had already climbed out of the chasm and were darting from boulder to boulder in jerky, contorted movements, chasing after the few laborers that had climbed out.

He was frightened in a way he had not been since he was a child. Back when a shadowy T. rex had haunted the outside of his window in a recurring dream he had as a child. He would often wake in a pool of cold sweat as the image of the ferocious tyrannosaur with glowing red eyes faded before his awakened vision.

But that wasn't real, nor could any of this be, he clung to the thought but knew that it was a thought on the same unsteady ground that he now clung so desperately.

He could feel the ground shift beneath him. It would soon give way if he didn't crawl to safety. The thought of leaving mankind's greatest find to a destructive fate sickened him. However, if no one survived this chaos, mankind would remain in the dark, but for how long, another millennium?

The thought of that troubled him more.

The wispy shade continued its slow approach towards him as the world seemed to fall apart around him. People were screaming yet none of it seemed to rise above the discordance of splitting rock and swirling wind.

He made one last ditch effort and threw the small pick axe at the figure which neither affected the figure nor stalled its approach. With no more options left, he scrambled backwards up onto the exposed fossil that had been uncovered. Cleaving to the find that could define his career and shake the field apart.

"What are you!?" he cried out to the figure that was now almost upon him. His voice barely audible to himself in the whirlwind.

The onyx figure made no verbal response. Its face began to contort in a twisted manner, stretching out with a long snout and raised eyes, much like that of a...carnivorous dinosaur. The deep ember eyes, however, remained fixed upon the paleontologist with cold resolve.

It was at last upon him, staring right through him, as if it understood every meek thought running through his mind. The figure's outstretched hand pierced through his leg with a sharp burning, scratching sensation, as if his very flesh was being peeled from the bone. A chill of pins and needles shot through his body as darkness began to tunnel his vision.

The sensation felt like floating in air until he realized that the entire dig site had collapsed into the chasm and he was in freefall. In his mind, it seemed like minutes were passing away as he fell deep, down into the shadowy abyss below. In his final thoughts, he knew that he would be lost to humanity, just like his discovery. He would be buried with it until someday, someone would find him with the truth that could shake the foundations of thought in the world. But now, only a veil of darkness fell across that truth— and his consciousness as well.

FIRST STAGE

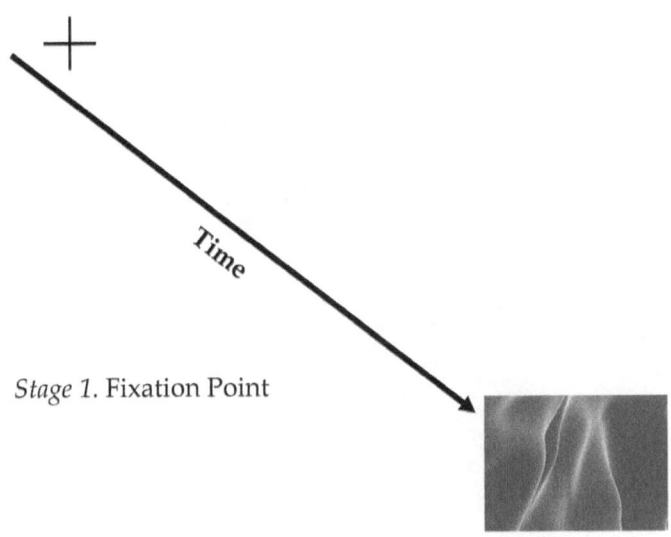

Stage 1. Fixation Point

"Subjects seem to be unaware of the myriad memories that lie just beyond the veil of consciousness...often reaching with all their mental might only to fix a fleeting glimpse of what is just beyond the spotlight of the mind's eye..."

Seeing through the Shroud:
Barriers to Accessing Total Human Memory
- Dr. Sebastian Silva,
Five years B.R.D.

1

Dr. Silva's Laboratory
Two months B.R.D.

Bash found himself staring across a shore of glimmering crystals. He knew he was really in his office but the daydream felt so real, like a flashback of a distant ephemeral memory that he could never quite fully grasp. He picked up a shimmering crystal and skipped it across the shore; each skip over the gems made a different tone that resonated in the manner of a mallet hitting bars of a xylophone. A warmth overcame him from an unseen sun as he closed his eyes listening to the sounds of waves rhythmically crash against the shore.

When he opened his eyes again, he was running, on a wooded path. He could feel the moss squishing between his toes as he was chasing something but could not quite make it out. He suddenly came to a pair of intertwined sycamore trees. To the right was a sun-filled clearing and to the left the path wound through a dense thicket of contorted trees that were covered with vines hanging down, obscuring what lay beyond. For some reason, he took the less tranquil path. He held up his hand over his eyes as the branches slapped over his face. The ground beneath his feet became cold and solid.

He removed his shielding hand. The light was dimly veiled and he was standing on a rocky ledge. Before him was a seemingly bottomless gulf. A sense of hopelessness fell upon him as he approached the edge. His heart thumped, and thumped, until the scene faded before his eyes to the thump of a knocking at his office door.

Dr. Sebastian Silva's office was half-lit by the buzzing glow of old fluorescent lights as his mind slowly came back to the present. Although the majority of offices were equipped with the latest energy-efficient, flexible OLED light panels, Bash (as his friends and colleagues addressed him) preferred the humming blue-radiance of phosphorescence that he had productively worked under through grad school and tenure.

Another light series of taps came at his office door. It forced him to gather his wits. He got up from his well-appointed leather chair and went to his office door. He opened the door to find his newly arrived graduate student, Aliyah Woods.

"Dr. Silva," the young student said, greeting him with a nervous half-smile.

"I told you Ms. Woods, you can just call me Bash."

"Oh yes, sorry. I'm...I'm here for our first meeting."

He looked her over. With white ruffled blouse and a pair of black dress slacks, she was severely overdressed for the occasion.

"Right. Come in and take a seat!" he said motioning her in.

Bash sat back down in his leather chair and watched his student meander her way to her seat on the other side of his desk. She stood reluctantly behind it clutching a brown leather-bound notebook.

The young lady was in her mid-twenties. Her slender frame glided across the room where only her chestnut brown hair seemed to ruffle as it fell back in waves on her caramel skin. In truth, her most distinct feature was her face. Its pleasing heart-shaped features were accentuated by dimples on each cheek and a little crinkle on the left-side of her nose. And when she smiled, the pearly-white teeth between her black cherry lips seemed to raise the lightness of the office by several orders of magnitude.

"You have such a beautiful office; I love the wood paneling and bookcase," Aliyah remarked in a soft voice.

"Thank you, I guess that's one of the perks of working hard to become a full professor—you get a nice, spacious corner office," he said, taking notice of an office that he had given little consideration for in quite some time. "Please, have a seat." He motioned to the chair before her.

She obliged and gently took her a seat.

"Thank you. I know I've said this before, but I'm so honored to be in your lab. You are like the father of the cyber psychology field and have done amazing things linking neuroscience, memory, and cyber technology with so many applications."

"Well that's nice of you to say. Though, to be honest, with the advent of virtual reality technology reaching a tipping point, there was really no choice but to take psychology into the virtual domain. Since so many people spend so much time in virtual environments in their free time, psychologists had to go where the people were to study them."

"May I ask, what got you interested in memory and virtual technology?"

He sat back in his leather chair and pondered for a moment over the query.

"That's a good question…" he began, still lost in thought, "…I don't know if I can point to a single antecedent to my interest in memory, but I would say that my own lifelong relationship with memory has inspired me to study it and push its limits. You see, since as far back as I can remember—which from what I've gathered is a lot longer than what most can recall—I have experienced very vivid, eidetic autobiographical memories. These memories are detailed images of the past that appear almost as if you are experiencing it in real-time. I would describe it almost like playing miniature film clips of episodes in my life, being able to describe fine detail of color, location, sounds, and even smells in some cases."

"Oh fascinating, I bet that can be both a blessing and a curse," she responded with sincere interest.

"Indeed. The memories can be haunting; sometimes I feel like my mind is like an empty mansion filled with corridors of unlocked doors just waiting to fly open and reveal some ghostly scene of my past that I thought had long been lost to the shadowy abyss of my subconsciousness. At any given moment, a door could swing open and I am instantly hurdled back into a flashbulb moment in my life that could go on to spread to any number of associated moments. The process whiplashes my mind across memory and time."

"So, you experience very intense flashbacks of your past?" she said, leaning in. Closer, he could see her brown eyes widening and filling with light. They held patiently to take in everything he was about to say next.

"Precisely! And sometimes more. In fact, just before you came in I had a flashback memory. Only I do not think that this memory was from *my* past," he replied.

Her eyes narrowed. "Uh...how can you have a flashback that isn't related to your past?"

"Have you ever heard of ancestral memory?" he asked, trying to test the bounds of his new student's knowledge.

"You mean like genetic memory?" she asked, not waiting for a nod of confirmation. "I know in the early part of the twenty-first century, like 2012 or 2013 there was an article in *Nature* authored by Callaway that found that the offspring of mice who were trained to fear stimuli were also fearful of the same stimuli despite having no prior personal experience with said stimuli."

Impressive, he thought to himself. It was that razor intellect that had made Aliyah stand out from the rest during the many laborious interviews. He could always pick out brilliance, even if it was harder to find as the years drew on.

Aliyah continued, "And I think more recent experiments, many decades later, have found that humans might also possess this ability to inherit memory through DNA ancestry, although only limited to implicit memory like making easier to learn how to ride a bike or learn a non-native language."

Most impressive. His new student had much potential and he felt pleased that he had picked her out over the many students who were falling over themselves to be in his prestigious lab.

"Do you see the picture hanging on the wall?" he said, motioning over his shoulder behind him.

"Yes, it looks like two intertwining trees…on some path…it's very beautiful," she replied.

"I took that picture fifteen years ago during my first visit ever to the town in which my parents met and grew up. However, I've seen *that* path and *those* trees in my memory for as long as I can remember. Despite never visiting that location I have 'seen' those two trees in my memory since I was a very little child. It always happens in the same way; I am chasing something down a path and I veer to the left of this unique pair of trees."

"That is odd, what do you think it means, Professor?"

"I have reason to believe that it is a past memory, not of my own, but of one of my parents. And I do not think I am the only one who has experienced this before. Throughout the centuries there have been many documented accounts of people claiming to have intense déjà vu or memories of past lives. What if they were experiencing a past life, not of their own experience, but that of relatives that came before?

"Jung would have called such a phenomenon something a part of the 'collective unconscious' but his musings from long ago only scratched the surface, lacked focus, and he never had the means to go deeper.

"Today, with some of the most advanced equipment in the world, this lab is on the cusp of a breakthrough. One that will reveal to humanity the existence of memories that transcend our own existence. Memories that have lain hidden but always just out of reach. But not anymore, the science we are doing here now will enable us to finally reach out and grasp them!"

Aliyah's head shook emphatically up and down, her eyes were sparkling.

"Wow, that would be incredible if that were true. To be able to provide evidence that people experience episodic memories of family members would be a truly groundbreaking finding. You could see yourself growing up through your parent's eyes!"

He shook his head, side-to-side.

"No. Unfortunately, with ancestral memories, it is somewhat a theoretical limitation that we can only see back to the point of birth when the genetic memories were transferred. So, I could not see my parent's memories beyond when I was born, but any time before that transfer point should be accessible.

"And that is precisely what we are trying to discover in this lab. What lies deep, beyond the realms of typical human memory. We endeavor to explore how to access every possible human memory that might be available for retrieval."

"How does one possibly plan to study something like that?"

"Come, I'll show you…" he said, getting up and leading his new student into the adjacent lab.

Like his office, the lab space was larger than that of the typical faculty member in the department. When he had been promoted to full professor he had demanded a bigger space that was directly adjacent to his office so that he could be close to his work. Being a well-known name in his field, he felt that he had earned the right.

The lab had high ceilings with three large picture windows overlooking the Hightower University campus that stretched out down the hill below. The room was filled with tangled wires that led from various supercomputers to an assortment of headsets and probes. Although messy looking, he was pleased to see all the equipment at his fingertips to achieve his dream. So many other dreams had faded, but he knew he was on the brink of achieving something he had been pursuing for decades.

"This is our lab space. As you can see, the equipment we have available, most of it custom built, is at the vanguard of technology for studying memory and interfacing with the brain on a neural level," he said, pushing back his shoulders.

He watched as Aliyah looked around with amazement. Her eyes darted to and fro at the expensive laboratory equipment, the fine furniture, and the fantastic view through the windows. Eventually, her eyes fell upon a prominent corner of the room that housed a large headset which hung over a black chaise longue.

"What's the purpose of this? I like the modern take on a reclining couch, very vintage," Aliyah asked.

He regarded the studded leather reclining couch for a few moments with quiet admiration. The couch was old, older than him. Long ago he had found it stored away in dusty, moth-eaten sheets in the basement of this building. It must have been a relic from perhaps almost two centuries before. When he had a graduate assistant help him drag the antique out, he found that the upholstery had succumbed to the ravages of time—or better yet, the teeth of rats that frequented the dark and dank places of the basement. *Sure,* he had thought, *I might need to reupholster it, but the bones are good.* The woodwork was in immaculate condition for its age and he relished the idea of the history that its once supple surface had supported over the centuries. Who could say what tales had been told, what secrets lay encapsulated within the hardwoods, that if loosened, would escape into an air, out of place and time—if woodwork could talk.

This reminded him of a long time ago, when some believed in the pseudo-scientific Stone Tape Theory, that events could be recorded in surroundings left by some sort of psychological residue from an intense moment in time. Supernatural phenomenon like ghosts were merely events being replayed endlessly from the stone and wood structures that had captured and encoded the intense psychological energy, analogous to a tape recorder that people find in museum exhibits from the twentieth century. But true science knows that the inanimate has no memory and tells no tales. The only recorder is between one's ears and it quickly succumbs to the teeth of time; fading away, or distorted through others, unless recorded in the digital ether of cyberspace.

Aliyah walked around the recliner with child-like curiosity. It pleased him to see his student take such a genuine interest in his laboratory. Even with all the accolades, most do not get to see where the science is made.

"May I sit?" Aliyah asked politely. "I've always wanted to sit on one of these psychology couches. There aren't many of these around anymore besides in pictures and museums."

"Of course! Take a seat. Lean back." he replied.

Aliyah kicked up both of her legs and shimmied into a relaxed position with both of her hands crossed over her waist. As a petite, pear-shaped girl, she looked so small lying on the couch. Her dark hair with golden brown highlights laid still next to her shoulders.

He noticed her eyes were fixated on the spherical head-piece that overhung the recliner.

"That is the crown jewel of our lab. Hanging above the couch is our sixth iteration of SEER goggles, or more precisely, Structural Extrasensory Extraction and Recollection goggles."

"What do they do?" she asked inquisitively, seemingly not understanding the meaning behind the acronym he had so carefully chosen for his most treasured research device.

"To give you the short answer, they help the user locate and recall memories. The SEER goggles sit over the user's head and then attach with an array of miniature probes that prick just below the epidermis…" he said, noticing her quizzical look at the array of pinpoint probes lined beneath the SEER device.

"Oh, do not worry about those. They do not hurt a bit. Feels like placing a stiff paint brush on your head…"

Her concern washed from her face but hints of perplexation remained subdued.

He continued, "The probes serve three primary functions. First, they send impulses to help map the mind to locate memories, mostly in the medial temporal lobe and hippocampus regions. Within the neural tissue, the machine searches for engrams, the biophysical changes in the brain that allow for the storing of memories, and marks them for analysis. Second, once identified, targeted impulses are sent to activate stored memories.

Lastly, the probes receive the activated brain impulses and decode them into the SEER goggles' internal viewing monitors that create a visual environment that is near-indiscernible from reality." His voice began to rise as he grew ever-more excited detailing the inner-workings of his machine. It pleased him to see that he had not lost his new student yet, so he went on.

"To provide a true porthole into the mind's eye, the aptly-named Mindsai machine is completely driven by the user's mind without anything added by the machine. The Mindsai simply decodes the mental imagery of the targeted memory and precisely stimulates the corresponding brain regions to access the memory using the brain's own biomechanical processes to reconstruct memory. Once activated, the memory is typically vivid and does not require extensive representation outside the mind. However, relying completely on the brain's mechanics can be taxing on the user. To solve for this, the internal mental image is amplified and projected within the SEER goggles for the user to see the memory with minimal effort." Normally, when he explained this process to reporters, their eyes just glazed over with incomprehension. Looking at Aliyah, she was so enraptured by the details that her eyes fluttered on every new detail. He fed her more…

"The goggles do not show a digital image, but rather an analogue of how we see…in reverse. You see, the Mindsai analyzes the activation of the occipital lobe from the reconstructed memory and determines what configuration of light would be required to make a similar activation pattern. The SEER goggles reinterpret this information, amplify it many times, and then projects images that match the memory signature," he said, pausing, for he was nearly out of breath in all his excitement. He leaned over on the machine to rest, trying to hid his fatigue. The metal housing was sturdy but gave his arm a chill from the hundreds of liters of coolant that flowed through its body.

Okay, time to bring it all together.

"When accompanied with a sophisticated algorithm executed on the quantum super computer behind you, the device is able to search for memories, activate them, and display them for the user in a very vivid, real-to-life reconstruction."

Aliyah glanced back at the massive computer towering behind her. Little bits of lights popped on and off in a rhythmic orchestration. Even when not in use, the machine seemed like it was thinking intensely. The machine had cost him tens of millions of dollars. However, being the patent holder on his Mindsai VR interface tech afforded him a generous source of research support that the university, flush with money from his innovations, was happy to provide.

"This is all so amazing! I've read so much of your work, but seeing it first hand is just fantastic. Even standing here it's still hard to believe what all this equipment can do," she said, her face in awe.

"It is amazing, indeed. For years, scientists believed that old episodic memories were eventually consolidated in the neocortex to increase the efficiency of encoding new memories. Thus, for all practical purposes, old memories faded as people created new ones throughout their lifespan. A dramatic example of this is what most scientists call 'childhood amnesia' that occurs around three to four years-old. It is believed that once a child develops language to describe their world, the memories built before language lose their meaning and are marked for deletion by the mind with a new way of explaining the world."

Aliyah looked at him somewhat uncertainly. Her face crumbled around the brow, her lips quivered in a reticent dance of the internal debate that of whether or not she would speak or not.

She started in a low voice, "I have heard that, about childhood memories…" Water filled the edges of her eyes. "I must be an outlier then since I have memories that seem to go back to when I was less than a year old. In some of my earliest memories of life, I can remember looking out behind the bars of a crib in the dark. My eyes were fixated on the shadow of one of my parents that came dancing down the hallway, aglow in warm yellow light. And strangely, sometimes I feel there are more memories before that one that I just can't seem to grasp."

He was intrigued but not surprised about this possibility. He too had experienced memories of his childhood before the age of four. He often recalled taking baths as an infant in the sink of his parents' and grandparents' home.

The newness of everything stood out in his mind from these moments; the sound of rushing water, the warmth of the water dribbling softly over his tiny back, the croaking sound of the drain that scared him into thinking that just somehow, if his tiny legs got too close, would fall down into the dark abyss of the drain that led to a mysterious place he could not fathom to guess—but he instinctually knew it was not a pleasant place to go. But the grandest part of these moments was the love he felt as his mother carefully lifted him up high from the draining basin into the fluffy gentle throws of a towel that coddled around him in a place of absolute security and warmth. The memory was an architype for joy and love for him that could not be rivaled by any that came after.

He smiled at those thoughts and spoke reassuringly to Aliyah's experience, "I believe the limits of the mind are near infinite, one only needs the right triggers or understanding of the mind to gain access to what lies buried deep in its recesses. Everyone has memories that might be inaccessible without the right key and I think our research has discovered that key.

We completed some pilot tests and have successfully documented the recovery of a fleeting memory after a delay of one year…And just last month we made a major breakthrough— we were able to recover not just a mental, freeze frame of a memory but an entire minute in vivid detail from over ten years ago!" he exclaimed. "Our test subject reported never feeling a more intense feeling of déjà vu."

"Oh, I'd love to see it in action. Could I try?" she intreated.

He admired his student's tenacity and bravery, but also noted the naïvety within the request. The machine was still in its infancy by technological standards. Many things still needed to be calibrated and worked out.

"In time, señorita. It takes many weeks for the computer to initialize the data mapping for a new test subject. But since you have me here, and you seem so enthusiastic about the project, why don't I give you a brief demonstration. After all, I could go on for hours on what it does, but you learn the most when you see the process hands on," he said not unkindly.

In truth, he loved every opportunity to show people what he had accomplished and where he wanted to go. He believed he was on the verge of a discovery that could change the very nature of the human experience, perhaps spring-boarding humanity into a major evolutionary leap forward. He wholeheartedly believed that humans are the masters of their own destiny, limited only by their own minds to innovate and find rational, scientific truth. And he relished his role as an intellectual trailblazer to unlock the full human potential. Sure, some might see his ambitions as arrogant and self-serving, but if humans were to reach a greater potential, someone must push the envelope to get the ball rolling.

He went over to the terminal of the Mindsai which interfaced with the supercomputer and the SEER goggles. He started to initialize the start-up procedure. More lights began to flicker on as the machine awoke from a restless sleep. Like all custom-designed machines, the Mindsai supercomputer lacked the elegant refinement of the devices afforded to the masses. But what was lacked in elegance, was made up for in sheer, unadulterated power. The computer used a dualistic doppelgänger design, with one half consisting of a 500-qubit capable quantum computer and the other half consisting of a classical supercomputer capable of achieving processing up to 200 zettaFLOPS. In combination, the Mindsai had the raw resources to analyze the entirety of the human brain in real-time.

He was proud to be the owner of only one of two such machines known in the world. The other one was owned by the government who utilized the machine to monitor the patterns of individuals across the globe with the ability to synthesize and predict behaviors, even on a crowd level in a manner of minutes. Given that nearly every aspect of the home and office were connected to cyberspace, gathering all types of information on citizens around the world was of little difficulty unless you were some sort of kooky primitive living in the quickly-shrinking backwoods of the world. Thus, in effect, there was little people could do to hide from the lidless eye of the virtual government domain.

Technically, the supercomputer that powered the Mindsai was on loan from the government, but given his contributions to science and some monetary pull that he personally applied to the powers that be, he had been granted access to utilize the device for purely academic purposes. Although he did, from time to time, use the machine's vast processing ability to win a few bets with colleagues.

"Now, what memory should we have a go at?" he asked lightheartedly at the touch controls of the computer.

"What about one related to your first week in graduate school, Professor? I would be interested in seeing how much better you handled it," Aliyah said timidly.

He considered her for a moment with one eyebrow raised slightly. His ember eyes peering at his young student inquisitively, trying to figure her out. *I wonder why she chose that memory*, he wondered. *I should be glad she did not choose others, there are some doors in my mind that are best left shut. If one of those doors should be opened, there is no telling where the spreading of activation would lead, what corridor of doors could fly open, playing events that should remain suspended indefinitely.*

After a few moments, he shook his head up and down with his lower lip pushed up towards his nose in nonverbal approval.

"Most appropriate, I would say. Although you might be surprised at my lowly beginnings," he chuckled.

Aliyah laughed, "Oh, I can't imagine that."

"You won't have to imagine much in a few moments once I get this thing fired up. Through our efforts, we have essentially created a time machine, allowing anyone to travel back in time to re-experience any memory they possess…" he said as he punched in a few more commands into the terminal. He continued, "With a few more months of research, we may have on-demand access to every memory anyone has ever experienced…and soon, beyond that, we may be able to glimpse ancestral memory for the first time.

"I have waited all my life to test the empirical possibility of such a phenomenon. Finally, technology and human ingenuity has reached a point in which my theory can be put to the test. I plan on doing a pilot test of that possibility in a month or so. You have arrived at an opportune time to witness history!"

"I'm honored to be here, Professor," the young woman said humbly. "Although I must ask, is there any risk to these experiments you are doing? Is there a possibility of brain damage or someone experiencing something so real that it could endanger them in the present?"

"That is a good question. I assure you, we have taken all the necessary precautions. The review board would not let us pursue our research if the parameters were even a smidgen near the danger zone. Over the course of a couple hundred experiments, the worst thing that has occurred was a headache or two and strong arousals of emotion caused by the memories that have been brought forth, which is to be expected. Other than that, we have had a stellar record. Besides, do you really think I would be willing to use the machine myself if I did not think it was safe?"

"I…I guess not," she responded, relaxing her posture.

He gave her a disarming smile.

To be honest, the review board had a hard time saying no when he leaned on the university president to pave the way for his experiments, he thought to himself. *But I know it's safe. I, myself have used it countless times without incident. Besides, without risk, there is no progress.*

He took a seat on the reclining couch and turned to Aliyah to provide additional instructions, "If you would like to see the memory I am experiencing, you can view it on the telewindow monitor over there." He pointed to a large viewing screen capable of real-to-life imaging that was positioned on the wall directly across from him. "It would be ideal to have you put on a set of SEER goggles yourself and experience the memory with me. Unfortunately, in our past tests of dual memory saddling we found that the Mindsai, for all its computational power, cannot support the generation of memory for two minds concurrently. It would require two Mindsai machines to accomplish such a feat and we are lucky to have just this one at our disposal." He let out a half sigh. Aliyah had turned back to listen to him directly, her eyes were wide as if they were sucking in every syllable of information he spoke.

"As the technology advances those will be future goals. But for now," he said, redirecting her gaze back to the wall, "you can view the reconstruction on the external monitor on the wall. We are still trying to get the calibration right so the image feed may not be perfect, but you should be able to see a decent visual representation of what I will be experiencing."

Aliyah nodded her head and walked over to a chair in front of the large viewing screen. The screen was currently black, save for some changing values indicating that the Mindsai was in the process of making the necessary calculations for the target memory that he had entered into the machine. As she sat down, Bash noticed a peculiar object that was hung about her neck, half-concealed. The object appeared to be a tiny crucifix made of a plain, unpronounced wood-like material. It had been quite some time since he had seen someone wear such a symbol of faith; there were not many who openly professed, what he believed to be outmoded superstitions.

You were married to just such a person once, his inner voice said betrayingly. But he did not want to think of *her*, not now. His wife had passed away from brain cancer over fifteen years ago. She had been devoutly religious in the most kind and unimposing way. She would have loved for him to feel the same way, but she respected his freedom of choice and the fact that he encouraged her to discuss her faith with him. *That was a long time ago, no need for these intrusive thoughts today*, he thought to himself, trying to refocus his mind on the task at hand.

"All right, here we go," he said ardently.

Bash grabbed the SEER goggles from above his head and carefully brought them into place. He could feel the tiny pin pricks of the probes as they settled into position. His entire scalp felt tingly, like it was in a sea of pins and needles. The tingling seemed to pulse in a wave over his head and down his back. It made him squirm against the cold leather couch.

Even though this was near the twentieth time he had been under the cap, the feeling of embarking on another trip still exhilarated him. He could feel his pulse begin to race as the machine was about to engage the commands he had entered a few minutes prior.

The machine slowly lurched into action with a dull electric hum. He closed his eyes thinking of the targeted memory. He could feel a slight tingling from the cap of sensors as they began to synchronously burst and connect with his mind. Like a tidal wave of consuming fire, his thoughts broke forth into a frantic search. His mind raced from random scenes of his past as the machine zeroed in on the chosen memory. Fleeting glimpses of past friends, loved ones, and beautiful triumphs flashed by him. The pace was white-knuckling, like being in mortal peril on a rollercoaster with life, literally, flashing before your eyes.

The roll of images started to slow down as his mind felt as if it was suddenly heavy-laden. He could feel his mind being pulled into a well of gravity, that pulled him down, deep into the recesses of memories he had not considered for the longest time. The mental mass of his being was descending into a singular point, becoming more and more concentrated, as if he were being smooshed into a tiny mason jar.

Eventually, the falling slowed and then he felt himself settle. Not too long after, the weight lifted from his mind.

At first, there was only darkness. But then each of the senses came to him starting from the lowest order. He could smell the musty scent of old books. This was followed by the dry taste of nervousness that was always present when he was in a new, unfamiliar setting. Third, he could feel a hard, uncomfortable wooden seat under his butt. Then the hush sounds of a library came over him. He could hear the soft murmur of students whispering and the shuffling of feet down the stacks. Lastly, since it was the most difficult sense to summon forth, his sight began to take shape. Like a dimmer switch that was slowly being turned up, the scene came into clarity and focus before him. He was in the campus library after his first day of classes as a graduate student at the University of North Carolina-Chapel Hill. Before him, on a tiny wooden desk, several textbooks and loose lined sheets of paper with his scribblings were strewn about.

In the back of his mind, he knew the Mindsai machine had locked in on the memory he chose but those thoughts were academic and seemed far removed from the now. The absolute realism of what he was seeing, what he was experi—re-experiencing was incredible. He had to correct himself because sometimes, even he could barely parse the re-creation from reality. The only real difference was the fact that his perspective was fixed to what was originally experienced. He was an observer without any real agency in the memory; there was no moving your head or body in a way that was incongruent with the original experience. It was an eerie feeling almost as if you were possessed in the body of another, but the other, was *you*, just in the past.

Bash, looking through the eyes of his past self, was in a cubby hole looking out at the stacks in the back of the campus library. The dull-blue fluorescent light of the ceiling fixtures discordantly mixed with the amber sunlight of the dying day which shone through a solitary window at the far end of the walkway. From the pale white drop-in ceiling, he could see the dust particles pirouetting in the air, falling aimlessly to the worn mint-colored commercial carpet. The place was quiet, only a faint echo of footsteps could be heard off in the distance. Not many students were ready to get down to work so soon after the first day of classes. It was syllabus week leaving the place still and quiet.

He glanced down. His advanced statistics book lay open alongside his scribbled notes he had taken in class. Formulas and Greek letters adorned his page like an ancient cipher. He had spent the whole latter half of the afternoon trying to figure out the model specification for a multi-factor structural equation model. He could have easily done it on his computer but this instructor was old school in every sense of the phrase. In fact, he was shocked the man was even functioning. The instructor looked like he was eighty years-old and had hobbled in with a cane with a tube protruding from his chest to supply him with some sort of insulin infusion. Some professors just hang on too long. Nonetheless, his homework was due in two days and he had only barely made any headway.

His fingers tapped aimlessly on the table beside his textbook. Perhaps their rhythm would unlock the key to the problem he had been grappling with, he hoped. The rhythmic beat seemed to sooth his over-taxed mind. So much had been thrown at him on the first day of graduate school. He had to adjust to a full schedule of classes, remember the names of fellow students in his incoming cohort, and most nerve-rackingly, figure out how he was going to teach his research methods section the following day to students who were probably just as smart as he. How in the world could I have the authority to teach something to students who were only a year or two younger than himself? The anxiety only seemed to increase the pace at which his index finger tapped against the wooden tabletop.

Suddenly, a loud noise rang out behind him. He whipped around. A book had fallen. No one else was around making its fall strange. He cocked his head slightly to try and make out the title on the book's spine. The lettering was worn on the pale green backing, but he could barely make out the title as *Days Gone By*.

After a few lingering moments, something else caught his ear. A faint sound that was out of place. It was his own voice he could tell, but not from this time. It sounded deeper, older.

The scene before him began to break apart and fade. A tunnel of blackness enveloped his peripheral vision and ever more quickly converged into the middle of his vision until all was dark. A floating sensation overtook him as the sounds slowly began to amplify and become clearer. He heard himself reciting a poem, and knew with mournfulness where his mind was taking him.

"—Forget me not my dear, I will remember you. / Though days, months, and years barrel down, / Behind a red door I place our every moment, every sight and sound. / On an autumn eve, under a blanket of stars. / A millennia's teeth couldn't diminish you in that French gown..."

His eyes cleared and he could see his wife, just as she was on the night of their tenth anniversary. Emma looked radiant sitting next to him curled under a fleece blanket leaning against the trunk of a felled tree. The campfire light flickered in her golden-brown eyes giving them the appearance of two tiger's eye gemstones. Only a tiny silver cross hanging between the creases of her hand-sized breasts could challenge the flickering in her eyes. Light brown hair hung limp over her smooth porcelain skin of her face. Her lips quivered slightly in the cool October night air as tiny wisps of her breath made their beautiful escape into the darkness and then vanished just as quickly as they had come to be.

The sea of stars in the sky somehow raptured his attention away from his beautiful wife. Each twinkling jewel shone with majestic resolve to the murky blackness that surrounded them like an encroaching shadow ready to envelop them all. He had chosen this remote spot of rural West Virginia because of its unprecedented view of the night sky, free from all the light pollution that scattered the celestial view. He had told Emma earlier that he was going to give her a thousand diamonds for their anniversary. When she first opened her eyes in this remote spot, she remarked that no earthly diamond could compare to these in the heavens.

Now, looking at the awe across her face, he felt contented to see the sight he had been most looking forward to seeing that evening.

"Bash…" Emma whispered in his right ear, "do you think you will remember this moment forever as well?"

"Like all the rest, I will not forget a moment my dear," he heard himself respond.

For a moment, he almost forgot that this was all a memory. *This must be what it feels like to be too 'in tune',* he surmised to himself. In the past, an insignificant minority of subjects reported feeling lost in their memory. Despite only experiencing the event for a short time, they did not remember that the present waited for them only a few centimeters away in true space. Due to its rare occurrence, he and his researchers had not really explored the potential issues that could arise from someone being lost in their memory without the ability to return to present reality. After all, that was kind of the point of the process, to make things seem as real as can be. Given his current feelings, perhaps it was an issue that warranted further examination.

Now, fully aware of his predicament, he needed to surmise a way back out of his memory state. He was way off script and did not have an inkling as to why.

First, he needed to stop the program. The machine must have lost its lock on the targeted memory, he began to realize. The one coming forth felt exceedingly natural and had overtaken the program's directive. Normally, when such events would occur and the recalled memory got off target, the entire process would disengage and the user would be thrust back without any issues. This time, the machine was still operating without tripping the fail-safe mechanism. *Curious,* he thought. *Very curious, indeed.*

Although he cherished this bittersweet memory of his wife, the thought of being stuck in it for an indefinite time made him uncomfortable. He did not panic, he just needed to think things through for a moment.

The moment was short-lived as his wife snuggled her head into his chest. Her hair fell over his arm as if it too was offering an embrace.

"Don't you wish this night would last forever my love," she said softly, in a voice that was far off and dreamy.

"We will always have it in here," he replied, patting her head gently. She closed her eyes and her contented face remained fixed.

After a long, admiring look, he found himself staring out into the woods that surrounded their campfire site. The firelight reached back a score of trees before falling off into a shadowy darkness. The engorged fire popped and crackled beside him in the quiet night. There was not much as a whisper of a sound out beyond the fire, save for the descending *wooo-ble-ble* trill of a screech owl somewhere off in the dark looking for prey.

Before long, a twig snapped. He jerked around, out of sync, and saw a wispy white figure of mist running away from him into the woods, darting quickly off to the side of two intertwined trees. And then vanished beyond.

He stared intently for a moment trying to process what he saw. He could feel his eyes bulging out of their sockets trying to capture every piece of light reflected from the trees. His focus was so zeroed in, he began to feel as if the darkness itself began to pulse in rhythm with his heartbeat. The pulse grew more intense with each beat until the very periphery of his vision slowly began to close in around him. A distant bellow of buzzers seemed to echo across the mountain side that were accompanied by strange but familiar voices that seemed quite out of place. His mind slowly succumbed to the darkness as he stole one last look at his sleeping wife, cuddled contently in his lap.

His return to consciousness was greeted by a French woman, or more precisely, the voice of his grad student's annoying ancillary artificial intelligence (AAI).

"...the man seems to be in good health with normal vitals for his age and slightly over-weight physique. Shall I pull up questions to discern his degree of mental faculties, Craig?"

"Craig, will you turn that thing off!? You kids could not think for yourselves nowadays to save your life. By the time that thing got to the right diagnosis I would be rotting in the ground somewhere," he rebuked.

"No, I think that will be all for now, Daisy," Craig replied dismissingly.

Bash still felt rather disoriented. A visual aroura occluded his peripheral vision with tiny semi-transparent squiggly lines. His head ached deep behind his left temple with a piercing pain that mushroomed when he shook his head too quickly in any direction. It felt as if he had just succumbed to a massive migraine, unlike any he had experienced before.

"You look like you had quite a trip," Craig said sardonically.

"I feel like I have fallen 10,000 meters straight onto my head," he replied.

"We were pretty worried about you there for a moment," Aliyah added, with more concern in her voice than Craig.

"What happened exactly? I came into the lab and saw you using the machine with her just sitting there looking kind of panicked," said Craig.

"I am not quite sure really. What did you observe from the monitor, Aliyah?" Bash said, trying not to color the events that transpired by offering an anchor point.

"Well...the machine started up and seemed to be working fine. In fact, it was amazing. I could see every detail of what you were experiencing in what looked like a library; I couldn't believe how clear and vivid the memory was. I can only imagine how it must be to experience, or re-experience, it firsthand." Aliyah paused and looked down at her shoes.

"Yes...and?" he urged.

She continued, "However, after a few minutes, the screen just went black and I couldn't see anything. I mean for a moment I could see the figure of a woman cast in what looked like the light of a fire but, like I said, it was only a brief look which was followed by darkness. After some time, I began to think something was wrong and called out for help. That's when Craig came into the room and got you disconnected from the machine."

He considered Aliyah's description of events silently for a few moments before speaking.

"The woman you saw, she w-was my wife."

"Even with only a short glimpse, I can tell she is very beautiful," Aliyah complimented him.

"Alas, she was…" He took a few moments for the words to solidify in his throat, words that pained him to think about, let alone speak with veracity, "Emma…died some time ago, of a brain aneurysm. It happened so quickly and then she was just…torn from me and no longer there. Just a hollow husk of the woman I loved."

"Oh my God, that's terrible, Professor. I am *so* sorry," Aliyah responded in a soothing tone that was genuine and kind.

"It's all right, that was some time ago. Almost two decades have past sinc—" He stopped abruptly, taking notice again of the cross that hung around Aliyah's neck.

"I think it was actually the cross around your neck there that triggered the memory for me," he said pointing. "You see, Emma wore a silver cross around her neck and I think seeing it on you reminded me of that."

"It must have been a powerful memory for it to cross-jump the system," Craig interjected.

"Indeed. It was the night of our ten-year wedding anniversary. We had decided to go to a remote mountain top in West Virginia to view the stars. It is a precious and bittersweet memory, for the weekend that followed, Emma was afflicted with her aneurysm and I lost her in the course of two days," he responded somberly.

"Well, if it is any comfort, the thin slice that I saw of her looking at you was one of complete adoration and love," said Aliyah.

"Thank you, you are too kind. But enough about that. We should probably do some diagnostics on the Mindsai to prevent it from jumping memories uncontrollably in the future. We cannot have people jumping around anywhere in their minds without some safeguards.

"Craig see what you can do in the computer system to add some code to prevent that from happening going forward," he directed.

"Uhh…sure thing. Daisy and I will start going through it all this evening after everyone leaves. Isn't that right, Daisy?"

"I am all yours for the night, Craig" Daisy responded again, in her French accent, emanating from a small device tucked over Craig's ear. It contained a speaker, camera, a processing unit, and a host of other sensors for the AAI construct to sense and interact with the world.

"Great Daisy, it's a date! Now, let's start by downloading the data from Bash's time in use. I want you to analyze the sensory array and tell me the moment the memory lock was lost and the order of sensors that unlocked, ordered by brain region and impulse magnitude…" Craig said to Daisy, as he walked off to a computer terminal.

Bash clinched his jaw and shook his head. A large percentage of the population had a corresponding ancillary AI to help them answer questions of varying complexity at any given moment during the day. These AAIs were not creative but could tackle and synthesize enormous swaths of data to provide insight for exceedingly complex problems. Most simply asked their AAIs to recall some fact with many conditionals or describe how something worked. He was opposed to the idea and did not have a personal ancillary device attached to his person. He found the whole idea of having access to vast amounts of synthesized information a crutch for people who did not wish to challenge their minds. The mind grows soft and feeble without use.

After Craig walked off, he noticed a blinking red light flashing from the machine. He turned to Aliyah, "And I also have a task for you, señorita."

"You do?" Aliyah responded incredulously.

"It may be your first day, but I like to get my students running quickly. I would like to invite you to the committee meeting coming up in a few weeks. This meeting is really important for deciding how quickly we can move on to the next stage of testing. However, I need some old lab notes stored down in the basement of this building to serve as reference for our proposal. And...since that red light is blinking over there on the Mindsai, I suspect we need a new fuse for one of the super-capacitors," he said looking over towards the machine. Craig was next to it tapping at the computer terminal with Daisy feeding him an on-the-fly assessment of the computer system.

"Craig, will you show Aliyah our storage space in the basement to get a new fuse for the Mindsai?" he requested in a volun-telling tone.

Craig didn't respond, being engrossed in his work.

"Craig... ?" he petitioned.

Nothing.

Bash was agitated. He liked people who worked hard but also liked those who listened.

"All right...DAISY! Tell Craig I wish to speak with him," he repeated. *Craig may be able to filter me out, but Daisy is always listening for a command,* he thought.

Daisy spoke in her soft French accent, "Craig, your attention is being requested by Professor Silvia."

"Oh...sorry...did you need something? I'm trying to make headway on the machine," Craig responded absent-mindedly.

"I was trying to ask if you would show our *new* student, Aliyah the basement storage area to get some of my old notes and grab a new fuse for the secondary super-capacitor," he said insistently.

"I...uh...can't Gabe do it?" Craig responded.

"I would really rather *you* be her guide, that would be my preference."

"Sorry, but I think my work here is a better use of my time, to be honest," Craig said softly, yet firmly, pointing to the computer terminal.

He was a more than peeved by his senior student's cheekiness but decided there had been enough excitement for the day and conceded to his student's wishes.

"Fine then, I expect you to have that finished by tomorrow then," he stated firmly.

"But—" Craig croaked, but was cut off.

"No buts, I want it done. You and Daisy work through the night if you have to, I am sure she loves sleepovers," he said looking at Craig with a firm eye before turning to Aliyah.

"All right, go down to the fourth floor to room four-ten and find Gabe Coleman. He is our undergraduate research assistant and he will be able to guide you down to the sub-basement where we place equipment, notes, and items of odds and ends in storage. I really appreciate your help and I think you will do well here. I will touch base with you in a few days to see how you are doing and I will give you a more formal briefing regarding the up-coming committee meeting," he said, starting to grow weary.

"Okay, Professor. I'll go find Gabe. Thank you so much for showing me around and I feel honored to be able to go to this important meeting. I'll see you later," she said. She smiled agreeably and turned towards the stairwell at the end of the hall outside the lab.

After Aliyah's departure, he looked around the lab. Craig continued to be engrossed with his work and the sun was hanging low in the Western sky. Not too far from the descending sun, he could glimpse the first lone star emerging from a darkening blue backdrop. *Oh, the stars have not changed a bit, that constant diffusion of light, but somehow, seem to have lost their glimmer in these past years,* he thought to himself.

He stood in a quiet pondering for a moment and then headed back to his grand office, the one he had worked so hard for, to gather his stuff to go home.

2

Bridging an Impassable Gulf
Two months B.R.D.

He left the lab around seven in the evening. For a tenured, full-professor Bash was leaving hours past what others of his status normally worked, which was scant in his opinion. For most, to be a tenured professor was a cushy job; come in for a handful of hours a week to teach or go to meetings and then spend the rest of the time 'thinking', err, sitting on your ass.

He had no doubt that his drive was the primary reason for his success. It was his hard work and determination that got him so far and opened many doors. He could have had his pick of being a professor at any prestigious institution of his choosing. Many had tried to lure him with large sums of money and fancy titles; however, he chose to stay at Hightower University. It was the place where he started. A place enveloped with so many memories he could not leave behind. Not to mention, the perks of being a big fish in a small pond allowed for an extensive network he could lean on and pull strings to allow for unencumbered research.

Academia reflected the modern state of society. Not many workers toiled in the fields or on factory floors since the Automation Revolution. Technology had freed many from work and provided the masses affordable leisure. The work that remained was that of engineers and scientists to devise ways to further advance society and provide entertainment. Whereas the work of old focused efforts towards the collective good, automation allowed people to focus inward. For many, the desire to remember and document every moment of life was paramount; status was often measured by the monuments that people built unto themselves in their own virtual domains. It was this commercialization of his research that kept him well-funded.

Despite the opportunity for a life of leisure that society could now afford him, he had remained, as some whispered in the halls, *desperately dedicated* to his work. He had never paid those hallway whispers any mind. Research was his passion, the only activity he found leisurely. His mind simply could not remain still, sitting at home twiddling his thumbs. Spending his days in some fake, curated world would have driven him mad.

Many would have been satisfied with his career accomplishments; a pioneer of cyber psychology, he had been the first to discover a brain wave algorithm to allow virtual reality technology to be accepted by the brain as seemingly real. Essentially passing the Turing Test of virtual reality technology, he had developed a device, the Mindsai mind-body interface, that drew on the mind's own faculties to drive virtual environments, making virtual reality indistinguishable from the real to the perceiver. What used to be run by a graphics processing unit, was now self-generated by the brain itself using his own program and physical interface. It was this breakthrough that propelled him into winning the Nobel Prize, only the second psychologist to do so.

He had also revolutionized the field of memory. Walking in the footsteps of the great neurosurgeon Wilder Penfield, he had just recently discovered a means to accurately map where specific memories were encoded and stored. Whereas Penfield had only unreliably been able to stimulate areas of the temporal lobes to bring forth vivid memories, he had discovered a non-invasive means to bring forth memories with great accuracy and specificity. His device and algorithm could identify the area of the brain where the memory resided and bring it forth, on demand, through intercranial stimulation. It still brought a smile to his face recalling the seminal moment when the world learned that a test subject could correctly recall a fifteen-digit mix of numbers, letters, and unfamiliar symbols engraved on the back of a silver spoon they had only been exposed to briefly a year before.

Thinking of these accomplishments was a private solace he carried with him as he slowly descended the marbled steps of the psychology building. A biting cool breeze brushed against his face as he passed beyond the protection of the tall sentinel pines that stood guard at the entrance of the building. Fall had arrived early this year.

Above him, the tree branches pattered against the building. Their taps made different sounds as the limps fell upon the brick and glass edifice. One of the branches obscured the name plate of the building, 'Hugenberg Hall.'

That limb needs a trim, he thought. Dr. Hugenberg had been a renowned cognitive psychologist at the turn of the twenty-first century, developing seminal work on the memory of faces. He continued to stare at the placard with Hugenberg's name. At one time, it was forged of solid bronze. But now, time had robbed the golden gleam and replaced it with the tarnished patina of an earthy brown. *People should know the name of this building and the great work that has been done in its halls*, he thought, and started his walk.

The breeze continued to blow from the East in its vain effort to catch the setting sun. In a couple of hours, darkness would follow and the air would become much colder, and still.

Responding to the unsettling chill, he pulled his heat umbrella from his satchel bag to warm him on his long walk home. The device had a length of thirteen centimeters for the cylindrical compartment that contained the heating element, battery, and disbursement fans. A press of a square red button released five long tubes that stretched up beyond his head and bent outward, then down surrounding the upper part of his body. Once the fans engaged, he was enveloped within a bubble of hot air that whirled forth from slanted openings in the tubes.

His walk home brought him through the center of campus which sat on a ridge that overlooked the Northwestern Virginia town of Talawanda Springs. The slant walk that carried his feet was hard and littered with the debris of crunched leaves. Students were a scarce sight; most had already retired to a bar or to their abodes in the virtual ether, returning to their preferred reality.

Only one young couple could be seen on a bench that sat adjacent to the Triangle Building behind Old Main. He huffed when he noticed that even the two of them could not disconnect from the digital domain; both wore augmented lens that shifted the environment around them and captured every living moment. He had even heard that some were now changing their own appearance in the real world to match their idealized, digital personas so that every reflection they saw of themselves was beautiful. Beauty was no longer a precious commodity when you could shape the look of yourself and your partner to be whatever you desired.

These artificial lives were never what he intended when he set out with his research many years ago. He wanted to help the mind experience the full potential of humanity, not replace it with a gilded shroud.

Despite these lamenting sights, he enjoyed his walk home. The sight of Old Main towering with its ivory steeples never lost its luster, even now in the chill air. From the front lawn of Old Main, he looked out to see the tiny town of Talawanda Springs resting below. Lights were slowly popping on like clockwork as the shadow of the ridge crept forward slowly over the town. He could see the path that he would take home, hugging the hillside in a serpentine sway through trees that came out near some solitary buildings on the town's outskirts. The setting sun flickered red in the waters of Lost Fork Creek that ran parallel to the academic mount and continued to sweep by the town center. These analog sights made his walk home memorable; every time was unique.

More than anything, his walk home was a time he could be alone with his thoughts and process many of the challenges that persisted to pick his mind. Many of his greatest epiphanies had come to him on his evening walk. Tonight, he wanted to work through what had gone wrong during his demonstration to Aliyah. His mind turned and toiled as he strolled along the well-manicured sidewalks and lawns. However, he found that he could not get his mind turned over, it just stalled and sputtered out.

His thoughts drifted away from his day, carrying him not forward, but back, inward. He found himself in a familiar place, what he often thought of as the manor of his memory. The venerable words of a Dickinson poem, that Emma had loved so much, trembled on his lips:

> *One need not be a chamber to be haunted,*
> *One need not a house;*
> *The brain has corridors surpassing*
> *Material place.*

In his mind, his conscious-self rested in a study. The study had an old-world look to it. Dark wood panels lined the walls in between the inlayed oaken bookcases that reached upwards to the impossibly high ceiling. A long black drape hung from another wall and looked as if it had not moved the slightest bit in a lifetime. Dust floated all throughout the air but never seemed to accumulate on any of the objects in the room; a globe, a model sailboat, a jar of sand—all relics collected from a past he treasured and could not let go. In a corner, the soft glow of the fireplace dimly lit the room with dancing firelight. Above it, sat a worn portrait whose visage had long worn from any recognizable figure of himself. At the room's center, sat a worn brown-leather chair that many of times had offered him repose; though solace had eluded him for some time. Looking around, he realized for the first time that, in a curious way, the study resembled his office. This revelation provided him a melancholy amusement for he knew that it was the other way around: his office décor was an attempt to mirror that which had always been present in his mind. Like his life's career pursuit, he sought to take the nonphysical and make it reality.

There were certain aspects of this study that he could not recreate, even though in his mind, none of it seemed out of sorts. The study was also surrounded by countless corridors that wound out in ways that would challenge the physics of real space. He was alone here, but not alone truly; the uncountable corridors contained a myriad number of doors that each opened up to a different moment of his past. There he would find familiar faces, voices, and feelings; some welcomed, some uninvited. For most, every day after an event the memory slowly fades to be more distant; for him, each memory was like it occurred yesterday, raw and enduring. Sometimes, when he sought solitude in his mind, it was these uninvited memories that would whisper down to his study and haunt him. Most of the time he could keep these specters at bay, but other times he could be overcome and drawn to doors he did not want to reopen.

Today was one of those days. His mind had strolled too close to a corridor he often found little pleasure in being near. He could hear the croaking voice reach out down the drafty hall, "Baaash, come closer..."

For a moment, he wavered. He knew what lie past the heavy burgundy door with peeling paint. It was Emma, or, one of his final memories of her when she was living. No, it was not the *final* moment, but perhaps it was more painful than the end, for it was in these moments that the last vestige of Emma remained before she slipped away into...into emptiness. After she lost her cognitive faculties, she ceased to be *his* Emma; the unyielding advancement of the aneurysm had assured that. Every other moment he had of her he had driven himself to remember, often indulging himself in them over and over. Yet, this memory held a darkness underneath its door that he painfully endured when it became unlatched and crept open in his mind.

Tonight, he felt drawn to open that door, to revisit a dark time for himself. His hand reached out trembling, to open.

His hand landed on a rusted wrought iron gate. Rods rose up from the metallic barrier, capped with ornate fleurs-de-lis. The cold metal met his flesh with an unpleasant kiss. A sign creaked in the evening breeze a few meters beyond the gate. The sign read: 'Grand View Cemetery, open from sunrise to sunset. If in-memoriam legacy port is non-active, please notify the groundskeeper.'

He had no recollection of how he got here from across the greenspace of Old Main. His mental disassociation must have led him to this place. He was unnerved by his lapse in awareness, but not surprised; Grand View Cemetery was where Emma's body had been laid to rest. In truth, Emma had ceased to exist long ago. The grave that marked her body was no more her than a bundle of sticks. The only thing that remained of her lingered on as encapsulated memories in his mind. As morbid as it was to imagine, little of her body probably remained, now, after the devouring teeth of the decades had taken their repayment for loaned time. The same fate awaited him; an inevitable reality that could not be changed—in a hundred years' time, his body too would lie in a casket somewhere, two meters under, decomposing to the bone.

His hands continued to falter on crown of iron as he looked wistfully across the sea of gravestones. It seemed fitting that the grave markers took up the appearance of stone teeth. *So many bodies devoured*, he thought.

With a fixed gaze, he slowly pushed opened the cemetery gate. The gate's screeching was slightly muffled by the leaves resting against the metal barrier that had been deposited there by a brisk breeze. Each leaf could have easily blown through the wrought iron fence, but their random dispersion had prevented the clot of decaying tree matter from exiting through the bars. They crunched under his feet as he moved down the central path.

He passed by the stone markers, row after row. Each had their own name, their own story to those who knew it. On the tops of many of the recent markers were flickering lights which cast a cold, unwavering blue glow. Unlike the eternal flames of old, these melancholy lights provided more than an ever-lasting light that endured through the days and nights. More than a symbol, these lights represented the legacy in which the person named, or their close associates, wished to continue perpetually. The in-memoriam legacy ports allowed visitors to access pictures, videos, writings, and other digital mementos about the person who once lived; to gain access, all one needed to do was connect their nexus device to the proper port on the desired place marker.

His face sneered slightly as he walked past the multitude of blue lights. It did not cease to amaze him the lengths people would go to find 'eternal' comfort with their carefully curated legacy. There is nothing significant beyond the veil of death, no matter how hard people try, nothing will survive. And yet, that is precisely why memory is so important; someday, his research would be the key to solving the centuries-old mind-body problem. Through the cataloguing of the vast memories of the mind, science will be able to provide a digital transference that would finally transfix across the gulf of physical death. Then, these grave repositories, filled with the human consciousness, would be a true legacy that would endure perpetually.

A hop came in his step. He never felt so driven to complete a piece of work. He knew he was near the edge of discovery; one that could change the very nature of humanity.

He continued his walk down the central path of the cemetery. The blue lights on the markers grew less and less frequent. He was passing into the older section of Grand View. Here, the graves were less polished and weather-worn. Up ahead, he saw the tree which signaled that he was close to where Emma's body had been interred.

The sycamore was old, maybe two centuries by some educated estimates. At its base, the tree's roots had dug deep over the years and had dislodged a few grave stones in their pursuit for nourishment and stability. The trunk was nearly four meters in circumference. It rose out of the ground with a stippled camouflage of silver, white, and cream bark which curled back onto itself in places. From the large central trunk, skeletal white branches reached out in contorted configurations over the grave stones below. Only a few stray leaves and a couple long-abandoned nests remained clutched at the very end of the finger-like limbs.

For a few moments, he regarded the tree, up and down. It had frequently caught his eye from a distance on his evening walks home—just like it had this evening. Reaching such great heights, the tree could be seen far and wide from almost any vantage in town. This was only the second time that he had seen it so up close. He had not been to Emma's grave since the day of her body's burial decades ago. Despite the intervening years, the tree looked much the same. *I guess once you are past a couple hundred years in age, things change slowly...if at all,* he thought.

He turned and saw Emma's grave a few yards away on the south side of the tree. The headstone had changed since he last gazed upon it. The writing had become less distinct and bits of green moss had crept up the sides, filling in tiny fractures of the stone. His eyes rested gingerly on the ending date recorded on the stone. The pain of that day, the funeral, the burial, and the months after could all be compressed in a single moment, a single memory.

He stood by her hospital bed, as she whispered out with everything thing that she had, "Baaash, come closer." Even in that final moment of consciousness, there was still a tenderness in her voice. She had beckoned him to come closer so she could see his face one last time; the aneurysm had disrupted much of her vision. Of course, he had obliged, much of his own vision was a slurry of blurry images from all the tears erupting from his eyes. He came as close as he could to her face, the warm expression that had summoned him remained frozen.

"Baaash, I can't see you," she said, her voice strained and weak.

"I am right here," he whispered, patting her arm tenderly.

"I'm so sorry."

"You have nothing to be sorry for," he replied.

"I do. I'm sorry I'm not going to be there. I'm not going to be there to take care of you. To see you achieve your dream, that I know you will achieve, you always do what you set your mind to," she said softly.

"You are a nurse, you have taken care of so many people. I wish you could take care of yourself. It does not make sense; how could we have missed this?"

With rationed breaths, each one taking her a little further away, Emma strained to speak, "Not everything in this world...is something...you can figure out, love...some things happen...even bad things. You have to have faith...to know...that it serves...some purpose. I just wish...I could...have been with...you longer..." Emma's voiced trailed off.

He could see the light, the essence of Emma, fading from her eyes as her world became dark. All he could do was sob and whisper in her ear, "I am sorry dear, I have spent so much time living in my work and in my memories, that I have not saved enough moments to enjoy *you*. I promise I will get you back...I will never forget."

In that moment, on the sixth of September, Emma was gone. A day later, her body followed suit—a delayed echo of finality.

He gazed, now, hollowly for some time at the stone-carved numerals. He did not know why he had come this way. She was not here, she had left him in that hospital room so many years ago. He had avoided this place because it was nothing more than a marker of bad memories. He began to speak, trying to make sense of himself.

"I know you cannot hear me...I guess I am saying this...why exactly am I saying this?" he paused, looking out across the headstones to the old brick wall that marked the edge of the cemetery, "...I guess I am saying this more for myself than for anyone else. I made a promise many years ago, one that I feel I am *so close* to fulfilling. Though many years have passed, it still feels like yesterday in my mind. Because in my mind, time has no distance; bouncing a ball as a child can seem as close to the present as that of brushing my teeth this morning. I wish you could see the work that I have been doing, Emma. Back then, these accomplishments were only idealistic daydreams.

"And perhaps you were right, I spent too much of our precious time together as a hermit in my mind, haunted by my memories. I wish I could have shared all those thoughts with you. I guess, even since I was a young child, I have always felt that there was something bigger than me...than you...than everyone. For so long, I could only scratch the surface of what it could be. Soon, very soon—damn I wish you could experience it with me—a million yesterdays will only be a push button away. For the first time in mankind's existence, no memory shall die, all will be able to be resurrected on-demand.

"Even now, it saddens me that my age has slowly began to fray the minute details of my memory of you. Since that day in September, a gulf has been fixed between us, that history and academic thought has deemed to be impassible. Yes, it is true, there is a great gulf that lies between us, but not one between the immaterialness of life and death, but that within the human mind. Yet, the human mind is material, and we have so much more control than we know. One only needs to find the right key and combination.

"I think I have found the key. It may have taken my lifetime, but it is finally hanging within my grasp. One that will bridge the 'impassible' gulf to you, and, perhaps, to that which has loomed over my life. Once I unlock my own memories, I will have the foothold I need to push behind a veil that has been cast deep in the back recesses of my mind, one that I have only seen flickers and glimpses behind. To be honest with myself, I do not even know if I can truly fathom the depths of ancestral memory. But I have a child's eagerness at what unlocking such memories might do for mankind.

"Emma, if you could see me now, I hope you would be proud of me. You had such deep faith in a higher power, a part of you that I respected, lived with, but never really understood. Even when that faith failed you, the day you died, you still clung on to it with such reverent resolve. Hell, I still half think you wished I would have shown some indication that I would come to faith in your last moments. In truth, all along, I wished you would have had more faith in me and my work. Everything that I am has been wrapped in the pursuit of unlocking the mind. The science is real, tangible, and I think, will change everything. I wish you could be here to see it."

He stood in silence, staring blankly out at the setting sun. The pointed shadows cast by the grave markers had grown long. With the creeping shadows shrouding his face, Bash took his leave. He did not know what had possessed him to visit this evening. Whatever his subconscious reasons were, he never felt so resolute about his life's pursuit.

The cemetery gate clanked nosily in the stillness. Like a child's naïve superstition, he made a conscious effort not to look back upon the graveyard for a fear of seeing some dark shadow darting in between the markers. He knew it was a silly thought, but he could never shake the feeling that it could happen at any moment. With eyes fixed on the stony path before him, he hastily made his retreat back across the arched footbridge that crossed loftily over the Lost Fork Creek, which was thirty meters below. His footsteps clanged across the bridge which had a metal grate deck for pedestrians to cross on. During the day you see down into the gorge below and see the creek's rushing waters tumbling towards the tiny waterfall downstream. Tonight, however, darkness had already filled the void and only the chatter of rumbling water echoed up from beneath him.

He was glad that he left when he did. The sun had already fallen past the horizon line. It was already difficult to see the serpentine path known by many as the Sage Walk. It was the one he often took to get back to his quaint little home in town. What light there was came from the lampposts placed in a uniform fashion on the side of the pathway. Their gentle glow lit the grey concrete of the path and little else.

The Sage Walk was flanked by old-growth trees that blocked most of the light cast off from the town. It was a claustrophobic feeling walking through the hardwoods at night. In the summer, the sound of crickets and other bugs would provide a somewhat comforting semblance of life, but now, in the fall, the silence was cold, and dead. The puddles of lamplight did their best to keep the encroaching darkness at bay. In between the lamps, the stringy shadows of stray branches gave him the feeling that darkness was only a flicker away from closing in.

He had always feared the dark, but never quite understood why. His educated mind told him that darkness was merely the absence of light, no different than the chill that had come due to the absence of heat of the setting sun. Yet, logic provided him little comfort here. There must be something primeval about the fear of the dark, the unseen, the unknowable. Something so deeply-rooted that the mind cannot escape it. Light reveals our world, all the truth and knowledge, while darkness shrouds it, just the same.

The path began to level out as he exited the last stretch of tunneled trees that put out the path at the foot of the hill. It felt relieving to put the woods behind him. Here the path was open under a lavender sky. The town's lights glimmered across the floodplain providing a comforting acknowledgement that people were near and he was no longer alone in the night. Now, if trouble would fall upon him, all he need do is cry out and someone would hear his need for aid.

The Sage Walk terminated in a three-way intersection of paths. To his left, a sandy path followed the heel of the ridge up to the waterfall that spilled over on the Last Fork Creek. People would often sit on the sandstone outcroppings to watch the water flow over the centuries-smoothed chute of stone. The water crashed downward fifteen meters into a large oval pool below. It had been one of Emma's favorite lunch spots. She could spend hours just gazing upon the rushing waters entranced as they slipped past her on their endless journey that stretch the bounds of time and space. She thought it was remarkable that a single droplet of water could have been drunk by a dinosaur countless years ago, and by virtue of a closed cyclical system, the same droplet could fall through her tiny toes dangling in the creek on a summer afternoon. She was always thinking of things so much bigger than herself. *If molecules had memories, they would be timeless,* he thought.

The path to his right was stony and worn. It led up a small hill to a tavern aptly called 'The Ebony Tower'. The Ebony Tower was an institution in Talawanda Springs. The tavern had been in operation for almost 250 years, the origins of which were lost to time. Some believed that the tavern had started as the first schoolhouse in the area before being converted to a tavern once a more appropriate location closer to town, that offered greater protection, was erected for students. Still, others suspected that the tavern had been used as a mortuary given its location on the outskirts of town near the Grand View Cemetery.

Whatever its true origins, The Ebony Tower had a rich history of being the frequent gathering place for faculty and graduate students of Hightower University. The Ebony Tower was a hole-in-the-wall place which the younger denizens of Talawanda Springs avoided for more well-appointed drinking locations. He himself used to be a regular patron at the bar until Emma's death. He now found little time outside work to waste away clinging to droughts of beer.

At the intersection, he could see the Ebony Tower's gas lantern flickering away in front the long rectangular building with a dark black wood façade. The lantern was sourced from a natural gas spring that derived somewhere in the roots of the adjacent mountain. The flame had been beckoning in patrons continuously for as long as it had been open. So long, that even the tavern's owners knew little on how it worked or how to fix it if it fell into disrepair.

The knowledge and craftsmanship of the tavern had been lost along with its origins. The front entrance was turret-shaped with black stone intermixed with white stones at irregular places. A pointed grey cone protruded from the roof which was capped with a weather vane in the shape of compass point. Most of the building was submerged below ground where patrons had to descend downward to gain entry. Overall, the building was a twisted reflection of the white marbled towers that rose up so majestically from Old Main, staring down upon the lowly town below.

This evening, he took the third path towards town.

As he drew nearer to town, he picked up his pace; his home awaited him. *I might have a warm toddy before bed*, he thought. It *had* been a most eventful day. Crossing the wooden footbridge over the creek he could see the electric candle lights in the upstairs windows of his home.

His home was a small two-story Tudor cottage. The outside walls were made of grey stone that were accented by two brick chimneys that protruded from the triangular roofs. In the center of the roof, directly above the entryway on the second floor, was a circular window that provided a view of the creek in daylight. It was a modest home for a person of his renown but it was the only place he had truly felt at home. He had bought the home when he was just starting out on an assistant professor's meager salary, not too long after he married Emma. He would have liked something grander in the more well-to-do part of town but Emma had loved the view of the creek so much, he could not refuse her. Even after her death, he felt he could not leave the place, too many memories had been lain down there.

Passing through the iron gate Bash strolled up the small brick footpath that led up to a mint green u-shaped door. He placed his hand on the latch and the door recognized him and let him in. He was so glad to be home, he only half-heartedly shut the door behind him, leaving it ajar. He set down his satchel bag and heating umbrella on the narrow entry table just inside the door. He then went into his study just off the foyer. With a push of a button to ignite the fireplace and a pour of a bottle of cognac, he collapsed in his chair never so relieved to be off his feet. The firelight glistened in his eyes that slowly began to glaze over. He could finally rest without any worries in the security of his home. Not even a forgotten open door could draw him away from his silent repose. On the edge of discovery, he felt he would need it, to cross the gap he would require every faculty he could muster.

SECOND STAGE

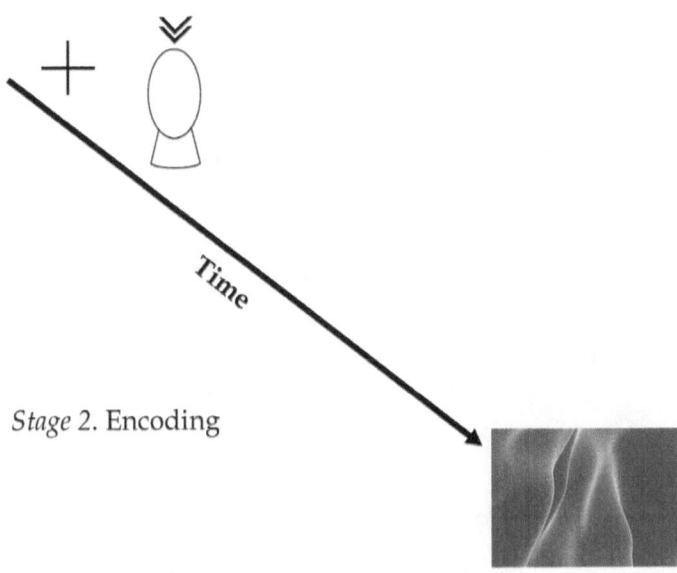

Stage 2. Encoding

"At any given moment, we are inundated with almost an infinite amount of sensory information, however, only a fraction of what we 'see' is processed and encoded into memory. It is a marvel of biological engineering that we do not miss out on greater amounts of information."

Seeing through the Shroud:
Barriers to Accessing Total Human Memory
- Dr. Sebastian Silva,
Five years B.R.D.

3
The Committee Meeting
One month B.R.D.

Aliyah got up earlier than usual. Today was a big day for her graduate career, even for one that had just begun a few weeks ago. Dr. Silva had invited her to a most prestigious committee meeting where renowned scholars of the psychology department would decide if Dr. Silva could test out theory decades in the making.

She felt so honored that Dr. Silva had asked her to be at the meeting. Not often were students permitted to observe the inner workings of faculty members. Usually such invitations were made with waving lips and idle hands, but Dr. Silva made sure she was available when scheduling the meeting. Even if she did not get the opportunity to speak a word, just being a fly on the wall and listening to the musings of great minds in the room was of rarefied air.

Since the semester started, she was loving her classes. Higher education exposed her to constant intellectual stimulation that she had hungered for her whole life. The knowledge of a multitude of scholars was there for the picking and she could not get enough of it. Sitting around faculty and peers to have group discussions regarding the merits of theory and practice challenged the very limits of her abilities.

Nothing seemed more idyllic than the prospect that, someday, she would find her own little niche in the ivory tower of academia. The thought of living a life filled with thinking up new and wonderful research ideas amazed her. It was a career in which academics could create their own Christmas mornings each and every day, unwrapping an experiment and finding the answer to the research question inside, months or years in the making.

She had always held a curious spirit within her. As a child of three siblings, she had been the one that asked her parents a constant barrage of questions. When her parents would take her out on errands, she would ask from her little fish-shaped car seat, "What was this?" "How does it work?" "Why do people do that?" It was perhaps a way for her to gain recognition. As the middle child, she often felt that asking questions was a means to make herself relevant, acknowledged, *present*. She knew her parents loved her deeply, but sometimes they would get caught up in the misbehavior of their youngest child, Amos, or the sporting success of their athletically-inclined oldest child, Troy. Then there was Aliyah, stuck in the middle. A well-behaved child, with a sharp intellectual curiosity that, for all they tried, her drudger parents could never quite fulfill.

To their credit, her parents tried the best they could, sacrificing a convenient commute to work so that Aliyah could attend the best school in the Cincinnati area. The pair were both blue-collar workers; her dad worked odd construction jobs and her mom did bookkeeping for the county fire department downtown in sight of the rolling Ohio River. It was a time when work was scarce. The Automation Revolution had just about reached its tipping point and many people found it difficult to find work. Her father was laid off six times growing up as his job began to be replaced by machines that could 'print' out structures on demand within tolerances that no human could match.

It was an uneasy and disruptive point in history. Engineers promised full automation without a need to work but the machines were not yet showtime-ready, and the promises went unrealized. The blue-collar workers were stuck in the middle between an ever-shrinking, dead-end job market and the promises of abundant leisure. Promises of the future do not pay the bills or pay for education.

It was not until the governments of the world began controlling the prices of basic necessities and offering a living wage did the birthing pains of the Automation Revolution subside. A complete revolution was not fulfilled as many had wanted; only certain number of blue-collar jobs were subsumed by machines. A vocal minority, sneeringly labeled neo-luddites, had halted a complete takeover citing the need for work was a basic human necessity on par with food and shelter. Some, including her parents, believed labor in the form of hard work was a virtue; to cast it aside completely, would be deleterious to the human soul.

In the end, only the less dignified jobs were taken from the hands of man and transferred to the mechanical; manufacturing, construction, farming jobs were all yoked to robotics. The intellectual and service careers persisted on, however. Humans were not quite ready to give up full control over the realms of labor, though most knew the halt would only last for a time. The younger generations of society marched to an unwitting drum beat of progress for its own sake. After the slow creep of years, the temptation of infinite leisure would seep into younger minds who did not understand the old virtues. At least, that's how she saw it.

It was these technological advancements that spurred her parents to implore that she got a good education in a field that could not be replaced by machines. That's what brought her to cyber psychology; understanding the human mind in the digital realms of machines was most lucrative. Since many younger adults spent a majority of their time in virtual worlds, studying them in these domains was the only practical direction the field of psychology could go. Not to mention, many titans of the technological industry found much to be gained monetarily through the understanding of the desires and decisions people make in the synthetic realm.

Her cyber psychology interests in college revolved around how childhood fears manifested in virtual reality. Dr. Silva's lab was so alluring because it offered her a way to conduct her research on childhood fears and phobias. Using advanced methods of memory retrieval developed by Dr. Silva, she hoped to test out ways to identify the origins of early childhood fears and then use the virtual domain to try to attenuate them by showing subjects that the fear was not threatening from an adult's perspective. It was only with the advances made by Dr. Silva and his colleagues that this research was now even possible.

Like with many psychologists, there was a lot of me-search in the research. The topic of childhood fears resonated deeply with her. As a child, she experienced several unsettling events that burned into her memory and stuck with her into adulthood. The two biggest standouts were trees and mirrors in the dark. They both creeped her out.

Her fear of trees in the dark started when she was young, perhaps six or seven. Around this time, she had a surreal nightmare. In it, she found herself walking through a forest, similar to one she saw in a children's picture book of Hansel and Gretel. It was an old growth forest with trees that towered upward in a sky-like canopy. The woods were shrouded in a velveteen darkness. Only the creaking of unseen branches pierced the silence. Then the dream jittered, as dreams often do, and she found herself running—barely out pacing her beating heart. Somehow, she knew she should not look back at what pursued her. So, she kept going, as fast as her incorporeal legs would take her. She ran and she ran. Passing little stone cottages with flickering lampposts at the door. Doors that would not yield to her in her endless flight.

Finally, at a lone lamp post, she decided to make a stand. She turned slowly to see her pursuer. She could hear the creaking of branches and scuffle of dirt approaching her. What she saw terrified her…the woods were walking!

Even in the dim lamplight, she could see the grey limbs swaying to and fro as they steadily marched towards her. At the front of the grim procession was a craggily old oak tree with a disfigured burl for a nose and two hollow eyes. The sockets contained nothing but darkness which contrasted starkly with the surrounding night. The tree lumbered, clumsily, towards her with thick roots, corrupted by the gnawing of termites. Closer and closer it came. There was no run left in her. There was only staring out at the edge of the lamplight to wait for the moving woods to cross into it. It was only a narrow branch that crossed the barrier of light. In the flickering glow, she could see the splintered fingers clutched together, seeping with a sticky black sap. As it came to reach her, the branches began to spread apart into an outstretched limbed-hand with three fingers of odd lengths.

Before the terror overtook her, her eyes opened.

Yet, she did not find herself out of the woods in her wakeful state. A two-dimensional afterimage of the scene she had just ran through was laid out upon her bedroom wall. In the moonlight, she could see the forest, the small feudal town on its outskirts with scattered lamps, and she could see trees...still moving! In a flash her heart skipped and her body froze. *This is reality, I'm awake*, she thought. But the trees continued to move within the scene on her wall as if they were still searching all the odds and ends of the landscape...for her.

Eventually, her paralysis faded and she jumped down from her tiny twin bed and grabbed her pink blanket to go sleep at the foot of her parents' bed. Darting out of her room, she did not hesitate to look back but she thought she heard a raspy whisper, not too unlike one that might echo up from the hollow of a large tree in the wind. She could not remember what it said and was glad of it.

Now, in the morning sun, she gazed out her apartment window. There was a silver maple tree in the front lawn. It did not seem so terrifying, now. The sunlight glistened through its leaves that had just begun to change a greenish-yellow hue. *As a child it seemed so scary*, she thought, noticing the wry smile on her face in the reflection on the window pane. Yet, she could still remember the fear she felt as a child, it was so real. When she was young, every tale, monster, supernatural event seemed possible. At some point, which she could not quite place her finger on, those feelings seemed to fade with age until they were but fleeting shadows of a young mind that did not yet fully understand the world.

Yet, on occasion, a singular guttural thought would emerge from her suppressed subconscious. One that offered up a simple question, a question she did not really want to know the answer to, *what if it was all real?*

That very question had reared its pestering little head only recently. What she experienced on her assignment from Dr. Silva in the Hugenberg basement with his research assistant, Gabe, threatened to shaken the foundations of her adult closure on childish imaginings. But she could not think of that now, not today. Today she needed to focus on the big committee meeting she had been invited to attend. She could not afford to let herself be distracted. Besides, it was probably nothing, just first week jitters.

The clear-blue skies helped calm her spirits. *A perfect day for a long walk to campus*, she thought, looking out the front door of her tiny apartment. She decided to walk in lieu of public transportation in the hope that her jitters for the meeting later would subside. A little heart pumping was sure to make some good use of the nervous energy. She grabbed her scarf on the way out the door and stepped out into a brisk breeze.

The fall breeze nipped at her nose as she walked across the courtyard of her apartment complex. In one of those rare moments of life, everything in creation seemed to shimmer with a numinous beauty. The simple splendor of a rustling tree or a songbird perched on a worn fence seemed to be on full display. Everything had an order to it, a part to play; even if it did seem an orderly chaos to observers trying to predict what a bird or squirrel might do next. Perhaps the seemingly contradictory, simple yet complex, design of nature was what made the world so fascinating and accessible. No matter what your level of understanding, there was something about the world that could provide tremendous joy.

These thoughts put a smile on her face as she exited the courtyard and began her day. Her apartment complex was located on the east side of town near Spring Lake Park and, like most days, her first order of business was to head to her favorite coffee shop. The typical path to get coffee ran directly through Spring Lake Park. The park was a generous green space about a kilometer square that sat at the bottom of a shallow depression in the middle of town. Nestled away, and surrounded by grass-covered hills, it was one of the few refuges people could go to get away from the modern world and the technology connected to it. A place for quiet thoughts, unstimulated by others, just the natural landscape. A little slice of tranquility she needed to remain connected to every day.

It was mid-morning and not too many people were about as she strolled down the path towards the lake in the center of the park. The water was an inky black color and had a bubbly appearance from the natural springs that sourced it, hence the lake's namesake. The path took her over an old stone bridge that bisected the lake. The stone bridge arched over the water, allowing pedestrians a view of the entire lake. She always loved strolling across this bridge. It had a rustic charm; the stones were misshapen and placed in an irregular fashion that marked the best that could have been achieved for the time in which it was built, sometime in the early nineteenth century.

Looking down at the water she could see little of nothing in the black murkiness. Only tiny green lily pads bobbled up and down, suspended on the smooth black mirror. At the edge of the lake, the tentacled roots of the cypress trees drank deep into the waters where a great blue heron stood motionless waiting for prey. Normally, she would enjoy just leaning over the edge of stone bridge and watch the herons stalk silently, cocking their heads to the side and plunging themselves into the water to pull up a fish. Today, she was too jittery to stand idly. She feared being too much alone with her thoughts would do more harm than good. So, she picked up her pace to the other side of the lake and climbed up the sandy path to Main Street.

Main Street of Talawanda Springs was typical for a small town in Appalachia. Most of the buildings lining the main avenue still had their original brick façades, though much worn for wear having lost their once deep red luster—only a faded salmon color remained.

In front of the store fronts, vehicles rumbled across the brick-laden pavement that lined a one kilometer stretch of Main Street. The storefronts were intrepidly local; there was a small-town grocery with locally-sourced meat and produce, a small craft shop sold home wares, and an antiques store.

The antiques store, Days Gone By, was popular amongst the students; many would buy small items to adorn their rooms for their vintage appeal. She enjoyed the store because each item was 'lived-in', it had a memory to it that seemed to have been lost in time. Someone, at some point, had a need for this item to help them in their everyday life. Now, these items were merely relics of bygone days, sought after for their looks since time had largely erased their original purpose or function.

She had bought just such an item because it fascinated her. It was tiny circular piece of laminated paper about four centimeters in diameter. She saw the circular piece of art labeled as a 'milk cap' in the display case of the store. Made of cardboard, it sat next to a thick disc made of translucent red plastic. She knew instantly she had to have the art piece. The label stated that it was from just before the turn of the century sometime in the 1990s. On its face was a beautifully rendered piece of art depicting a cartoon rabbit flying a carrot-shaped ship into space. To her, it was beautiful, but she could not figure out its purpose. As a solitary piece of art, the best she could do was assume that it was used as pendant to be hung around the neck. Optimistically, she believed that someday she would find out what her astro-rabbit was meant for, but for now, it would sit in a place of honor in a frame above her mantle.

She continued down the street passing the Moon Tunnel alley, the Masonry Street Theatre, and the tall brick courthouse, known as Carlisle Hall. At the end of the street, the corner of Main and Tower Road, was her favorite little coffee shop, aptly named Corner Café. The shop had a rounded front of brick that framed the tall, curved glass front windows. A sage-green awning made of heavy cloth was propped up by a pair of shiny brass-capped wood poles, which provided shade for the outdoor tables and chairs. She could already smell the delicious aroma of coffee spilling out into the street as she grabbed the handle to the double doors.

The inside of Corner Café was just as quaint as its outward façade. The aged brick was exposed throughout the interior walls. The narrow-planked wood floor was also original to the building and creaked slightly as patrons shuffled about in queue awaiting to place their orders. What she admired most was an arch-shaped stained-glass window that stood above the front entrance. The window's glass was a mixture of greens, yellows, browns, and whites illustrating a tree with a wide canopy and rolling hills in the distance. At the right time of day, the eastern sun would shine through the window casting a soothing blend of filtered light across the shop's interior. It was so bright and welcoming, that the tree seemed almost pleasant to her. Unfortunately, standing in line today, the sun was not quite right for the effect.

There was a delightful baby that drew her attention, however. He dangled happily from a chest harness of a young lady standing a few people up from her in line. The baby's wide blue eyes were fixated on her yellow pea coat. He gave her a big smile. She answered back with a puckered face. When a man buried in his nexus device stumbled between them, bumping the mother, the baby's playfulness subsided. The warm smile turned to a frown and his eyes stared with displeasure at the man.

From the baby's reaction, she wondered if they, in their innocence, had an innate sense of the 'essence' of others. At such a very young age, were they sensing the good and bad auroras of people? Could they see other things that we have forgotten in our childhood amnesia? Being so close to their own creation, maybe young children possess a lingering connection and perceptiveness to a world which becomes occluded with age, as the weight of the human world settles upon them. It is only in the period of newness that we are sensitive to and influenced by forces we can no longer see. After all, it was well-documented that babies had many abilities that seem to fade with time and development like the ability to distinguish a complete set of phonemes that served the basis of all languages. It was only after time immersed in an environment, hearing a certain language around them, that they begin to lose the ability to produce and discern sounds that underlie other languages. It begged the question: what else could the very young discern that adults can no longer?

She enjoyed these little thought experiments. They helped her to generate new hypotheses of the world around her. Many of her greatest ideas came to her just by observing the natural world. For some, it might all seem like a random assortment of events, but she felt there were patterns to discover that might connect to a greater meaning. One need only look.

Another benefit of an active mind was that time speeds by more quickly. Before she knew it, she was at the front of the line giving her order to the barista.

A cup of chestnut praline latte.

Caffeine was a graduate student's basic necessity, perhaps above food and water. Cup in hand, she pushed out into the street. She still had a few hours before the big meeting. An abundance of time was good, for she was going to take the long path to the office; maybe by then she would feel ready. The meeting was coming, it was only a matter of passing time.

Aliyah stared at a drawn-looking face in the mirror that was her own. She was in the restroom just down the hall from her office. The big committee meeting would be starting within the hour. She had rushed into the restroom as soon as she felt her nerves begin to buckle within her. Her stomach was turning over onto itself as if it was a wad of string that had become impossibly tangled together. The nauseated feeling had brought her to the brink of throwing up several times. The thought of going into the meeting with barf on her breath almost scared her more than the meeting itself.

"You can do this, you're a graduate student now. Less than one percent of anyone in the world has the same privilege as you," she quietly spoke to herself, splashing warm water onto her face.

She whispered a brief prayer, "God please be with me this afternoon. I pray that I can get through this meeting without any health or career-ending problems. I wouldn't be here in this privileged position without you Lord, you deserve all the credit. I trust in you to guide me and provide me strength, amen."

After a few moments, she felt a warm, soothing sensation run down the back of her neck onto her shoulders. She liked to think that this was some sort of response to her prayer, but her analytical mind took over and began to dismiss the feeling as just being 'in her head.' Either way, she did feel calmer and the twisting sensation from her abdomen had subsided slightly, at least for the time being.

She studied her face in the mirror. It had begun to slowly recover its normal, lively color. The lines of her face curved around her rounded nose and reached out to the dimples that framed her mouth when she smiled. She could only muster a smirk in the mirror now.

Examining her face in this way was entrancing; for a few brief seconds she almost felt disassociated from herself, like she was looking at someone else, who was strange to her. Only when the lights began to flicker somewhat did she come back to herself.

The realization she lost a few seconds of time startled her. She did not quite understand how she could be so fascinated by her own reflection.

In truth, mirrors were the second thing that frightened her, particularly, gazing into mirrors in the dark. Another fear borne out of her childhood. This fear, she recalled, largely originated from a sleepover experience she had as a prepubescent kid. It was strange, she had such fond memories of her sleepovers with friends, but now, remembering one in particular seemed to put a pox on the rest.

The one in question was like many of the other sleepovers that she participated in as a pre-teen girl; trying on new makeup, clothes, and prank calling some potential love interests. As the night dragged on, and the hours grew late, the fun settled on more mystical enterprises.

It first started with the guessing of fortunes. Who was most likely to get their first kiss? Who would end up with the new cute boy in class? The silly games eventually evolved into a game with more serious stakes: TRUTH *or* DARE?

She could picture it almost as clearly as she lived it. All nine of the girls sat in a circle cross-legged. In turn, each spun an empty beer bottle that her friend Chelsea had fished out from the waste basket in her kitchen, most likely a deposit of her dad's.

Round and round the bottle spun adding randomness and suspense to who would be in the hot seat for the simple, exclusively binary question. All of the girls that had preceded her that night had chosen truth. The collective had learned that Sarah had stolen a ring pop from the grocery store a week ago, Stacy had let a boy feel her budding breasts in a movie theater last summer, and, most shockingly, Josie had admitted she had lost her virginity at age twelve to Jamie out in the baseball dugout of the park near everyone's houses.

Due to choices that had preceded, when the bottle's lip finally slowed to a stop in front of her, she cried out, "Dare!"

The choice of the dare rested with Amanda. She was a pretty girl with locks of curly blonde hair that shaped a sandy white face speckled with sun freckles. Her parents were wealthy so, of course, she was quite popular.

The bold red lipstick that had been crudely applied earlier in the evening smeared as her lips curled over themselves. It took some time for her to contemplate what the dare would be. Everyone could tell that she was trying to craft in her mind one that would truly be worthy of the first dare of the night. Aliyah could sense that the decision had been quickly, but the longer Amanda drew it out, the more attention remained on her, and the more it tortured her in a stew of suspense.

Eventually, something apparently came to the girl, Amanda's face suddenly exploded into motion.

"Okay, okay everyone, I've got a good one. Aliyah, I want you to go in the bathroom downstairs...with a candle...lock the door...turn out the lights...and...summon Bloody Mary!" Amanda dared with a fiendish grin upon her face.

A collective gasp moved throughout the group. She could not process much else of the moment since she was mostly in shock of the task that had been laid before her. She knew she might have brought this upon herself earlier when she had mentioned to the group that she had always felt a little uneasy around mirrors.

Before she could re-gather her wits, Chelsea had already returned with a skinny candle already lit. The wax was dark red and sat on a tiny porcelain holder with a little ring that her fingers slipped through and clinched tightly. The giggling gaggle of girls escorted Aliyah to the door that led into the basement. Looking down the steps, all she could see was darkness.

Amanda offered some parting words: "Don't forget, you must look into the mirror and say 'Bloody Mary!' three times. If you don't, we will know because we will be listening from the top of the stairs. We know you can do it, and who knows, maybe Mary will be in good spirits and reveal your future husband...good luck!"

Aliyah turned from the sea of grinning faces none the more encouraged. She took a deep breath and stared down into the depths. The shadows moved with the huddled movements of the girls behind her who whispered incoherently amongst themselves. The amber kitchen light only reached down about a quarter of the way down the steps. The rest faded into the darkness. They were the same wooden steps but the darkness made them look less stable, less secure.

One step at a time and then you'll be down there, she thought.

Stiff-legged, she began her decent slowly. She kept her face forward, not wanting the girls to see her face that was losing its color or her lips that were starting to quiver together. No, she needed to focus on her feet. Each footfall downward was a jarred up through her body. The descent down to each step felt as if she were plunging meters below the ground level even though the steps were barely larger than her tiny feet. When she reached the edge of the light, there was little contrast between it and the dark. The light of the candle offered only a faint outline of the path before her. With a brief pause, she crossed into the dark.

With each step, her bare feet feebly tapped out before her trying to find the next stair. Like a blind man's cane, her toes tapped against the wood before plopping down on her heels with the rest of her weight. The air was becoming cooler now. The light of her candle slowly was the only source of light, an undependable one at that. She felt as her eyes widen as they adjusted to the new surroundings. She thought of her parents who, if they could see her now, would have shown strong disapproval for the summoning of any spirit. "You should never dabble with the occult, you never know what you might bring upon yourself," she heard her mom say in her mind. "The Bible teaches the dead are asleep, ghosts can be nothing more than a demonic lure, to draw you in and oppress you. Don't let them in. What's dead is dead, Aliyah," she heard her dad add.

She tried to stay focused and push her parent's foreboding words aside. After all, she was just having a little fun, and had never heard of someone getting hurt from these silly games.

At the foot of the stair, she looked out into the murky darkness. She needed to find the door to the basement bathroom. Though she could still hear giggling emanating from the top of the stair, her friends might as well have been kilometers away, now, across a black expanse. Even their implied presence provided little comfort to her on this dark quest. *I had to be different, I had to choose* DARE.

Fumbling through a cluttered corridor of sporting equipment and laundry baskets, she finally found the entryway to the basement bathroom. A glimmer of light came out of the room and startled her. She caught her breath and realized that it was just the light of her candle reflecting back at her from the large mirror within.

"You've come too far to chicken out now," she whispered to herself before stepping over the threshold and pulled the door shut behind her.

Inside, her measured breaths seemed to pound against the confined space of the half-bath. She set her candle down on the countertop of the sink. In front of her, the full-length mirror spanned the double vanity. The candle light flickered to and fro making the shadows dance in the background behind her. The air in the bathroom was stale and cool.

Being alone in front of the quiet mirror made her feel uneasy. To cut the tension and, chiefly, to give herself a sense of control over her reflection, she made a face with her tongue sticking out. Her reflection did the same before her, in perfect unison. She almost laughed at the silliness. Mirrors were a funny thing really. A trickster that we conveniently ignore, for what they show us is not reality but, by nature, a distortion of such. Maybe that is why people attribute so many mystical things to mirrors, the human mind cannot be tricked, not fully, it must be able to pick up on the subtle distortions and decode the reflected self is not truly what we should see.

Silence befell her once more. A silence that she did not want to let build. For each passing moment, added a beat to her thumping heart and out into the encroaching walls. These thoughts only served to stall the task before her. Enough thinking, it was time to get down to business.

"If you are going to do this, might as well get it done with, nothing will happen anyways," she whispered.

"All right…Bloody Mary…" she paused and looked around her. Nothing had changed. Had she really expected there to be any?

"…Bloody Mary…" she paused a bit longer, knowing now that the process was past the point of no return. One more time, with feeling.

"…Bloody Mary!" she exclaimed, emphatically. She was at the precipice of adrenaline and felt ready for anything.

Her body clinched towards its core in preparation for a swift flight. She held her breath as the reverberations of her voice fell away.

Only, nothing happened.

The candle light continued to flicker softly. A 'haaa' sound slipped between her lips as she let the last remnants of air escape from her lungs. She had been holding her breath to listen to the continuing silence.

Still, there was nothing.

After what seemed like several minutes had past, she decided that she had fulfilled what she had been dared to do. She disengaged her gaze from the mirror and reached for the candle holder. As her hand reached out she could see out of the corner of her eye that it's mirrored twin was very much unlike her own. It was onyx black with a nebulous shape that only approximated her own. At the end of the mirrored black hand was what looked like three finger tips, each with their own flickering flame. She tried to blink to assure herself that what she was seeing, this visual anomaly, was not real. Yet, with all her might, her mind would not let the form go. She feared that closing her eyes would allow whatever she was seeing free reign around her. Another part of her worried that even if she did close her eyes, the bigger fear was seeing that the entity still remained when she opened them once more.

With eyes, steely and focused on the candle, she grabbed it and brought it up to be in between herself and the dark figure in the mirror. What she saw surprised her, it was just her, or rather, the typical mirrored visage of herself. Nothing was slightly out of the ordinary.

She sighed a breath of relief. It might have just been the shadows playing with her strained eyes.

The candle flickered out.

All that remained were a pair of glowing red-ember eyes in the mirror. Lidless, they stared without blinking and floated in the darkness attached to an unseen, wobbling head. She could not help but to stare back into them and see a flame, like her candle, spark at their center. The trance burned into her and she could feel herself falling forward, towards the mirror.

She blinked and turned to the door. It began banging loudly. It was all too much for her to take. She screamed in heart-pounding terror. She closed her eyes and lunged to push through the door. As she did, the door gave way, but not to her own weight. She found herself lying on the basement floor with the entire group of girls crowded around her laughing and mimicking her with pounding motions on the nearby walls. All she could do was sob uncontrollably. It was over, she was surrounded by real human beings. Yet, she dared not tell them what she had seen. She had been humiliated enough for one night.

In the fifth-floor restroom, her reflection stared blankly at her in the mirror. She shuddered at the recollection of her childhood. Even now, the reflection of shadows that lurked at the edges of the mirror made her feel uneasy. As a grown woman, her mind had largely dismissed what happened as an imagination that was tricked under uncertain circumstances. There was plenty of psychological research on perception, specifically pareidolia, that finds that the mind simply cannot handle randomness and does its best to create familiar patterns, shapes, or figures out of nothingness. Perhaps the scariest thing of all, is nothing, for it gives the mind the carte blanche to do anything, allowing imagination to take full control.

Yet, for whatever strange reason, this logic did not dissuade the fact that mirrors in the dark scared the hell out of her. She still felt a sense of vulnerability gazing into a mirror, not knowing at what moment her mind might create another anomaly. One that might depart from its one-for-one following of her movements. The anomalies she encountered with Gabe a few weeks back had definitely filled her quota for the year, but she tried to ignore all that and focus on her research, and importantly, the committee meeting.

She looked at the time.

"Oh my, it will be starting shortly," she gasped. Aliyah took one last glance at her 'look' and started off down the hall to the stairwell.

Once on the first floor, she navigated her way to the 'Sebastian and Emma Silva Grand Conference Room.' A gift, generously donated by Dr. Silva and his late wife.

The conference room was as majestic as the name implied. The room was in the shape of an equilateral triangle set on the eastern corner of Hugenberg Hall. The two outward facing walls were almost entirely composed of two meter tall picture windows that overlooked the river valley below. At the center of the room was a giant hardwood conference table made of mahogany and surrounded by fine, black-leather chairs.

When she entered the room, she was so awed by its grandeur that she did not notice that most of the committee had already arrived. Coming to her senses, she realized that she needed to find a seat. Most of the well-appointed chairs around the conference table had already been taken by the committee and she was too afraid to sit so close to these prestigious members of the university's academy. So, she decided to sit down in the very back of the room on a modest wooden chair underneath a very nicely-framed print of 'Relativity' by M.C. Escher which depicted a series of staircases going to a vast number of corridors in a seemingly impossible arrangement—the staircase that one figure walked was on the underside of another staircase that a similar figure was walking.

Just as she began to take her seat, she heard a voice call out to her warmly.

"Hey, Aliyah, what are you doing sitting all the way back there? Lean in and sit with the rest of us, you are just as valued as all these old fossils," said a man behind her. When she turned around, she immediately blushed when she recognized the voice belonged to her adviser, Dr. Silva.

Dr. Silva was a handsome man for being late in his middle age. He had dark black hair, thick eyebrows, dark-brown eyes, and a large, arrow-shaped nose. His face was square-shaped and a honey-beige color. It was mostly obscured by the roughness of a neatly trimmed beard that time had made mostly grey with a few splotches of black color that remained mostly in his mustache and around his chin. He was wearing a rather dapper tan, camel-haired sports coat, navy dress slacks, and a white dress shirt that was unbuttoned down to the middle of his carpeted chest.

Just after she had turned to face her adviser, another voice came from behind near the entrance to the room.

"Now, Bash, insulting our age is not a great way to start of the review of your proposal. Besides, Dr. Edmonson has been emeritus for longer than I have been here and I've been a professor here for nearly twenty years."

She glanced back to see a pale-skinned man in his late fifties with a full black beard, bushy eye brows and a hairline that had largely receded to the top of the man's head. He had a gentle appearance; his cheeks were full, nose was big and rosy, and his small mouth opened slightly with a playfully roguish grin.

Dr. Silva acknowledged the man, "This colleague, who I regret to call an *old* friend, is Dr. Christopher Irving. He is one of the last purely cognitive psychologists.

"And, come on Chris, this is not an evaluation *per se*, but rather a necessary process to stamp my go-ahead," Bash replied through a crooked smile.

"And who is this that you have invited to this meeting?" Dr. Irving inquired.

"This is my new student, Ms. Aliyah Woods. She just started, but I already know she is a future rising star," Dr. Silva said proudly, giving her an encouraging nod.

"Well it is nice to make your acquaintance Ms. Woods. I look forward to seeing great research from you," Dr. Irving replied, kindly.

"Thank you, Professor, I hope I can live up to these lofty expectations everyone is setting for me," she replied.

Dr. Irving departed to find his seat at the corner of the table. Dr. Silva remained with her and was smiling and waving to the last few committee members that were shuffling in before turning back to her.

"Be confident in yourself Aliyah, I meant what I said. When the time comes, you will do great. Just follow my lead if you need help."

Bash went to take his seat on the opposite side of the table from where Dr. Irving sat. She was left standing alone mulling over his words. She really did not have the faintest idea what he had meant by them. *I suppose he was just trying to settle my nerves before the meeting*, she thought, and looked for a remaining seat.

She sat in the last open chair that Dr. Silva had presumably saved for her next to him. Once in her seat, a man of East Asian descent, began to speak at the head of the table.

"Good afternoon! Thank you all for making time for this committee meeting, I will be acting as the chair to facilitate discussion on the merits of Dr. Silva's proposed experiments. I think it is very fitting we are having this meeting in this wonderful conference room, it underscores Professor Silva's career-spanning contributions to the university, of which he passionately *continues* to do. Now, I do see some unfamiliar faces around the table, so let us begin with some introductions before getting down to business. I will start.

My name is Doctor Jéan Chan and I am the Dean of the College of Arts and Sciences. I have been at Hightower for almost twenty-five years now. I started out as an Assistant Professor of Chemistry with research that focused on super-conducting meta-materials. I moved to Associate, then Full, before becoming the

Head of the Department for five years. This year will mark my ninth year as the Dean of the College."

Dr. Chan then turned to a middle-aged man sitting to his right. The man was blue-eyed, light-skinned with a rosy-hue to his face. Remnants of blonde hair split apart at the peak of his forehead like a bunch of cornstalks leaning over in opposite directions with little wisps of strands fluttering about. A gap between the man's two front teeth was noticeable when he began to speak.

"Hello everyone, my name is Doctor Timothy Larson and I am the Head of the Department of Psychology. I have been here at the university for over twenty years now. My training was in clinical psychology which led to a fruitful career studying conduct disorders in children. As Department Head, I have endeavored to foster new, and innovative research that pushes the boundaries of scientific thinking. This has placed our department among the top institutions in the world and we are especially proud to have such a well-acclaimed scholar among our faculty," Dr. Larson gestured over towards Dr. Silva who replied back with a gracious nod.

Next to Dr. Larson was Dr. Irving.

"Hi. My name, when I can remember it, is Chris Irving. I have been with Hightower University too long for some, and not long enough for retirement I am told. I am a cognitive psychologist who studies the sharedness and unique experience of visual perception. I also want to thank Tim for choosing me to serve as the representative from the department, I know it is a thankless job, but I am willing to be the final sucker you asked who said yes to do it."

The room let out a brief moment of muffled laughter as Dr. Irving leaned back in his seat.

Next in line was Dr. Silva.

She could already feel the cold sweat begin to ooze between the folds in the palm of her hands. Once Dr. Silva introduced himself, it would be her turn. She was intensely nervous and began to rehearse in her head what she would say. *Just keep it simple*, she told herself. She would state her name, who she worked for, her year in school, and maybe her research interests. But how technical should she get? This audience is not full of psychologists so she needed to be broad, but not too broad or she would sound dumb and…her ears perked up in synchrony with the hairs on the back of her neck.

"—I think my graduate student is next," the voice of Dr. Silva rang out. It took a few moments of processing before Aliyah realized—it was her turn!

"Ga-good afternoon, my name is Aliyah and…I um…I am a first-year student in Bash's, I mean, Dr. Silva's lab," her heart was racing a million miles a minute as she searched for the words to describe her research interests. Amidst the throbbing in her neck, she found some words, "My-my research interest is on the effects of childhood fears in virtual domains."

She looked around the room to see only gazes of feigned interest and half nods of acknowledgement. She had stumbled but made it through.

The people that followed after her seemed to keep things short, though admittedly, it was hard to focus on anything as her elevated heart rate gradually slowed to a more relaxed state.

Dr. Sara Winters, a wide-framed woman with cats-eye glasses and curly golden hair simply stated her name and title as the university's Director of the Institutional Review Board (IRB). The IRB was the main institutional body that decided whether research was ethical and could be conducted without great risk to human participants. They were the gatekeepers, without IRB approval, a study could not be conducted.

Next to her was an IRB associate named Britt Catalán who had a dreamy look to him. He had pale blue eyes, raggedy thick brown hair, and a scruffy beard. He simply stated his name and the fact that he had just started on the IRB in the last six months. She was raptured by the smooth sound of his voice and wished he could have gone over his whole life's story then and there. Everyone else seemed so old and drab by comparison.

The last to go was a Lance Simonson who apparently was the university's legal representative. He was a middle-aged man with light skin, a large nose, and a protruding chin. Something seemed off with the man; his eyes darted back and forth as he spoke as if he was checking to see if every word he spoke was received without reservation.

From circling the room, the speaking was back to Dean Chan.

"Great. It is so good to get a chance to meet new faces. Now let's get down to business, shall we? I know everyone has read the proposal, are there any questions? I do not want to take too much of your time before we vote this afternoon."

A few seconds of silence passed before Dr. Irving cleared his throat to speak.

"I did have a few concerns after reviewing the materials submitted by my colleague," Dr. Irving paused.

She looked over to Dean Chan who had a dull look on his face. Nonetheless, he subtly nodded for Dr. Irving to continue with his inquiry.

"My major concern with this proposal is that we honestly do not know what might happen when the machine is pushed to dig deeper into the recesses of people's memories. From the description of recent findings, it has only been proven to find glimpses of memories as far as ten years back, for a few moments, what you are proposing is several orders of magnitude greater than what has been approved so far for your research."

She looked at Dr. Silva. If there was any hint of irritation by the critical question, he did well to conceal it with a courteous grin.

"I conducted a test just a week or so ago and was successfully able to go back several decades. My new graduate assistant, Aliyah, was witness to the remarkable achievement."

Dr. Silva turned and gave her an encouraging smile, not too unlike the one he had flashed Dr. Irving moments earlier.

"Were there any issues or irregularities of this test?" Dr. Irving pressed once more.

"Not at all, it all went as planned," Dr. Silva replied.

"I apologize, I meant to direct my question towards Ms. Woods," said Dr. Irving.

She instantly felt the collective gaze of the committee. All eyes were on her, searching, waiting for a response. Yet, it was Dr. Silva's stare that easily blotted out the rest. His face had a stern appearance that seemed to offer guidance in her response, screaming "everything went over fine."

However, she remembered what had happened that evening and how the machine had seemingly malfunctioned making it difficult to disengage. *Surely, that was not normal and was something that should be reported,* she thought before doubt swiftly followed after. *Maybe that is normal when you reach a high level of scientific inquiry. I do not want to derail a potentially revolutionary scientific discovery.* She was a stranger in a strange land and felt that going against her adviser, a man with more experience than the years she had been alive had the judgment that she should follow.

So, she acquiesced.

"Yes, everything went the way Dr. Silva described, no issues. I am still new to all this and it was exciting to see the machine safely in action."

Dr. Silva smiled pleasantly at her response while she caught a deflated sigh flash over Dr. Irving's face who settled back in his seat.

"Ah, Aliyah, do not sell yourself short. You are brilliant and there will be many, many big historical moments that I will make sure you are apart of," Dr. Silva said in a relaxed tone.

The IRB Director spoke up after glancing at Dean Chan, "I really could not find anything too concerning in the proposal myself. Though, out of personal curiosity, I would like to hear more about what your theory is about. It sounds so fascinating."

Dr. Silva sat up straight as if to prepare himself for some a well-practiced performance.

"Of course, I like to use a colorful analogy. I posit that our memory is like a bottomless well. Each memory is like a photograph cast in the water to float. As time passes, most pictures sink further and further down, until the natural light, our conscious awareness, can no longer reveal them to us. My machine acts like a powerful flashlight that can reveal depths that are not able to be seen with natural light. So far down into the deep that we can see into a past that goes beyond ourselves."

"I thought our memory was not limitless and that old memories are overridden by more recent memories unless they had special importance," Lance stated from across the table.

"Sure, many people experience memory in such a fashion. However, with the right triggers, a play of light, a smell, a sound, even memories that had been thought to be lost to time can be recalled in vivid clarity. My device acts as that trigger. Using sophisticated targeting algorithms, my machine can lock onto a memory and stimulate its activation within the brain. It really is not too fantastic to believe when you think about it. We need not look any further than the multitude of cases of people who display hyperthymesia. People with this remarkable gift, what lay people term super-memory, are able to recall every major and minor aspect of their lives. Give them a day and time and they are able to go back and tell you precisely what they were doing and what was happening in the world with great accuracy. Hyperthymesia is a proof of concept in the natural world for my device. I am merely looking to be able to bring the same opportunity to everyone else who was not born with such a remarkable trait."

"Eh hem," the cute IRB associate, Britt cleared his throat. "What do you mean go beyond ourselves?"

"That is a great question. Now, I know this might seem somewhat fantastic, but I am referring to the possibility that we might be able to uncover ancestral memories using our apparatus."

"Ancestral memories?" Britt inquired further.

"Yes, sorry. We theorize that ancestral memories are those which are passed down, genetically, to offspring. Similar to how a child receives traits of one of their parents, like blue eyes, or excellent hearing. We posit that memories also get passed on through genes.

"Most of the time, like many biological traits, people are unaware of these memories except for the occasional flashing of an image or vivid day dream. Things like déjà vu, feelings of past lives, and the circumstances in which people can suddenly speak another language or play an instrument they never learned might be scattered manifestations of these types of memories, buried deep within our memory. Typically, not consciously accessible on demand.

"Indeed, there is already precedence for this possibility in the natural world as well: many scientists believe that genetic memory might be the explanatory mechanisms for why migratory animals know where to travel and why primitive, instinctual behavior like fearing fire is baked in at birth. Perhaps more convincingly, experiments with rats have shown that rats with a memory for a complex maze pass down their experience to their offspring who have never navigated the maze," Dr. Irving replied with an exacting authority.

"That is all so fascinating! What you speak of is an actual time machine that the laws of physics have denied us for so long. We could be able to see the past if what you are saying is right; it would be a revolutionary discovery, a new era of enlightenment," said Dr. Chan enthusiastically raising his hands in the air as if he were conducting his own symphony unto himself.

"Sometimes that light of discovery is an on-coming train. You can be right, and then you can be dead right," Dr. Irving countered bleakly, who looked back intensely at both Dr. Chan and Dr. Larson.

"Now, now, Dr. Irving. Let's not get hyperbolic. We all know that Dr. Silva has spent much of his illustrious career developing these ideas. Bringing the university unprecedented funding and prestige. I think it is safe to say that if anyone can do it and succeed without incident, it is he," said Dr. Chan, instructively.

She sat there, quietly in her seat. She was enjoying the intellectual debate between the top minds of the department and university. Each point and counterpoint added to the crucible of ideas, slowly being broken down until some sort of logical principle was reached. Most of which was over her head.

Dr. Silva leaned in and whispered, "I think all is going well."

"Are these things normally this contentious?" she asked, trying not to let the others hear.

"Oh sure, you will find that academics like to throw around their intellect to puff their feathers. In the end, having a dean on your side is the only real feather you need to have in your cap," Dr. Silva answered with a slight wink to his right eye which was obscured from the rest of the table.

She pulled back from Dr. Silva, puzzled. She leaned back in her cushy leather chair that paradoxically yielded little comfort. Again, she felt she did not quite understand what was really going on. Seeing the inner workings of how research is conducted through the administrative channels was all still very foreign to her. She felt so out of place and wondered if anyone else noticed.

She scanned the faces around the table. Dean Chan's face was propped up between his thumb and index finger. He had an unassuming dull-expression as Dr. Irving made another forewarned critique. The Department Head, Dr. Larson had a similar expression, but was worse off for hiding it. He constantly shifted back and forth in his chair making a series of creaking and cracking sounds. Dr. Winters, the IRB Chair, also seemed adrift in thought; her blue pen tapped incessantly on her pad of paper. She only could catch a few glimpses, but the pad of paper in front of her seemed to have various scribbles of drawings at its margins. Not what she would have expected from an administrator supposedly taking note of the merits of an important research project. Lastly, she came back to the face of the young IRB associate. Britt's face seemed restless and about to crack forth with questions lying beneath. When Dr. Irving took a pause to catch his breath, the young associate spoke up.

"I'm sorry, but no one seems to be asking about the ethics of conducting this research. Sure, it sounds like it could open up so much knowledge, but as a review board member, I must ask if we might be exposing people to a whole new level of risk with such an experiment? As far as I can tell, we don't fully understand a lot of what would happen as it is mostly theoretical at this point. The question must be asked: what are the unintended consequences of having a complete access to memory and, if real, ancestral memories? I could imagine that opening that door could harm participants by making them obsess over the past and never want to move forward with their lives. Has no one stopped to wonder why we might have these natural limits? I'll also use an analogy from the natural world: in nature, there is a reason why trees don't reach the sky; growing too high would cause them to fall from their own weight—"

Dr. Winters interjected surgically as soon as Britt finished. "We need not belabor again the value that this research can have. I appreciate your concerns Britt, but as Chair of the IRB with over fifteen years of experience, I am fully comfortable with the science that is being conducted here. I have had a long relationship with reviewing Bash's work and *not once* has he caused the board any concern with his research."

Dr. Winters finished with a rebuking glance at her young associate and then turned and smiled at Dr. Silva.

"Oh Sara, it is fine. We should have these discussions and I welcome the feedback. However, we must balance our concerns with the scientific pursuit of inquiry. A scientist needs to be free to pursue questions, seek out evidence that holds great significance for humanity. Some of the greatest discoveries would have never seen the light of day if we were not willing to go breach beyond the line of uncertainty.

"To your point though, I think knowing our past is the only thing that can propel us forward. You need to know where we have been to advance and build upon our past achievements. I always like to quote Cicero here, 'Those who know nothing of what happened before they were born, are to remain forever a child.' Those words still echo with truth today, if we do not try to understand our past, humanity will be forever stuck making the same old mistakes and coming to the same conclusions," Dr. Silva said, tapping the top of the table twice with his fingertips.

Dean Chan spoke before anyone else had a chance to respond, "Well put, I think that really sums up the necessity for this research. I'm looking at the clock here and see that we are running out of time…so unless anyone else has something further to add, the committee members will take a vote for a simple majority. If you approve of the project proposal, say 'Yay' and raise your right hand."

'Yay,' the chorus rang out as all the committee members, save for Dr. Irving, marked their endorsement.

Dean Chan continued with a pleased look to his face, "And any 'nays' for the proposal?"

"Nay," Dr. Irving said affirmatively.

"Well it looks like the 'Yays' have it. Dr. Silva, you have the committee's approval to begin your experiment."

"Thank you all, I am honored to be able to conduct such significant research here at Hightower. There are so many great scholars here that we are surely the envy of so many institutions," Dr. Silva replied.

"Yes, we are. Now, that brings us to a close for our meeting. Please check your calendars for our next review," Dean Chan concluded as he began organizing his papers to leave.

She felt as if a great accomplishment had been made, despite not fully understanding the process behind it all.

One by one, the committee members pushed back from their places. Dr. Silva immediately went over to go carry on a cheery chat with Dr. Larson and Dean Chan by the head of the table. There was much congratulatory patting on the back and hand shaking along with several furtive glances over towards Britt and Dr. Irving who were engaged in what looked like a kindhearted conversation.

She was left alone at the table. She did not really know what to do with herself now. She *did* know she was not going to bother her adviser in his big moment. This was a culminating moment for him and she had the wits about her to know that a first-year graduate student by his side now would only be an unwelcomed audience. He had done her a kindness by allowing her to sit in and soak up the experience. She would do the same and step back and let him soak up the achievement.

She waited at the table until she felt that the remaining people in the room were distracted. With gazes turned, she slipped out the back through the double doors out into the hall.

4

The Old Woodlot
One month B.R.D.

The hallway was quiet.

Not wanting to linger by the door, Aliyah walked down the hall. The freshly-polished tiled floor rang out the soothing rhythm of her high-heeled footsteps. The hall led directly to the atrium at the entrance of the building.

The rectangular atrium was magnificent. By day, it was filled with the light that filtered down from a diamond-shaped skylight. The skylight was made up of a dozen interlocking widow facets, refracting the light that shifted throughout the day. Now, in the evening, the light was a faint crimson that contrasted with the pearl white glow of the polished marble floor. The floor was scattered with lounging chairs and reading lamps placed in neat squares on either side of the walkway that connected the central stairs to the front doors. Above the ground level, the space opened up all the way to the fourth floor. People walking on the upper floors could walk around the atrium from all four sides and peer down at those below.

Upon entering the space, she smiled at Mr. Jones, who was finishing his floor waxing in front of the central stairway. Mr. Jones, who went by 'Skeeter' to his friends, was the building's custodian and did his best to keep the halls and rooms in pristine condition. He was a homey-looking man with steely grey eyes, thin lips, and a receding white hairline that made a sort of peninsula shape on the top of his head. Like his faded blue jean-jacket, his face was worn from years of hard work. Not much unlike her own father.

Mr. Jones was a rough man to those who did not know him well but was friendly once he felt comfortable around you. She would always wave to him in the hall or flash him a smile—even the roughest of people will wave back when one waves. She thought he appreciated it, being noticed.

"Good even'n, Ms. Woods," he said, politely stopping his buffing machine so that she could pass up the stairs.

"Thank you, the floors look great!" she replied, pointing to the mirror polish that he had diligently attained.

"Why thank'ye, not many people seem to take too much notice. I figure they gots plenty of big ideas troubling their minds than the polish of a floor they walk over every day. Not many folks notice where they walk."

"Well, I think it looks lovely. Besides, having a mind looking to the sky is nothing without steady footing," she said, parting ways up the stairs.

"Thank'ye kindly…and take er easy."

She climbed the stairs up to the fourth floor and slumped down in one of the lounge chairs. It felt nice to have a moment of quiet, free from the potential gaze of those who could shape the trajectory of her professional career. She closed her eyes to rest for a second. She felt the squishy fabric against her back. The seat was not as expensive as the leather meeting room chairs but was so much more comfortable.

She heard talking below.

The moment of tranquility soon evaporated. The committee members must have begun spilling out from the conference room, she could hear the cacophony of conversations and deep-bellied laughter quickly filling the large atrium space. She leaned her head slightly to the railing to peer down to the first floor. She was careful not to be noticed.

She could see the remaining committee members heading out the doors of the building. Dr. Silva and Dr. Irving were entangled in a lively conversation and exited out together. As Dr. Larson bid farewell to Dean Chan, he nearly slipped and fell on the waxed floor. He gave a firm reprimand to Skeeter before retreating gingerly to his office.

Lost in her observations below, she felt an unexpected tap on her shoulder from two unknown fingers.

She whipped around.

"Ahh! You scared me," she exclaimed, trying to catch her breath.

"Sorry Aliyah, I didn't mean to give you a fright," Gabe replied behind a round face, almost baby-like if not for the dark stubble covering the bottom half. His baby-blue eyes were kind but subdued behind a mop of hair. The sandy-brown hair was thick and feathered out over his ears like little bird wings. His hair today was unusually disheveled, like a bird in molt, which highlighted the uneasy look on his face.

"Gabe, it's fine. I was just lost in thought. What's the matter? You look like you haven't had any rest for days."

There was little doubt of that, his skin looked pale and his eyes were drawn and sunken.

He did not reply immediately. She tried to search his face for an answer. His eyes darted back and forth trying to avoid her gaze until he could not hide from the question any longer.

"I dunno if I want to say. It sounds crazy and I'm hoping *I'm* not crazy," he muttered, picking at his thick, collared shirt.

"Gabe, you can tell me anything. I'm not going to judge you. My mind and ears are open. Go on…" she replied, trying to be delicate. She motioned to the empty chair next to hers for him to sit and be more comfortable.

He sat down slowly.

"Thank you. You're much more approachable than everyone else in the lab. If I told Dr. Silva or Craig, they would laugh me out of this place for sounding so anti-scientific."

"You won't get any laughter from me, just attentive ears and an open mind. I'm still new to all of this too, remember, so I really can't be one to judge."

His eyes locked on to hers and his face loosened slightly.

"All right…here goes then…do you remember a few weeks back, when we had to go down into the basement to find those records for Dr. Silva?"

"I recall that, yes," she replied, remembering the creepiness of the basement and *those* sounds that they had heard.

"I know we haven't had much time to discuss the basement but I just wanted to retread a few things to make sure what I am going to tell you makes sense."

"Sounds fair to me," she replied. The thought of revisiting that evening compelled her to shift in her seat.

"Okay, I'll stick to the main points, but please stop me anywhere you find a discrepancy with your own account."

She nodded her head in agreement.

"From what I recall, you came down to my desk in the late afternoon about two weeks ago. You told me that Dr. Silva needed a few old records from his storage space in the sub-basement. So, we went down into there and went to the area where Dr. Silva archived his documents and stored old equipment…" Gabe paused for a moment until she gave him a nod of concurrence. He continued, "…at that point, we began looking through a lot of different file drawers trying to find the right set of documents. It took a few minutes but eventually we found them and right as we were turning to leave the room, you jumped at an old one-way mirror leaning against the wall…"

She remembered this moment vividly. She had turned around and right before she began to leave the room, she swore she noticed a flint of a shadow move from the corner of her eye. It was then that she turned to notice the mirror which startled her in the dim basement light.

He went on, "You knocked into me and as I reached out to halt my fall, I leaned into a rack of metal storage shelves. Though sturdy, the shelves couldn't withstand the quick force of my weight and they all fell over into the wall. After checking you were all right, I pulled back the shelves into their original position to find that they had made a tennis ball-sized hole in the wall. Upon closer inspection, we realized that the area in the wall wasn't the true wall but a poster board that had been placed over a recessed place in the wall..."

"Yes, I remember, the poster board had faded and accumulated so much grime and dust over the years it didn't look any different from the rest of the walls of the room."

"...However, the curious thing was the grains of salt that poured out of the hole. You said we should leave it be but I was curious and pushed aside the poster board. Behind it, we found a small bag of salt with a spot that had been punctured by the shelves. I wouldn't have thought more about it until I noticed a glimmer of something that looked golden protruding from the white grains. Pulling the object out, we were both amazed; the object was circular, just a bit larger than a half-dollar coin. The gold-colored outer edge was carved in the shape of a snake eating its own tail with two blood red crystals for eyes. Encircled within was a jade-colored tree with branches and roots that intertwined and connected into one another in a continuous circle.

He paused and took a deep breath through his nose.

She sat quiet, remembering what happened next. She half-wished that he would just stop there and not continue on.

But he continued, "Right when I picked up the object, I told you I could hear a faint sound of music. At first you doubted me and told me to check if I had it playing from my nexus device, like I usually do during the day, but I told you that I had left everything in my office. The music was faint, barely audible. It almost sounded like some of the really old songs my grandparents would listen to."

"I know. At first, I didn't hear anything besides the creaking of pipes. I thought you were just trying to freak me out more after the whole mirror thing. Then I heard it. A waffling sound that danced in progressive octaves up and down. It sounded like that weird organ instrument that you see in museums and in old films. It got louder, fluttering towards some unseen climax…and then…just as suddenly as it had begun…it stopped."

She could see that that Gabe was encouraged by her shared account. His posture was more relaxed and his face had even returned some of its natural color.

"After the music stopped, we both swore that we could hear giggling and a child's laughter. We knew we were the only ones down there and after that we decided to just run for the stairs and get out of there."

"I still don't believe it, but yes, that's how I remember it too," she reluctantly reassured, looking at Gabe and then back at the floor with a half shrug.

In the pause, she noticed how quiet it had gotten in the atrium. Mr. Jones must have finished his work because he was no longer buffing the floor below. Not even a muffled footstep or conversation could be heard anywhere in the building. The atmosphere had returned to silence, its natural state, not unlike the one that had preceded that haunting disembodied laughter she had heard in the basement. She did not want to let the memory back in her mind for fear that she could not banish it again. The tension from the stillness drove her to speak.

"So, now that I have confirmed what happened, was there something else you wanted to tell me?"

"Yes, thank you. Knowing that you also experienced that 'unexplained' stuff is reassuring. I know that at least I'm not losing *all* my mind."

He paused to think for a moment. He looked right through her as he twirled the wing of hair next to his ear with his right index finger.

"Perhaps, I'll start with a question: since that night, have you noticed anything else strange that's happened to you?"

"Umm…not really. I have been pretty stressed out of late but nothing out of the ordinary…although I have been remembering some frightening episodes from when I was younger. I kinda figured it was just related to being scared now reminding me of when I was scared as a kid," she replied, not wanting to disclose too much of her anxiety she had in the restroom just hours earlier.

"…very interesting, it can't be a coincidence…" he replied, trailing off again in thought.

"What coincidence?" she asked. His pieces of cryptic statements were not making any sense.

"I know you study childhood fears in your research, did I ever tell you that I had an imaginary friend?"

"No, you did not," she replied.

"I did. His name was Mr. Pickles. He came to me from my closet when I was just six-years-old. He looked like a small boy with pale skin and jet-black hair and a face that was oval-shaped not unlike that of a frog which reminded me of a pickle for some strange reason—kids draw strange connections.

"I knew, even being so young, that he wasn't like other people I had met from the start; he had unusually large pupils that were midnight-black, so black that they reflected no light.

"Oh, and the fact that Mr. Pickles didn't have a face; no nose, no mouth, just those two wide black circles for eyes. That was a pretty good indicator he was different," he said, his voice had developed a hint of a quiver in it.

"You know, it's perfectly normal to have an imaginary friend. Many children report having them come and go early in life before eventually growing out of it," she said, trying to make him more at ease.

"I'm not too sure what I experienced was normal. At first, Mr. Pickles was innocent and mostly just told me stories about great warriors of the past, stuff that I was interested in as a young boy. Then, after a while, his stories began to get darker. He would go into gruesome detail of death, fighting, and killing. For instance, one time I was out playing in my sandbox and he told me that I could practice being a warrior by killing grasshoppers. He told me to get a glass jar and catch them in my mother's garden, and when I did, to bury them in the sand so they would suffocate. For any that made it back to the surface, I was to rip off every one of their legs and watch them roll around in helpless agony.

"I did as he told me, I collected about a half-dozen grasshoppers and buried them in my sandbox. When the first one reached the surface of the sand to get its breath, I didn't want to dismember it. I can remember it as clear as day, for when I refused, Mr. Pickles's demeanor instantly changed to anger; it was as if a cloud had blocked the sun over just my little sandbox. Everything got darker as he yelled for me to finish the job. 'Pickled peppers, pick them, peck them, watch them throwing.'

"I was so scared that I did as he said, crying, plucking each leg from the poor helpless grasshopper's body and watching it squirm in distress, spitting brown tar on my fingers."

"Oh my, that's terrible," she gasped, trying her best to shield from him how disturbed it really made her feel.

"Yep, Mr. Pickles said it was good practice. He told me that when I get older, my job would be to kill people using these skills. He would be there along to help guide me and identify my targets, my helpless grasshoppers. I tried to tell him that I didn't think I could do it; my heart couldn't take it. He chuckled at me and told me that I would get used to killing after a while, when my heart grew dark, there wouldn't really be any other choice. It would even be *fun*."

She sat in her chair with her mouth half open. She had never heard in all her interviews with children, anyone report such a disturbing story.

Her lack of response gave her away.

"I know, I would be shocked too. I was so traumatized by the sandbox incident that I went to my parents to tell them everything Mr. Pickles had told me. Of course, they never believed that he existed, even after pleading with them to make him go away. They wouldn't do anything besides tell me that I may need to see some sort of therapist. I asked if this so-called therapist would come over and kick him out of my closet and they told me that's not how it worked.

"I couldn't understand so, I don't know how I got the idea, but I went to my closet and commanded Mr. Pickles to go away, that he was no longer welcome in my house. At the same time a hissing sound began to emanate from my closet, like that of air leaving a balloon, and I demanded more forcefully that he leave. This time, a loud whip of air went by me and the entire room got brighter, like a black sheet had been cast off my windows letting in the natural light. I knew he had gone."

"Wow, that's an amazing story. You were so young!" was the only thing she could think to say.

"Yes, I thought it was the end of the story…for the longest time afterward, I thought it had all been the fabric of the imaginings of a little boy. Up until a couple of weeks ago, I thought none of it had happened. But then I saw *him*."

"Mr. Pickles!? You're imaginary friend!?" Her heart began to race.

"Yes, after our basement incident, I woke up that night and saw him, sitting at the end of my bed, just as he was, not aged a day. What's worse, I was frozen in fear and couldn't move my arms or legs. I was stuck, just watching him blink those big dark black eyes.

"After a few minutes, I would blink and he would be gone without a sound. But every night since, he comes to my bed and just stares at me. I fear that he eventually is going to speak, he's gonna say that he's back to do what he told me he would do, get me killing people. I don't want that to happen, but I don't know how to be rid of him," he said, collapsing his face in his hands just as the tears began to bellow up from the corners of his eyes.

She got up and comforted Gabe at his side. She didn't know what to make of his story quite yet but could definitely see that something was affecting him. Her heart was still racing as his story had brought back into light doubts of her own childhood memories. Memories long-locked behind walls that she preferred not to scratch against; of things that she knew, that she hoped, were not real.

Later that evening, Aliyah was still working late in her office. Preparing for the committee meeting, the meeting itself, and, importantly, making sure that Gabe was in a good place before she sent him home, had soaked up much of her working time. There were still dozens of pages to read on *Advanced Neural Matrix Analysis* and *Barriers to Accessing Total Human Memory* and, not to mention, a project plan proposal that Dr. Silva wanted in two weeks. But somehow, the numbers on the clock had just flown by; seemingly, 6:20 p.m. had turned to 8:30 p.m. in a blink of an eye—such was grad school time.

The hour finally had become too late for more work, the marginal gains had reduced to skimming of paragraphs with little comprehension.

She really could not focus anyhow; all she could do was think about the strange story that Gabe had told her. Sitting at her well-organized desk, her mind was a jumble; replaying over, and over again, Gabe's story and their encounter with that mysterious object. Questions echoed out in her mind: *How did that thing get there? Where did it come from? Could he really be seeing a childhood imaginary friend?*

Unanswered, the questions itched in the back of her mind. A pesky irritation in a place she just could not reach. Usually, she would unravel the solution with careful reason and thought. A problem would be laid out with the facts, opinions, and speculations and see how all the pieces went together—present and missing. But this problem seemed beyond her ability to decode.

She was also still very worried for Gabe. She had told him before parting earlier, that he could contact her if he needed someone to talk to. She wished she could have done more; he had been so upset and frightened.

At least he was not shaking any longer when he left.

It was almost impossible not to believe him. *How else could something affect someone so?* she thought. Gabe was smart and an exceptionally hard worker; so much so that he could easily be confused with a graduate student. She wondered if him trying to do so much had finally broken him down. It would not be unheard of for a high-performing student to have some sort of psychotic break when under so much self-imposed stress.

Yet, that really did not fit him. Up until this point, he seemed to be managing things just fine. His demeaner only changed *after* their time in the basement.

Gathering her things, she shut down her work station and locked the door to her office behind her. The hall was quiet, which was not too unsurprising for the late hour. Only graduate students lingered in their offices at this time in the day; the faculty had long since gone home—it was by tenure's right. For grad students, there were always things they could be doing to forward their career and little time to do it. She was exhausted and it was time to go home. Every step down the hall brought her closer to home, to food, to some rest.

Up ahead, an obstacle to her relaxation presented itself. Craig had just turned around the corner and was walking with a purpose in her direction. His wavy black hair bounced atop the large-frame designer glasses that occluded a pair of beady eyes that were now fixed upon her. His face typically carried a half-smirk but tonight it looked much more irritated. She was so exhausted and really hoped to pass him by with just a forced smile and a simple 'hi' without much more.

"I'm glad I caught you," said Craig, his dark eyes were determined and looked tired against the burgundy-hued bags holding them up underneath.

So much for a run by, she thought.

"You and Gabe were supposed to get all those documents for Dr. Silva a couple weeks back. He mentioned to me that we still don't have one of the calibration manuals needed for the Mindsai machine. So, now I'm asking you, did you guys even go down to the basement like you were instructed?"

Waiting, Craig stood there, picking at the black stubble that ran down his neck, remnants of a patchy beard that he was oft to mess with when restless or in thought.

"We did go down there…" She bit her tongue to force herself to pause and think. "…We got the notes that Dr. Silva requested but ran out of time to find the manual."

"And why didn't you go back to get it later?" he pressed, giving her a look of contempt. "Were you too busy preparing for your *big* committee meeting that Bash asked you to attend? For what reason he would invite a first-year, I don't know."

"I'm not one to speculate on the intentions of others. He asked me to go and I was honored to do so," she snapped back.

"Well good for you…" he trailed off, losing his train of thought for a moment and continued to dig at a shaving nick at his Adam's apple.

"What was I asking again, Daisy?" he asked his AAI companion.

"You were asking why *Aliyah* did not retrieve the *Mindsai manual* from the *basement* from a suspense date of approximately *thirteen days* ago," said the French-accented AAI voice.

"Right you are! So, why is it that you guys didn't go back down to get what was asked of you?"

"Honestly, when we were down there, some strange things happened to Gabe and I and he is frankly still shaken up by it."

"Strange…?"

"Yeah, Gabe almost got hurt from a falling storage shelf and then we both heard some strange sounds down there that freaked us out."

"Strange sounds, really Aliyah, what are we, preteens? You were asked to do something and you didn't do it and your excuse is some *strange* sounds were heard. I know you both are new at this but you're both supposed to be scientists, it's a fucking basement, there are all kinds of creaks and sounds down there. Nothing strange about it."

"I'm telling you, these weren't natural or explainable. And I don't admit that easily," she said emphatically, trying to put a little distance from Craig who had aggressively encroached into her personal space.

"I guess it's really not a surprise that you would believe in such superstitions, you do believe in a mystical spaghetti monster in the sky who created the universe, don't ya?"

"Excuse me?" She was so taken aback by the sharpness of his tone that she truly only heard the first half of his statement.

"Oh come off it, you wear that archaic symbol around your neck representing some old system of beliefs that has no place anymore. I can't believe people, especially those espousing to be scientists, can still blindly believe the veracity of a book written by people so far removed from the events they were writing about…And that reminds me, in fact, from the diagnostics of the Mindsai machine, Daisy and I determined that it must have been Bash seeing the cross you were wearing that day that disturbed the machine's processes; a silver cross on a shadowy background was the only discernable image that we could recover after he experienced the targeted memory. Good job fucking it up."

She took a few blind steps backward, trying to lean away from Craig's aggressive posture.

She was almost too stunned for words. She was visibly shaking and wanted to slump away like a shrinking violet. She had never felt so attacked for anything. Sure, she understood a few people, especially younger people, did not share her beliefs. Many young people of the day had traded the worship of the divine into worshiping themselves within their own virtual social kingdoms. In these realms, people could acquire the attention and tribute from like-minded people and AI alike—worshipers surely outnumbering that of any king of antiquity. But she lived in the real world, and devoted her worship to that in which could not be depicted by some machine. She did not flaunt her beliefs and certainly did not deserve to be ridiculed for something that was so important to her identity.

For half a second, she thought about retorting back that it was largely possible that the writers of the books of the Bible were able to do so, with great accuracy, using spiritual gifts of super memory. Like Dr. Silva stated in the meeting, dozens of contemporary cases of people with super memory, or hyperthymesia, who can remember almost every autobiographical moment of their lives was certainly proof of the human capacity to remember great details. It would not be too much of a stretch for divine providence to unlock these gifts for chosen individuals to write and document the important events of biblical history down to the exact things that were said.

Yet, the half-second thought past by without even an utterance from her mouth which was still agape. She knew any argument would fall on deaf ears and a hardened heart.

"What? No response? Come on Aliyah you need to be fast on your feet if you want to stay in this lab. Bash doesn't like people who can't think quickly," Craig said, shaking his head in a mocking motion.

Tears were welling up within her. She could feel the warm wetness circling the perimeter of each of her eyes. She did not...no, she could not, let Craig see that his bladed words had cut her deeply. Not here, not now.

"I'm sorry, I need to go. If you want that manual, you'll have to get it yourself. I'm not feeling well enough to get it," she said with a quaking voice. She felt a single tear rolling down her cheek and turned abruptly to leave before the levy broke. Staying to fight would have gotten her nowhere and only made her first year in grad school that much harder.

To her relief, he did not pursue. Through her strained breathing and quick footsteps, she could hear him chuckling and making comments to Daisy. That stupid French accent rang down the hall, mocking her.

A tiny laugh filled her chest after she had turned the corner of the hall; she actually felt angrier at the AAI than she did at Craig.

Pushing open the doors to the back entrance of Hugenberg Hall, she felt a weight lifted from her. The cool night air instantly enveloped her in a calming embrace. The rhythmic chirping of crickets sang in chorus, one last mournful crescendo of lament, a coda before the cold befell them all. She was finally alone, free to let her guard down…and cry a little in peace.

The sidewalk stretching away from the building was narrow and in disrepair. Cracks and fissures feathered out as a result of years of winter expanding and contracting, slowly wearing away the unnatural structure that trespassed onto the landscape. In places, chunks of concrete had crumbled away at the edges and had found their way into clumps in the patches of ankle-high grass next to the walkway.

The sidewalk on the rear side of the building did not see much use by students or faculty. Most were probably not even aware of its existence. She counted herself among those who rarely traversed the path; she had only taken it once before when she wanted to explore other parts of campus. Tonight, however, her reasons were simple, with tears rolling down her face still, she merely wanted a path where she could head home, unseen.

The crumbling path led directly into the patch of woods that comprised the western portion of campus. Called the Old Woodlot, the woods were a thick composition of old-growth hardwoods. Tall pines could be found closer to the cliffs that jutted out from the ridge.

She began walking, not really noticing her steps. Her mind was still busy ruminating over the day. The basement…Gabe's 'friend'… Craig. The thoughts that frightened her most were the seeds of doubt that seemed to sprout forth more with each passing week. Doubts about whether she had made the right career decision, about whether she was cut out for grad school, about whether she could be so far from her family. It was toughest being away from her family. After moving from her hometown in Ohio, she was a seven-hour trip away, missing out on family gatherings and seeing the steady pace of age change the nature of her parent's faces she used to know so well. Faces that had almost begun to lose familiarity as the weeks stretched between when she saw them during their weekly video calls. Not having that family support system added a layer of difficulty to an already formidable task of being the first person in her family to attempt to obtain a graduate degree.

She knew well that, if she let these doubts creep in, it eventually would be crippling. She was not going to let that happen. She would honor her father's parting words that he gave her before leaving for grad school:

"You've already made us so proud, just continue to keep your eyes on the prize."

Stopping in her tracks, she repeated the encouraging words in her head. Then she declared loudly, out into the wood, "I'm just going to keep on swimming!"

Her voice bounced off the trees that seemed to pay no reverence to her declaration—they had no ears to hear it. They only rustled their leaves in silence.

She pushed the doubts from her mind and took in the sereneness of her surroundings. The path was dimly lit in the fading light. The lampposts had only recently sprung on. She could still hear their electric hum as they warmed up in the cool night's air. The trees that surrounded her on both sides towered above. She looked up and could see their sturdy boughs sway from the westward breeze that rustled the leaves at their tips. A harvest moon was on the rise but she could only see slivers of its pale-orange glow filtering through the branches of the cross-hatched canopy.

A winged shadow streaked across the moonlit backdrop.

Probably a bird trying to find a place to roost, or a bat starting its night; *the twilight was truly a time of transitions,* she thought, gazing intently into the branches trying to get another glimpse at what might be moving about in the night.

Only inanimate shadows remained, unmoving.

She continued walking down the path. The pools of lamplight appeared to get brighter as the night grew darker. The trail at her feet had turned from solid concrete to a grey mix of dust, stone, and woodland debris. These signs signaled she was approaching the heart of the wood. Coming around a large oak tree that had diverted the path slightly, she was at a T-junction. Her path home was to the left. To the right, she was not too keen on. She knew it led to the living communities on the north side of campus. And she had also heard it connected to the path leading out to the cliffs, a place town's people affectionately called Devil's Leap. The cliff outcropping stood nearly one hundred meters above the valley floor. At its foot was a sulfur spring-fed pool whose depths had never been officially assessed.

The promontory of Devil's Leap had received its name from tales since the town's inception that people who dared to gaze from its craggy point would hear whispering voices from the surrounding pines. There was no definitive account of what the whispers spoke of; some say you can hear the people who jumped screaming all the way down, others tell it as the devil himself trying to lure you to the warm pool below—with promises of a great reward. One consistency of all the stories was it was said for those who lingered too long teetering at the edge would be driven to madness by the voices and take a fatal leap to the pool below.

She briefly gave a weary glance down the path to the right before swinging her feet onto her chosen path on the left, to home.

The trees grew younger as she drew away from the heart of the wood. The canopy was lower so that she could see the full glory of the moon. In the moonlight, she could see the brush was much thicker here. The competition for light was on a more even setting when tress are young and not quite at a height to dominate everything below. She felt a little bit claustrophobic but could tolerate the feeling for a little while longer.

She picked up her pace, sensing she was nearing the end of the path. The beat of her shoes on the ground was almost soothing. So soothing, that the light seemed to be dimming in her eyes. She opened them wide to compensate for the lack of light. There was no change in brightness. She knew that it was not sleep encroaching upon her now. She saw the lamplights were beginning to dim. With each quickened footfall, dimmer and dimmer the lights became. By the time she had gone the length of a fallen tree trunk, the lamplight closest to her was nearly out. Only a faint cool grey glow remained. She could barely see the path before her if it was not for the moon.

She whipped herself around to see from whence she had come. The lights behind her were out or imperceptible from where she stood. She was concerned. She did not want to have to feel her way out of these woods tonight.

Her gaze returned to the lamppost nearest to her. The light was there still, but clinging for its dear life, fluttering ever-so slightly. Then, suddenly, the light began to flicker wildly. The others too, in perfect unison. Their lights intensified to a bright blue light and flickered so quickly that the light gave off a white strobe effect. Her hand sputtered in slow motion as she reached it out in front of her. She could feel her heart begin to race in time with the light, not knowing if she should run or hide. Her leg muscles clinched tightly as she prepared for flight, ready to push off down the path to make for an exit.

There was a bursting sound and then all the lights were out. She was in darkness.

After her eyes finally adjusted, she could see that only the pale moon allowed her to discern any of her surroundings. *I could probably make it with the moonlight*, she thought in between her pounding heartbeat.

With one sense gone the others became more acute.

She listened.

Nothing.

She tried harder, perking up her ears to focus on any sound.

Still nothing. Not even the tiny scampering's of a field mouse or the flutter of leaf. There was not a sound to be had in the wood.

She looked up at the moon that was still rising. She felt companionship with it, in the silent vacuum of space, with no light to shine of its own.

Woo…Woo…

The sound of a distant train whistle pierced the silence. She nearly jumped out of her skin.

"Automated, or not, I wish I was on that night train right now, anywhere but here in the woods in the dark," she said under her breath, as if hiding her voice from other prying ears that could be listening. It was ridiculous, really. There was no one there to listen in the dark, she knew that, yet anything above the threshold of a whisper felt strangely risky.

The train's whistle grew fainter as it disappeared into an unseen distance. The heavy silence quickly filled the void that it left, at least until a light breeze started blowing from the east. Unlike the breeze from before, this one was different; it only traveled at head height near the forest floor. She knew because she could not hear or see the branches swaying above in the trees. It was also extremely cold, not like the chilly breeze of fall that she had felt before, this one was icy as the coldest winter's day.

Her eyes were now better adjusted to the low light of the moon and she could see the leaves rolling over themselves across the path. Some even floated up into the air at shoulder height to pirouette in an eerie dance of amorphous form. Even in her frightened state, she was almost enchanted by their performance.

The feeling was short-lived, her trance was broken by a rumble coming out of the east where the breeze had come. The rumble was building in strength. It did not take long before she realized that it was coming towards her!

She had no time to run, no time to prepare, when the gust hit her, she never had felt so cold. The stale air smelled of rotten eggs.

The smell was bad, but the sound that followed was worse. The blast of air around her made a deep, guttural growl that vibrated the very innards within her. She screamed uselessly as her voice was carried in every direction by the cold blast of air. *You can't yell at the wind stupid*, she thought frantically.

Her next thought was to run. She really did not care where, as long as it was not here. Her feet were under her and she was running as swiftly as she could. God knows what direction. It had only taken a few strides before she was off the path. She reached out her hand to push aside the nearly invisible branches that swatted and scratched at her face. Down at her feet, twisting vines tugged at her legs, making her stumble forward in constant deceleration. She could not hear or feel the cold air anymore but she did not want to stop, not until she reached some sort of civilization.

As she trudged on through the dark, the undergrowth lessened and the trees grew further apart. The ground beneath her feet became sandy, then gravellier, and before she could process it, she was standing on solid rock.

She stopped suddenly as a blast of warm thermals lapped her face in greeting. She knew where she might be. *It must be a stony outcropping from the ridge*, she gulped hard, *please, not Devil's Leap*.

With legs spread apart in a readied-stance, she looked up to see in front of her. There were no longer any trees, only the blackness of the ridge's edge a few meters away.

That was close, she thought. *I could have run straight over the edge!*

She raised her eyes up from the black abyss and looked at the moon. It was now fully unobstructed, shining nearly parallel with her position on the rock. It was a beautiful sight to behold under different circumstances.

She turned around. She wanted to see what lay behind her, what she had been frantically running from. She could see many loose boulders and the wood's edge only ten meters from where she stood. Even more, she could see the faint, soft-white outline of a path glowing in the moonlight.

A way out!

She exhaled deeply.

Then, something else caught her eye. It was faint at first, but it growing in size and intensity. A light was passing between the trees. As it drew near, she could see that it was a blue orb of light!

The light that emanated from the orb was fiery blue at its edges that turned to a bright white at its center. The orb was completely silent as it slowly floated between the trees, shrouding their bark in blue translucence. On the ground, directly beneath the orb, little wil-o'-wisp-like sparks were brought forth from the ground. It silently hovered and pulsed as it approached, with no signs of anything else around it to explain its source.

She was frozen in her feet and could not move. The orb was hauntingly beautiful, but like staring into the sun, she had a visceral feeling this beauty was dangerous and not to be gazed upon without a price.

The orb reached the tree line and stopped, seemingly unwilling to go any further. It floated and sputtered in place as if it was mutely considering her. Closer now, she could see the rich blues and whites pulsate over its surface in rhythmic motion.

After what seemed like a few minutes, without any noise whatsoever, it floated perpendicular to where she stood and disappeared into the trunk of an old oak tree. The light was completely absorbed and darkness fell back into the wood.

Still frozen in place, she stared dubiously out into the night. Her eyes felt as big as her coffee saucers trying to pick up even the faintest hint of light or movement.

She waited, daring not to venture back to the tree line where the orb had halted. Some unseen horror could be lurking anywhere in the gloomy shadows.

She felt she was still being watched. Her eyes darted from left to right, right to left…scanning… searching for any lingering indication that something remained, waiting for her to make a move.

There was nothing.

Finding feeling and control return to her feet, she crept forward. The loose stones and leaves crunched loudly beneath her feet. So loud in the silent darkness, that surely people from town could hear her step.

She stopped…and watched…and listened. Still nothing. The woods were still…but unnaturally so. The terror did not feel like it had passed.

She took another step towards the path at the edge of the trees. Before she could lift up her other foot to continue her slow march, a blast of cold air hit her smack in the face. Her eyes closed for a split second as an autonomic reflex but she quickly forced them open wide to see where it was coming from. The trees swayed and buckled from their great weight; their branches rattled without heed. Louder and louder the clamor rose. She could feel the noise run through her toes as the ground vibrated beneath them. The sounds were soon accompanied by darting shadows among the trees. There were figures! They had distinct, purposeful movement to them, jumping in disjointed movements from tree trunk to tree trunk until…her greatest fear became realized…

She saw that the trees were moving!

Her mind raced trying to process the sight before her eyes. She could barely fathom any of it. The pines were slowly encroaching on the rock promontory, past their original line of demarcation. Their roots reached forward like leathery whips snapping to each new foothold. Their pine needles whistled in the wind, incoherent at first, but slowly growing to a faint raspy whisper as they edged ever closer. A great creaking and cracking drew her eyes to her left. The grand old tree that the orb had disappeared into had begun lumbering towards her from the place that it had probably stood for centuries. Its large branches twisted and turned, all stretching out towards her with a multitude of crooked fingers. All the while staring at her with faceless bark.

The trees approached without the slightest sign of wavering. She stepped back slowly being ever mindful of the dark edge that lurked only a few meters away. Soon she would be in their woody reach, then what?

The whispers began to whirl around her along with a torrent of decaying leaves. She could make out the voice, or was it voices, she could not say. It did not matter, the raspy whisper frightened her to the bone just the same, because it knew her name.

"Aliyah...We are the watchful night, we are a child's deep fright. Eyes and ears, yours don't deceive, we need not belief. We wait here always and ever, always and evermore... Evermore ... EVERMORE!"

Her heart beat out of her chest. She scooted back so more. She felt the edge now. Her back heel teetered over the side. Time was up, there was nowhere else to go—darkness would envelop her here or below.

The grand oak tree was almost to her now, its woody hand outstretched and pinching.

She closed her eyes almost to resign herself to her fate. The whispers maddingly filled the air with growing fervor marking the creaking approach of her doom. A doom that had waited in her darkest dreams and in basement mirrors. It was real, it was not really a surprise, she had always known it, deep down. She had chosen not to believe, to bury the knowledge only a child would accept. But choices do not change reality, it was about to grasp hold of her now.

At least...until...a tune sprang to her mind. No, not a tune, a hymnal from church she recalled as a child. It was like a ray of warm white light in her mind, the only thing she could see and focus on. The words took hold of her and spilled from her lips. She sang so loud that she thought the whole valley could hear it.

"Praise God, from whom all blessings flow / Praise Him, all creatures here below / Praise Him above, ye heavenly host / Praise Father, Son, and Holy Ghost / aaaaamen.

"Now be gone! You are not welcomed here!"

And when she had finished, a light shone on her closed eyelids. It created a warmth inside her like that of a cozy campfire. She feared the orb might have returned which made her hesitant to open her eyes at first. Yet, something told her that the danger had passed. When she finally opened her eyes, the trees were all back in their natural places, the voices and the wind had ceased, and the lamplights...yes, the lamplights...had sprung back on to light her way home. She did not hesitate to get on her way.

5

Philosophies from The Ebony Tower
One month B.R.D.

Carefully watching his footing, Bash descended the moss-covered steps that led down to the entryway of The Ebony Tower. At the bottom of the stair, a massive swamp-oak door guarded the entrance. Cut from a single tree trunk, the door was large and dark in color. Even the countless years of age had not much weathered the sturdy slab of wood. He could still distinctly see the tight parallel lines of the grain, a testament to the tree's once long history.

Ahead of him, Chris gripped ahold of the wrought-iron door handle and pushed with considerable effort to open the door. The door creaked and moaned on its hinges as if to announce their presence to the underground tavern that had served the town for hundreds of years as a place for drink and merriment.

On the inside, The Ebony Tower was illuminated with a mix of gas-fueled lanterns and Edison-style bulbs, though illuminated would be overly-generous for the place. The air had an earthen smell to it and had a cool draft that swept across the low-hanging ceiling that was bolstered by thick, black beams of wood. The walls were covered with a grey barn siding that had been graffitied heavily with the etchings of past patrons. Hung on them, were translucent telewindows, broadcasting the college football game. The image was so clear and full of depth, that it was absolutely indiscernible from the real thing. It was like looking through a window to any part of the world. Though in the tavern, the out-of-place telewindows were typically only a portal to mundane sporting events.

Chris chose a spot in the back of the tavern for them to sit. It was directly adjacent to the grand fireplace that was alight with a healthy supply of giant logs.

Walking through the maze of tables and chairs, he could overhear an elderly couple discussing that another massacre had occurred in Jerusalem with nearly 500 dead. This news was unfortunately not out of the ordinary, as violence was a constant. Due to the frequency of their occurrence, most news agencies did not report deaths unless they rose above 200. The whole of the Middle East had been in constant instability since a terrible earthquake, caused by a large meteorite, had struck the region decades before. Many of the historic sites had been damaged and the Islamic holy site, the Dome of the Rock, had been completely destroyed. The nation of Israel had taken advantage of what they deemed divine providence and decided to remove all remnants of the Islamic site in favor of building their own holy temple on what they had always claimed to be their Temple Mount. The surrounding Islamic nations took the blasphemous actions of Israel with great indignation and unified in a constant state of subversive conflict with the more powerful Jewish state. With constant sabotage and disruptions to construction, it had taken more than a quarter century for the Jewish Temple to be built. The temple was now nearly complete, which explained the uptick in violence in the news.

Given the history of the region, this was one case in which memories are perhaps best forgotten. *Open wounds never heal if you keep peeking into them*, he thought.

His mind turned. Most of these wounds were based on folklore and myth; if one could see into the past, with an objective lens, then perhaps, disputing parties would bow out to the sword of truth. His research could be a vehicle for peace if all disputes could be set up against an unfiltered eyewitness, even if that eyewitness was taking the stand from hundreds of years ago. Seeing the memories of ancestors from long ago presented boundless possibilities. Maybe he could win a Nobel Prize for peace as well.

He smiled as he took his seat across from Chris.

From his seat, he could watch the dancing fire. He reached for the center console of the table to turn on the cone of silence distributor nested directly overhead. Bash flipped through the menu slowly, passing by 'Telewindow 1' ... 'Telewindow 2' ... 'Telewindow 3' ... 'Telewindow 4'—all options that would transmit the audio of the various telewindows across the room to their table with near-perfect clarity using directed soundwaves. Finally, he arrived to the setting category he was looking for: 'Cone of Silence.' He was presented three options, (a) open cone (no noise attenuation), (b) half cone (fifty percent noise attenuation), and (c) full cone (one hundred percent noise attenuation). He selected option 'c'. Immediately, the surrounding clamor of the tavern fell silent, as if all sound had been sucked away by some vacuum nozzle. He could now converse with Chris undisrupted by the loud noises that surrounded them. Additionally, starting from a few steps away, they were now completely unheard by surrounding ears due to the cone's noise-canceling field that surrounded their table. In plain sight, the cone of silence was their own private sanctuary.

"Good idea," remarked Chris, as the sounds around them fell away. "I can finally hear myself think without the chatter of these young girls squawking about their latest virtual fashion creations."

Chris motioned to the group of girls who now appeared silently laughing at one of their nexus devices the group was enthralled in.

He turned back to his colleague. It was Chris who had proposed that the pair go out for celebratory drinks. He found the suggestion odd at first, given Chris's tough criticism of his project during the committee meeting. Now, though, after having considerable time to ponder about it on the way down, it was not really too strange at all.

His friendship with Chris stretched back decades to when they first arrived as newly minted assistant professors. Much of their early research had been collaborative, studying the interplay of cognition and perceived realism of virtual environments. Their collaborations had also been somewhat adversarial. He often found himself on the opposite side of hypotheses from Chris. Yet, they could always feel free to speak their minds and not hold anything back. Though contentious at times, the research was always better for it.

To say that they were merely good colleagues in those times would be a disservice to his memory. Outside of the lab, they would frequently hold dinner and cocktail parties—his Emma and Chris's Jessica became fast friends in their own right. That is, until Emma's death. And by the time Jessica died suddenly in an accident by an automated vehicle a few months after, things never really were the same.

Their friendship slowly waned and faded as they grew apart. After Emma died, he threw himself into his work and had little time for friends, old or not. Life was too short, what happened to Emma was certainly proof of that. There were so many things he wanted to accomplish. Big dreams and goals he had been pursuing his whole life. Not friends, colleagues, or even death would prevent him from falling short.

And it had been worth it. Look at him now, he was on the very edge of the biggest discovery of his life, perhaps for even all those who came before him.

It took him a while, lost in thought, to register the tall glass of beer bubbling up in front of him. Chris had already ordered a round of drinks. He really had not intended to drink tonight. Or even be in a bar for that matter. He had only come to figure out why his old friend had treated him so critically.

Smiling, Chris raised his tall glass of beer. He raised his and smiled just the same.

"Cheers, old friend," Chris said, clanking their glasses together.

"Cheers," he replied, somewhat begrudgingly.

He took a sip of his beer. The carbonated drink was cool and tickled the back of his throat as it slid its way down.

"Ahh...it's good to have a beer after a long day. It loosens the body and the mind—a true elixir of life. The ancient Egyptians knew that when they discovered it 3,000 years ago. And yet, that simple discovery has not changed much across the expanse of so many years, even with all our modern tinkering, beer is still just water, yeast, sugar, and grain. There's a simple beauty to that," Chris mused, before taking another generous swallow.

Pleasantries aside, he finally had a moment to truly study his old friend. The years had indeed changed his face but it still rang true to the man he had known for so long. To many, Chris always looked outwardly content. However, not even the passing of decades of falling out from one another could rob Bash of his discernment to see that, buried underneath the jolly exterior, a sad smile was rooted underneath the veneer. Chris's eyes showed intense longing and, on his face, regret lurked at the corners of his closed-lipped smile. The look pained him to see and made the first question barely lift off from his lips.

"Chris..."

"Yes, my friend?" Chris's eyes were now fixed on his own. Open and searching to predict what was about to come out of Bash's mouth.

"Chris, I have to know why you were so antagonistic in the meeting today. It felt like you were deliberately trying to undermine my research. I know we go a long way back, and *you*, of all people, should know how much it means to me."

He had gotten it all out and was surprised he had done so without interruption; Chris was apt to interrupt when he had a point he wanted to interject.

This time, Chris was quiet and listening intently. His head might have raised slightly from when Bash began, but his face had barely changed from before. His eyes were glazed over as if the mind was away searching or hiding, Bash could not tell. The silence between them made him feel more and more uncomfortable as it stretched out between them, slowly forming an ever-wider space that was not seen, but was, indeed, felt.

His question hung, suspended, in a still air with no response to support it. He was prepared to ask it again, to keep his query aloft. For he had to know an answer. A demand he would make of an old friend. His lips pursed forward to speak just as Chris began his reply.

"Sorry to keep you waiting. I wanted to gather my thoughts and fully consider your statement before I spoke. I do so, because, I deeply value our friendship. Sure, we have drifted a bit as we have traveled down this river of aging—I recognize that—but it does not change the fact that you are a person who has left heavy footprints on my life and you are very dear to me, Bash," he said, his eyes wide and unblinking. Water had begun to flood the corners, but the tears were kept at bay.

He continued.

"With that said, I spoke up today because I am genuinely concerned about where this research is all heading. You are pushing for so much, so fast, that I do not know if you fully grasp what you are experimenting with here. Just one small misstep with these types of systems you are dabbling in could change people irrevocably. We are talking about people's very memories, what makes us who we are.

"I know you have climbed high pursuing this goal for so long, but Bash, my friend, I fear you are developing an Icarus complex on me. Rarefied air is certainly sweet—and you have tasted a euphoric slice of it—but it is also thin, perhaps not meant for us."

The pointed honesty of Chris's statement dug into Bash. He had been prepared for an attack, but not one that undercut him so deeply. It was not so much the content of Chris's words—he already knew how he was going to respond to them—it was that they had come from a friend who he thought knew him so well.

To make Chris understand, he would have to try and make a clear and factual case, his friend had always appreciated a logical composition of facts.

"Chris, even after all these years, you are a good friend and I appreciate the concern. I do. We did not get a chance to go into much detail in the meeting today…"

By design, he thought to himself.

"…but, Chris, we are there. We have done all the tests, simulations, and calibrations. The data we compiled from our last test was the last link our system needed to devise an algorithm that is accurate, stable, and to your concerns, completely safe. Moreover, in all our tests, with dozens of subjects, not one has experienced any ill effects."

"That is fine, but how can you possibly know what your messing with? No person or computer can predict what no one has ever glimpsed before. Your potential new world of discovery could have an entirely new slew of parameters that make all prior predictions inconsequential.

"Besides, even if you are able to get a view of these *ancestral memories*, how do you know they are true and not some sort of reconstruction derived from what your machine's algorithm *thinks* should be in your ancestral past? Perhaps the Mindsai is merely a modern-day version of Theseus's ship; each memory a reconstruction, in the same form of the original but never a true analogue."

"Did you not listen at all in our meeting? These memories we have activated are near-perfect in accuracy."

"Yes, for something in the order of a handful of months, but when we are talking about expanding across years and decades, I would imagine much more needs to be reconstructed. The more distal the memory, the more noise is added to the signal."

"Come on, Chris, you know everything we experience is a reconstruction of the world around us. Even something as simple as seeing the color red is different from person-to-person.

Perception is relativistic between persons, but within, there is something definitive. That is the great accomplishment of the system I have devised; we are able to peel through the mind to activate memories just as they were originally perceived with no filter, in perfect clarity."

Chris shook his head and stared wistfully at his beer.

Bash allowed a moment for a response, but none came from his friend. He was ready to dive deeper. He had a feeling that his friend was not being completely forthright with his concerns.

"So, what is your real critique, Chris?"

Chris took another long swallow of his beer and clanked it down on the wooden table. His lips smacked as he sorted through his thoughts silently. While, to others, he looked as if he was stalling, he knew his friend was crafting a well-thought retort that would have taken others hours to formulate. For Chris, it only took minutes. This was a characteristic that had first drawn them together into collaboration—a quick mind, though apt to be adversarial.

Chris began to tap the table, a sign he knew well that Chris's thought process had finished.

"To be completely honest, and I will be frank, I think you might be chasing after a specter," Chris said sternly.

"Umm...how do you mean?"

"For as long as I have known you, and it has been a long time, and even before that, you have been pursuing a knowledge that rises above all the bits and pieces we as scientists have been able to put together in psychology. Over a thousand of years of study and how far did we truly get in the study of the human mind? Do we really understand the aspects of human nature any more now than those who came before us? Over the years we have gained glimpses of a truth, an understanding, but as a complete picture, psychologists still have no holistic synthesis of how it all fits together. But you my friend, you have been pursing something grander, qualitatively on a different level than all the pieces before.

Your research truly seeks to unlock a door at a higher level of understanding of the human mind, past and present."

"I see nothing wrong with seeking to unlock the vast trove of knowledge locked away in human memory."

"Except…what if the ascending path ahead is closed to us?"

"I really do not understand what you are getting at, Chris. Are you dismissing the entirety of scientific study?"

"No, not at all, but I might be dismissing the assumption that has held your dream aloft for so long."

"Oh yeah? And what assumption is that exactly?" replied Bash.

"The assumption that we, as humans, can ever fully understand ourselves."

Bash moved in his seat restlessly. He was surprised that the man across from him, an educated and knowledgeable man, was now putting forward the kind of nonsense that crept up from laypeople who often tried wrap up undercooked philosophies in the guise of intelligentsia.

Bash prodded his friend, "What, that people are too stupid to figure ourselves out? How can a professor of psychology say such a thing given the vast amalgamation of evidence that we have learned?"

Chris spoke replied calmly, "My friend, I do not think you are grasping my central thesis. I did not say that humanity is stupid or unintelligent. We are the most intelligent beings on this planet— most of the time," he chuckled. "Yet, the point I want to emphasize is that the human mind is limited and perhaps incapable of fully understanding itself. We may be able to deeply study different facets of the human mind and have a working understanding about how they operate, but we might not possess the capability to see the greater picture and put together the myriad set of parts into a cohesive picture. Simply, we are cognitively closed off from that greater perspective—the mind cannot understand itself!"

"I truly fail to see how you can believe that, through our science, we are able to develop a universal model of the human mind. Eventually, with enough data, the picture will be completed."

Bash swirled his drink restlessly trying to cover up the nerves that were flaring within. *Why did* he *need to defend psychological science to this man?*

Chris smiled gently and leaned in closer.

"That is my point, even with all the data, we will not have the vantagepoint to see the whole picture. Consider this thought experiment: imagine everyone in the world could only stand a centimeter away from an elephant. Sure, each observer could report on the wrinkly grey texture in great detail, but could they put all that information together to understand the gestalt whole?"

"No, but—"

"They could not. It would take an observer who could see from ten or further meters away to see the animal for what it is and how the small, detailed parts fit together. It is quite probably the same for the human mind, without a mind's perspective, on a higher plane of existence; humanity is just pieces on a chess board seeing the diagonal paths of a single color, missing out on the horizontal and vertical paths which connect the black and white squares into a complete, multidimensional picture."

Bash did not have words to respond to his old friend quickly this time. He felt his mind stretching in a dozen directions trying to process his friend's twisted logic, and importantly, how to refute it all. He needed to defend his research, his life's pursuit, science. In many ways, he felt hurt that his friend was implying the impossibility of his endeavor. Chris knew how much it all meant to him.

Bash could feel his feet braced against the sticky wooden floor; he had unconsciously triggered himself for flight. He was too tired to discuss topics that were of no real merit. No time for things that would detract him from his goal.

For whatever reason, his feet held firm. It had been decided, he would fight this argument to its natural end. He still respected

Chris that much, at least for the happy memories of Emma they had all shared together.

He cocked his head side to side. He was ready to continue with the only question that could follow Chris's point.

"Okay Chris, if we cannot obtain this level of understanding, what kind of 'higher' mind would we need? Could an advanced computer not fill this gap, after all?"

"I anticipated that you might go in that direction. Your Mindsai machine is quite impressive and can do so much, so quickly. But I am afraid even an advanced computer system is limited by the same flaw as us…" Chris replied.

"Okay, and what is that?"

"The human mind."

Bash, feeling irritated, "I do not see how. Computers are now capable of processing more information, knowledge, than any individual or group of individuals could in fractions of a second."

Chris nodded his head only slightly. Looking past Bash, his eyes seemed focused on something out of view.

"I do not disagree in the truth of that. It is clearly self-evident. But what you speak of in terms of speed and processing power is a quantitative difference, not qualitative. A machine is merely a supremely optimized human extension, able to operate quickly with vast amounts of data that is *quantitatively* more advanced than the human mind. Yet, these machines are still limited by our own thinking. For, to build those machines and the logic unto which they operate is derived from the human mind. And like us, they are unable to reach a higher, qualitatively-different understanding of the mind they are a product of."

"Well then, if you eliminate anything connected with humanity, to reach this higher understanding it would have to what…be the mind of…of God?"

"You have discovered the truth that has persisted throughout time, my friend. To understand the holistic nature of the human mind would require a higher level of existence that is only accessible in the realm of God, a higher mind able to create those beneath."

Bash had anticipated this sort of response and left little time for a pause.

"To be honest Chris, I am surprised you would espouse such a point of view. We had so many conversations years ago where you adamantly professed to be agnostic to the existence of some supreme being that created the universe. But now, I see, you are going with a convenient, if not intellectually lazy, explanation for the world."

Bash sank back into his seat. He felt puzzled and a bit troubled by this new revelation of his friend. He wondered where his friend's mind had gone over the years to succumb to such backward musings. *Would this have happened if they would have remained closer?*

Despite Bash's disengagement, Chris continued talking, "Yes, you remember correctly. Time is a process, ever-working on us all. In my aging years, it has come upon me that one can say that they are agnostic, sitting on the preverbal fence, but one cannot live as one. You either live as a believer on faith or not, there is really no in between. My mind took a side, a side that it had always known but feared to acknowledge.

"After Jessica's death, things changed. I felt like there had to be something bigger. To suggest otherwise, would be giving into human hubris. That I could devise a complex system of explanations for a complicated world when the most parsimonious explanation might be the true one.

"And that is why I wanted to speak with you tonight. You are a friend, and I do not want your ambitions, though noble, to blind you to the bigger picture…the risks.

"I wish Emma was here. She had a beautiful faith in you that kept you grounded. For her, and as a friend, please consider you may be venturing into an area you might not want to go."

The crow's feet around Chris's eyes were stretched with concern and his hands were clasped on top of one another, silently pleading, or praying—he could not tell.

For a moment, he had almost lost what they were talking about. It was as if a friend had stepped out from the past in front of him. The filter of time all but removed. With it, memories of Emma came flooding through a fissure. He found himself walking down that old familiar corridor in the mansion of his mind. The doors of happy memories were open wide. He could see her, her face, her smile, the beautiful shape of her body.

A warmth swirled through him. He could see Emma dancing in a field of sunflowers in her springtime dress of robin egg blue. He could see her dancing at the sink as she washed the dishes in her tight, athletic pants. The ones he loved because they revealed so much of her beautiful form and left just enough for his boyhood imagination to run wild.

He could see…a burgundy door, with peeling paint…no, he did not want to be there. He wanted to run back to the happier doorways. Times of joy, not sadness. Yet, his incorporeal feet would not yield beneath him. The soft voice came, as it always did, "Baaash…come closer…"

He was back before the memory drew him in further. Chris was still there. The same kind-hearted face beaming at him as if no time had passed at all.

Thinking of Emma, he realized that Chris too had lost someone special, Jessica. She had died suddenly when an automated vehicle veered off the road due to a sensor that had misperceived the lines on the road that had shifted due to a crack. She died instantly. The loss, only happening mere months after Emma's death, weighed on his friend, a pain he endured for years.

Maybe speaking of Jessica would make his quest finally resonate for his friend, he thought.

"If you could see Jessica again, would you?" he asked.

"Of course, she was the light of my life," Chris responded, without hesitation.

"Chris, that is precisely why I want to pursue this. It is my only shot to see Emma again, my family. I do not care what the costs are. This is bigger than me. Bigger than all of us. If I am successful, and I am highly confident I will be, this could open up a whole new level of understanding and allow us to never truly lose the ones we love."

At first, Chris's face wound up as if to counter, but soon relaxed and melted away into a sad smile.

"If that is what you truly want, I guess I cannot dissuade you. Though for the record, I tried my hardest. Though if I can say one more thing and that will be that: if you do go down this road, do try to be safe. Know when to turn back."

"I will do my best," he said, to appease his old friend.

Then, there was nothing left to be said. He felt the conversation was won, but the satisfaction of winning eluded him. Sure, he had succeeded, but was such a dark victory really worth pushing their ailing friendship further in the grave?

They continued to sip their drinks together. The stillness gathered in the ambers of their conversation.

In his restlessness, his eyes wandered. He could see the young girls were still enthralled in their devices. Silently laughing and giggling. Their eyes were transfixed. Even a fire alarm probably would not disengage them. At the adjacent table, a group of men appeared to be silently yelling at the football game on the telewindows. Hightower's team had committed some sort of grave foul. Then his eyes crossed over a man seated in the far corner of the room.

The man sat alone, a few tables off to his right shoulder. The man was staring directly at their table.

He redirected his gaze quickly to seem as if to not notice the man. After a few seconds, he planned to scope the area again and, sure enough, the man was still looking in his direction. Even in the low light, he could discern the man's cool eyes, like two blue precious stones both fixed and unmoving. The man's gaze bored right into him, as if he had been watching for some time.

How long though? Had he been there the entire time? He could not remember noticing the man when they had come in. Though he would not have noticed a black bear sitting in a booth being so lost in thought the whole evening.

He turned back to Chris who was still sipping on his beer, eyes distant and glassy, appearing to be humming something to himself.

"Chris, who is that man sitting off to my five o'clock? He is just sitting there staring at us. Have you seen him before?"

Chris's eyes narrowed slowly, coming back down to regard Bash once again.

"I had noticed him for a while now. I have seen him in here a few times before," Chris said, disconnected in thought.

"Does anyone know who he is? Where he comes from? Judging from that ratty, old-looking pea coat he is wearing, he looks like someone from straight out of my childhood. But the age is not right; he could not be much past thirty."

"Hmm...yes. He does look a little bit out of sorts, doesn't he? I asked the barkeep one night when I saw him in here. He told me that the man was a sort of drifter who only came in once every blue moon. Always sitting by himself, at the same little table, and ordering a single glass of Italian wine. The barkeep said that he could never really recall the man speaking with anyone. The college crowd saw him as a weird oddity and preferred to talk about the man amongst themselves. However, he did proudly state to me that he once asked the man a question, about where he lived, after serving him his usual glass of red wine."

"What did he say? Doesn't look like one to disclose too much about himself," Bash asked.

"The barkeep told me that the man was quite enigmatic. He said the man told him he has lived far and wide, behind a cobbler's door, up in the seven ridges, on seas of sand, and, now, under the stars of creation, where man's makings cannot blot out the natural light."

"That's pretty out there," said Bash.

"The barkeep thought he was a little kooky; not just one of those kooks who uses their virtual devices to escape to a time before the internet; no, this man was the real deal. Completely disconnected from society and technology, and in his opinion, reality. Though he did not think him dangerous, he was always kind to him. And tipped well, always left a silver dollar."

"And no one knows his name?"

"No, no one can figure that part out. The man appears to have no digital footprint. He is truly off the grid somehow. But I have heard students refer to him as 'The Man with Sapphire Eyes.' "

"That fits him well, his eyes are quite striking. I can still feel them burrowing into the back of my head."

Chris's eyes shifted to look for the man they had been discussing.

"Funny you should say that because he is no longer there!"

He jerked his head around for his own confirmation. The man's seat was indeed, empty.

"Where the hell did he go?" Bash waited for a response but received none.

"Ah...Chris?"

"Good evening," said a velveteen voice, far removed from that of his friend.

He turned back around to see Chris still sitting in his seat but now curiously looking up to his right. The Man with Sapphire Eyes now stood next to him.

"I don't mean to intrude. I overheard your most-stimulating conversation from my seat and wondered if perhaps I could join you to add some of my own harmonics to the dialogue?" the man said politely.

Bash looked to the center console at the center of the table.

How did he overhear us? The cone of silence is still on, he wondered, still trying to process fully what the man had said. The man carried an accent that he could not quite discern completely. There were notes of British, Italian, and perhaps a Middle-Eastern dialect that were unfamiliar. His Middle-Eastern ethnic appearance provided some basis for this assumption, he was sure.

"Please, take a seat," Chris said, without hesitation, giving Bash a quick look and half shrug.

"Thank you both kindly," the man said, taking a seat between him and Chris. The light from the grand fireplace positioned on the other side of him cast an aura-like glow to his silhouette.

Now that the man was closer, there were more details for him to study. The man's coat was clearly outdated and over worn. He could tell now that the grey color was only a figment of what was once a deep black, now fraying at the edges. Around his neck, the man wore a metallic yellow scarf with blue accents that looked like little stars. The man's face was youthful, he surely could not be much past thirty, but it also seemed to carry a great weight upon it, especially around those eyes...

Just like viewed from afar, the man's eyes were a crystal blue. He could see facets of his iris glimmer as they trapped the light into their deep wells. The man's hair was jet black and unkempt, probably curly when in a cleaner state. The man wore no jewelry save for a tiny leather cross which hung from a string around his neck. Like the rest of him, worn and faded.

"New faces, new ideas, are always welcomed in The Ebony Tower. What about our conversation interested you? Surely the academic speak cannot be the most interesting thing in a place like this," said Chris, half-jokingly. "Tell us, friend, what sparked your fancy?"

"You are most welcoming," the man said, pausing before leaning forward in his chair. A solemn thoughtfulness enveloped his face before he spoke, in an almost poetic cadence.

"Memory is a tantalizing mistress, so close, but elusively just out of reach. Both blissful in our glories and cruelly haunting in our miseries.

"And what is sadder than the experience of regret? The replaying of a single event, long-concluded, yet persists on for a thousand what-could-have-beens. I know regret all too well, she is truly an old bedfellow. I once did something terrible...perhaps unforgiveable...and I have paid for it every day. It only lasted a brief moment—a mere flick of the hand to move quicker with taunting lips—but that was enough for it to be burned into my mind so clearly, that it endures eternally...never fading. Another thousand years could pass and it still would be like yesterday to me.

"It is a curse that I bare, a brief mistake that happened forever ago, but carries the weight of a thousand lifetimes."

Bash straightened up in his seat. The man's statement piqued his curiosity beyond the trite mystery of who he was and where he came from.

"That's a very interesting account of your experience with a memory. It sounds very near to how I experience memories, so vividly, that I feel that I am there, in the moment as if the images are moving in front of my own eyes again," said Bash.

The man turned to him and cocked his head.

"Hmm...I overheard much of your talk of memory. Do you truly believe that you can travel into the past, to see memories of your forebearers?" the man asked, sounding more concerned than curious.

"Oh yes, it is quite possible. In fact, we will begin testing that possibility here at the university in a couple of weeks. The experiment could be the breakthrough that opens up a whole new well of knowledge for mankind, a true paradigm shift in our evolution. Not by nature, but by our own hands."

"Yes, tinkering in the dark as if we have the knowledge to know where we are going," Chris added.

Bash gave him a stern look of disapproval before the man beside them spoke again.

"Why is this plane of knowledge so important for you to reach?"

Bash was eager to respond, "Without new knowledge mankind becomes stagnant, limiting progress. We cannot be satisfied with what we have achieved, though we have achieved much as a species. We are at a point where nearly any pleasure or fantasy can be played out, on-demand, in near-real clarity. Despite our progress, though, we are still animals bound by physical desires. We know an animal with a lever that taps pure pleasure in the brain will continue to heedlessly pull that lever every time until all progress and concern fall away to that singular desire—at least until the mind and body are utterly destroyed.

"So, you see, we must advance from where we are, or risk falling into a technological slumber from which we may have no desire to awake."

The man sat motionless without any indication of his current feelings towards Bash's remarks. He simply stared at him as if he was studying not the words but Bash himself. Eventually he spoke with great clarity and precision in his voice that did not waver the slightest.

"Yes, knowledge may reveal much for you to see, but yet still you may be blind if you cannot discern the illusions of this world from truth," the man replied, narrowing his eyes on him.

Bash was growing uncomfortable. It was one thing to be questioned by a friend, but now he was being questioned by a stranger he hardly knew who looked as if he rolled out from under some rock in the hills. It was time to cut the crap and get to the man's purpose.

"You speak in riddles, why not speak plainly? Are you afraid that doing so would expose your points to being falsified?" Bash retorted.

The man struck back quick and prepared.

"You sound as if you are searching for knowledge when it is *wisdom* that is far more valuable. Your science can tell you all about what a thing is but nothing about its worth, its meaning, or its propensity to inflict great evil. Knowledge is the test of if something is possible, while wisdom places that knowledge into context asking whether something ought to be brought about.

"Wisdom is a true understanding of the meaning of the world. The light from the lamp of knowledge is merely an illusion of understanding, without the wisdom to know how to wield it, feed it, and place it in areas of good use, lest it burn everything down.

"Many believe that, since the beginning, it has been the relentless pursuit of knowledge that has been a recursive folly of mankind. Our histories tell tales of the Tree of Knowledge, the

Tower of Babel, Atlantis, the Roman Empire, and the Automation Revolution; all for the sake of knowledge and progress, and not the wisdom and foresight to see all the unintended consequences of that pursuit—"

Bash replied, "You speak of myths and conjecture, without looking back, with our own eyes, free from historical filters, we will never know their veracity. How can we not try to look deep within ourselves to that knowledge? Knowledge that has been distorted and lost to us. Knowledge that is our own to claim back. Our civilization is much wiser and civilized than that of centuries ago. Yet, progress needs to be made to prevent atrophy, we must always have a goal for growth and understanding."

"Is this truly progress?" the man gestured to the girls fixated on their devices. "Pride…vanity…slothfulness, they are all the same now as they have been since the beginning. You assume the passage of time means we have also progressed with it, casting shame on your ancestral brethren, but if you look back, you will see it is all the same. As the wise King Solomon put it, man is the same, just using new ways to do the same things but cloaked in self-gratifying virtue—there is nothing new under the sun."

The apparent biblical reference did more to discredit the man than help him in Bash's eyes. *Where are all these religious people coming from?* he thought. Talk of virtue and sin had no place in a scientific discussion on the merits of his experiment. He was ready to wish the man a good night and go home. It had been a long day and he was tired. Too tired to listen to these half-baked philosophies. But before he could offer a reply, the man continued.

"As a fellow traveler on an endless road that offers little respite, I will leave you with this: it may be better to leave these memories you seek in their grave. Who can tell what ghouls you may resurrect in the minds of others by digging to such depths, to be haunted endlessly by the past that cannot be changed. With the penance I carry, I would wish it on no one.

"Some memories should remain suspended in the amber of time from which they were wrought. There is a reason we do not vividly remember such things. The gulf is fixed and not meant to be crossed. I fear once you look back behind the veil, you might not be prepared to take on the responsibility of that knowledge, the dispensation could be a weight that drags your mind down to depths you cannot imagine...In truth, I came here to warn you that—"

The man was interrupted immediately by a low rumbling that seemed to bellow out from within the earthen walls of the tavern. Bash could feel the table begin to shake forth before him. He got up out of his seat and stood over by the fireplace. The lights were flickering on and off in quick succession. Looking over at the girls' booth, with each interval of lightness, he could see a new expression of fear that had befallen each one of their faces. They were all screaming, silently.

On the back of his legs, Bash felt a cool draft. The air slithered around his ankles and curled its way up his thigh. He turned to see that the fire was still very much ablaze with a large log on a bed of white-hot embers. From appearances, the fire looked hot, but yet, he felt cold. The frigid draft was emanating straight down the chimney chute and out into the tavern.

The sounds around him fell away and all he could hear behind him was the muffled clamor of the patrons. It was as if all sound and heat were being extracted from the room in one giant inhalation. The coals glowed hotter and hotter as the draft whisked across them into the room, carrying with it smoke and soot. He raised his hands to protect his eyes from the ash.

Through the cracks of his fingers, he could see something was, it was moving in embers! It looked to be the wind at first, navigating its way through the burning logs from the back, but now he could see a long slender shape writhing in the fire. It was a glowing snake like that of one of his childhood nightmares.

The snake's scaled body was composed of flakes of embers and its head was black as coal. When it opened its mouth, tiny forked wisps of flame shot out. Its fiery-red eyes stared at him, tracking his position and every slight movement of his horrified face. The snake was coming forth, straight at him, as if it planned to emerge out of the fire. He was frozen in fear. All he could do was stare into the flames and watch the flamed serpent approach him slowly. The scene was playing out and he had no control over his own part in it.

Just as the snake was about to come to the edge of the hearth, a low-pitched guttural growl came from the fireplace. He did not have time to react, for it was followed by a great booming sound that traveled down the chimney and filled the room with a blast of icy-cold air. The force of the sound blew his eyes shut and he could see nothing, no tavern, no fire, no fire snake, there was just the darkness, the cold, and the deafening sound that rattled through his core. It lasted only for a handful of seconds and then was gone.

When he managed to open his eyes, the fire was extinguished. The sound and cold blast of air had subdued the fire and blown the once burning logs across the floor in front of him. They laid there smoking and would have been cool to the touch if he had dared pick any of them up.

To his great relief, though, there was no longer any sign of the fire snake. It had vanished with the fire and, he reasoned, it probably was a smoke induced hallucination anyways. The whole thing was probably an earthquake. He remembered from his reading of the great quake in Israel that they can occasionally release toxic fumes and strange noises.

This peace of mind allowed him to turn his back on the fireplace and observe the room. Most patrons were still huddled on the floor with their hands over their head. Chris laid flat on the floor with his own chair overturned upon him. But the chair that stood between Chris's and his own was empty with no sign of its mysterious occupant.

Just like the flames of the blazing fire—the Man with Sapphire Eyes was gone!

THIRD STAGE

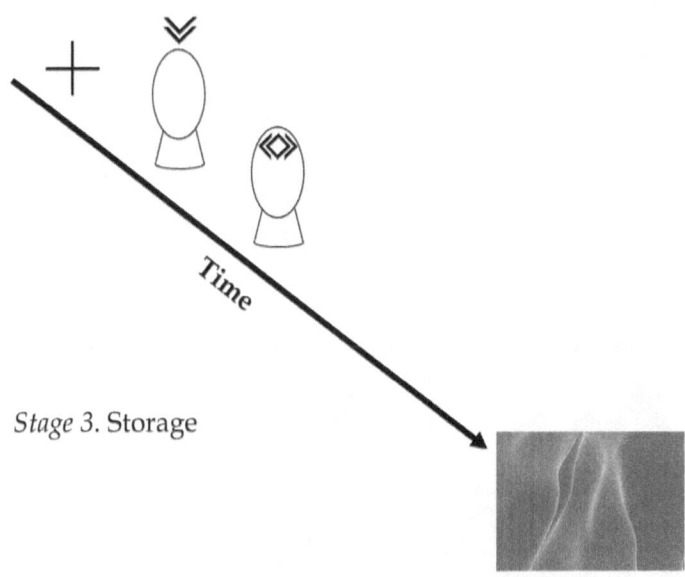

Stage 3. Storage

"Memory is the most valuable thing we possess; it silently guards our past and enables us to have a future, without it, we are but beings in an infinite loop of uncertainty."

Seeing through the Shroud:
Barriers to Accessing Total Human Memory
- Dr. Sebastian Silva,
Five years B.R.D.

6
Basement Archives
One month B.R.D.

The lights in the hall were beginning to dim as the building was winding down for the undemanding hours of night. Few bodies remained in Hugenberg Hall having left for the day—except for Craig.

It was going to be a late night. He was compiling simulation data for the planned experiment in a couple of weeks. Even for the state-of-the-art supercomputer, the simulations were taxing and took several hours to fully complete. The simulations ran best when the building was empty which is why he chose to stay for the evening; the network was wide open with plenty of bandwidth to utilize. After all, much needed to be done. Without much help from Aliyah, the new graduate student, there was more work he had to ensure got completed in time. Bash was not one to like missing deadlines, especially for a project as dear to him as this.

With each passing day, he found Aliyah to be a weak addition to a lab as prestigious as Dr. Silva's. He truly could not fathom why she had been selected for the lab without more extensive credentials. Well...besides coming from a home of drudgers, who were a class of people who received special treatment to enter the high-thinking sectors of society, despite having little technical expertise. Some societal stewards believed that entrance into lofty education could provide drudger groups a means away from the labors that defined a less civilized era in history.

Drudgers were the antipathy to modern ideals. Typically, drudgers were those who, puzzlingly, made the choice to continue toiling away in jobs connected with basic labor. Drudgers performed jobs that were mostly dispensable with the advent of advanced robotics, though a few worked in areas robotics had still yet to fully infiltrate. They were a dying breed of people who believed menial labor was some sort of cherished human virtue. This belief was in stark contrast to leisurists, a societal majority who performed no work outside of leisure pursuits of art, sport, and virtual enterprises. Leisurists represented a culmination of human progress by casting off the chains of labor that were once necessary for survival. Leisurists were free from production to consume the fruits of societal advancement and principled humanism. This progress was ensured and sustained by the third group, the intelligentsia. Comprised of technicians, engineers, and civic stewards, the intelligentsias helped develop new ways of leisure and technological delights for consumption while ensuring that the basic needs of society were well-managed and cared for.

Craig came from a strong family of intelligentsia. His father, a quantum computer engineer, and his mother, a supreme civic steward of the Seattle region. From a very early age, he was stimulated with intellectual thought and conversation. His father's career developing the latest quantum computer architectures was what inspired him to pursue his own academic career. He had early success in the second year of undergraduate studies publishing research on the synchronization of virtual environments and bio-metrics. By the time he arrived to Dr. Silva's lab, he had published a dozen articles and was one of only a handful of scientists in the world that could program for a computer like the Mindsai.

The fact that Aliyah was chosen for such a high-status seat at a committee meeting, for perhaps the biggest experiment of the century, seemed utterly preposterous—she had only just arrived! The girl knew nothing of the machine, how it worked, the potential problems that could arise, the risks. Besides Bash, there really was not anyone better to inform the committee about the technical aspects of the Mindsai. He was disappointed that he was not there to support Bash's efforts. It was not his fault; Aliyah could be quite persuasive with her innocent charm. Bash must have pitied her, because she was not chosen for her expertise, seniority, and merit; the things that matter.

Aliyah was certainly too busy attending meetings because she had not provided him any help on the project thus far. Even when he asked her in the hall earlier in the evening, all she could give him were excuses. She just kept stalling and stalling until an upswell of crocodile tears gave her an out. Leaving him with many tasks unfinished.

I'll have to go down to the basement tomorrow to get those papers, he thought begrudgingly.

His eyes turned back to the monitor. The status window flashed incessantly: twenty-three percent complete...twenty-three percent complete...twenty-three percent complete. This was going to be awhile.

He grabbed for his tall mug of coffee with the phrase 'mind ambrosia' inscribed on the side. A few sips of the warm liquid hit the back of his throat, filling his empty stomach. Almost instantly, he felt a tingling shot of alertness travel up his spine into his head. He also felt a heaviness in his bladder. Like a well-refined algorithm, a few drinks of coffee and he needed to take a piss.

The restrooms on the fifth floor were just down the hall from his office. He would not be long so he let the compiling program run on its own. He stepped out into the quiet hallway. The motion lights above lurched on in synchrony as he strolled his way down to the restrooms, around the corner and past the elevators.

As he turned the corner, Craig came upon an unwelcome sight. A sign stood in his path that read 'Cleaning in Progress.' Just inside the door he could hear the rattling of a push cart.

Why would the janitor be here this late? he thought. He really did not want to have to walk all the way down to the restrooms on the fourth floor. They were dark and less clean since the undergraduates had access to them.

The restroom door swung open quickly. Skeeter, the building's janitor, emerged wearing a denim shirt and oil-stained pants. His eyes stared at him, making him uncomfortable.

"Why are you here so late, son?" the janitor challenged.

He stared blankly at the old janitor. Skeeter was a drudger in every sense of the word. A man with no discernable aspirations, Skeeter lowered himself to clean the mess of others, doing the work only fit for a machine. The university felt it would be bad optics to not employ people that identified with a menial work ethic. Sure, everyone's basic necessities were met by social planners, but some people wanted to work and demanded jobs to do so. Thus, jobs were held open for these masochistic luddites.

At home, his mother had done the same thing when he was a kid. Being a civic steward of the community, she hired a drudger to do the housework to show the community that they were not going to exclude anyone from fulfilling their cherished identity. The housekeeper was quiet and attended to her work mostly well…No, he did not blame the university for trying to keep up gentile appearances. There was the quiet assumption that society would tolerate and accommodate these strange holdover ideals for a time. The unspoken expectation was that the drudger lifestyle would slowly die out after a generation or two.

Craig found it hard to like the chiseled-faced janitor. He was a crudgy old man with clothes that belonged in some sort of redneck time capsule. The man always seemed to have a look of contempt on his face. It was not his fault that the man was living as a drudger. Janitorial work was the few occupations that had not been completely subsumed by the ever-progressing Automation Revolution. The man should have just given into a life of leisure long ago.

He felt a tingling pressure on his pelvis once again. This time it was sharper and more localized. He needed to piss, and soon.

"How long are you going to be working in the restroom?" he asked incredulously.

"As long as er takes, son," Skeeter spat back. He gave Craig a sideways glance and then returned to mopping back and forth over the restroom's tiled entryway.

This was not the answer he was looking for. His need to use the restroom was vast approaching the point where he might not make it to one on another floor. His legs began to shift and buckle as he attempted to stave off the pressure of his overfilled bladder. The sharp pain now felt like an ice pick burrowing into his lower abdomen.

"Daisy, how valuable is my time?" he asked, thinking that maybe he could provoke the janitor to leave. It was a psychological strategy that had worked very well for him in the past with people he wanted to get out of his way.

"It is hard to calculate such a vast quantity," Daisy replied.

Skeeter stopped mopping and leaned on the handle. He just stared at him with his squinted steely eyes.

"Come again?" said the janitor.

"It is hard—"

Skeeter cut Daisy off short. "I ain't talking to your machine, son. I don't take kindly to people thinkin' they are entitled to everything."

Craig's feet began to tap in quick groups of three as he tried to hold off the dam that was about to burst in his pelvis.

"You may think I'm stupid, boy. That I am not even worthy to walk these halls. But I have my Bachelor's degree...at least that's what they called it in my day, before changin' it to an Affiliate degree due to some people's weak sensibilities about genderness. It was in business. And I'm quite happy, thank you very much."

Craig bit his lip as his patience was nearly extinguished. He needed to go.

The janitor mistook his expression of urgency as a slight.

"You can wipe that shit eatin' grin off your face right now, 'cause it ain't funny. How big a boy do you think you are?"

Craig remained silent and looked past the janitor to the bathroom. Sweat was beginning to bead around his glasses. He could not let himself piss down his leg here in the hall in front of Skeeter of all people.

Unaware of Craig's dilemma, Skeeter continued, "If I was a younger man, I would whoop that ass-smirk'n grin right off a you. Back then it weren't nottin for me to whoop a wise-assed boy who needed an advanced degree in manners."

Craig was about to burst. He could feel little dribbles of urine begin to soak in his underwear.

His time had run out.

"I've got to go!" he said, pushing the janitor aside and running into the restroom.

He heard him call out behind him. "Just needed to say so. I've actually been done for ten minutes now, just waiting to see if you were ever going to be as civil as you like to think you are and ask politely," the janitor said, chuckling to himself. Craig could hear him pushing his squeaky cart away down the hall, humming some old tune.

He frantically rushed to a stall. A few drops of urine saturated the top of his pants as he rushed to relieve himself at the toilet. The stream of urine was coming out with such great force that he feared for a few moments that his urethra might not be able to handle the pressure, that it might burst forth. The bio-mechanics held, however, as frothy orange urine splattered down into the toilet below. He could feel the sprinklings hit around his ankles. It was no matter. The slow emptying of his bladder was a sort of ecstasy. It felt as if a bucket of bricks had finally been tossed off his stomach.

A few solid minutes went by and he was done. He shook out the last remnants and then went to the sink. The first sink he came to had a long, thick strand of hair protruding up from the drain from some prior female patron. The left-behind memento irked him strongly, so he went to the next sink which appeared to be in good order. He placed his hands beneath the faucet and waited for the flow of water to pour over his hands. When the water emerged, it was warm, infused with cleanser and moisturizers which soothed his hands.

He cupped his hands to gather a pool of water to splash in his face. His eyelids slowly grew more fluid as the warmth from the water melted away their gumminess. Fatigue was trying to encroach in on him, but he would not have it. Not tonight. There was too much thankless work to do.

He raised his head to look at himself in the mirror and admired his reflection. The water slowly dripped down from his face. His eyes did indeed look tired, yet, they were determined, nonetheless. The life of an academic is always on-going, for the wheels of science do not slumber. It was an encouraging thought.

Before exiting the restroom, he noticed a powered spray bottle filled with cleaner left against the entryway. Skeeter must have forgotten it as he was leaving. Their conversation already seemed ages ago to him. The crescendo of a crisis often has a funny way of distorting the sense of time. Once released from the pressures of the situation, you often forget how bad it was in the moment when the mind is so singularly focused. Now, staring at the dirty spray bottle, he unexpectedly felt regret in his renewed state of mental clarity. He knew he should not have been so combative; members of the intelligentsia need not act in the manner that he did. *The power of the situation is truly real*, he reflected. Between the letdown of not being able to attend the committee meeting, staying up to work late again, and then the physical pressure exerted on his bladder, it was no wonder he had lashed out. There really could not be any other explanation. As an upstanding person, he always strived to be well-intentioned...highbrowed...good. If all these things had not converged upon him today, he found it highly unlikely that he would have acted the same way. He hoped the janitor, even with his own faults in the exchange, would come to the right attribution, that a person in real need of relief would have little patience. This was a naïve theory of mind that most laypeople could understand.

He returned to his office. Everything was just how he left it, including the status bar, which had only gained a few percentage points in completeness. He sighed a heavy sigh and sat at his desk to re-check the processing efficiency of the compilation program. It was bouncing between ninety-six point seven five percent and ninety-nine point eight seven percent. At this rate, it might be early morning before all was completed.

He slouched back in his seat.

The compiling would not require much input for a while, so he might as well get comfortable.

On cue, the lights in the hall slowly dimmed off from inactivity. His eyes were also dimming, the warm watery revival of his eyelids had surreptitiously faded. They felt heavy now, as they creaked in slow intervals between being closed and half-shut. Each cascading effort to open them fell further and further short.

His mind was beginning to slip. His head felt floaty and light, as he began to lose his grasp on awareness. Consciousness was falling beneath the waves into a dysphotic realm where experience was nebulous and incorporeal, fleeting and ephemeral. All perception of time and reality was distorted in this half-conscious space. If he awoke, the dreams that he dreamt would slip quickly from memory to be more pieces of feelings rather than events.

He remembered this sensation, like a distant dream from his childhood years. In those times, he would sleepwalk, especially after a period of extended wakefulness. It was when the fatigue finally became insurmountable that he would fall into a sleep-like state where his consciousness ventured into a space between sleep and full awareness.

On one such occasion, after staying up late with a group of friends at his home, he arose in the middle of the night to sleepwalk. He could still recall the surreal feeling of walking in a dream. The feeling of gliding through space without complete control or awareness of what was happening. It was like watching a movie through one's own eyes as a semi-passive observer.

He watched himself float down the hall, passing a large picture window that let in the silvery-shining light of the moon which filtered through the silhouette of trees just outside. After this point, things became fuzzy and his memory seemed to blackout and skip.

His next thought was seeing a dark outline of a basement door. He remembered just staring without blinking or taking a breath. It stood there before him, stoic and unmoving. He felt a strange feeling as if the door was watching him, as if it had an essence of its own that vibrated with life. A cold, tingling feeling began to move through him. This visceral feeling made the door seem to pulse within his limited visual perception. The pulsing slowly grew until eventually the silence was broken by the sound of rattling and uneven air emitting from the cracks underneath the basement door. He could not discern if it was a dream or real. Yet, in his mind, dream or not, he knew he did not want to go investigate, but his body lurched forward.

Nearer to the door, in the uneven movement of air, he heard the sound of whispering. It was unintelligible at first, just wispy sounds, like the fluttering of a moth's wings, that barely rose above the noise floor of the silent room. But as his ears strained to pick up the noise, the sounds grew louder and clearer. As if whoever, or whatever, was making the noise, knew that his ears were trying to listen. Finally, the whisper registered in his mind into a recognizable word.

"Craig…Craig…" said a voice that floated up from beneath the crack of the door.

Only silence filled in thereafter, like it had all been a mistake or a misperception of his mind.

What happened next still eluded him. His next conscious thought was the sound of his mother's voice shaking him awake. He was somehow in the basement with all the lights turned on. She told him that she found him screaming, alone in the dark, still in a state of sleepwalking. He had no knowledge of it. He thought it all had been a dream.

Now, in his office, he had that feeling once again. He had almost forgotten it. The memory, much like the sleep-walking behavior that had begotten it, he had out-grown by his teenage years. It had all become a distant echo of childhood, something that might have been more imagined than real.

The sleepiness was growing. It brought with it a sense of dread. A dread of losing control, into a realm where his scientific mind was a stranger and could not explain perceptions not tethered to a reality he understood. But as much as his semi-conscious mind struggled for wakefulness, a slumbering sleep was pulling him away.

Pulling him down.

Down.

DOWN.

All seemed inevitable until a radiant white light penetrated his mind. His eyes jerked open in alarm.

Was this it? Was he dying?

All seemed to go white as his vision was overloaded with light. His heart jumped and blood rushed to his head. At the threshold of consciousness, his visual field was a foggy blur of half-sleep. Speckles of red and purple glimmered and flickered across his eyes.

Still trying to focus, he noticed a dark shape dart across his visual field. With a clearer mind he would have guessed it to be a figure made of shadow, but in his state of hypnopompia where he was coming out of sleep, all was a hazy flood of visual stimulation.

When his vision did finally acclimate itself, he could see a light had come on in the hallway at max brightness. The brightness of the light filled his pupils and pushed away the foggy haze of slumber. The light had jolted his system to a state of alertness no different than if he had just jumped down from a cliff in a mid-run.

Now awake, and clear of mind, he wondered why the light in the hall had sprung on so late in the night. He turned to look at the computer monitor. The status bar was now at thirty-three percent which meant he must have been dozing in and out of sleep for a little while. He turned back his attention to the light emanating from the hall. It was bright, much brighter than it usually was in the evenings with people about.

His ears perked up to listen for who might have triggered the lights to come on at this late hour. There were no sounds of footsteps or talking. Not even the soft closing of a door. He pushed his ears hard to try to capture even the slightest sound of a draft moving through the building. This time there was some sort of pattern that rose above the normal sounds of machine humming in his office. It was faint, but had a discernable, repeating rhythm to it.

"Baa Baa Buummm…Baa Baa Buummm," the rhythm went, not unlike that of old-timey music. The sound was too faint to hear from his seat, so he sprang up to his feet to investigate with Daisy in tow.

Stepping out in the hall, he noticed a radiant white light shone down upon his head at his office door. The change in light from his dimly lit office made his eyes squint tightly in response.

He surveyed the hall.

Only one half of the hall was lit up, the other half was still dark and without movement. On the light side, the lights continued down the corridor to the far end where the elevators and stairs were. There was no sign of anyone who might have tripped the lights to come on. There was only that repeating beat that had grown louder and more distinct:

"Baa Baa Buummm…Baa Baa Buummm…"

He listened through a few sets of repetitions. It sounded as if the beat was coming from down by the elevators on the light side of the hall.

He turned back to stare longingly at his office. It looked homey and serene; a place far removed from the unexplained. He took a half step forward to go back to work and dismiss the disruption. Deep down, he really did not want to know what ebony shadows lurked in his ivory tower.

He stopped.

He knew that it was his charge to ensure the expensive equipment on this floor was safeguarded while he was in the building. To have someone steal or tamper with the delicate proprietary equipment would be disastrous for the planned experiment. One missing or broken part could set things back months, if not years. Bash would never look at him the same. And when it came time for his own academic appointment, he might not receive the recommendation he would require to have a successful career. With that in mind, he pulled shut his office door and pressed his nexus device against the door panel to lock it. The bolt clanked loudly and it was secure.

He slowly began to make his way down the long corridor, stepping in and out of the bright cones of light shining from above. The light contrasted with the darkened offices and labs that he passed by on his left and right at staggered intervals. Each door's tiny rectangular window was like a small black event horizon, concealing what might lay within. He knew they were empty, just like they always were at this time of night.

He tested one door's handle just to be sure.

It was locked.

As he edged further and further down the hall, the sounds grew louder.

"Baa Baa Buummm...Baa Baa Buummm," the beat continued, on and on.

He knew he was headed in the right direction but was still at a loss for where the sound was originating. With so many intersecting corridors, offices, and labs on multiple levels, sounds could bounce between any number of surfaces before reaching his ears. For now, though, it appeared that the relay of lights correlated with the growing sound. So that's what he followed.

He finally reached the end of the hall at a T-junction. The lights were on, but only going down the hall to his right. The sounds were much louder now. He could hear them emanating from just around the corner where the hallway zig-zagged. He knew he must be close.

He approached the corner cautiously and slowly peered around it, hoping not to jump whoever was the cause of the music. He gripped the corner of the wall and pulled his face around.

The hallway was empty...

He exhaled deeply with relief but with a new breath, uneasiness swiftly swept back into his gut. He knew the null finding meant that he must continue to investigate.

Above him, the trail of lights stopped right at the elevator bays. One was closed, but the other was curiously stuck open.

He moved closer to get a better look.

Once he was about three meters away, he stopped and squared his feet so that he could peer directly into the elevator compartment. The recessed lights were bright inside, illuminating the dark wood paneling that made up the bottom half of the car underneath the square mirrors inserted at the top of the three walls. It was the mirrored interior which confirmed for Craig that there were no occupants inside. It was completely empty.

He stood motionless in front of the open elevator doors. Doors that would usually close after about ten seconds without user input. He checked the warning light, and it was not illuminated, indicating that the doors were staying open for no apparent reason.

He stepped forward, into the car to complete his examination. He looked around the elevator and did not see anything that look peculiar or out of place. The buttons were all unlit and he could find no signs that someone had been there to tamper with the elevator's systems to create those strange sounds and keep the doors open.

The elevator was quiet.

He realized that the rhythmic beat had stopped. Thinking about it, he had not heard anything since he walked around the corner to where the elevators were.

But why now?

Everything was silent. The air was still and unmoving. He could only hear the sound of his elevated breathing, in and out, in and out.

"Owooooo!"

The sound of a man howling pierced the heavy silence. Then, even louder than before, the beat came back with great force from within the elevator:

"Baa Baa Buummm! Baa Baa Buummm!" it went, hurting his ear drums.

The beat, of what he could now identify as a strumming guitar, seemed to be slightly out of tune. It was enough for him to identify its location. The sounds were not coming from the elevator's speakers but seemingly up from within the elevator shaft. In another wave of sound, a voice rose up through the floor right at him!

"Hey there, Little Red Riding Hood / I don't think little big girls should / go walking in these spooky old woods alone…Owwwooo!"

Like the beat that came before, the lines repeated over and over again in an unending loop. The repetition froze every part of his body. He could feel the cold sweat creep down the back of his neck. His legs began to shake and buckle as fear took hold. The sounds that had emerged from the elevator shaft were now all around him. All he could think to do was cry out for Daisy to know that she was still there.

"Daisy! Daisy! What is this music!?"

"The song being played is titled: 'Lil' Red Riding Hood' by the group 'Sam the Sham and the Pharaohs' who were a band from the mid-twentieth century who gained notoriety for this song and another novelty, 'Wooly Bully.' Shall I play a sample for you?" Daisy replied in a calm voice, seemingly oblivious to the situation he faced.

"NO! NO!" he replied, clinching his teeth.

Then, before he could engage his legs to move, the elevator doors slammed shut and the text on the elevator console illuminated in red.

Sub-basement.

The elevator lurched as it began its plunge downward. He grabbed on to the brass railing at his side to adjust to the sudden acceleration. His head was full of blood—and terror.

"Daisy! Call"—he stumbled and lost his footing as the elevator jerked in its rapid decent—"call the campus police!" It was the only thing he could think to do.

"Right away, calling the campus police," Daisy replied in the garbled noise of the elevator and music that continued to repeat.

In all the sound and motion, he could not hear a connection.

"Craig, it appears that a connection is currently unavailable. Shall I try again?" Daisy reported.

"Yes! Call again! This is an emergency!"

Daisy's time to process was much shorter this time around. He knew instantly the response was not one of salvation.

"I'm sorry, Craig, the connection is still unavailable. I will ping your request periodically as I standby."

He did not bother to respond.

The elevator had come to a halt and his eyes were now fixed on the elevator console. The status screen read 'Sub-Basement.' Instead of a chime, a last "Owooooooo!" rang out and faded into a steady silence.

For the moment, the elevator stayed motionless at its unsolicited destination. He remained fixated on the elevator doors which were still closed. He tried his best not to stare too long at the doors for fear that his gaze might trigger them to open. Into what peril he did not know. So, he shifted his sightline just off center, rapidly moving his eyes side-to-side. Yet, even the sides of the car left him with little refuge from fear. He dared not linger too long or gaze too deeply into the mirrors that surrounded him either.

He looked at the console, which was now unlit again. He had little confidence that it would work but he figured he had to give it a try. So, he tapped the console to get back to the fifth floor.

No response.

He leaned back against the railing, running his hands up through his hair. He felt the dampness from the sweat that now covered his head.

Krrrrrrrrt!

He heard a scratching sound coming from the other side of the door. He could feel his temples pulsing up and down from the intense flow of blood. His mind was askew, trying to grasp for a singular thought that might offer a solution to this impossible situation. So many ideas flashed by him but all were bubbles just out of reach.

Then the doors opened, just as they would in normal operation. He clinched at the coming sight, but nothing was there, just a dimly lit corridor.

He went forward cautiously, steadying himself on the elevator's doorway and looked around the corner—more empty corridors.

He exited the elevator.

A column of air smacked him square in the face. The air was stale and had a musty smell of old electronic equipment and rotten egg.

He followed the long corridor ahead until he came into a large archive room filled with rows upon rows of metal stacks. Each compartment contained assortments of old books, file folders, computer storage devices. On one shelf, of a professor he did not recognize, a Dr. Czardo had a creepy looking child's doll among other toys from what was probably once a developmental psychology lab.

He continued down the center aisle, passing the tall metal stacks that varied in their state of clutteredness. Some had stacks of papers and folders while others had old surgical instruments. He went on until he found a small room that was an offshoot from the main archival room. A dingy bronze plaque read 'Dr. Silva' above the doorframe.

He stepped inside.

The floor of Dr. Silva's archival storage vault was strewn with old yellowed-papers and manila file folders. One of the stacks was obviously out of alignment with the others and he could see a gaping hole in the wall.

Those two made a real fucking mess of this place, he thought. He was still annoyed that Aliyah and Gabe had not finished their assignment. Now that he was here, maybe he could find the file that Bash had requested and make the best of his unexpected situation.

He began to search through the clutter. He picked up a few loose pieces of paper. The first, an old experimental log, was covered in dust. Shaking off the parchment, dust particles snowed down in a grey-tinged cloud through the air and deposited on the floor softly. Holding the page under the light, he could now see the hundreds of inscribed participant numbers, dates, times, and simple notes. He smirked at reading one comment that read: "Participant showed up with an air of alcohol on their breath and clothing, recommend exclusion."

Behind the old log, he found another page that had a simple, lighthearted phrase "It will be fun" repeated over and over. He assumed both were from some long-forgotten cognitive experiment.

He shuffled through the papers a bit more until he realized that, on principle, that it should be Aliyah and Gabe who should be cleaning up this mess. He would take it up with Bash personally if he had to. Bash would be disgusted with the state of his archival records. Besides, with all this dust everywhere, which could damage the electronic archives stored on the shelves, the space could use a good cleaning.

He went over to the wall to examine the hole that he had noticed earlier when he entered. Coming closer, he noticed that the hole was in fact a gap created by a recessed portion of the wall that was about a shoe-length wide and went back about a meter deep. A fine white dust could be seen flowing out of the depression.

This piqued his curiosity. He knelt down on his knees and dipped his hands in the unidentified substance. The coarseness of white grains grated his skin. He brought up a pinch to roll around onto the surface of his nexus device.

"Daisy, what is this stuff?" he asked.

"Stand by…analyzing…the substance you are referring to is sodium chloride or salt. This particular mixture has trace elements, less than one percent, of zinc, iron, and potassium. The substance is non-harmful," replied Daisy.

"Thanks, that's what I thought it was. But why would a huge clump of salt be sitting in Bash's archival vault?"

A glimmering sheen caught his eye. A small sliver of a curved metallic object was sticking out from deeper within the nook. Bracing himself against the gap's opening, he stretched out his fingers. His fingertips just barely grazed the object. Determined, he pushed his full body against the opening and a single finger was able to hook the object and drag it out. Before he could even lay his eyes on it, he could feel a cold chill coming off of it. The metal stuck to the inside of his fingers with an icy embrace.

Object in hand, he pushed back from the opening and got to his feet. He brushed the last few remnants of salt from the object's surface. It was indeed metal; it had a goldish hue to it with certain parts covered with black blemishes. He guessed that it was made of bronze or iron pyrite. It was cast in the shape of a snake coiling back onto itself around a jade-colored tree with interlocking branches and roots. He was instantly overcome by it—he had never held something so…unique…so old.

Craig held up the object at head height for Daisy to see. The ruby eyes of the snake glistened in the low light.

"Daisy, can you identify this?"

"Searching stored databases…" she replied quickly.

There was a pause as she searched. Even though Daisy could not connect to the outside world, her internal storage of information compiled from history, museums, and science were still vast.

"Sorry, this object does not meet any known artifacts. From what I can tell you, the snake appears to be cast in iron pyrite in a configuration like that of an ouroboros, an ancient symbol of infinity. The tree, shaped in jade, appears to match with several ancient cultures as a symbol of knowledge."

"Wow, I wonder how old this thing is? And how did it get here?" he said aloud.

A small, metal protrusion sticking out from just behind the head of the snake caught his eye. He placed his thumb on it and felt that it displaced slightly from a little pressure. With more pressure, the piece moved until it clicked and then...

POP!

The head of the snake turned outward away from the end of its tail.

The action of the mechanism made him jump back and he almost dropped the object. Just as he tried to catch his breath, he felt his hand, that was holding the object, growing cold. His fingers and palm began to tingle, not unlike the feeling of holding an ice cube for too long. The tingle quickly turned to be a sharp pain, like an array of needles pushing themselves deep into the flesh of his hand. The pain grew until it became unbearable. He placed the object on a nearby shelf and then immediately stashed his hand into his armpit to regain warmth.

As he warmed his chilled hands, the object began to vibrate, violently side-to-side upon the shelf. What little light there was in the room also began to flicker in unison, creating a strobe effect. Everything around him—papers, dust, old hard drives—began to whirl in slow motion as the flashes of light captured the objects in a slow, silent dance.

The serpent-shaped object was the only thing he could focus on to remain balanced on his feet. The ghastly object gave little comfort. Its ruby eyes began to glow red and he could feel a chilling breeze emanate from the object which fed into the whirlwind that had surrounded him. The whole room began to feel like he was at the center of a winter's storm.

The rattling escalated louder and louder. At a crescendo, a large blast of cold air filled the space around him. The force of air brought him down to the floor. He had never felt so cold...and alone.

In a shrieking sound, the frigid air around him wailed at deafening levels. It sounded like screaming, but he was quite sure that the screaming was all his own. He knew that if he lingered on the floor for too long, this all could very well be his final memory—dying by himself, screaming. A part of him lamented that perhaps it was better this way. To just let go to the cold and all the fear would be over. The cold was beginning to numb all his senses...and it was strangely comforting.

Another part of him remained resilient. There was too much he wanted to accomplish than have it end in this dusty old basement. The thought was enough to tend a spark within him. A sudden rush of energy shot from his brain to his freezing limbs. The energy was enough to prop him up against the wall and hobble out the vault's doorway.

His hobbling turned into a dash as he found his way back to center aisle of the stacks. He brushed up against several shelves as the flickering lights made it difficult to run too quickly. The stacks of archives flickered in and out as he desperately scrambled to reach the corridor he had come in through before. Behind him, he could hear the whirling of more objects as the breeze had entered the larger archival chamber. He also could hear the sound of heavy footsteps.

"stomp...stomp...STOMP...STOMP..."

The stomping came from the same space behind him. He dared not turn around to see what was in pursuit. More than ever, he wished he had chosen to stay in the comforts of his nice cozy office. The choice was now so far out of reach, he could not double back, he could only try to go forward.

He reached the corridor he had come through and sprinted down towards the elevator. The doors were still open. Even at a full sprint, his steps seemed to sludge across the concrete floor.

He reached the elevator and placed his hand on the adjacent wall, gasping for breath. He had made it!

Turning around a dark cloud of shadow was filling the other end of the hall from where he had come. The ebony darkness was absolute and it seemed that no light could penetrate or escape it. He could still hear the stomping sound coming from within the dark mass, but he could not see the source of the sound.

The approaching darkness filled in closer, and stomping grew louder with each meter of its encroachment down the corridor. He could barely stand to watch. He wanted to throw himself in the elevator car, but that would be little use if it was still inoperable.

Just as he was going to make a last, desperate leap, the stomping ceased. The lights all went out except for a couple of dim emergency lights within the elevator car. The basement filled with darkness but nothing compared to the absolute blackness that glided heavily down the corridor towards him.

His vision went black and starry. Motion fluttered in unusual patterns in front of him in the dim light. As his eyes became more adjusted, the hallway itself appeared to pulse with a heartless beat. The walls seemed to be moving in-and-out in the same rhythmic beat he had heard before: Baa Baa Buummm. Baa Baa Buummm.

This had to be in his head, it could not be real. *Could it?*

The walls kept up their pulsations as wispy streaks of dull lights began to emerge from them in circular shapes. One-by-one, a sea of eyes emerged from the walls—contorted and jumbled upon one another with links of ebony strands of shadow. The eyes looked upon him with a dead stare, fixed and unmoving. Drips of streaking silvery-blue light formed misshapen grins and snaggled teeth beneath them. The mouths opened and shut in mute moaning expressions like a fish uselessly gasping for air out of water.

As he watched grimly, he went to jump in the elevator but found that he could not move. His legs were frozen to the concrete floor. He was being forced to watch.

As the phantasm materialized before him, it triggered a hint of recognition. Unlocked deep within his mind, he felt a recognition of this scene from before. Whether from a dream, a memory, or some half-dream somewhere in between, the flicker of familiarity was there. It did not matter from where it came, it was real, just as real as the image being fed to his brain in this moment.

Something else began to take shape in the shifting void of eyes and teeth. A swirl of black particles, like a faint black mist, came out of the dark mass, coalescing in the center of the corridor. The black mist expanded until it almost reached the ceiling. The particles then seemed to thicken out of thin air, revealing a tall and broad figure.

His eyes blinked rapidly as he tried to make out what now stood before him, as the figure's features were indistinct at first. He could tell that it was massive, with a large head and muscular upper body. It was when it took its first step forward, that he saw the hairy head of a bull emerge from the shadows with two massive horns protruding outwards. Underneath the head, the body was that of a man, bare-chested and beefy. The body was supported by two massive legs that terminated in cloven hoofs. Their steps pounded hard on the concrete floor as it approached, sending up tiny sparks. But it was the creature's eyes which glued his attention. They glared at him as dark red ambers in the darkness. Softly glowing, just enough to pierce the silky blackness that surrounded it.

To his shock the creature began to speak, not through its mouth, but through Daisy!

"Been a long time, Craig, a long, long time it has been," the entity said, in a low voice filled with static from the speaker in the back of his ear.

He was terrified to respond. Maybe if he didn't the thing would go away. Just like a dream to be forgotten…again.

The entity continued, "You don't remember…but you haven't forgotten. Dig deep, you will find us staring back in the black. I can show you, show you it all, if you would like. There is so much your grown mind has hidden from you. Let me pull back the veil."

He stood, unblinking in the threshold of the elevator, pondering what to do. He could not run. He couldn't hide. Perhaps acting agreeable and appeasing the entity was the only way he would see his office again.

"I'll…I'll do whatever it takes," he said, voice quivering.

The entity grinned, revealing its yellow, triangle teeth—rotten and covered with decay. It then pulled from the darkness the snake-adorned object and reached out with a black three-clawed hand.

Daisy spoke again, only this time, her normal, comforting French accent had returned, "Craig, you are just going to take it, aren't you? I need, we need, you to take it."

He stepped forward cautiously, his legs were wobbly and his hand was trembling. He reached out and grasped the object in his hand. It was still cold, but bearable to touch this time. The cold seemed to stretch up his arm and into his body. Everything felt like tingling, even in his head; he felt things were disconnecting. New thoughts were coming forth, floating up deep from within.

"C'est bon, Craig; oui, c'est bon," praised Daisy.

He heard a sound behind him. He turned completely. It was the elevator springing back to life. He looked back over his shoulder. Everything had disappeared, there was no abhorrent entity or sea of grinning faces anywhere to be seen. It was just a dimly lit corridor with a cool draft brushing across his face. He grasped the object tightly in his hand. He was ready to return to his cozy office.

7

The Mindsai Experiment: Unbounded
One day B.R.D.

The view of Talawanda Springs was softened by the mist. The town below had been reduced to vague outlines, traced out by shades of blue and grey. Nothing seemed to be moving besides the slow breath of the misty fog rolling across the landscape. The mist was cold and dense; it clung to the skin like wet cloth. Every inhalation brought with it thousands of chilling droplets that tingled his throat and weighed heavy on his lungs.

Bash took a deep breath. He could not shake the feeling of drowning breathing in this misty air.

No matter, only a little further to go, he thought, as he crossed the damp lawn of Old Main.

He felt a bounce of excitement with each step. Today was to be a defining moment of his career. Today he would show the world the proof of a concept that had grown in his mind for the majority of his life. Something, through his own experience, he knew to be true. The Mindsai experiment would validate ancestral memories for the world to witness. Probably changing the course of human history in the process.

Like any cutting-edge research, the experiment required a test case. Rather than subject others to any potential risks, he had put forward himself as Case Zero. If the experiment was exploring truly uncharted territory, then it should be he who helmed the pioneering expedition. At least, that is what he had told his lab group. Truth be told, he did not anticipate any risks; safeguards upon safeguards had been put in place.

Though he would not admit it to anyone, he wanted to be the first for truly selfish reasons. He had waited a lifetime to finally grasp the fleeting images that had been flashing in his mind unpredictably. Now, he finally had the opportunity to connect the images that had eluded him for so long and put them in fluid motion.

His mind would be the first to fully bridge the deep gulf of memory and perceive any number of past events. He could see his parents who died so early in his career. He could see childhood adventures with friends who had long since faded from his life. And, of course…he could see his Emma again.

The true test would be pushing past his own memory and see what lies beyond in the void of ancestral memory. In the mid-twentieth century, man broke barriers of physics in the air and space. In the early twenty-first century, man broke barriers of the digital realm with the internet and quantum computers. Today, he would break barriers of the mind.

These thoughts clung close, giving a certain spring to each step that he took as he approached Hugenberg Hall. Coming up over the rise next to Old Main, he could see his building standing tall against the backdrop of brown woods. The misty fog had largely dissipated as his walk had taken him to a higher elevation upon the mountain.

He studied the features of the building he had spent such a large portion of his life within. Today it looked completely new, as if he were setting eyes on it for the first time. The edifice of red and brown brick cut through the thinning mist in the dull, early morning light. It was a grandiose structure built in a time before the Internet. Though repurposed and remodeled over the decades, the building remained true to its heritage as a broad, rugged, and aged structure, one that possessed its own unique history.

He had stopped to admire the building without realizing it. He felt silly for considering the place he had seen almost every day of his life for a quarter century. Shrugging off his brief bout of nostalgia, he walked through the wide glass double doors.

The atrium and corridors were quiet as he made his way to his laboratory. It was fifteen past nine so most students and faculty were in the midst of lessons and lectures. As he walked, his mind was aflutter trying to run over a checklist of tasks and processes that needed to be in place for the experimental procedure: (a) the Mindsai was operational at optimal levels, (b) the Mindsai's quantum processor was compiled and fully calibrated for its repurposed use, (c) the SEER goggles were cleaned and fully configured for his test run, (d) the emergency power and auxiliary systems were functional, and (e) the SEER goggles were connected to a supply of fresh recording units with full capacity available. He fully expected that Craig and Aliyah had gone over this list several times over before he arrived but rehearsed it to ensure he could find confirmation. He knew, any deviation from this expectation would quickly erode his cheery mood.

He arrived at the door to his laboratory and paused a moment. He wanted to listen to what might be happening within. He had told his lab group to be there early in the morning to make the specified preparations and there should be much clamor of productivity within the lab. He smiled silently when he heard the scuttling of feet and the tapping of computer keys—it was a good sign. So he pushed the door and entered.

Aliyah was just inside the entryway fiddling with a power control unit. She was in a stripped powder-blue twofer dress wearing a slim brown belt and a solid navy skirt. She quickly greeted him.

"Good morning, Dr. Silva."

"Good morning, Aliyah. Are we ready?" he asked anxiously.

"I think so," she said softly. Her smile seemed strained.

He looked over her face closely. It was drawn, and an area under both of her eyes was dark.

"Are you all right? You look so tired," he inquired.

"Oh, I'm fine. I just haven't been able to get much sleep lately," she paused, looking down to fidget some more with the power converter. Her eyes eventually returned to meet his after some thought and a shrug. "Perhaps I'm just too excited for what we're going to be doing today."

"Well, if you feel too tired, do not push yourself. This is a very delicate process and we do not want you hurting yourself or others if you feel you're not up to it."

"No, no, no. I'm fine. I've got my coffee right here," Aliyah implored.

He chuckled. Her retort had assuaged most of his concerns.

"Where are Craig and Gabe?"

"Oh…Craig is in the back room there just making some last-minute checks and calibrations…and Gabe…well, he really wanted to make it, but has taken ill," said Aliyah.

"Hmm…I see. That is unlike Gabe, he usually would be here no matter what."

He tried to read Aliyah's face for a response, but she had already turned back to her work.

"Well, all right, the major players are here at least, and it looks like you have been doing your checks I see."

"Yep, I've been following your checklist you gave us to the letter."

"Excellent. Let me check on Craig and then we can get started."

He continued to walk through the lab, passing by the reclining couch. The SEER goggles were hanging neatly above, looking almost brand new after a thorough cleaning. *That checks another box on the list*, he thought.

Further back, the Mindsai machine was quietly humming along. The monitor was flashing a diagnostics screen that appeared to be almost complete. All looked just how he expected things to be.

In the back of the lab, he found Craig in an unlit supply room looking rather unkempt. His hair was greasy and disheveled. The wrinkles in his shirt and pants gave off the appearance that he had slept in them overnight. And around his neck, he was wearing a piece of gold-chain slipped beneath his untucked plaid shirt. Any type of jewelry was pretty uncharacteristic for him.

Craig was flittering around with some cables and electronic storage devices while mumbling to himself—or Daisy— unintelligibly. He did not even notice that Bash had entered into the doorway.

He tried to gain Craig's attention, "Craig! What are you doing?" But Craig merely stopped for a moment as if he had heard only the slightest whisper from far off.

He tried again, a bit louder, "CRAIG!" This time Craig whipped around in a fright and almost dropped the delicate storage device he held in his hands.

"Oh…I…didn't see that you were there," Craig said, the piece of hardware trembled in his hands. His voice was distant, like his mind had not fully returned from what he was previously doing or thinking.

"My, you look terrible. Are you all right?" he asked.

"I…I'm fine. I just…haven't been getting much sleep, that's all."

Aliyah said the same thing, he thought.

Craig added, "Good news though, we are all ready to go today, ri-right Daisy?"

Daisy responded on cue, but in a voice that seemed hoarse and imbued with a hissing static, "Yesss, first-order compilationsss have been completed and all diagnosticsss are within target parametersss."

"Yes…good, when you are done here, Craig, I want you to come and show me your final calibrations on the machine, okay?"

"Sure," Craig responded with a shrug and went back to fiddling around with the storage device in his hands.

I hope I have not been putting too much pressure on these kids, he thought to himself as he turned to walk back to the main laboratory space.

He had noticed that Craig and Aliyah had both been a little out of character these past two weeks. Aliyah seemed to be avoidant, coming into the lab less frequently. When asked why he had not seen her as much, she told him that she just preferred to study at the campus library where she could think better. Craig, on the other hand, had been in the lab constantly. He was there when Bash got there in the morning and when he left in the evening. He suspected that Craig was staying late through the night tinkering with the machine and running an exhaustive list of simulations.

He had meant to talk with Craig about easing up his workload. Though he appreciated the oppressive work drive for the experiment, he did not want Craig to burn out, or worse, make a mistake due to an exhausted mind.

To think about it, he too had been uneasy ever since that night at the Ebony Tower a couple of weeks ago. A night he had spent with Chris, whose presence in the weeks had eluded him. He had tried his hardest to push what happened from his mind that night: the man with sapphire eyes, the guttural sounds, the snake he saw—thought he saw—in the fire. Yet, despite how hard he tried, the images kept creeping back to the forefront of his mind.

It was that damn ironic process…the more he tried to not think about it, the more attention he brought to it from his internal monitoring. He snickered to himself. Thinking of Dostoevsky's white bear certainly seemed more pleasant than a red-eyed snake.

He pushed these thoughts aside as he reached the Mindsai machine. The events of today should be more than the distraction he needed to put such things, that probably did not happen, at bay. He pulled up the status menu on the computer's terminal and all looked to be at optimal levels.

His heart fluttered. For so long, this experiment had been an abstract idea, a wistful notion that needed to be pulled down into reality. Now, for the first time, his moment had reached a concrete stage and he could feel the nerves contracting in the back of his throat.

Aliyah walked in just behind him.

"Do you want to get seated so we can get started shortly?" she said.

"Excellent idea, let me hang up my coat and kick off my shoes."

He went over to a chair and draped his coat over the back and then sat down to pull off his shoes. Standing in his grey wool socks, he rolled up the sleeves of his royal blue dress shirt and shuffled over to the reclining couch to take a seat.

Not too long after, Craig entered the room and quietly began to punch away at a computer terminal for the Mindsai. He watched him intently as Aliyah prepared the SEER goggles suspended above his head. An illustrious focus had returned to Craig's eyes as he scanned the screen line-by-line. Whatever his brief lapse in presence had been about, for the moment, Craig was composed.

He redirected his gaze above and watched Aliyah move the equipment with the most delicate care. She placed her hands gingerly around each of the three main data cables that protruded from the top of the headset. The cables were a twist of black, red, and blue wires. The two-gauge-sized wire looked large in Aliyah's small hands. She carefully lifted up the SEER headset a lowered it down onto his head. A shock of electrostatic hit his scalp.

"Oww!"

"Sorry, did I poke you!?" said Aliyah, jerking back the headset.

"No, no," he said, waving a hand. "I think it was just a built-up charge from my socks rubbing against the floor. Please continue," he looked up over his shoulder and flashed her a smile.

The expression of surprise melted away from her face. She then nodded in acknowledgment and waited for him to turn back around before proceeding.

As the SEER goggles came to a rest, he felt the tiny metallic pins within the cap nestle into the nooks of his scalp. Aliyah came before him to check the fit. Her eyes darted to-and-fro to ensure everything was in place. She then pulled down the goggles over his eyes and the room became hidden to him. There was only darkness and his thoughts.

"Does it feel secure?" her disembodied voice sounded out in the void.

"It feels great," he answered.

She acknowledged him with a simple pat on the shoulder and retracted away. He could hear her footsteps trailing off in front of him and off to the right. The sound of a rolling chair marked that she had taken her seat at the monitoring station.

"How are things looking Craig?" he asked, blindly.

"I think we are all set to proceed," Craig replied.

"Good, good. Aliyah could you start the recordings?"

"Umm…we are recording…now," she replied. Her voice was fainter now, though only meters away.

He had rehearsed in his mind for several days what he would say in this moment and he was glad to make it a term of record.

"Well, we have all worked very hard to get where we are today. I have spent decades trying to defend the possibility of what we are attempting today and I could not be prouder to have a team so highly skilled as the two of you.

"With that said, today we shall all make history together— opening a whole new realm of science and knowledge. For so long, science has been focusing on how the story ends, people want to live forever. But science is not quite there yet. I hope to offer us a means to see how the story began. For the first time, we can see the faded text of time-forgotten chapters and prologue. See what truly set the world in motion and uncover all the ideas and knowledge that have become lost. Yes, today we embark into an undiscovered realm—beyond the veil."

After he had finished, it was Aliyah's weary voice that reached out to him, "Please be careful, Professor. This is just a first attempt, no reason to push for it all in one trial."

"Thank you, Aliyah, for your concern. But let's get things started before you all talk me out of this," he replied.

"We know there's not a chance of that happening," Craig chided in.

"You've worked for me too long," he replied. "I am ready when you are."

"All right Bash, I have started the sequencing. It will engage in a minute or so. Make sure you're situated."

He pulled down the electrostatic earphones to isolate himself from the room. The two cups slipped over his ears and then the silence mixed in with the darkness. His senses were now isolated from the lab, ready for the Mindsai and SEER goggles to engage. He raised his thumb up blindly from his reclined position to give an indication that he was ready.

Waiting there, in complete silence and darkness, he stared off into the swirling patterns of fussy noise caused by the resting electrical signals of his retinas. The phosphene light show was without form. Dull shades of green and blue light pulsed and danced across his visual field in random patterns. He thought if he stared long enough he might bring shape to the formless void. And for a moment, he imagined that he saw the rough outline of his study. Though he was sure all was pareidolia, bringing structure to a stimulus without order. Soon the experiment would begin and the signal would break through the noise.

His thoughts turned to the procedure, going over each critical step. The process would start simple. During the first stage the Mindsai would calibrate to a memory a week ago, then a month, then a year. In the second stage, the machine would be instructed to progress further and further back at known memory junctures in his life. Finally, the third stage, the Mindsai would target an ancestral memory not of his own making.

For this first attempt, he had chosen the memory that had been haunting him for all his life. The memory of a path, a chase, and the two intertwined trees. He had waited his whole life to know who it was that he was chasing and where the path led. Soon what was once fleeting images would be revealed to him in crystal clarity.

It seemed that several minutes had passed by in the darkness. *What was taking the Mindsai so long?* he thought. It was easy to lose a sense of time in the machine; time by definition, was relative within it. The visages of light were still swirling and pulsing in their dance. Tiny blobs of cool green had now joined the fray, emerging from the black background. Just more artifacts and noise, echoes and afterglows.

He then felt a tingling sensation starting at the back of his head and moving slowly across his scalp. The flickers of light in front of his eyes were now all flashing in a uniformed pattern. The Mindsai had initiated the experiment.

He felt the burst of energy rush through him. A multitude of images began to flash quickly before his eyes. They were all going too fast to pick out any familiarity. He then felt himself being pulled down into the well of the first calibration memory from a week ago. His senses came to him in relative succession. He had discovered early on that the younger the memory, the easier it was for the machine to stimulate all aspects of the memory in synchrony.

Before his eyes, he saw nearly a dozen pairs of eyes staring back at him. They all belonged to the young-adult faces of his students. He was standing at lectern of his introductory course on cyber psychology. It was early morning and the sunlight made the electro-polarized windows glow, casting a defused amber light across the small room.

He was lecturing on the methods of interfacing between the brain and virtual environment simulators. The student's faces were raptured in attention. He always had good success at explaining psychological concepts by using student-relevant issues as the vehicle for illustration. He was just about to go into a comment on the nature of virtual perception when all began to fade away. The sound of his voice trailed off steeply as the treble tones were lost in the whirlwind of images that began to flutter before him again. The machine had already begun to move on to the next memory. These initial steps were only for ensuring calibration and he needed not linger on them long.

It was not too long before the images slowed down at the next memory juncture. He heard footsteps walking on a solid surface and before another thought crossed his mind, the world quickly came into view. He was walking home on a sidewalk with a cool breeze brushing across his face. He had just met with his new student, Aliyah, for the first time that afternoon. It was about this time he had drifted off into one of his flashbacks in his mental study.

He did not see the study now, though, he was just walking across the grass in a kind of sloppy zig-zag pattern. Up ahead Grand View Cemetery had already come into view. The rows of headstones with their dull blue lights stood as pale markers in the fading light.

Once he had reached the outer fence, he was impressed by the clarity of the memory. All was still fresh in his mind and the reactivation seemed to be in perfect fidelity.

At least until he noticed something out of the corner of his eye. His memory was focused on the sign to the cemetery but he saw a black shape move at the very edges of his field of view. He independently redirected his gaze to inspect the movement at the left edge of what was his peripheral vision a month ago. His eyes strained to move as the scene began to become blurred at the limits of his view. He stared intently for a few moments until the anomaly became visible once again. A dark shape darted amongst two tall headstones at the far northern side of the cemetery. The shape was fuzzy and moved too quickly for him to discern it for what it was. One thing he knew, he did not notice it a month ago.

The shape moved again, and this time, it crept just a little further into his visual field. The shape was like that of a figure, undulating as a thick black shadow. Parts of it contorted in unnatural ways that he could not find any natural explanation for. The shadows around it were in a perpendicular position to the entity and this shadow was not a static inanimate part of the scene.

Had it always just been out of view for the whole time? he thought. But before he could get a better look, the machine lurched onward to another juncture of his past. A cascade of flashes went before his eyes. The next memory would be a year back. Then the jumps would come in wider intervals.

Out of the darkness, he heard the quiet pattering of computer keys. Slowly he began to feel the tactile pressure of the smooth keys beneath his fingers, their flat square surface depressing and rebounding on the soft ends of his fingertips. The world then slowly faded into view. He was sitting at the terminal of the Mindsai. The display screen was showing an array of activity, monitoring the feedback from a participant reclined just a couple meters away. The participant was a man, in his late twenties. He was one of the first to test a memory recall back to beyond the year mark.

The man was laying still on the reclining couch. Across from him, the monitor showed one of his memories where he was looking at a series of symbols. The group of circles and lines looked like an alien language, as they were intended not to be recognizable. They had been presented to the man almost eighteen months prior by Craig. It was a remarkable moment. One that led to a cascade of progress and fine-tuning of the Mindsai so that it could go further and further back.

His eyes were fixated on the monitor. He could feel his heart racing as the moment overtook him with excitement. Periodically, his eyes would dart back from the memory viewer and check out the myriad measurements indicating the performance of the Mindsai connection. All were flowing in without any hiccups. He could barely keep his mouth from hanging agape.

He looked over to his young graduate assistant, Craig, who was also monitoring the progress of the experiment. Craig looked up as well and met his eyes. Craig's face instantly opened up with wide eyes and a bobbing head that could barely contain the gleeful excitement.

After the exchange of looks, he returned back to the monitor. The participant was now staring at a younger version of himself, who was giving him instructions of what to expect for the second session to occur in eighteen months. His face looked serious and professional but without a hint of tedium. It looked like a man who truly enjoyed his work.

Slowly, the memory began to lose its clarity. Tiny dark spots emerged in his vision as the scene faded back into the neutral state of darkness.

Whoosh! Another cascade of images flickered before him. This time he would be going much further back. He could feel a heaviness within his mind pull him down as the Mindsai pinpointed the targeted memory. Like traveling a number of fathoms beneath the sea, the pressure continued to build as he went further and further back. Only when the images began to decelerate did the pressure begin to subside.

First, there was nothing, then, after a few moments, a mix of sweetness and earthen tones rushed across his nostrils. It was followed by the rush of a warm breeze falling across his face, carrying the sugary aroma in a delayed sensory echo. The sloshing of water timed in with the gentle sound of creaking of wood. His head felt as if it were rocking back and forth. It was summer time and he was on a boat.

A waving white cloth appeared in front of him. It was the main sail of a boat. Not just any boat, it was the eleven meter sailboat that Emma's parent's owned so many summers ago, 'The John B.'

The image cleared and he could now take in the magnificent craftsmanship of the sailing vessel all over again. The deck was inlaid with a mahogany-stained teak wood. The large white mast protruding from the small cabin towered above him, fixed with a sloop-style white sail rigged at the fore and the aft. Directly to his right was the large wheel fitted with brass knobs upon each of the spoke ends. To his left, he saw Emma, reclining in her two-piece bathing suit, reading a book.

This was their first summer after they were married. They had visited her parents for a week on Lake Champlain in New York to have some rest and relaxation—though it had really been for his sake. He had just started his tenured job and was so immersed in his work that Emma felt like a distance was growing between them. She had practically demanded that they take a week off to rekindle some intimacy. He had told her times he could be free for her, but some research issues always seemed to pop up.

At last, on another pledge to take time off, Emma finally told him, "Your promises are made on waving lips and idle hands, Bash."

The bite in her words wounded him deeply but also cleared his eyes to see her genuine desire to spend time with him. So, the next week he cleared his schedule. At the time, he did not see that a whole week was necessary, but now, oh how he wished that that week of summer could have lasted forever.

He looked out over the bow, they were anchored in a small, secluded inlet. Only a few boats had passed by that day so it was their own little slice of arcadia. He sat straddled on the edge of deck with one foot dipped down into the lake. The water lapped at his leg and presently, a school of little minnows had ventured up to nibble at his toes.

He lifted up his leg and decided to stand up to stretch. The warm summer wind blew through his dark brown hair and he could feel the kiss of sun rays against the back of his neck.

Emma looked up from her book, smiling, in quiet repose. She beckoned for him to come over to her. Eyes fixed in yearning above her sunglasses.

He complied without hesitation and dropped to his knees next to her on the bench. She lifted up her hand to gently stroke the curls that winged out above his left ear. He leaned in to embrace her with a kiss. She kissed him back with all the passion and want of someone helplessly in love. His heart fluttered.

Without a second thought, he lifted her up with a tiny yelp and proceeded to carry her down to the cabin below. His heart was racing as he steadied his footing on the rocking deck. Her eyes were filled with insatiable desire. He could feel her mid-section quiver in his arms. He walked down the few steps into the tiny cabin below carefully ensuring that she did not bump her head. Once inside, he tenderly laid her upon the twin-sized bed tucked away in a nook at the bow and then took a place beside her.

Starting with her inner thigh and then up across her side, he slowly traced the lines and contours of her porcelain skin.

She never could tan right, he thought.

His fingers reached the strap of her navy-striped bikini top and slowly began to nudge it down the smooth slope of her shoulder. She exhaled heavily. Farther and farther down the strap went until it fell in the crevasse of her elbow. He then went over to her other shoulder and kissed along with his hand to remove the other strap. Her breathing quickened and her lower body rose and fell with each breath.

With both straps at her side, he soaked in the reveal of her perfectly round breasts. Modest though they were, he took pleasure in cupping them with his right hand as the other removed the bikini top from view. Then, starting in the valley between her breasts, he gently kissed her abdomen with little pecks. Down…down…down he went, until he reached the edge of her bikini bottom with his lips. He pulled up a hand to hook two fingers in the garment and pull it down ever so slightly to kiss the tender skin just below her panty line.

She let out a soft moan as her breathing had intensified more. He could feel his own arousal beginning to throb within his tight swimming shorts. He took both hands and removed her bottom and then took in the beauty of her naked form. The curves, the soft skin, the smooth hair now partially covering her breasts.

He leaned in to embrace her and—

The scene dissolved quickly into darkness. A weight pulled on his feet and yanked him abruptly downward. He could still feel his heart pumping rapidly and a dull ache in his loins.

Another rush of images began to speed by rapidly. The weight upon him felt heavier than before. There were only a few more target memory junctures to go before he reached the true test of the experiment.

A tinge of aching pain sprang from his forehead as the Mindsai settled into the blackness that preceded the next memory. After a time, it gave way to the faint odor that he had not smelled since his college years. It was the soothing smell of fruit and flowering plants from a tropical breeze air-freshener.

He felt a deep breath take in the scent that mixed with a damp gust of cold air. This was quickly followed by the spattering of rain drops as well as a stiff sickness in his stomach.

When his sight returned, it was blurry. Something was wet and pooling in his eyes. He felt his chest shake uncontrollably back-and-forth. He was crying.

His hairy arm came up and wiped the tears causally from his face, leaving still, a starry residue of bent light at the corners of his vision. But he could see now out in front of him. There was a window, propped half open. The window panes were thick and cross-hatched with pale-white muntins. The peeling paint of the signaled the wear and tear they had received over the many years of being housed in a dormitory building. He recognized the window instantly, he was back in his freshman dorm, Dickerson Hall.

He moved closer to the window and continued to stare blankly outside at the concrete slant walk below. He could feel the cooling wind blow on his face carrying with it an earthy scent. The rain had just come to an end and a sliver of crimson light had broken through the clouds as the sun was setting in over the woods to the west. The courtyard was empty and only the twirling mists of steam moved about from vents in the sidewalks.

He knew this moment well. It was a late afternoon in April, just a few moments after a break up with his girlfriend, Katie. They had both spent the last two hours talking on his bed. Katie had told him that, after six months together, she did not think they were a good fit any longer. He had begged and pleaded for another chance and, for her part, she had politely listened. Yet, throughout his desperate pitch, she just stared right through him, without any glimmer of expression for his words to find hope in.

Eventually, after exhaustive, circular discussion, he could not find the right words or the perfect line to turn things around no matter how hard he searched. He realized it was over, a decision had been made without him. He learned then and there that a woman's determined heart is not easily swayed. It was one of the many first lessons he had received that year.

Now, all he could do was watch out the window, waiting to catch one final glimpse of his first serious relationship slipping away out a side door of his dorm. He muttered to himself, "Why?" over and over again, as if doing so a miraculous answer would present itself to him from the world.

His arms trembled uncontrollably as the finality of the situation was sinking in. He could barely stand.

Katie finally emerged from a side door three-stories beneath his room. She was wearing her little black fleece jacket that contrasted with her wavy auburn hair—she looked as beautiful as ever. She slowly began to walk down the sidewalk, her brown-leather boots making splashes in puddles as she went. Her steps were slow, maybe they were indecisive.

His hope swelled. He could not let his mind provide an unfavorable interpretation.

She reached a lamp post and stopped just as it kicked on in the waning light. The lamp cast an amber glow on her dark outline. She turned around and looked up at his window. His heart jumped as he could tell that she saw him. He did not know what to do. Should he wave? Should he cry out? Should he tell her to wait and run down and embrace her?

Before he could make a choice of response, a half-smile ran across her face. It looked tired and forlorn as she lingered there for a few moments. The leftovers of rain dripped at the edges of the square light fixture above her head. All-the-while his heart and mind urged her to start walking back, to have a change of heart. He was trying to will her into action with all his mental might.

She never moved. She just remained sadly still.

A few more moments went by before some cheerful voices off in the distance broke through the calmness. More people had begun to emerge out into the world after the rain.

The breach of quiet seemed to have shaken Katie to action. She raised up a hand and waved a half-hearted goodbye.

His heart sunk.

Katie turned and continued her walk up the sidewalk, this time with purpose. She then faded in and out of view. All that was left was the playful conversation between a couple who were heading out to go uptown from another dorm across the courtyard. Their voices carried in the misty air while he slumped to the floor sobbing just before everything began to fade to black once again.

Again, a multitude of images went before him, but not as quickly as before. The machine was straining to dig deeper, back into his earliest memories.

The pressure in his head seemed to be intensifying as he went back further. The pain radiated from his right temple to encompass his whole forehead feeling like a metal band was constricting inwardly. It was similar to the feeling he got when trying to recall something that he just could not bring to mind, like when something was at the tip of the tongue. Only now, the intensity of the feeling was a hundred-fold and much more painful.

He found himself smelling musty air mixed with hints of potpourri and cedar that could only be from one place—his grandmother's living room. Another few moments passed in darkness and he began to feel the thick carpet wedging between his toes as he felt himself scooting across its soft surface. In his hand there was something solid…wooden, being pushed along an unseen path. The soft melody of classical music came in slightly muffled from another room. Finally, the scene illuminated in a giant wave of light. He was on his hands and knees pushing a tiny wooden train across wooden tracks that he had constructed across the floor of the living room. The tiny black engine with a red smoke stack squeaked along as it went around corners and up over bridges. In the middle of the maze of track stood a large formation of wooden blocks. The blocks, of mismatching colors and sizes, had been carefully placed to form a one meter tall tower which provided overwatch of the trains below. For a kid, it was a marvel of engineering.

He continued to loop his little black engine around the circuit of track, picking up cars along the way using magnetic bumpers. The large picture windows that surrounded the room on two sides filled the room with the ambient glow of a late morning sun. Outside, tall sycamores looked in with grey squirrels bouncing from their branches.

He felt a strong sense of coziness and security. Here, he was alone within his own world of imagination. He knew somewhere his elderly grandmother was working away at some household chore, maybe preparing him a hot dog for lunch—he loved how she would cut it into circular pieces for him.

Watching through his young eyes, he could remember what it was like to have everything be so new, so unexplored and unmastered. Time seemed to go by so slowly. A morning seemed like days of adventure.

Thinking on it, now, he felt he was on the cusp of recapturing that feeling all over again.

Suddenly, the scene dissipated from view. A disembodied voice came out from the void, it was Aliyah.

"All right, Professor, we have gone through all your targeted memories with no deviations from optimal levels. We are now going to engage in the experimental phase unless you signal an objection…"

There was a pause for a few seconds.

He made no response; he was ready to proceed.

"…All right, we are instructing the Mindsai to recover the targeted ancestral memory now. Should commence in a few minutes. If we notice any issues we will abort the program immediately. Good luck, Professor!"

Again, he waited in darkness as the machine prepared to sling him beyond the veil of personal memory into the uncharted parts of the mind. He was nervous, but ready.

A warming sensation propagated from the back of his head. His entire scalp felt like it was ablaze as his mind strained to cope with the increasing demands from the Mindsai machine. To use an old computer analogy, the Mindsai was overclocking his mind to bridge the gap between his own memories and those of his father. At least that's what he believed the owner of the target memory to be.

In addition to the feverish heat, his head and body felt as if they had been injected with lead and were falling into a great gravity well. An enormous pressure was pulling upon him, this time the weight was not downward, but imploding inward, into his core.

Bits and flashes also went before his eyes—his dad's office globe where he had marked places he had been—a toddler's tiny piano—a blue blanket—a dark place with a dim red hue where he felt suspended in a warm liquid.

Then there was only a gloom.

His head continued to feel like it was going to crush in upon itself. The pain was starting to become intolerable. Physically, the mind could only take so much strain if things progressed at this same rate. This thought sent his mind into frantic concern. *Should I turn back? Abort the experiment?* But something inside him was telling him to keep going, to come closer. The time to turn back had long since passed so he pulled together every last ounce of resilience to push on.

The pressure intensified. Everything about him felt like it was collapsing into a singular point no bigger than a cell, like some sort of singularity.

There was a great acceleration. It took hold of him thrusting him down what seemed to be a long vacuum tube. Though he could not tell, there was only a void of blackness. Even the flickers of light had ceased their dance in front of his eyes. In fact, there did not seem to be any light at all, the darkness was absolute.

Without a sound, a singular point of radiant white light pierced through the void at an immeasurable distance. It was brighter than anything he had ever seen, but it did not blind him at all. His senses could take in every bit of its radiance.

Starting out no more than a speck of dust in size, the light grew and expanded slowly. Larger, and larger, the white sphere expanded. It was hard to tell if it was growing bigger due to his approach or its own.

And then, in a flash, he entered the white orb. An indescribable array of iridescent color burst forth all around him. He was awash in a rainbow of colors, some translucent, some not unlike a flame, and others he never had experienced before. They surrounded him and seemed to give off a unique resonant tone in his ears as he looked upon them.

And then, just as quickly as they had flashed into existence, the colors disappeared. For a brief moment after their departure, he saw a celestial scene of dozens of revolving planetary bodies, stars, moons, and comets arranged together in a form unlike anything he had ever observed from science. The planets were grouped together around a tiny blue planet that looked to be covered in water. The other planets were much bigger and arranged in a ring with a star above the blue planet and a moon below. But before he could get his bearings, they were lost again to darkness.

The darkness swirled around him once more but the pressure upon him had halted. It actually seemed to be lessoning by the moment. Across his body, his limbs felt lighter as a sense of expansion set over him; even his mind felt lighter. It was a delightful relief.

Once the floaty feeling had past, he was again left alone in the dark. There were no sounds, no sights, no smells...nothing. He could only feel the thoughts wrestling in his head. *Did it work? Where was he? When was he?*

There was no indication of time or space. He could have been experiencing everything for minutes or hours—it could not be known. But whatever may come, *something* had happened, which was quite remarkable in itself.

Time passed and he waited.

And waited.

And WAITED. For something, anything but this void.

Then something did change, it was subtle, but even subtleties of something in a void are apparent. A very faint whiff of fragrance entered into his mind. The aroma grew in strength and overpowered the nothingness. First, there were notes of light dew smelling of damp long grasses. Then, a subdued mossy scent came from below him. Finally, above him, the sweet smell of new growth filled the air.

A steady breeze streamed past his face. He could feel it contouring around his nose and ears. He was moving through the mass of air at a solid pace. He could feel the ground beneath his feet. It felt squishy and crunchy with each long stride that he made. He was running somewhere outdoors. It felt and smelled like spring.

His sight confirmed his suspicion. The newly budding leaves were rustling back and forth on their green branches. Through them, rays of golden-yellow light filtered down in streaks from the early morning sunlight. The woodlands around him were lush with new growth; green ferns and umbrella-shaped mayapple plants covered the forest floor around him.

As his sight cleared more, he could see that he was running down a worn path. Even before the fuzziness had completely faded away, he knew the scene before him. He had seen flashes, glimpses, and flickers of it throughout his life. Now, however, it was as if an occluding haze had been lifted and he saw the memory as clear as if he were experiencing it in real-time.

He had done it! He had reached an ancestral memory!

Further ahead he could see that he was chasing a woman. He could only see the back of her body as the rest was still blurred. What he could tell was that the woman was wearing a pair of tight blue jeans and a white shirt layered with a long oatmeal-colored sweater that stretched down beyond her back pockets. On her feet she wore navy running shoes that she was using quite effectively in her evasion of his pursuit.

Trying to catch her, he hurriedly jumped over logs, ducked under limbs, and dodged the branches of undergrowth to try and get a good look at her. He could see his father's strong scarred hand grasping around the small trunks of trees as he steadied himself over the uneven path. The tell-tale scar stretched from the knuckle midway up the bottom segment of his right ring finger. The scar looked fresh and more vivid now than he ever had seen as a child. The many intervening years must have had a fading influence upon it.

The chase continued and he made up some ground as he turned around a bend in the path. The woman up ahead must have sensed his advancement. She turned her head to check on his progress and, when she did, his heart nearly jumped forth.

He recognized the sweet face of his mother instantly, though it was so much younger. All the familiar features were there. Her round face, the dimples on her cheeks, the striking hazel eyes, and the wavy light-brown hair that looked so soft and silky. She looked beautiful, in ways that pictures he had seen could never explain. She flashed a sly smile as she increased her pace to be just out of his reach.

She was leading him down the path. Every few dozen meters she would turn her head to check again on the progress of his pursuit. He could feel the raw power his legs possessed and, at the same time, the degree to which they were being restrained from overtaking her. He kept just enough distance to maintain the act.

"Cora, how long do you think you can keep this up?" his father called out in between heavy breaths.

"What's wrong, Henry, losing your confidence?" she jeered back over her shoulder.

There was a playful gentleness in the air, that of youthful innocence. An intense electricity tingled across his skin. Every movement felt elegant as if time were passing in slow motion. His heart was beating a million miles a minute. A surge of warm tenderness took hold of his body. It was a powerful moment; it was no wonder why it had transcended down to him. Memories like these get encapsulated in a way that people will remember them to the end of their lives.

The chase continued down the path until they came upon a fork. The path divided at the feet of two sycamore trees which were twisted in and around one another. Their branches were an interwoven mess of grey wood that made it difficult to tell from which tree they belonged.

His mother had stopped just beneath the tree's tangled boughs. He reached her position and wrapped his strong arms around her waist, picking her up off her feet in a spin.

Cora shrieked gleefully in the silent wood before he set her down gently facing him.

He stared deep into her hazel eyes. The star burst pattern of her eyes flickered between locking with his and looking down at his lips. He felt his own lips roll between one another to moisten them together. He reached out delicately with his large hand to cup her small round face. He kissed her sweetly on the lips.

The moment felt of pure bliss but he was conflicted. The experience of living through his father's memory was surreal and he felt a voyeur observing the intimate moment shared between his parents. It was a strange feeling kissing as someone else, especially when it was your own mother.

Cora's gaze broke away to look down the path to the left. He followed it.

The path led into a clearing. White and gold wildflowers bloomed on a green-leafed carpet under the radiant yellow glow of the morning sun. Beams of light stretched out in all directions from the trees lining the clearing's edge.

On his own, his eyes shifted to the path on the right-hand side of him. This path led deeper into the wood and was less-inviting. The trees were much larger and older, blocking most of the sunlight from their impressive canopies. The path also grew narrower, restricted by an ever-encroaching thicket of woody shrubs. Only the passage of large animals could keep it at bay but their passage seemed to be forgotten and the overgrowth seemed to be near its reclamation.

As he turned back, his vision flickered and morphed suddenly in a peculiar undulation. The Mindsai appeared to be struggling with its feed. Yet, things were neither blurry nor faded as they often could be when a lock had been interrupted.

No, the actual environment was present, but changing! The temperate woodland greenery was giving way to a lush variety of tropical fauna. Green plants with large bouncy leaves now carpeted the forest floor. The trees were now double in size both in height and girth. Flowering plants of every color abounded near his own height in the garden-like habitat.

He looked up.

Even the two intertwined trees had changed. Both were now species of trees that he could not identify. Whatever they were, they were the most magnificent he had ever seen. The grandeur of their beauty was awe-striking. The trees seemed to radiate a glow with some sort of white luminesce. The tree that stretched out to the right was covered in a silver bark as smooth as ivory keys. The leaves on its branches shimmered a brilliant green like large heart-shaped emeralds. Protected among the leaves were nearly a dozen varieties of peculiar-looking fruit. The fruit were of an assortment of different shapes and beautiful iridescent colors of yellow, green, purple, and blue that seemed like they would provide for any manner of satiable need.

He looked up, hanging just above his head was a shimmering, semi-translucent blue fruit. It was filled to its seams with a liquid like a hanging tear drop. He somehow knew that if could reach it, it would fulfill even his most voracious of thirsts.

Turning his head to the left, the other tree had a dark-burgundy bark with deep recesses in between the rib-like ridges that ran up the length of its trunk. Its trilobed-shaped leaves glimmered golden in an unfelt breeze. The way in which light flickered off their waxy sheen made them look like thousands of tiny lamp flames lighting up the surrounding area. Hidden among its limbs hung just one variety of fruit. The fruit were circular in shape, all a deep blood red. These fruits gave off a soft ruby glow, that enticed his eyes and made his mouth lust for a bite of their juicy-looking flesh.

The light from the two trees seemed to affect his vision as well. A noticeable black ring had appeared at the periphery of his visual field. The ring slowly tightened inward towards the center of his vision. Squiggly lines formed at the edge of the darkness, blurring out the surroundings.

He felt as if he were going to pass out or go blind.

When the tunnel of darkness had engulfed nearly a third of his sight, his gaze shifted back to where Cora once stood when he last saw her. A woman was still standing by his side but it was no longer his mother. In his growing tunnel vision, he could only see from the woman's shoulder—now bare—up to the top of her head. The woman's face was foreign to him; it was darker than his mother's, perfectly symmetrical, and like the two trees, her skin had a glow emanating from the skin without any imperfections.

The woman was perhaps the most beautiful one he had ever seen. Her hair was jet black with sheens of red, brown, and golden-blonde streaks. Her eyes were like radiant pools of cat's-eye stones. A computer simulation could not create anyone of such beauty, even in his wildest dreams!

The woman began to speak but no words came out. The darkness closed tighter and tighter until the magnificent scene had gone. It was like fainting, but he was still fully aware of himself.

A sudden flash of light burst like the popping of an old incandescent light bulb.

He blinked his eyes rapidly trying to acclimate to the light. He could see the tall windows inside his lab and Aliyah at his side speaking to him.

"Professor, you're back! We're so sorry, we had to do it, we had to pull you back!"

Bash was seated in front of the review monitor. The screen displayed a scrolling red alert along with a raw video feed of what appeared to be a large blue and white orb descending into an old-world looking city.

"What's going on? Why is there a news feed up on our experimental monitors? Where's the recording of the experiment!?" he asked with a dazed and puzzled look.

"Sorry, Professor, the alert came in over the network just after you began. We debated it for a while but something big was happening so we decided to end the experiment prematurely," Aliyah said. Her voice was anxious.

"Prematurely?" he inquired further.

"Yes, not too long after you made history seeing your mother through your father's eyes—we captured all of it by the way—or, to be precise, just after your father caught up to your mother in front of that twisted-looking pair of trees."

"So, we did capture the first documented recall of an ancestral memory, you are sure?"

"That is correct, it came through perfectly."

"What about after?"

"After?" Aliyah looked confused.

"Yes, the tropical garden, the shimmering trees…the beautiful woman?"

Aliyah shot a confused look at Craig, but he did not say anything.

"Um…no, nothing was recorded after. Our last image received on the feed was you looking into a woodland clearing. After that, the Mindsai disengaged and we removed the SEER goggles. A few moments after that, you were here blinking at us."

"Oh, hmm…that is interesting. We will have to delve deeper into that in a larger discussion…but tell me, what is happening here that was so important that you felt ending the biggest experiment of this century was absolutely necessary."

She told him about a flash alert that had come up on her monitor. A news report came in regarding an unidentified mysterious pulsing blue orb that was descending on the Israeli city of Jerusalem. Coinciding with the object, a wave of rolling power disruptions was being reported all across the globe. She emphasized that it was the uncertainty of power disruption that had led her to halt the experiment early. Even though there were back-up generators available for the lab, she explained that she did not want to risk a momentary power fluctuation during the sensitive experiment.

As for the orb, civil and military reports could not identify it or its origins. Estimated at one hundred meters in circumference, it had landed in the center of the Middle-Eastern city. The landing site was near the controversial Jewish temple complex that was near completion. Many Jews, Muslims, Christians, and secular people had gathered around the object after it had landed and waited for it to open or make some sort of sign.

He quickly turned on a large telewindow in the lab. A news headline in crisp bright red lettering instantly flashed across the bottom of the window: "First contact with alien life or messenger from God?" The message hung there, seemingly suspended in space behind the scene of onlookers. The text looked like it would block their view if they were to turn around and see the rest of the world who was now witness to this event.

An even larger mass of people was now gathered around a stone plaza overlooking the pulsing sphere. From this feed, he could see the multitude of heads swiveled to one another in discussion of the object before them. It was much larger than the images of it from before in the air. The glowing orb towered over the plaza, casting everyone in a white-to-blue glow as it pulsed within the recesses of itself outward in a rhythmic motion. Some people cried, some were quietly praying together, while others stood clutching their tiny children sharing a look of childlike wonder.

Despite the large numbers of people, an uncomfortable stillness had taken hold of the crowd. Only a few stray whispers and murmurs were audible through the telewindow.

The quietness seemed to have taken the animal life as well, for there was not a sight or sound of bird, dog, or cat of any kind near the viewpoint into the plaza. Only the soft blue glow of the orb bouncing off the ancient buildings, some still visibly cracked from the earthquake years earlier.

The uneasy tension felt around the world grew until a noise, like a deep, gasping breath, exited on all sides of the orb at once.

Yeahuuuuuuh!

The noise was quickly followed by a large rush of air which pushed out across the spectators. People braced themselves and their children as the blast of air sent hats and hair flying about.

Then, just as sudden, a bright beam of light saturated the image feed. He could barely make out the edges of the plaza that were furthest away from the orb. People covered their eyes with their arms in an attempt to shield themselves from the white brightness.

When the intensity dissipated, an opening could be seen on the lower portion of the sphere near the ground, in the shape of oval about four meters tall. In the opening, light was beaming out in all directions in a great blueish-white luminance.

Of great importance, the light revealed an unworldly tall figure standing silhouetted in the middle of the opening with two open hands held outward, up high. He and the world gasped at its revelation.

FOURTH STAGE

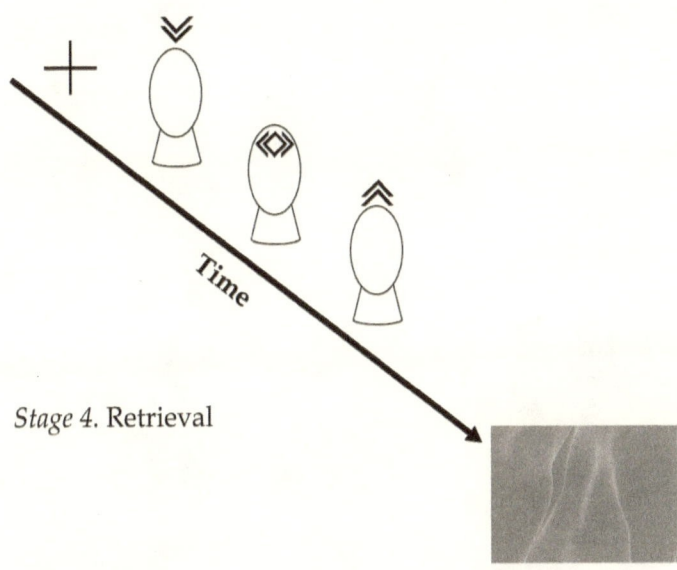

Stage 4. Retrieval

"Memory recall is a curious process; a vast store of memories lies just beyond our reach waiting to be snagged into consciousness. Once constructed, memories are nebulous, filled with noise and distortion—making desires into reality and displeasures into myth."

Seeing through the Shroud:
Barriers to Accessing Total Human Memory
- Dr. Sebastian Silva,
Five years B.R.D.

8

Revelation Day
Zero Point

The figure seemed to glide down from the bright opening in the orb-like structure. Aliyah's eyes frantically tried to focus through the telewindow to see the figure but she struggled to see it. The figure was enveloped in a shadowy umbra created by the near-blinding light coming from the opening behind it. The light pulsed out with great intensity in all directions with an effusive blue glow.

It was so similar to—

The figure landed onto the cobble-stoned plaza, doing so with a graceful final step. It was then that it stepped out of the piercing light. The natural light fell upon the being revealing its true form for the first time to the world.

The being was not a grotesque green blob from outer space or some hairless grey little creature; no, to the shock of a world of vigilant onlookers, it was something that hit closer to home, a distorted reflection of us all—it was a man!

But somehow, it was more than a man, at least, any earthly man that she had ever seen. The being was alien, in the sense that it was not human, but its foreign nature was remarkably beautiful. Standing roughly three meters tall, he was slender with a musculature that one of the great masters could have chiseled an ideal out from stone. The being's hair was midnight black and had a pair of piercing eyes that looked like amethysts with fiery hues. His skin was without imperfection; mildly tan, and looked as smooth as a newborn's bottom with not even a hint of a freckle or mole. The skin also had a soft shimmer to it, giving off an aurora of glowing blue light similar to the light it had come out from in the orb. In one body, it was as if the being were an amalgamation of all the best features of mankind strung together without discord.

In contrast to the simple beauty of the being's physical features, its garments were simple, plain, and surprisingly, not too alien. His body was covered shoulder to feet in a hooded-robe without design or adornments. The robe appeared to be white at first glance, but as she stared longer through the glowing lights, she could tell that it was a false white like a hint of yellow cream had been mixed in the fabric.

The being took a few steps out in the plaza. It was now in full view under the late afternoon sun in Israel.

The gathered crowd had fallen to a hushed silence. The intervening moments felt like an eternity as the whole world held its collective breath to see if the being was friend or foe.

Raising two, long outstretched arms, the tall being spoke.

"Marhaba! Shalom! Greetings!"

Audible gasps could be heard in the crowd. For some, their mouths hung opened wide while others cupped their hands over their mouths in apparent shock.

The being continued. Its voice was filled with a smooth, wispy elegance that seemed to transverse the plaza without need of amplification. Her ears eagerly consumed each deliciously sweet word—each poetic syllable rang with an enchanting tune.

"To commune, my means are legion; I shall speak to you to be familiar. I am *Phosos*, the morning star in the sky and the one at the dawn of the universe was I. For I endured many a time, and times, replete; watchful of all incomplete. Your cries have been heard, for the need is great, and the time, it has come, for my reveal."

Phosos paused briefly for a moment. His eyes flickered about the plaza and she thought she saw them glowing a soft red but could not rule out the setting sun beaming into them between the crumbled roofs of the old city buildings.

Phosos continued, his intonation changed, now more resolute:

"Fear not, harm is not my intent; knowledge I shall gift. Gifts that shall be given freely unto you all. Order, purpose, meaning, I shall restore once more. Once you all were united as one race, one tongue. Now you find yourselves scattered, so lost and adrift. Many now seek an escape in worlds of your own creation. Time to return, I have come to redeem this world."

Phosos paused again.

Her mind instantly accelerated in all directions, trying to process every word that the being had said. But, before she could get a grasp on one coherent thought, the being started again.

"I say, all who desire health shall be healed, need sustenance shall be filled, seek leisure shall have repose. No one shall want, or toil, or ail in New-Eden. I shall provide all in our earthly paradise. It is upon you all; you need only receive it.

"I ask you all only for your devotion to my wise binding law. A *true* covenant to unite you all in ever-lasting harmony.

"Some will resist utopia, there are always contrarians, but if they reject these gifts of peace, then fiercely they must be dealt."

As Phosos finished, the power flickered on and off all around them while the telewindow feed remained strong. She could see out the windows that adjacent buildings were also suffering from power irregularities. Then it seemed to stabilize just as Phosos continued speaking.

"Long have you been led astray; today you shall stand as one, evermore."

"Ooooamph!" A deep blast of a horn rang out from all sides of the orb when Phosos paused.

"OOOoamPH!" It rang out a second time, deeper than the first, and not as audibly loud.

"OOOOAMPH!" The horn rang out a third time, this time the sound was not so much heard but, was so deep in frequency that she could *feel* it through the telewindow.

In concordance with the sound, another opening, larger than the one that Phosos had emerged from, opened around the original. Another whoosh of air broke against the spectators watching on.

The feed from the telewindow zoomed in over the shoulder of Phosos to anticipate what else might appear from the orb. Bright blue light screamed out from the newly opened cavity. Many had to shield their eyes.

She waffled her weight back and forth on her feet. Beside her, Craig and Dr. Silva watched the broadcast with barely a blink.

Phosos's voice drew her back in to watch as well.

"Your sacred texts, your *God*, misled you of your origin and coexistence with creation. In truth, immense time sundered you from this *old world's* genesis; a truth your science has only glimpsed. Yet, so you know the power I offer, and my eternal age, I shall join what time has separated—behold, a beast of old."

Phosos's pronouncement was echoed by the appearance of three grey blobs in the light. Two taller shadows flanked a smaller shadow in between them about half their size. The shrouded figures moved forward at leisurely paces. When they came out into the plaza, exiting the light, a collective gasp waved across the crowd. The two tall figures were identical to Phosos in nearly every way: both were tall, carried dark hair, and had impeccable skin and musculature. The only discernable difference she noticed was that they did not have the same shimmering-blue glow emanating from their skin.

The two Phosos-like beings walked in unison, with their torsos turned towards one another as they appeared to be carrying an object between them. As they ventured further into the plaza, Aliyah could see that they held two long poles that terminated in each of their hands. The poles were made of a bronze-looking metal that was duller than gold. Hanging from the poles, between them, was a large, rectangular chest made of the same material. It looked to be of great weight but the two beings seemed to stride with it effortlessly.

The chest was embellished with a multitude of creatures, some Aliyah recognized, others she did not. She saw cattle, camels, deer, and fish. One creature, larger than the rest, caught her eye. She had never seen such a creature before, besides in one of her old natural history lessons. Its skin looked scaly, like the foot of a chicken. Embedded on the side of its head were little black stones for eyes that looked over a beak-shaped snout. Starting just behind its eyes, a feature sloped upward in the shape of a half-cone forming a type of frill at the back of its head.

She could not believe her eyes; it was a dinosaur!

The dinosaur looked to be a type of triceratops but without the three horns sticking forward from its head. The only horns that were visible were ten horns that protruded out from the edges of its back frill.

Her mind tried to process the meaning behind the symbol. A creature that had been extinct for an unfathomable amount of years was now being displayed on the side of an alien's metal chest. She wondered if Phosos or his kind saw such creatures directly to inspire the artwork. If so, he or his race must be of great age. Yet, before her mind settled on an explanation, her eyes glanced back at the tall beings standing beside the chest. The conclusion was clear, anything could happen now that alien beings had entered the world.

Another object drew her attention. Protruding out of the chest was a peculiar looking tree. Standing about three meters tall, the tree had peeling strips of bark that twisted in a glossy-smooth spiral up the tree's trunk. Its bark had the color of the greenish patina of copper. At the crown portion of its trunk, the tree had a center split which equally divided six main branches on each side. These branches twisted and curled downward like a willow and intertwined with a mirrored set of six roots that arose out the dark black soil from which the tree rested in. There was little foliage or signs of greenery, only a few gold leaves with spotty black edges clung to the limbs. The whole tree resembled a contorted ball of woody branches.

The crowd was clamoring at the sight until Phosos began to speak. This time, the two Phosos-like beings also spoke in unison with Phosos as if the triad were speaking with one voice. If the voice of Phosos had been powerful, the addition of the other two beings made his voice sound thunderous.

The crowd quickly fell silent.

"So long, misled have you been by your own beliefs. Ideas and faith, and doctrine time twisted, diluted. A *God* you worshiped over many millennia. One that divided and led to killings in *His* name. Lost and scattered you are on your own devices. Here am I, without distortion of time, writing, or mind; present, proximal, and much providing, am I. Greater than the gods that led you to be astray, I, of purer spirit, come to provide for all. To be the Provider, everlasting, to all nations, as one."

The crowd let out a collective gasp but even before it had completely been exhaled, Phosos went on:

"Behold, the Tree of Unity and Provision, a symbol. For once nations branched and split, but I shall unite all in the roots of one people in peace evermore. Six continents, one Provider, six provisions—food, shelter, clothing, health, purpose, peace—salvation. Thus, listen...see...forget your differences, forget your past, devote yourselves to a common future. I will be the head to guide you, as one body.

"So, I speak to all, the time has come to unite."

Phosos fell quiet and watched the crowd around him. His steely eyes still showed traces of fervor from his compelling speech. He seemed to be waiting for something but she could not recognize what that could be.

At least, not until a small number of groups of people came forward from the gallery of onlookers. Among them, were people of different faiths: Orthodox Jews, Muslims, and a Christian. The three Jewish men wore traditional black cloaks and kippah caps while two Jewish women wore headscarves with white blouses and knee-length skirts. The six Muslim men were dressed in ankle-length Thobes with matching white turbans while the eight Muslim women wore full-length black tunics with black headscarves. The solitary Christian man approached with the party in khaki pants and a white button-down shirt, sleeves rolled, and a slender black tie.

Once the party had reached within shaking distance of Phosos, the members astonishingly removed all vestments and symbols of the faith that separated them from one another. The Jewish men cast off their kippahs and tzitzits. The Jewish women and Muslim men and women all removed their head coverings. Finally, the Christian man tore from his neck a golden crucifix that hung from a chain and threw it before the feet of Phosos. Then, they fell to their knees, some leaning to kiss the ground, in veneration. Hailing the being: "Phosos, The Provider!"

Phosos seemed pleased by these gestures for he approached with long outstretched arms. For each person, he quietly touched their forehead and traced out what appeared to be the six branches and six roots of the tree with a single unifying trunk connecting the two parts.

The crowd was moved by the act as well. More people approached, one-by-one. Though Aliyah noticed a few people slipping away discreetly. In a few short minutes, almost the entire assembly could be found bowing before Phosos to pay homage to his promise of a New Eden.

She stood there, a world away, lost for words. Her mind, her closely-held beliefs, were all askew.

The frost was creeping along the edges of her office window. Little white crystals fanned out into beautiful feathered patterns like a flattened array of icy trees. She had been standing there for several minutes now, just staring aimlessly. A reflection of her face hung suspended within the panes, blank and subdued. Outside, in the grey light of the morning, squirrels pranced up and down the sturdy oak trees gathering leaves and bits of branches to make their winter nests. For them, the world was still much the same as it had been three days ago. The sun still rose, it still set, and the wind blew a chilling breeze upon them foreboding the winter cold to come.

She stood there, in her warm loose-knit shawl, thinking about the transformative events that had transpired. It all still seemed like a fantastic dream that she could not quite wake herself from. In just three short days after Revelation Day (A.R.D.)—as it became called—the world had come together in ways not thought imaginable. Almost overnight, nations of the earth, their peoples, all major religions had devoted themselves to the vision and new world plan set forth by Phosos, the godlike alien being.

Though in truth, there was little choice to be made in the face of a superior being that offered to provide so much and asked for, what appeared on the surface, to be so little—collective leisure and devotion. The only requirement that people relinquish their governance to his judgment and set of laws. For the detractors to this New Eden would be dealt with harshly. The militaries of the world had been given a strict two-week deadline to stand down and disband. There would be no need of weapons and armies under Phosos's cloak of protection.

Another shock that she had learned in the last few days was that the other beings on Revelation Day were not in fact like Phosos but some sort of artificial robotics that Phosos claimed to have adapted from humanity. He instilled in them, his image and his advanced mind as an artificial intelligence. This AI was somehow interconnected between robotic beings and connected to his mind, allowing himself to be omnipresent through their artificial eyes. They were declared by Phosos as the Hands of Provision, operating at every step in the means of production. They were to be the drudgers and societal stewards all in one unblemished form.

The Hands of Provision were to make any work by mankind obsolete, or more precisely, prohibited. The people of New Eden were commanded to focus on leisure and their devotion to each other—'Branches and roots, one sturdy trunk: unity and provision.' No longer would there be a gap between the rich and the poor, the intelligent and the dumb, male and the female, all were equal and united. A new golden age was to be ushered in, only this time, without end.

To achieve this grand vision, it was the Hands of Provision that would help monitor and enforce order and help provide the food and services needed by humanity. And, as a symbol of unity, the citizens of New Eden were to accept a branded mark on their right wrist which would signify their devotion and right to obtain sustenance without cost—for money now had no value. There was also no need to work or pursue science and new technologies. These were relics of a fallen society and were needed not with the great provision.

There was no place for the religions of old either. Twisted by time, humanity's selfishness, and desire for power, the old-world religions were deemed by Phosos to be vain constructions by man that feebly attempted to understand universal values. Phosos offered a purer form of existence that accepted all regardless of any individual characteristics, wants, or desires. As long as one devoted themselves to New Eden, they would be accepted and included.

She struggled with these revelations. The very foundations of her faith had been shaken. She did not know what to believe anymore. She saw, as did the world, the tangible existence of a being like Phosos. He was real, he had power she did not understand, and, importantly, he promised what people, including herself, had been crying out for over so many centuries. She wanted peace and sustenance for all, how couldn't she?

To her embarrassment, doubts had crept into her mind. She did not want to entertain that, just perhaps, her beliefs were based on a millennia-long game of telephone. The possibility that things really did get twisted, misinterpreted, and molded to serve those in power so much that the original message had been lost to time. Like many, she couldn't know; she was not there to see it.

She could see Phosos, and that evidence was undeniable.

Despite these thoughts, she just could not resign herself to abandon her faith, at least not yet. Many of her colleagues had already gone to provision stations to get what was being called 'unified' with their provision symbol upon their wrist. Craig had received his own the day before. As for Dr. Silva and Gabe, they had been strangely absent the past few days and she could not account for their whereabouts. Their absence was concerning, but so was everything else that weighed heavily on her mind in these moments.

She turned her gaze deeper into the hollow of trees. The space within was dark and still filled with an occluding morning mist. In contrast to the edge, the deeper woods were completely still, without signs of life. Only the grey twisting of branches and shifting shadows were noticeable.

Even with Revelation Day behind her, her mind kept returning to that night in the woods. No matter how hard she tried to push it aside she constantly relived it all...the sounds...the trees...that light.

She remembered the orb vividly. It was hard to forget. The orb from the woods was many magnitudes smaller than the one that descended upon Jerusalem, but it was very similar in shape and appearance. Both pulsed with that eerily dead, blue glow like the strobing of dull antique florescent lights. The pulsing had a rhythm; two quick flashes and a long drawn out fade from bright white to the darkest midnight blue.

A branch from a nearby tree tapped the window from a gust of wind. It sent the squirrels reeling back to the safety of the sturdier branches.

She shuddered.

Even thinking about it in the safety of daylight in her own office made her feel uneasy. There seemed to be some connection she could not make between the orbs; it was discomforting.

Turning back from the window, she stared at the screen of her computer which was playing back a series of analyses from Dr. Silva's big experiment.

With all that had happened, she had placed little thought on the success of the experiment. Dr. Silva had achieved a trans-generational leap in memory retrieval. The readings and visual recordings all confirmed that he experienced a memory of his father that preceded his birth. It was an extraordinary moment to witness and one that would have been trumpeted in every outlet of the world, if not for the arrival of Phosos.

Like many journeys into the unknown, there were unexpected findings along the way. Several data anomalies were recorded during the experiment. Just after the experiment was terminated, as Dr. Silva reached the point in the memory where he was looking down one of the paths, the readings showed a stream of data accounting for what would have been nearly ten minutes after the experiment had been disengaged. Typically, as she understood it, the Mindsai uses a sophisticated algorithm to stimulate the part of the mind being targeted to retrieve a memory. However, with the machine disengaged, the readings were indicating that Dr. Silva was experiencing a very vivid memory deep within his mind without the aid of the machine. Dr. Silva's own mind was generating a deep-seeded memory and feeding it directly into the sensory array. So much so that, the battery of twenty, petabyte-sized storage devices were filled to capacity. This strange event accounting for nearly ninety-eight percent of what was recorded.

Stranger still, when analyzing these data stored on the devices the computer decoding program was unable to read it readily. Her computer showed that the Mindsai was still, nearly three days later, trying to unravel the data into a meaningful pattern. Even with the large data streams of prior experiments, the Mindsai could usually decode them in a period of a dozen hours or less.

But if it was taking this long to crunch the numbers, the patterns, she guessed, must be immensely complex.

As she pondered over these mysteries, a figure darted into her peripheral vision…

She quickly turned to face the office intruder. It was Gabe, looking tired, disheveled, and frightened. He desperately gasped to catch his breath.

"Gabe! I haven't seen you in days, what's the matter!? Are you all right!?" she asked franticly.

Gabe slowly got control over his breath. His hands waved in circular motions as he geared up to speak.

"I…need…your…help," he sputtered.

"Okay, okay, what do you need!?"

"I…I…can't get away from him?"

"Who?" she asked, though she feared the confirmation of her suspicions.

"Mr. Pickles," he replied.

She took in a deep breath and exhaled just the same. She thought the pause would help her think of what to do, but even the long breath wasn't enough.

"Can't you just tell him to go away? You know, like last time?"

"Believe me, I've tried…and tried. He won't go away. No matter what I say, he shows up at the foot of my bed, whispering endlessly about the bad things he wants me to do."

Gabe face was trembling, his eyes were dark and face looked gaunt from lack of eating.

He went on, quivering, "And for the last three days…he has started to appear…during the day. I've seen him…in the courtyard outside my dorm…behind trees on my walks to class, in the communal bathroom…there's nowhere I can go to escape his presence.

"On my way to see you, I just saw him on a bench along the sidewalk. He told me he wants me to destroy Dr. Silva's machine!"

Gabe was markedly distressed. His eyes wobbled back and forth as if he was trying to catch his balance. His hand was quivering with uncontrolled shaking so he pressed it into her desk to try to gain control over his body. As he did so, the shaking transferred up through his arm and into his shoulder.

"The Mindsai? But why?" she asked.

"He tells me not to look back, the past is dead, the pleasures of *now* are fully-satisfying," he blurted out.

Gabe's whole body was shaking terribly as he tried to keep on his feet.

"Gabe, why don't you take a seat?" She motioned him to the small brown sofa in the corner of her office. He took a seat gingerly and it seemed to relieve some of the strain. His shaking lessened.

She was perplexed by the specificity of the entity's demands. Why would it care to destroy a man-made machine? What was there to gain? Could Mr. Pickles really be that focused or was this just another call for aimless violence?

Perhaps a world without the Mindsai wouldn't be such a bad thing.

The intrusive thought flickered in the back of her mind. It had been there for some time but she had been reluctant to allow it audience. Given recent events with the basement archives, Gabe's Mr. Pickles encounters, and the woods—*those woods*—she already had begun to doubt the benefits of opening up the world to face childhood terrors. There was little sense of trying to alleviate childhood trauma if the terrors of childhood were real after all. Maybe breaking down walls within our minds to suppressed memories was unwise unless we know why they were put up in the first place. It was also possible that the Mindsai experiments were the source of these disturbing occurrences.

She looked back at Gabe. His eyes hung low in their sockets but his breathing had steadied and he looked more calm sitting in the sofa. Breaths came in and out at uniform three second intervals. It had probably been days since he could take unguarded breaths. Even a few minutes of repose in her office must seem like a well of refreshment after nights without sleep.

He could rest as long as he needed. She could not leave him alone now, not until they figured out what they might do next.

Outside of Gabe and herself, their predicament might be of little consequence amidst the world-wide upheaval that had swayed governments, cultures, and religions alike. So, what they were going to do she had not the slightest clue. While Gabe rested, she needed time to analyze and process. With enough thinking, maybe she could develop a plan.

About twenty minutes past before a sound rang out in the adjacent lab room. Startled by the unexpected sound, she looked to Gabe to see if he could confirm he heard it as well.

Gabe was snoring softly on the tiny sofa. Apparently, he hadn't noticed a thing.

The sound came again.

She froze, trying to listen closely to what was making the noise. Her ears slowly picked up on a rhythmic humming from an unknown distance away. It was almost chant-like in its cadence with harmonics that varied from low to high. Interspersed the drawn-out notes, she heard the sound of metal-on-metal clanking. The repeated impacts gave off a certain oscillating "wwowwow" resonance similar to a tuning fork.

She didn't know what to make of these sounds. They certainly were not normal sounds to be coming from the laboratory space. It was likely that someone was moving equipment around in there, but, as far as she was aware, there was no reason for anyone to touch the equipment.

She paced behind the door, biting the corner of her lip until it began to throb. In her gut she knew that Dr. Silva would want her to investigate. Neither he nor Craig had been in the lab today and with the priceless equipment in there, she needed to ensure a stranger was not meddling around.

She glanced back at Gabe. He was still sound asleep. A half smile had emerged from his drawn and tired face.

"You rest, I'll investigate," she whispered softly.

Walking towards the door, she realized that she did not know what she would do if she did encounter a stranger. She had little time for a plan; her feet were already outpacing her thoughts as she slowly creaked open the door.

On the other side of the door, the humming clearly sounded low and throaty. No longer muffled by the door, the clanging sounded more like a pinging from jarring metal.

She stepped further out into the main lab space.

All she could see was the blinking lights from the equipment. She could still hear the humming but it seemed to be disembodied. It took a few moments before her ears narrowed down the source.

She turned towards the Mindsai. The sound seemed to be emanating from just behind it.

She stepped quietly towards the machine, trying to conceal her approach. She looked down at her feet to ensure she did not step on anything that would make noise or trip over a wire.

One foot in front of the other, heal to toe. One foot in front of the other...

The sounds suddenly stopped.

Her foot froze in mid-step, hoping she was not heard.

She waited breathlessly in the stillness of the room. The increasing silence rose with her uneasiness. What if no one was there and she had imagined it all? What if there was someone or *something* there? She couldn't decide which scenario was more desirable in the moment.

"Please don't be Mr. Pickles. Please don't be Mr. Pickles," she began to repeat as inaudibly as she could under her breath.

"Whose Mr. Pickles?" said a familiar voice behind the machine.

Craig's head popped up with a toothy smile. His eyes looked cold and overly focused on her. In his left hand, he held a peculiar pick accompanied by an equally peculiar hammer-like object in his right hand. Both were made of the same metal that was often used in medical equipment, though what their medical use was she couldn't say. The metal appeared to be some sort of stainless steel in composition, but they were speckled at their terminating ends in a dried reddish-brown patina. They were cast from a solid piece of metal about the length from Craig's elbow to the bottom of his hand. The pick had a long-rounded handle that tapered off into a fine point at one end, like a spike, and, at the other end, had a crescent moon-shaped handle. The hammer had a similarly rounded handle that flatted slightly at one end and had a tiny indentation for holding with a thumb. At its terminated end, the hammer's head was in the shape of a rounded hour-glass about the size of a half-sized drinking glass.

"Whose Mr. Pickles?" Craig repeated.

All she could do was stare at the metallic items in his hands that dully glimmered in the lights.

"Do you know a Mr. Pickles, Daisy?" Craig asked.

"No Pickles on record, no *zo*," Daisy replied in a deeper voice without her normal French accent.

"What are you holding and what were you doing back there," she asked, pointing beyond the machine.

Before Craig, or Daisy, could reply, Gabe's voice croaked from behind her. He was awake.

"They appear to be an orbitoclast set, though outside of a museum, I don't know how you came in possession of them. No one has used those psychosurgical instruments in over one hundred years!" Gabe said. The sound of grogginess was still noticeable in his voice.

"Orbitoclast?" she asked. She had never heard of such an instrument. The warm blush of embarrassment crept across her face as she acknowledged her lack of historical understanding despite being a semi-professional psychologist.

"Very perceptive, Gabriel. Very perceptive. They're just some old lobotomy tools I found in the basement archives. There's a lot of nice old stuff down there. You should come with me to check it out," Craig answered.

"I think I'll pass on that offer," Gabe replied.

Craig turned to Aliyah. His eyes were bored their focus into her own eyes. His gaze made her instantly uncomfortable. Her thoughts were sent scrambling, like a school of fish trying to evade a predator.

"Umm…yeah, I don't think I'll be venturing down there again," she mustered forth after a few moments.

Craig's stare remained unmoved by her response. His hand fidgeted with the metal instruments, rolling them back and forth between his thumbs and palms. They dangled down precariously with each movement.

Just as she began to turn away, Craig spoke up, not breaking his gaze from her for a second.

"Tell me, where are your unit marks? I don't see them on either of your wrists. You have been commanded to receive them, for New Eden."

Craig was not wrong. Phosos had decreed for all peoples to receive the unity tree mark as a symbol of unity in New Eden.

The process was completely painless. People only had to go to select locations where a machine would shine a specialized blue light on the wrist that burned at a layer beneath the skin and the nerve endings. After a period of a few minutes, a dark red mark of the six-branched/six-rooted unity tree would well up from beneath the skin and remain as a permanent symbol of citizenry in New Eden.

She could see that Craig had a mark. However, his mark was unlike those she had encountered on other people's wrists. For one, it was not really on his wrist but more centered on the palm of his hand. Also, the mark was peculiarly discolored in non-uniform shades of red and white like it had been seared into his skin rather than as a result of a precision mark-making device.

Her eyes darted back to Craig's which were, narrowed, still intently waiting for her response.

She looked back at Gabe, but his eyes were already downcast on the floor, avoiding any chance of eye contact, and support. Her mind scrambled to put together a response.

"I...um...sure, I have...um...thought about it. I ah...just haven't found the time to process all these recent events. So much is changing, so fast, I don't know what to make of it all yet."

Her response seemed to fall flat. Craig's forehead unwrinkled and his mouth turned to a frown.

"Daisy, what happens to those who reject the unity that our Provisioner Phosos and New Eden offer?" Craig asked, looking down at her with his lips half-smirked.

A hiss and popping sound came from the speaker before Daisy spoke in a low, gruff voice.

"Those who reject the provision of New Eden will be plucked out like weeds. A garden cannot grow when strangled by the roots and leaves of those who will not grow and fertilize paradise. Dissenters will be exiled or, if necessary, disposed of."

The response was not foreign to her. She had heard much of these decrees and warnings during the past few days. Though Daisy's rendition was much darker and disturbing than the others. She did not care to hear much more from Daisy or Craig. She needed to turn the focus back on him.

"Craig, exactly what were you doing back there behind the Mindsai?" she asked once more.

"What business is it of yours?" he snapped back quickly.

"I am a member of this lab and that machine's security is as much a responsibility of mine as it is yours," she replied, trying to stand her ground. Craig's eyes flashed a flicker of fury.

"You think so?" Craig snickered, in half snorts. "You've never really been a part of this lab...and, I don't think you ever will be."

"And what is that supposed to mean?" she said.

"Yeah Craig, knock it off. You're being a real jerk, more so than usual," piped Gabe, coming next to her side. His posture was alert and his eyes were glimmering with energy and resolve.

"I mean, come on, you really think that you belong here...that you're smart enough to be in the lab of one of the greatest minds of psychology? Face it Aliyah, you're a token child lifted up from drudgery to be good PR for Bash's lab. Just to keep inquiring eyes of regulators and would-be critics looking elsewhere," Craig said, twirling around the hammer around his index finger.

She could not find words to speak. The pit of her stomach turned in a twisting pain. His words had struck her deep, to an old wound that had always been there, one that could never really heal. It was the realization that she did not earn her place above being merely the daughter of a drudger family. She had tried her best to push that thought down and obscure it from her mind but she could never escape it—the feeling of being an imposter here, in this lab, in graduate school. So many things had worked against her: being a woman, being black, and coming from a home of people who labored and worked so hard to provide for themselves. Due to these characteristics she could not control or change, she felt she could never truly know if her achievements were her own or due to some misplaced pity from powerful decision-makers. This was a truth she tried to hide deep within herself, but now it had been dredged up to the surface, exposed to the air. Despite all her hard work, and the things she absolutely *knew* she had earned with true merit, she couldn't help to feel her pride slipping away from her, leaving her naked and bare.

She looked over to Gabe. Water had set in the corners of her eyes and she could barely make out his face. All she could see was a wordless shake of Gabe's head side-to-side.

She took a deep breath and wiped the tears from her eyes, and then turned back around.

Craig's face was still frozen in a callous grin. She felt the tips of her nails dig deep in the palms of her hand as they clinched tightly together in a building rage. *Sticks and stones, they're just words,* she thought, trying desperately to restrain herself into composure.

Without rebuttal, Craig continued:

"The sad thing is, with New Eden, we'll never get to see you fail and expose you for the fraud that you are. There is no need for science anymore. There's no need for this machine. All will be provided for."

"Z-O-Z-O-Z-O-Z-O," Daisy interjected, in a sort of gasping voice.

The string of letters made little sense. But it frightened her. She felt a coldness slip into the room. Her instinct suggested that something was amiss and that evil was imminent. She wanted to run, but her feet would not move.

"That's right, Daisy. Its time," Craig said. His grip on the hammer became firm and he raised his other hand that held the long metal pick. Positioning the pick over the main control terminal of the machine, he began to tap forcefully onto it.

TING! TING! TING!

A flurry of sparks flew up all around Craig as the pick drilled deeper into the heart of the Mindsai. A terrible crackling sound of crunching metal and disconnecting circuits came out from within. Air coolant bellowed out of the fissure and fell heavy to the floor around Craig's feet.

She cupped her hands over her ears and yelled.

"Stop! Stop! What are you doing!?"

Craig paid no attention to her and continued. Once the pick had reached its length into the machine, he jerked it out and proceeded to make another hole. He kept going at a feverish pace. The Mindsai was sparking and flashing red warning lights all over. It was beginning to look like a mangled piece of swiss cheese.

It all seemed to be slipping out of her control. She had to do something. She couldn't just let Craig destroy it all. It was Dr. Silva's career. It was one of a kind…

Then a most desperate thought popped into her mind, *Oh my God, it was the only key to corroborate Phosos's account of the past!*

Before she could act, a grey figure darted before her. It was Gabe. Just as Craig was about to hammer down the pick into the interchange box between the Mindsai and the cables leading to the SEER goggles, Gabe grabbed the spike with one hand and threw a fist into Craig's face.

Craig stumbled back on his feet. His mouth hung open dumbly for a few flash moments before closing tightly, baring his teeth.

All she could do was watch as the two struggled over the Mindsai that was still sparking and oozing coolant. The lights in the room began to flicker as the damage was creating rolling power fluctuations.

Eventually, Craig overpowered Gabe's hand and placed it flat against the machine. Taking the pick with his other hand, he pushed it into the backside of Gabe's hand and leaned into it with all his weight. A series of loud crunches came out as the slender piece of metal drove deeper. Almost immediately, bright red blood began squirting out all over the machine and Craig's shirt. Gabe cried out in pain and desperately grabbed at the pick, trying to stop it from going any deeper.

The two struggled as Gabe held the pick at bay from going any further. His time was limited. The loss of blood was visibly weakening his grip. If the pick went any further, he might never use the hand again.

She jumped forward, without thinking, and pushed Craig as hard as she could onto the floor. He fell back and hit the ground with a heavy thud next to the Mindsai. Craig looked like he was going to get up and strike back against her but the flow of heavy coolant had pooled over his face and it seemed to knock him unconscious.

She turned back to Gabe who had managed to rip the metal pick from his hand. Blood was gushing from where the pick had exited in his palm and fragments of white bone were visibly protruding from the wound. Gabe clutched his damaged hand with his other, placing his thumb and fingers over the holes. It did little use as blood continued to pour out around his fingers and dripped into dark pools on the floor.

"Gabe, we need to get you to the doctor!" she said.

"Yes, it looks like I need some treatment, and so do you by the looks of it," Gabe said, pointing to the side of her arm.

She looked to where he was pointing and saw a circular ring of blood about three centimeters in diameter was forming beneath her shirt. Craig must have hit her with the hammer as he fell to the floor.

"Yikes! I guess we both need help."

"And so does the Mindsai," Gabe added jokingly.

"Dr. Silva is going to lose his mind when he sees this. I don't know what got into him, I've never seen Craig lash out like that."

"I'm not sure either, but I think it has something to do with that ouroboros trinket I saw around his neck," said Gabe.

"What are you talking about?"

"I'll show you."

Gabe walked over to the door to grab a scarf that was hanging on the rack and looked back to her.

"Do you mind?"

"Go ahead, you need to stop the bleeding."

He then walked back over to Craig who was still lying motionless on the floor. The coolant was beginning to dissipate and she could see the snake-encircled tree trinket around Craig's neck.

"How did he get that!" she gasped.

"I'm not sure, but I think it's what has caused him to go berserk. I think it has something to do with Mr. Pickle's recent appearance too. Everything was fine until we stumbled upon this thing. We need to get it off of him and get rid of it."

She nodded in agreement.

Gabe leaned down to grab the ancient trinket from Craig's neck. Just as he touched it, he jerked back quickly in shock.

"What's the matter?" she asked.

"It's ice cold. It burns to the touch," Gabe replied. "I'll have to hold it by this chain he has on around his neck. It's kind of a pretentious chain, really. Not one that is good for concealment."

Gabe picked up the chain and slowly began to shimmy it up over Craig's head.

"LET IT GO!" came a voice near Craig.

The sound startled both of them.

She looked to Craig who was still unconscious on the floor.

"It must have been Daisy, I haven't seen Craig move a centimeter," she said, with an encouraging motion for Gabe to continue.

He nodded and then pulled more forcefully on the chain until it was off completely over the head.

Craig's eyes jolted opened wide, staring up at the trinket that dangled from Gabe's hand above him. His eyes were fierce and menacing.

"Give that back!" Craig said in a deep voice.

Gabe stumbled back and turned to her. Gabe took a few big steps and grabbed her arm to run. They both bolted out of the lab doors into the corridor as they heard Craig behind them in the lab trying to desperately get to his feet.

The two of them ran down the stairs and out the front doors of Hugenberg Hall. They both stopped, gasping for air on the steps.

She looked around to gather her bearings. The sidewalks were mostly empty since the university had suspended classes in light of the events of Revelation Day. There truly was not a soul to be seen. Even if there were people walking about, it would be difficult seeing them in the thick mist that still hung about.

"We should...head...into town," Gabe said, in between breaths.

"I agree, which way should we go?" she replied earnestly. She did not want to linger in front of the building for too long. Craig was sure to come after them and the quicker they could depart and put distance in between them, the better.

"We could take the Sage Walk, that's probably the most direct route," he replied.

She didn't have any objections.

The pair set off along the sidewalk, walking quickly. The mist was growing so thick that Craig could approach them from any direction and they would only have a dozen meters to react. So, they huddled together closely for security.

As they turned the corner of the child learning center, they heard something in the enclosed playground.

It wasn't the sounds of approaching footsteps like she feared. No, the sound was more mundane. It sounded like metal slowly creaking in a back-and-forth rhythm…

They both peered their eyes over the low fence to see through the mist. As the mist swirled, they both could barely see the outline of a swing moving on its own accord. The swing moved steadily in a forward to back motion. There was no passenger in the swing's seat nor was there a person to be seen in its proximity. The air was without a breeze leaving little explanation for its animation.

They both exchanged expressions of puzzlement.

The swing slowly lost its momentum and came to rest.

Silence began to return around them.

"Hehehehehe…"

The giggling of a child echoed from where the swing had stopped. The sound was unsettling; they both knew no child was present here. No *real* child at least.

Before long, singing came upon them from the swing set. The tune was playful, like a nursery rhyme, but it sounded distant in place and time.

"It's raining, it's pouring, the old man is snoring," sang the child's voice.

"We better get out of here," she said nervously.

"No, wait…look!" Gabe pointed back to the swing.

Amidst the two hanging chains she could see what looked like a small boy wearing a black polo shirt floating above the swing seat. The figure did not seem to have any legs, just a vaporous shadow. The face was sunken in without features, except for two yellow eyes that glowed in the mist.

"Is that—"

"Yes, it's Mr. Pickles," Gabe replied.

The rhythmic singing continued and began to move around them, seemingly just out of sight in the mist. The singing crossed the playground, then the fence, and moved until it seemed to be right behind them. She did her best to track the singing out of the corner of her eye while still remaining fixed on Mr. Pickles sitting motionless in the swing.

Then the singing stopped and Mr. Pickles disappeared into the mist, his burning yellow eyes being the last to fade away from view.

She did not want to turn around, but knew she must. Grabbing Gabe's good hand, they both turned.

Craig stood in front of them. He his face and arms were bright red from his long exposure to the Mindsai's coolant. She could already see pieces of skin starting to peel back in little curly-cues on his arms and face. In his hands, he held the metal surgical hammer and lobotomy pick; the tips of his fingers had already begun to blacken from extreme frost bite. On his face, his mouth was closed without expression. Yet, his eyes were fixed and blackened.

Craig did not speak, but Daisy did, in a growling voice.

"All night, all day, let the blood spray. In houses, in fields, and woods, let them run, run. Kill them, *it will be fun*, fun. Give them a chop, with la guillotine and watch heads roll, eyes blink, but nothing comes out of lips clink, clink..."

Without wasting a second more, Gabe and Aliyah both ran as fast as they could down the sidewalk. She did not dare look back over her shoulder. The sound of Daisy's maniacal voice was confirmation enough that Craig was in pursuit.

The two of them ran down the sidewalk until Gabe quickly pulled on her arm to dart onto an adjacent path, trying to lose Craig. She had not seen this path before and had to duck down low due to the thick underbrush that had built up at its entrance.

The path descended sharply down the ridge. The rocky slope made it difficult to keep her footing. Her feet skidded on the gravel constantly as she followed Gabe who was trying to keep up a quick pace. After some near falls, saved by a quick bracing hand, she found it helpful turning sideways and seeking out root outcroppings to steady her controlled fall down the mountain.

And if the loose slope wasn't enough, both sides of the path were lined with a tangled brush of leafless undergrowth that pulled and prodded at her clothes all along the way.

She gave a huge sigh of relief once they both reached the bottom of the ridge. They were both tattered, scraped, and out of breath. However, the flight wasn't finished. Above they could hear the snapping of branches and rolling rocks.

Craig had found their trail!

Leaving no time to waste, they both pushed northward.

The dirt path, now at the foot of the ridge, hugged the slopes that increasingly became more and more sheer. The cliffs began to tower above them on their right, casting shadows over the cypress trees that grew in the black bog that followed the other side of the path. With each step that they took, the ground became squishier under their shoes. The bog had encroached itself under the path that looked as if it had not been tended to for years.

The path began to narrow sharply as they passed underneath a cliff several hundred meters above, forcing them to walk in single file. She feared that the path might become impassible and they would need to double back. That was not an option. She could still hear a voice on the air coming behind them. She could not make out the words but did not need to. Craig was still hot on their trail.

Up ahead, Gabe gasped and stopped suddenly.

"What's the matter, Gabe?" she asked.

"We might be at the end of the line here," he said plainly.

She pushed through the brush to get up beside him, the smell of rotten egg wafted across her nostrils. When she reached Gabe's side, she nearly face-planted on the wet stone. Gabe's good hand had steadied her arm and averted a nasty slip.

The path had opened up and terminated at the edge of a large pool about fifteen meters in diameter. The water was murky, stagnant, and mostly still.

Looking down, her reflection jeered back at her quietly. Tiny ripples fluttered through the visage as the mirrored surface was disrupted only in places where baseball-sized bubbles broke up through in murky yellow hues. The depths seemed bottomless and she could not find any sides heading downward. There was only a small ledge, covered in an orangey-yellow slime, about a half meter below the surface. It jutted out a meter over the dark murky depths.

To her right was a sheer cliff towering upwards many hundreds of meters and on the left was a thick foggy bog of trees.

Across the sulfur pool, she could see the path continuing onward. It was where they needed to be, but there was no way to get to it.

"I've never been down here but I think we are at the sulfur pool beneath Devil's Leap," Gabe remarked.

"Why would the path just end like this here?" she asked.

"I think it's supposed to wrap around the edges of the pool but it looks like the trees and underbrush from the bog have reclaimed the space," he said, pointing to a thick nest of wood, thorns, and black mud.

Off in the distance, they both could still hear the unintelligible chatter of Daisy approaching with Craig.

"What should we do?" she asked. She felt trapped and frightened. There was no telling what Craig would do to them if they got caught.

After surveying the surroundings several times over, Gabe asked, "Can you swim?"

"I can tread water all right," she answered unconfidently.

"That should be good enough. Here, hold this while I go first and find the best way across." He handed her the chain with the ouroboros trinket dangling below.

"Be careful, it looks really slippery," she said, as he stepped out onto the ledge.

"Well, at least the water is warm," he called back with a half-smile after dipping in one of his feet and swirling it around a little.

Gabe then slipped into the pool and made several nice sidestrokes before reaching the other side. All wet, Gabe pulled himself out of the water onto the path. His clothes steamed vigorously in the cool air.

"Okay, your turn," he called across the gap.

She wrapped the trinket around her wrist in a simple knot and then stepped gingerly down onto the submerged ledge. The water soaked her pants up to just below her waist, but it was warm. She slowly stepped out to the end of the ledge.

Looking down, all she could see was darkness. *Just keep your eyes on the prize*, she thought.

She turned her head to look at Gabe as she pushed off from the ledge into the water. Using a bicycle motion, she treaded through the water towards the other side.

She was making good progress until she had reached the center of the pool. Her feet suddenly began to feel tired and heavy. It was like she was trying to churn through a jar of honey.

Twisting around in the water, all sides now looked so desperately far from her. From beneath her, she felt a growing cold spot filling in around her. With it, a swarm of bubbles came up from the depths and bounced off the side of her feet, legs, and her paddling arms.

At least, she thought they were bubbles.

When she looked down, each 'bubble' was staring directly upon her with cold, lidless eyes. Each eye glowed inky yellow in the dark water.

"Aaahhh!" she shrieked in dismay, splashing her hands downward to lift herself out of the water and try to get a little farther away from the eyes.

Below the floating eyes, hovering five meters below, a dark mass, had formed just beneath her feet. It was much darker than the bottomless depths of the pool and she could tell that it wasn't just a play of the light. It was moving side-to-side in a sort of figure eight pattern. From it, black shadowy tentacles that shimmered with strange light anomalies reached out for her feet. She could feel a scratching sensation on the ankles of her foot. It felt like woody branches trying to take hold of her leg!

She panicked. All semblance of proper swimming had left her mind. Her arms were now flailing violently to keep herself afloat and away from the thing below.

In between splashes, she could see Gabe's face drawn in complete shock. His mouth was moving but she could not hear him over the churning waters.

The eyes had now breached the surface in front of her. They bobbed up and down with the waves, swiveling in all directions, but always trying to return their focus on her, following her every movement.

She did not have any choice but to swim backward to the ledge where she came. Kicking her feet, she drew herself backward away from the scratching shadow below. She kicked and she kicked as hard as she could until her back hit the edge of the pool with a thud.

Quickly turning around, she scrambled to get herself on her feet. As she put pressure on her right foot, it slipped on the ledge and her face plunged into the now frigid water. She dared not open her eyes.

She tried again, more carefully this time. She reset her feet and slowly put pressure on her legs when she felt stability. Her body rose out of the water and she grabbed a nearby tree root. It was slimy but it was anchored enough to pull herself up on the stony bank.

Breathing heavily from exhaustion, she saw Gabe pointing at her and shouting. She could not make it out over her loud breathing.

A hand came down tightly on her shoulder. She looked over and saw a hand blacked with dead flesh. Her breaths stopped and Gabe's alarmed voice came through over the pool.

"Aliyah! Look out!"

Craig spun her around and pushed her forcefully against the ground. Her head cracked against the stone and she could feel the warm, dampness of blood pool through her hair.

Craig looked even worse off than the last she saw of him, if that was possible. Running through the woods had scratched his face to be almost unrecognizable. Long flaps of bloody skin were peeling back from the sides of his face.

Despite its mangled nature, his face still managed to produce a mangled smile.

"Why do you run? Don't you know I will find you, with Daisy there isn't a place you can run or hide," Craig said grimly. "And I'll be taking this back."

He untied the trinket from her wrist and placed it back over his head and around his neck. In his left hand he held the metal hammer and pick. She tried not to stare at them but could not help it.

"Ah, yes. I brought these with me for a lesson I was preparing. I bet you have never seen a real lobotomy before." He tapped the metal pick against her forehead lightly with the tip.

"Daisy, please describe to Ms. Woods the lobotomy procedure. Don't spare any of the gory details, I want our participant to be fully informed before obtaining consent for our little experiment."

Daisy began, "The procedure calls for the orbitoclast pick to be inserted just inside the socket of the eye on the orbital roof. It is then turned slightly upward against the bone lining the back of the socket. Using the surgical hammer, the pick is lightly tapped until it splits through a half-centimeter of bone to the brain where the psychosurgeon can sever the connecting tissue—"

"Thank you, Daisy, I don't want to give it all away," Craig said with a cackling cough.

"Daisy is right, normally it should be transorbital, through the eye, but maybe today we experiment, go through the nose up the nasal cavity…"

Craig inserted the metal pick into her left nostril. She could feel the cold metal scrapping across the membrane in her nose and placing intense pressure on her sinus cavity. His hand was unsteadily twisting the tip of the pick back and forth in her nostril. One premature slip would cause irrecoverable damage.

Her mind was fluttering all over the place. She could barely process what Craig was saying.

Craig twisted her head to the side. Now she could see Gabe looking across at her. He was frantically looking to her and back to the murky waters before him which were still bubbling tremendously. He seemed trapped in an impossible place of indecision.

Craig continued, whispering in her right ear. She felt warm droplets of spit fall down onto her earlobe. "...or maybe, we go through the ear canal. Sure, some memories and other functions might be lost; maybe you even lose who you are, but your future, not your past is what matters. In New Eden, we will shape your clay mind anew."

The cold metal slipped in her ear and wriggled around like a wild cotton tip. The pressure was excruciating. It built and built against her head like she was tens of meters under water. Then with great release, she felt her ear pop and all sound became muffled and unclear.

My God! My eardrum!

"However, being this is my first time as well, we should stick to the tried and true method..."

Craig flipped her onto her back. Her eyes quivered at the metal pick hovering centimeters above. "Now, I'm going to need you to keep yourself still. This is a very delicate procedure and any error introduced on your part will cause significantly harmful deviations."

Craig took his right hand and forcefully held back her eyelid on her right eye so she couldn't blink. Then, with his left hand, he lowered the metal pick downward until it was a black blur in her eye.

The cold metal slipped slowly along the edge of her eye. A rainbow wave of colors radiated outward from the pressure that the pick placed on her exposed eyeball. The pressure also caused her vision to double with slight misalignments of the terrifying image before her.

After a slow insertion, the pick came to a rest on the backside of her eye socket. With her left eye, she saw Craig's face flash a pleased expression and then he drew up the hammer above her. The hammer came down with a light tap on the crescent-shaped end of the metal pick.

Ting!

She felt the pick lurch forward slightly. Her eye radiated in waves of color.

Then another tap. Ting!

The pick dug deeper. The colors in her eye were growing in intensity.

Another. Ting!

A tingling sound began to radiate from the front to the back of her skull, reverberating under her skin.

She wanted to sob desperately, but restrained her gut with all the control she could muster to keep herself from shaking the instrument precariously in her eye socket.

TING!

She could now feel and *hear* the bone fracturing from the tip of the pick.

Oh God, please help me…I don't want to lose myself.

TING!

Craig let go of the pick and it stood upright, on its own, lodged in her eye.

He then stroked down the pick with a finger to feel the small indentations that marked its depth in the skull.

"Good, one more tap and I think we'll be through!" he said with a devilish grin. "Then we'll push it in a few centimeters wriggle it around a bit to sever that frontal lobe of yours. It will be fun!"

Craig pulled up the hammer once more. He held it steady in position for one last tap into her skull. He was ready to strike…

She closed her eyes in anticipation of the final strike. Her eyelids slammed shut, even around the pick.

All went black.

These might be the last thoughts I have, she pondered.

She waited for that final tap…

Happy memories that defined her flickered in her mind in the fading moments.

Suddenly, the pressure holding her down released and she rolled over to her side. She cracked open an eye to see what had happened. The world swirled with black spots and flashes.

Her sight eventually cleared enough to see from where she lay that Gabe was beating back Craig with a tree limb. Toothed with thorns, the branch tore deep into the already peeling flesh of Craig's arms and legs. Blood seeped all around them on the rocky platform.

Joyous tears came to her eyes.

Craig, however, was unphased by the surprise assault. He swung back wildly at Gabe with the metal hammer as Gabe tried to grab ahold of it with his injured hand. He had no luck and Craig only forced Gabe backward onto his heels. Near the edge of the pool, they struggled in a mortal dance trying to gain position over the other.

In the fray, something else caught her eye. Standing out in shadows of the bog, amongst the trees, she saw a small pair of legs sticking out of the black muck. She blinked hard trying to make sure it was not an artifact of her affected vision. But there they were, a pair of legs attached to a small pale body whose oval head was faceless besides a pair of beady black eyes. Mr. Pickles was watching on intently. As she stared back, his vacuous eyes shifted directly upon her. In the cone of his gaze, the world got darker, like a thick cloud had blocked the sun. A mouth wasn't visible but she could *feel* in her mind that an evil grin stretching across the entity's face. The presence of wickedness instantly turned her stomach sour. She turned back to the fight at the edge of the pool…

Finally, with one dire swipe, Craig struck Gabe square in the nose. Gabe stood there after the strike with a confused look until his body fell with a hard thud to the ground a few meters away.

His eyes remained open wide in an unblinking stare of complete unconsciousness.

Craig began approaching Gabe's defenseless body, twirling the hammer in his grip.

I have to do something.

Opening her eyes wider, she saw that the orbitoclast was still firmly lodged into her eye. Before she dared to move, that would need to come out—carefully. With double vision waving back and forth, she lightly grabbed the end of the pick and delicately pulled out the instrument. Again, she could feel the metal rubbing against her eye sending a spray of color and flashes across her visual field. Centimeter by centimeter she gently coaxed it along until the severing point was out. However, once free, the sharp point slid before she could react and caught the edge of her eyebrow and forehead. Blood trickled down from the gash.

She paid the wound no mind; she was glad to be free of the brutish instrument and cast it into the mud.

She planted her hand on the stone to push herself onto her feet. She could see Craig towering over Gabe about to strike him once more with his hammer. Gathering what strength she had left, she lunged forward and pushed Craig with all her weight.

Craig stumbled back in surprise and wobbled precariously at the edge of the water. Daisy cried out a deafening shriek, "Faux pas!!!" that echoed up the cliff face.

Craig lost his balance and fell, face forward, into the water. His motion was instantly halted by the rock shelf below causing his body to became ridged from the sudden deceleration from hitting his head. And with one last large burst of bubbles, his body sank into the dark depths of the pool out of sight.

Then everything fell silent.

She rushed over to Gabe who was struggling to get up. His body was covered in the foul-smelling muck of dirt, dead leaves, and stagnant water. She pulled him onto a dry patch of the path and sat him up.

"Uhh…what happened? Where's Craig?" Gabe asked groggily.

"He's gone," she replied, motioning towards the sulfur pool with her head.

"And the ouroboros?"

"Gone too. It was around his neck."

"Good," Gabe said and then looked at her face more closely, "your eye…"

"I'll be fine, might have a scar but I can see all right. There's just a lot of sparkles in one side of my vision but I'll manage. Do you see Mr. Pickles anywhere?"

"No, I think he's gone," Gabe answered with a sigh of relief.

"Great. I can't believe we got through that; I was terrified."

Gabe nodded in agreement.

"Though to be honest, I might be more scared to tell Dr. Silva what happened to his lab," she said in jest.

Gabe cracked a smile and she helped him to his feet.

"Let's get you to a doctor, we still need to get that hand of yours checked out," she said.

It would be a long way back to town, through the woods. But they had survived an ordeal and the woods seemed a little less frightening at the moment.

9

Operation Hivemind
One month A.R.D.

A bright morning sun filtered through the dusty blinds. They once had been a bright white color but were now only the shade of yellowed egg shell from years of exposure to the sunlight and little attention. The windows were set in a modestly-large office that was decorated in drab mixes of grey-painted metal and beige-painted walls. Most of the furniture and equipment as outdated by a decade or more, but it was reliable, and that's all the U.S. Army really cared for. Things moved slowly in the Army, if at all.

He sat quietly with hands clasped together overtop his legs that jittered lightly on the floor. The industrial grey-toned carpet wasn't quite thick enough to fully camouflage his nervous excitement as he waited in a red velveteen chair just outside the office of Brigadier General Samuel T. Sturgeon.

He checked over his uniform, to give the freshly-pressed olive garb one last look over before his meeting. He scanned his sleeves ensuring that no fuzzies had latched onto it during his long walk from across post. On his right shoulder, his fingers traced the seven-pointed gold oak leaf, signifying his rank, 'Major.' He moved his fingers down and across his chest. On his right breast pocket, he passed over a patch that depicted a dove hovering over an open text with the Latin words 'PRO DEO ET PATRIA' inscribed underneath. They translated to: 'For God and Country,' the motto of Army chaplains.

He gave a quiet, bittersweet smile as he knew that his duty would soon be coming to a close. After fifteen years of service, today would be his last day. He was rather puzzled why the commanding general of the Kansas post had called him in during the standing down of the division garrisoned there.

The executive officer, a major as well, sat typing away at her computer terminal. She did not pay him one glance until the clock struck twelve-hundred when she stood up without a word and went over to knock at the general officer's door. A muffled sound was barely audible but she cracked the door open and popped her head in.

"A Chaplain Dean Wilkins, is here to see you, sir," he overheard the XO say.

A distracted voice replied from within, "Good…send him in."

"Chaplain, the general will see you now," the XO said sternly.

He nodded politely and got up. On his way through the door, he tried not to step on the scatter of papers that had piled up there. Official letters of memorandum and unit rosters lay discarded and disregarded at the foot of the door.

Within, the office was large, even for a BG. Compared to the spartan décor of the reception area, the general's office was luxurious. The walls were covered in cherry wood paneling. On the floor, the carpet was intricately woven with insignias of the Army, the Fort Riley post, and a singular silver star commiserate of his rank. The general, a man of imposing physique, looked small behind the large wooden desk. Slouched over, he was enthralled in a mess of paperwork.

"Please, take a seat Chaplain," the general said, without looking up.

Chaplain Wilkins took a seat in a plush leather chair in front of the desk. Next to it, a circular wooden table, positioned artfully in view of visitors, was piled high with stacks of challenge coins— tokens of the general's many accomplishments and ceremonial connections. He sat and studied the general, waiting for him to begin conversation. General Sturgeon continued to pour over the surface of his desk. The desk's surface was one big interactive telewindow, currently cluttered with an assortment of news reports, EXSUMs, FRAGOs, and other assortment of technical force-readiness readouts. The crow's feet around his eyes twitched slightly as his eyes strained to read.

The general let out a heavy sigh, palming his brow with his large hand.

Few officers reached the heights of general officer. The general was a man in his mid-fifties, but the years of service in the cavalry branch had aged him well beyond his years. His face was sunken in around the check bones and covered in pockmarks. His hair, white with black streaks running throughout, was high and tight, probably the same style it had been when he had joined nearly a quarter-century ago. Folds of skin drooped down over his eyelids giving his cloudy-grey eyes a constant look of fatigue. In the service of his country, his body had been ridden hard and put up wet.

The general took a few more moments reading before raising his head and clasping his hands upon the desk.

"I bet you are wondering why I called you here, Chaplain," the general began.

"My counsel is at your disposal, sir," he replied.

The general smiled and leaned forward. "Do you know what today is?"

"Today is the suspense date for our standing down orders," he replied.

The general gave a half nod.

"Yes, today is the day our damn freedom dies," he paused and looked down at his desk. "And, hell, I would prefer chaotic freedom than peaceful dependence."

He did not know how to respond, so he sat quietly and remained politely attentive.

"Do you trust this celestial provider, Phosos?" the general asked sharply.

Chaplain Wilkin's seat creaked loudly as he leaned back.

The question had taken him off guard, a feeling he had almost forgotten. His stomach felt uneasy and he found it difficult to see a clear path in his mind.

There had been many unexpected questions across his ten-year career as a Protestant chaplain. Questions of sin, regret, salvation…even the metaphysics of heaven.

On the surface, the general's question was deceptively simple. However, behind that veneer, there was a great weight to it, for the consequences of its resolution were serious and affected the entire division.

"Sorry, sir. Please give me a moment to gather my thoughts."

The request left no impact on the general's grey eyes. Unmoved, he simply leaned back and said, "Carry on, Chaplain."

He took some time to think about the question, and after thoroughly pondering his response for the general, he spoke.

"I don't claim to be a sage of wisdom, but in my opinion, there is something truly illusive surrounding Phosos and his motives we can't see past."

The general's eyes began to focus on him with interest.

"Usually, when so much is provided, much has to be taken away. There always seems to be strings attached and I fear a silk veil is being pulled over everyone's eyes. The people are certainly willing to be blind if it offers personal comfort without end."

He paused, and shook his hands, palms facing the ceiling.

"Afterall, how can you say no to a real-life Santa Claus?"

General Sturgeon was now leaning as close as he could towards him. Pleased, he looked as if he had heard what he wanted to hear. His bottom lip had scrunched up making his mouth in the shape of an inverse-U and his head shook up-and-down ever-so slightly.

But he did not speak a word. The general only sat still in his chair, waiting and watching with his pale eyes cast down upon Chaplain Wilkins.

"And sir, if I might add..." he began, concerned too much of his opinion had slipped into his advice. *A dangerous truth.*

"Carry on, Chaplain," the general said attentively.

"Well, we also must temper ourselves. Recognize that although we don't know much about Phosos, or his true motives, what we do know is that he is a very advanced being. If there is any evil, it is best that we leave it up to a higher power to resolve. It is in *His* hands."

"Is it not true that we would be relinquishing all our security, our freedom, OUR FAITH to this bastard of infinite provision?" the general said pointedly.

"But sir, we would merely be but dust in the wind going up agains—"

"Chaplain, have you seen these headlines?"

"Sir..."

"Phosos and his robotic providers have embedded themselves in every facet of our society."

The general pointed to his computer desk and began to read from it.

"It says here that they will provide all the food and sustenance we need...

"There will be no need for engineers and scientists because they will provide solutions to any of our problems...

"There will be no need for doctors because they will provide any healing that we shall need...

"And...there will be no need for social stewards because Phosos is instituting a system of social credits. 'Every person's good- and ill-actions will be tracked continuously to ensure that all citizens are in compliance with the spirit and laws of New Eden. Those who lose enough credits will be barred from the use of technology, then the public space, and if egregious enough, forced to live *without* provision,' " the general said, reading aloud snippets of news reports from across the globe.

"Sir?" he asked, trying to jump in to speak without interrupting.

"Carry on, Chaplain," the general replied.

"Sir, what are your concerns?"

"My concerns are that this is not how things have been done. I don't think humanity can live without work, to be left to decadence and dependence. Look here," the general magnified an internal intelligence memo. "This says that Phosos has taken residence in the newly built temple in Jerusalem. Jews, Muslims, and Christians alike are united for the first time in centuries. Many are hailing him as some sort of messiah who has come to save mankind. And Phosos, for his part, has declared himself truer than any god that has come before."

The general tapped his index finger vigorously on the screen.

"I'll level straight with you; I'm not a very religious man, by any means, which is why I called you in for your professional assessment. To be honest, my staff had a hard time finding a chaplain given that the Army had been phasing your ilk out over the past five years. You were the last one on post.

"I called you in here today, the last day potentially for all of us, to see if you agree that my instincts are right and that this Phosos is some charlatan. Give anyone one free miracle and people will willingly deceive themselves for anything that comes thereafter. That's my fear, and I think you might agree."

Wilkins did not know what to say. He had a sense of what he thought the general wanted him to say, but he hesitated. Like the general, he had similar inklings about the true nature of Phosos, yet he feared that to voice this opinion would be a voice of rebellion. It was a tough position to be in as a chaplain; he served God and his country. His theology pushed him to say to wait and come what may, for God will take care of his flock. False prophets and messiahs had come forth before and were cast aside in the dustbin of history.

Yet, unlike those claiming the divine before, this entity had great power and global influence. For his country, for the very society that had progressed for thousands of years, he feared that willingly relinquishing all responsibility to this unknown entity was foolish without question.

The time was nigh though, a decision had to be made before all weapons were pounded into tools of leisure and provision. There would be no second opportunity to choose.

"Well, Chaplain, this is your chance to speak. Speak up!" the general insisted impatiently. He tapped his large fingers restlessly on the desk making new images pop forth brightly in similar intervals.

He thought it over. It was not his place to provoke conflict, only to nurture the living, care for the wounded, and honor the fallen, that was the chaplain creed, that was his role. Even if his personal convictions stated otherwise.

For him, the days of conventional battles had long since passed. He still remembered, sitting in that small-town recruiting station, watching the dazzling images of helicopters and tanks firing off volleys and rolling through a staged battlefield. Fighting was a Soldiers purpose, their duty. But after his asthmatic condition manifested in basic training, he had fallen down a different path, distant from the bravado and glories of Army service. He was a man of God, and his duty was to serve the well-being of his Soldiers. His gun and shield were one in the same, a Bible. His adversaries were often immaterial.

It was a lonely fight, but he always kept marching.

"Sir, in my opinion I believe we must see what comes and follow the orders given by command. If this entity is truly exposed as something else, then he will be diminished like all those who have tried similar tactics before, but we must honor the intent of our governing authorities," he said full-throatedly.

"You would willingly surrender all freedom to this entity who desires nothing but worship and obedience?"

"Sir, I have faith that God will guide and look after those who seek Him…no one can enter the mind and control that choice," he said firmly.

"Well, I simply don't agree. A choice has to be made, and made quickly. We must deal with this entity as we have dealt with other would-be creators of new world orders—

Hitler…Stalin…Li. We must strike them head on before they can get too much of a beachhead," said the general, his voice raised in fervor. He then leaned forward across his desk, pointing his finger at Chaplain Wilkins.

"And don't undersell the U.S. Army either, Chaplain. I know you don't get to see it much in action but our AI and robotic technology are quite sophisticated."

The general ceased wagging his finger at him. He smiled, or smirked. His face looked like that of a boy about to attempt to be the first to perform a great feat of his manhood.

"Besides, this being has hardly been tested. With people throwing themselves down at his feet, it has been a cake walk for him so far. Throw in some good resistance from a world-class superpower and we'll see the true mettle of The Provider, sure enough. We'll see if this Santa can fight or wallow away and let us decide our own destiny."

"But sir, if I may."

"Carry on, Chaplain." The general's eyes remained fixed and unblinking.

"Sir, Phosos seems to control every aspect of the world's infrastructure, trying to match him with technology may not be the right approach. Maybe the most innovative thing to do is to be primitive in our tactics. Simply refusing to comply, non-violently, may force this seemingly benevolent being to reveal its true colors. If he uses violence against you, that may sway the hearts and minds of the masses that this provider isn't the sanctified being that he claims to be."

The general sat up straight in his seat, reminding him that formalities of rank had returned.

"Chaplain, I appreciate your red teaming this situation, I really do, but strategy-making is not your role here. I have an innovative plan, and it's now or never," replied the general.

"Yes sir, understood."

The general rose out of his chair. He responded quickly to his feet in kind.

"I thank you for your candor, Chaplain. You may be dismissed...or...if you so desire, you can come with me and see how humanity isn't going to lay down and be domesticated."

The offer took Wilkins a few moments to contemplate. He had been fully prepared to stand down from his post at seventeen-hundred hours. Going with the general was just delaying the inevitable and also ignoring direct orders from command. Yet...the inevitable was a purposeless place. Unlike many of his fellow Soldiers, he did not have a family or a home to return to. His residence, his food, his family, had always been the Army. Walking out that door now would be into uselessness, away from a life that he had known so long. This meeting, even if the general barely heeded his advice, had fulfilled his purpose as a tiny cog in the large Army machine. Walking out on the Army now also meant facing a choice, to take the symbol of New Eden and be apart of another large organization or reject it and be on his own for the first time. The Army was a comforting delay, and who knows, he thought, he might still be able to be of some service.

"Thank you, sir. I kindly accept your offer," he replied, welcoming the opportunity for delay.

"Good, I likely will need a man like you to keep morale when we venture into these troubled waters."

The general motioned him out of the office into the anteroom. Without a hint of doubt, the general dictated to his XO to send out orders to his subordinate leaders that Operation Hivemind was a go and they should have their units at full readiness within the hour.

His XO complied without hesitation and ran to an adjoining room to carry out her orders. There was no indication that she might buckle at orders that flew in the face of the bigger command.

With the orders handed down, the general led him through the hall and then down some stairs. They descended several levels before entering a long hallway with minimal lighting and only a single door at the far end. As they walked, the general remarked about the state-of-the-art systems that had been put in place in the facility they were walking into. He nodded at the general with courtesy and the pair walked through the narrow doorway. Above their heads, a plaque read: 'The Hive' in gold lettering.

Three colonels and a dozen officers of lower ranks immediately came to attention as they entered the room. Chaplain Wilkins tried his best to inconspicuously catch his breath.

"At ease, and carry on, we can waste no time today," the general said with a dismissing half-salute.

The Hive was primarily a bunker about twenty meters square, filled with blinking electronic equipment and telewindows. In the center of the room was a large circular wooden desk shaped like a donut with three chairs at its center. Its surface was embedded with the same interactive telewindows as the one he saw in the general's office, only much larger. Wrapping around the space above, was a continuous set of telewindows, each displaying a complex assortment of technical feeds and readiness levels. Mostly lit in yellow, the readiness levels were indicated by shades of green, yellow, and red from brigade down to the squad unit level.

He stood in awe at the central hub that was the command and control center for the entire division. Here the general would have a perfect view of his forces and real-time feedback for their progress. At his fingertips, or from the command of his voice, he could put into action the most sophisticated system known to man.

After putting his troops at ease, the general walked to a colonel standing by a large computer assemblage. The computer was unlike any that he had ever seen before. As one unit, the machine stood two meters high, three meters long and two meters wide. Two massive black electrical bundles connected into the adjacent wall. Their innards glowed and dimmed with an oscillating yellow light that he guessed must be carrying the massive amounts of data to the Hive's telewindows. Above the machine, a single hose dropped down from the ceiling carrying what looked like some sort of liquid coolant. He could see a small white ring of frost surrounding the hose from where it met the grey drop-in ceiling tile. The machine itself was painted a drab olive green and was largely unadorned except for a couple of terminals affixed to its side. The word 'HIVEMIND' was inscribed on its front plate in gold lettering with a picture of a bee spiraling off from the last letter.

"Colonel Richardson, status report!" General Sturgeon barked. The colonel standing next to the machine's main terminal had thinning dark hair that did little to hide the gaunt-looking face covered in lines.

"Sir, all HIVEMIND systems are in the green. However, our troop strength is less than optimal. My captains are reporting many of their Soldiers AWOL. They—"

The general interrupted with an incredulous tone, "AWOL colonel?"

"Yes sir, many of the force have abandoned their post to accept the provision of New Eden, especially when word got out that HQ had ordered a stand down."

"Cowardly sheep. Luckily, the main portion of our force capabilities has no need of provision," the general sneered, curling his top lip back on his teeth.

The general turned to Chaplain Wilkins.

"Wilkins, from where you sit, I'm sure you've never seen a machine like this before."

"No sir," he replied.

"It's called a Human Interactive Volitional Electronic…" the general paused to think.

"Sir, Massed," the colonel added.

"Yes, I always forget that one…Massed Information Networking Device, or HIVEMIND for short. We love our acronyms."

Chaplain Wilkins looked over the machine once more to show interest even though he had already thoroughly examined it.

The general continued without prompt, "Only three machines like this exist in the world. One is used by the Department of

Virtual Domains and the other is in Virginia being loaned to some academic," he said rolling his eyes sideways.

"He must have some strong strings in the government to get that kind of pull. These devices are the fastest computation machines known to man and were developed for complex military applications. We keep this one here in Kansas as it is easier to secure in the middle of the country, but can be utilized from any post in the world."

"Sir, what does it do?" Chaplain Wilkins asked.

The general smiled wryly as if he had been praying for him to give him the opportunity to brag about his equipment he had under his control.

"It's machines like this that have kept us out of work, Chaplain; no power in the world can provide overmatch against it. The relative peace the world has enjoyed for nearly a decade— or stalemate to be more accurate—wasn't achieved with bombs and bullets but with AI and algorithms," the general paused reflectively. A smile slid across his closed lips.

Before long, a thought seemed to pop in his eyes and he shook his head side-to-side, "You know, I hate to say it, but it was engineers and computer scientists that won our current state of stalemate since the Seventy-Two Hour War with China. The patterns and strategies were so complex and adaptive that any side with such technology can only hope to achieve a draw. And that's why we need to keep attention on these machines, to keep the balance."

Chaplain Wilkins continued to admire the machine. It was easy to see that it was put together with careful precision, but obviously larger than need-be for the stresses that it needed to bear for military-grade operations. Placing his hand on the cool metal exterior, he could feel the pulsing hum of the intricate circuitry within. He had heard of previous iterations of the technology but in his line of work, had never found it important to know much about them.

"How does a HIVEMIND work, sir?" he asked.

"If you want the ticky-tack details you can ask an SC but it works by connecting our force of infantry and mechanized drones together in an integrated network allowing for independent pieces of intel to be synthesized into a collective hive of instantaneous information," the general motioned to the donut-shaped desk in the center of the room.

"From this central Hive, a commander can see every angle of the battlefield in real-time. Equipped with military-grade nexus devices, every Field-Grade Officer down to their lowly Privates can provide input from the field utilizing their unique vantages of the battle environment instantaneously. Together, the force turns into a collective consciousness that feeds inputs into the system that can be processed and then directed back to direct individual Soldier actions.

"Have you ever heard of the 'wisdom of the crowds' or WOC phenomenon, Chaplain?"

"No sir, I don't think I have."

"Well, Chaplain, the idea is that, a complex problem can be solved with a large unit of diverse people who are enabled to provide feedback on the best course of action. An example, would be a county fair where people are asked to guess the number of marbles in a large glass jar. No single individual guesses the right number. Sure, some come close, but no one, not even an expert in physics is typically spot on. Yet, aggregating the group's guesses is right on target, almost exactly so…" the general stated before trailing off to look across the room.

In the moment of pause, Colonel Richardson elaborated further.

"Chaplain, to add to that, the WOC process is quite simple. It requires that (a) the units of people be sufficiently large to harbor a diverse set of perspectives, (b) opinions are made independently without undue influence from other unit members, (c) knowledge is not overly centralized, and finally, (d) all the independent inputs of information are aggregated and synthesized to come to the best decision possible.

"For the longest time, such an idea was infeasible for the Army. There were difficulties with aggregation and synthesis on such a large and complex scale, but with the development of a new class of HIVEMIND machines, aggregation and synthesis were operationally achievable.

"Designed at first for human Soldiers on the battlefield, it was the integration with drone technology that revolutionized the WOC process. Drones could be deployed in high numbers with many perspectives of the battlefield; it was difficult for any adversary to match without similar technology.

"But that was for conventional adversaries, with this new threat we mig—"

The general piped in, "It was a radical approach for the Army but it worked. The chain of command remained intact but it allowed for commanders to reach out and gain insight from anywhere they wanted to bring force."

The colonel's face began to redden and his eyes twitched in rapid succession. At the first opportunity he could find, he raised his head to speak.

"And if I may, sir…" the colonel began. His teeth bit down on the inside of his lip as he waited.

"Carry on, Colonel," the general replied with an abbreviated nod.

"…Sir, might I suggest that we limit drone usage for this operation. We don't fully understand the alien's capabilities at this point. Intelligence is sparse and with all the other commands standing down, we really don't have any updated int—"

The general cut the colonel off. "Drones are how we have always done it. What we don't need to do, is to over-think things outside the box right now. We've already built an impeccable box and we will continue to perfect it."

"Yes, sir," the colonel replied, rubbing the back of his neck.

Just then, a lieutenant colonel, who had kept his distance during the conversation, reluctantly came forward to address the general. His steps were careful and planned, as if he were stepping into a toxic chemical spill that had oozed about across the floor.

"Sir…"

"Yes, carry on, Colonel," the general replied.

"The seventeen-hundred deadline has elapsed, sir."

The general gave an acknowledging nod and walked over to the center hub. He took his seat in a large black-leather chair so that he was surrounded by the monitoring telewindows. For a few minutes he sat surveying the screens. His fingers tapped with little drum beats on the chair's padded arm rest. Then, after confident shake of his head, he cleared his throat to speak and pressed a button on the desk to all under his command.

"All right, listen up. We've passed our deadline to stand down. To all of you: I appreciate your duty and courage to continue to serve your great country. I won't lie, we face an uncertain enemy. But like all those who have worn the uniform before us, we will go out and meet the enemy with the same warrior ethos; placing the mission first and never accepting defeat. To keep the American way of life, and our freedoms, requires our sacrifice and courage to tell the enemy we shall never say die! Hooah!"

"Hooah!" the room went up collectively and then proceeded to buzz about their tasks.

Chaplain Wilkins walked closer to the hub to get a better view of the battlefeeds. The windows displayed feeds from Soldiers on the ground and the vantage of the drones holding their formation above the troops below.

Through one of the feeds, he saw a squad of Soldiers rallying together in an industrial sector on the north shore of the Kansas River. Across the river, the tall buildings of Topeka loomed large on the horizon. Voices of the squad leaders on the comms spoke of taking the Hands of Provision center located just across the river near the capital building.

Each Soldier wore a speak-easy headset, or SEH for communication. The headphones allowed speaking in loud environments using algorithms and AAI to discern what frequencies to filter out or amplify. Gunfire and certain ambient noise would be filtered out leaving human voices and footsteps to be amplified. These comms fed into a heads-up display on the Soldiers visors which were miniaturized telewindows. The visors allowed information to be displayed on the transparent lens in both passive and interactive forms.

Some of the Soldiers were also equipped with the latest M88 'brick gun' while others carried the decades old mechanical M4 carbine from the Desert War Era. The brick guns, only prototypes when he had gone to basic training, were electronic battery-powered rifles. They got their name from the small bricks of caseless ammunition that could be linked together like plastic blocks. Each brick could carry twenty-five rounds and also served the dual purpose of acting as a dischargeable heat sink when all rounds had been fired and the magazine was ejected from the rifle. The barrel of the guns had five bores and could shoot up to three hundred rounds per minute and, when placed in 'five-shot' mode, could fire all five bores simultaneously. Soldiers jokingly referred to this setting as the BYL shot, or "blowing your load."

On another window feed, a large room could be seen with nearly a thousand operators seated at large-windowed terminals. He figured these must be the drone operators. From discussions with Soldiers that trained in this military specialty, he had pieced together that drones were operated in squads of three. One drone would be directly operated by the operator who flew the drone remotely via terminal. The other two drones would be autonomously linked to the lead drone mimicking its movements and taking commands as needed. If the lead drone were to be damaged or destroyed, the operator's control would switch to the nearest drone in the squad.

Next to the feed of the operators, several feeds cycled through footage from the drones in the field. The drones were a dull grey color with a slender T-shape about the size of a large motorcycle. A rotary fan was embedded near the end of each arm keeping them aloft. Cameras and sensors were placed at the top and bottom of the 'T' allowing the operator to toggle between directions quickly. Like their Soldier counterparts on the ground, the drones were armed with their own variant of the brick gun with three hundred and sixty degrees of coverage.

The drones looked to be hovering near a large warehouse-like building just a few hundred meters above the Soldiers. There looked to be nearly a thousand drones in a tight, coordinated formation. Some looked down on the troops to monitor their position while the drones at the perimeter looked outward to scan the horizon for potential adversarial movement. Besides the occasional interest by civilian onlookers who had been pushed back a safe distance, the environment looked pretty normal and calm.

Chaplain Wilkins looked back to the general. The general's index finger was slowly drilling into his right temple. His face was sneering and eyes were fixed on a map at his desk displaying the operating environment with the collective information feeds of Soldiers and drones in the field. He tapped back and forth examining different routes using the tiny blue dots and triangles that represented the ground troops and drones, respectively.

He leaned back in his chair and folded his arms. He sat for a few moments and then leaned forward to type out a question that he sent to the thousands of Soldiers and drones in the field: "What is the best route of approach across the river?"

After about thirty-seconds, the map began to populate each Soldier's synthesized response on a heat map overlay. The blips came in and began to change to warmer shades of color as consensus was found in certain areas.

Once the input had been synthesized, the bridge area along Topeka Boulevard had changed to a bright orange while the other surrounding areas tapered off in shades of blues and yellows, including the bridge to the east.

The general scanned the map for a few moments, stroking his scrunched chin, and then marked his command on the screen. A green line stretched out across the Topeka bridge. Within seconds, the Soldiers and drones received a green overlay in their personal feeds showing the order to cross the bridge. They all began to slowly march across the river.

When they had crossed the bridge, the Soldiers fanned out over several blocks for their approach of the target. The Hands of Provision center was now only a half-dozen blocks down the boulevard. Overhead, the drones advanced forward in three tiered waves. The first wave of drones would be the tip of the spear, making first contact. It was amazing to watch the multitude of drones hold a near-perfect formation. With their down-folded wings, they looked like a flock of osprey swooping in towards their target.

It did not take the drones long to reach the center. Once they did, they all held position overhead. Down below, no movement was detected. Over the comms, the operators awaited their firing orders. The general scanned the feeds and the map before he gave his order.

"This is General Sturgeon, Squad Delta SEV-EN SEV-EN through Delta WUN-AIT-AIT, you may chop the tree when ready."

Before the order could be executed, a squad of drones began to veer off from the larger formation. On the screen, three blue triangles drifted backward and to the west of the rest of the drones that were still holding steady.

"What the flying fuck is that drone squad doing, Colonel!?" the general cried out.

"Sir, I don't know…" Colonel Richardson attempted to reply nearby.

"It's your damn job to know, get me the operator of that squad now!"

But before communications could be made, two more squads of drones began to drift off from their position. Even within these squads the drones seemed to be pulling off from one another.

Six more squads split off…then twelve…then twenty…

"What's going on out there?" The general's eyes were wide with disbelief.

"We're not sure, sir. Reports are coming from the operator bay that they are losing connection with their drones," a sweat-faced major replied from his terminal.

"Order them to fire, while we're still in control," the general shot back without a moment's hesitation.

Before the order could be relayed, a bright blue light blinded the array of telewindows that were displaying the first wave of drone feeds. When the flash dissipated, the feeds were dark.

The feeds from the second wave of drones showed that the bright beams of light had totally destroyed a majority of the first wave drones. The beams of light were originating from a pair of alien entities on the ground.

"Get those things moving and take evasive actions before we lose everything!" the general yelled desperately.

"Sir, I'm not sure we can outrun the speed of light," the colonel replied shaking his head in disbelief.

All of a sudden, the rest of the drone feeds went black. The only feeds that remained were the Soldiers on the ground who had just reached their holding position outside the target zone. From their view, the drones that had survived the original light attack were flying around erratically in odd formations. They were slowly massing together in a blob with about a half-dozen outstretched branches.

The mass hovered in place as it grew larger and larger as it added new drones to its collective. Once the drones had reached an uncountable number, they began moving in unison downward…right towards the Soldiers staring up from the ground.

The drones began to attack the Soldiers as a swarm of mechanical bees. Like an AI possessed, the flying crosses systematically eliminated any and all the ground forces in their targeting frame. The Soldiers on the feed were fighting erratically. The surprise and fear on their faces spoke volumes of the betrayal from their once angelic overwatchers. Soldiers darted back and forth among the buildings trying to dodge blurs of light and projectiles. They tried to return fire but many of the advanced electronic M88 brick guns seemed to be failing to operate. The only ones who could fire were those equipped with the mechanically-operated M4's. So many were getting hit and falling to the ground that the others had to leap over the ruined bodies of their brothers in arms.

It didn't take long for the staff in the Hive to realize that the numbers and advantage of the carbon-fibered drones were too much for the Soldiers to overcome. Chaplain Wilkins could barely bring himself to watch the slaughter. The feeds were splashed with the blood of Soldiers being shot from all angles from the nightmare above. The once graceful birds of prey had turned into hell-firing imps.

Some Soldiers cursed the sky while others huddled and waited for it all to end. The last feed that he could watch was that of a pair of Soldiers running down an alleyway trying to escape the open spaces of the streets. The young private up ahead was running at full speed to cross the next street when a drone clipped him right below the neck. The Soldier following his battle buddy caught the severed head on reflexive instinct. Through the feed, the head's eyes were wide and in shock, looking back at where his body had fallen to the ground. Sorrow filled those eyes as the realization of what had happened to him sank in. His mouth opened and shut, as if to try to speak, but nothing came forth. His eyes began to slowly shut as if to sleep. At this moment, in shock, his buddy yelled.

"Mark!"

The eyes shot back open, fixed on his buddy, as if he had heard the call of his name. Yet, they could only stay open for a few seconds. Soon the eyes began to gloss over once more and the lids shut over them. The feed did not last much longer before a few flickers of blue light turned all to black.

All the feeds had gone dark. The general's face was blank as he stared at the map before him. The last few dots had faded from the battlefield and the swarm of four-thousand triangles persisted. They had a new heading now, a path that set them straight towards Fort Riley. Operation Hivemind was a complete and utter failure.

In the nerve center, staff and Soldiers were running about. The general had made a broad announcement that everyone was released from their duties. Some Soldiers rushed home to try to be with their families, others left to find a place to hide out, and a decent few chose to stay and make a final stand on post.

Chaplain Wilkins could only muster up an unfocused gaze at the world moving around him. As the people scampered about, so did his thoughts in the mirrored world inside his head. What was there for him to do now? He had discharged his final duty and there was no task left to complete, no place to go, no one to provide counsel. His thoughts went by in a blur before he could pin one down to commit to an action.

The general's raspy voice pierced through the haze.

"Well, we tried, Chaplain. We tried. You are free to be dismissed like the others, there isn't anything left for you to do. You have served your oath well, for God and Country. Maybe you can get out before it's too late."

"And you, sir?" he replied, realizing the weight of the general's final remarks.

"I shall stay at my post…come what may," he replied solemnly and turned to find a seat in his chair. He returned to staring at the map as the triangles scooted in closer. The fight had fled from the general's eyes. A man's face that was once strong and chiseled with confidence, now signed his own resignation.

Chaplain Wilkins regarded the general with a final salute and left the man to have his repose in his formal greens.

He ran down the hall as fast as he could. He could barely hear his feet as the alarms rang out all around him.

As he climbed up the flights of stairs from the Hive, he could feel a change come over him. A marker had been passed noting his transition to something new, though he lacked clarity to know exactly what that was. He did know that his years of Army service had come to an end. He had kept his oath, faithfully.

He paused to catch his breath. He could feel the wheezing air burning through his windpipe with each exhale as he leaned over the metal rail. Then, in between sucking breathes, a realization struck him.

When fighting a superior force, going in with a big burst of effort is not the best response when outmatched; your forces simply cannot keep up in a marathon match. However, there is a role for small, focused engagements. Little sprints here and there that optimize your resources, that collectively provide a large impact on your adversary.

He laughed. The raspy cadence bellowed throughout the stairwell. It sounded like a different man. He realized that he didn't need to be in the Army to do what he had always set out to do. Now released from duty, he could fight on his own standards. He peeled off the chaplains' patch from his breast pocket and clinched it tightly between his fingers. He could still see the faces of the poor Soldiers who had just been mauled by their own machines—an alien wolf had come amongst the flock in a god's clothing.

With his thumb, he traced the Latin words that had defined his career. A career that was now finished. "For God and country," Dean said allowed. He had done his duty, guiding his flock in peace. Now, with no one left to defend that peace, it was time for the shepherd to fight that which would devour everything; there might not be many others to do so.

For humanity, he thought.

Dean's grip loosened and the chaplains' patch slipped between his fingers. It fell downward through the slats of the metal grate at his feet. He watched as it spun in a blue and yellow blur until it hit an unseen platform below.

Now empty, his fist clinched hard. He felt a renewed vigor welling up within him. A space that had long been left vacant was now filling with a fighting purpose. Even his breath had returned at full strength as his mind began to plot his path forward.

There would be peace when the job is done, he thought, and then climbed up the last few flights of stairs.

Topside, alarms were wailing across the post. Red and yellow lights flashed from every building. Dean looked to the east and saw a dark black cloud moving over the flat plain. The drones, massed in the thousands were coming to finish the job. He turned his head west and saw a group of men gathering around a pile of old M4 carbines. He felt the fight return to his face that had been lost for so many years.

He sprinted westward, towards the group with a mind springing with rejuvenation. Each step with a full set of lungs. Somehow, someway, he was going to find a way to carry on.

FIFTH STAGE

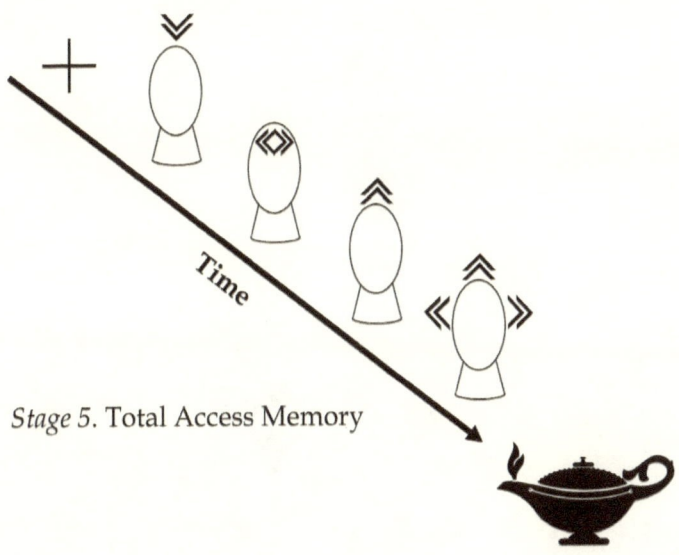

Stage 5. Total Access Memory

"...And all at once, a spreading of activation went through all my memories—and others—and every past moment became the present, which lost its meaning with the unbounding associations—"

Unpublished laboratory notes
- Dr. Sebastian Silva,
unknown originating date

10

An Interview with ZoZo
One month A.R.D.

Sleep stalked him. Bash's head jolted back upright against the chair in his study as he fought its encroachment. His tiredness wanted to embrace rest, but his dreams as of late—if they were dreams—had been uncontrollable and disquieting. Images of unfamiliar people and places intruded upon his dreamscape. They were all vivid, like the images he experienced in the Mindsai. But how they came to his mind now, disconnected from the machine, he could offer up no hypotheses.

Though strange, some of the imagery was pleasant. In one vision, he had looked through the eyes of a callused-handed man who was turning over flat rocks in a steam. The rocks felt slimy underneath his fingertips as he lifted them slowly, one-by-one. Underneath a particularly large triangular stone, a small brown crayfish wriggled away in a cloud of silt from the unwelcomed introduction of light. He heard a tiny gasp next to him. A young girl stood knee-deep in the softly-rolling waters. The polka-dot pattern of her rubber boots matched her freckled faces that was curiously looking on at her safe distance.

Many others, however, were not so pleasant, and terrified him. He tried not to think of them now. The night was still dark in the early morning hours and he could still see the afterglow of disturbing images that only got more vivid when he closed his eyes. An imprint of a face still lingered in the back of his mind...

Earlier that evening, a dream had taken him to a desert. There he approached a large white, triangular tent. His approach was drawn out with each step as if his leg were lame with some sort of limp. He felt it drag slightly over the tiny rocks and sand on the ground. When he reached the tent's entrance, he pulled back the heavy canvas with dirty fingernails, clumped with mud. As he entered, he felt his index finger slither up and pressed firmly against his hushed lips. Inside, an old woman was bathing in a small metal tub. Her face was pale white and oddly shaped as an elongated oval. On her head, she wore a strange gown and a frilled black cap that tied beneath her chin, doing its best to control the wispy strings of white hair. Behind her, figures of shadow flickered about the tent walls as the singular candle struggled to light the dark space. With one steely-eyed look upon him, she clasped her hands against her wrinkled-worn face and opened her lips in a wide oval shape. An ear-curdling scream pierced through him.

He awoke in a bath of cold sweat and still tasted the dusty air on his lips. The images had made him too frightened to nod off. The visions were not his own anymore. There was no telling what strange body he would drift into or what scene he would be forced to witness. Were these images real? Was he going mad? Had the Mindsai turned on something in his brain that wouldn't resolve on its own? He had no answers for these questions. He needed to go into the lab to do more tests.

For now, though, he was content to stay awake in the soft white glow of his study's telewindow. A news correspondent named Walter, an AI construct, was outlining recent events. AI had long ago replaced human news anchors because of their capability to nearly instantaneously synthesize the news and report it factually, without bias. What they possessed in speed, they lacked in character that only human imperfections afforded.

Walter's voice was perfectly pitched as he pronounced each word in a soothing southern accent. He was reporting on the continued repercussions of the failed military coup that had happened two days ago somewhere out in Kansas. Thousands of 'disaccorders' had been killed in the attack which had sent ripples around the world. The complete failure of a hegemonic power had squelched any other would-be armed insurrections. The reporter added that every nation's military had now peacefully disbanded.

His eyes began to droop as Walter moved on to a new edict directed by Phosos for New Eden.

"Today, Supreme Provider Phosos has issued forth Provisory Number sixty-seven, declaring that virtual environments will be augmented with Hands of Provision AI to ensure unity in all aspects of our New Eden. The Hands of Provision will provide accurate corrections to past events to reflect history as it truly unfolded. All historical simulations will be updated with this new record by the end of this week," Walter stated in great voice. Behind him, a flash of images showcased glimpses of these historical revelations, tagged with the headlines: 'Catholic priests conspire black plague to sway public to the Church' and 'Missing link? Ape-humanoid revealed at last.'

The images then transitioned to a map of the Mid-Atlantic region.

"Now for your local weather forecast."

He did not hear the forecast; his mind was still entangled in Phosos's new edict. History was being rewritten by an entity offering an omniscient view of humanity's past. It had only been a few weeks and it already seemed that such things were commonplace, accepted without question by all peoples of the world.

He then realized, that in all of the success of the Mindsai Experiment, he too had tacitly accepted recent events on their face without much question. He had not had the time to process or grapple with New Eden, unity symbols, and the like.

His scientific mind now searched for validation to this new world view in the waxing hours of morning. *How could it be verified?* he thought.

It did not take him long to circle back to a solution. One that had occupied his mind for so long. It was simple, really...

He chuckled softly in his chair; the leather upholstery squeaked with its own little jollies.

The Mindsai was the key. Given its success, he could validate such chronicles of the past by corroborating them with actual memories of the people that lived it.

"Yes, the Mindsai could be a touchstone. First, though, I need to get these intrusive flashbacks under control," he said to himself aloud.

A yawn came on uncontrollably. He exhaled most of the air in his lungs and leaned back into the chair.

Before long, his eyes began to droop once more. Each eye blinked out of unison as his mind grew heavy. Then Bash closed his eyes for what he had intended to just be a second.

Sleep snatched him. And in the wake of the darkness, the flashbacks began again.

He awoke with the sun glimmering into his eyes off the copper waterspout that ran just outside the window of his study. The clock showed that it was mid-morning. His brief shuttering of the eyes had turned into hours of sleep.

As the mental grogginess lifted, the visions that had haunted his dreams became apparent. Unlike dreams, that would wane from focus when he awakened, these images became more vivid with time. A wave hit him as the lives he never had flashed before him in a blur...a horse-drawn wagon on a stone bridge...a bunch of lush grapes on a sun-soaked vine...a hedgerow with gunfire crackling toward him...

They were all too much for his mind to bear. The memories had been fine in a controlled environment using the Mindsai, but now, the unbounded cascade of memories was starting to blur the boundaries of who he was.

One need not be a chamber to be haunted—

Emma's words rose above his scattered thoughts. He needed her. It was a cruel oppression that he could not be plagued by memories of her soft face in place of the others. She had kept him grounded; now, firm footing was hard to find.

"Come closer."

The sound broke the silence. His ears perked up instantly. The voice, unequivocally Emma's, had not come from within his head, but out in the hall.

He waited, trying to shake off the impossible arrangement of familiar tones and inflection.

The voice hushed from the hall again, "Come closer..."

His gripped the leather arms of his chair to brace himself. His breathing had begun to quicken as he debated whether to run or respond.

The voice of Emma grew more direct, "Baaash...come closer to me."

KAR THUD!

He jumped to his feet. Something had fallen in the hallway. He looked to the door, holding his breath, but there was no sign of movement in the adjacent space.

"Hello?" his voice creaked.

For a few heart-pounding moments, he stood stiff, arms limp at his sides. His fingers twitched in the air as if they were trying to test it for some sign that had passed. He stretched his hearing out into the hall, but not even the faintest noise could be heard now. Instead, the two legs beneath him began to rattle violently and he had to brace a hand on the chair to keep balanced. Under a firm grip with his other hand, he got his legs under control and started himself towards the hall. His steps were shaky as he leaned forward on the balls of his feet.

The hallway was empty. The only thing that drew his eyes was the sparkling sepia tones of light filtering in from the kitchen. The little breakfast nook with a wooden bench was stacked with old grocery sacks that he had been too remiss to move with so much going on. The bench was surrounded by a gorgeous bay window that overlooked the back garden. The spot had been one of Emma's favorite places to read her books in the mornings after breakfast. He smiled faintly. Turning around, he studied the front door. It was shut and securely fastened as he had left it the day before. Besides some large dust bunnies clinking to the molding, the hardwood floor was bare. *What a cluttered place I have wrought*, he thought, but nothing appeared to have been moved at all.

He ran his hand up through his hair. He could still feel damp sweat plow up on the webbing of his fingers. All he could do was stand there, staring at the door in a daze.

The daze snapped like a hard blink. Suddenly, the door before him changed to a dark red color. The once smooth texture now looked worn and neglected with peeling paint where the edges met the frame. He looked away briefly, and then, just as quickly, it reverted back to its normal hue of minty green. The door had not been painted red since Emma—

"Come closer," the voice whispered behind his ear.

He jumped, hitting his back on the door with a hard thump. The impact expelled nearly all of the air from his lungs. Gasping for breath, his eyes focused narrowly down the hall. It did not look the same as before, the hallway was no longer bathed in early-morning light. In fact, it seemed drained of color altogether. His eyes peeled further until he recognized that he no longer could see back to the nook, the kitchen had become completely obscured by something dark filtering the light. And then, more unsettling still, his mind registered that something was moving nearly imperceptibly in the middle of the hall. That something began to draw form in the shadowy mist. It grew darker and taller and it wasn't long before a slender shadow figure was towering over him with arms disproportionally long hanging down motionless at its side. Its legs contorted in an uneven stance on the flat floor.

He stared into its face, or at least where a face rightfully should have been. He could find no discerning features. No eyes, no nose, no lips. Yet, somehow, a voice came from the figure.

"Closer," it hissed.

In a frenzy, he pounded his palm against the surface of the door, trying to pat out for a handle. All he could feel was rough paint. As the figure floated forward, his pats turned into a wild rubbing motion. He could feel flakes of paint rolling up all over his hand like gnarled teeth trying to clinch it to the door. Then, his palm finally slammed into cold metal. He twisted the knob and pressed the release to dart out into the sunlight. He didn't dare look back.

Out of habit, he found that his feet had carried him about halfway up the Sage Walk. So many years of walking it had made the journey nearly automatic. It was just as well; the lab was the only place he really could go. Reconnecting to the Mindsai was the only way he could re-center his mind and escape these images.

"Those grad students should have never aborted the experiment," he muttered to himself. Alien or not, unbounded, his mind was bursting with activations that opened doors to so many memories.

As the incline drew sharper up the path, he had to ease his pace. His heart was still racing but the heat he had worked up running was beginning to dissipate in the cold air that had been held at bay all around him. Sucking in breaths, the trees around him seemed to pulse, but it was not from his rapid heartbeats or the blood vessels in his temples still throbbing. A heaviness pulled down on his head. He thought he would faint right there in the middle of the concrete walkway. And just like that, another flashback enveloped him.

The path was gone. The oak trees had morphed into towering monstrosities like the redwoods he once saw out west, only these were much more numerous and rugged-looking. Their canopy rattled as a pounding rain splashed down through overhead. Next to him, a giant fern brushed against his forehead as he crept low to keep out of sight. *Of what?* he thought. His right hand was shakily clenching a long wooden pole. It was capped with a long, slender spear tip made of some sort of mustard-hued metal. Despite the rain, he could feel the sweat dripping down from his brow in the hot and humid air.

He heard it before he saw it. The deep breathing sounded like an enormous bellows that filled through the woodland floor, wheezing in and out. His view panned upward above the thick white mist that clung heavily to the forest floor. At first, he only saw the limbs, leaves, and the trunks of the trees. The rain splashed in his eyes making him blink uncontrollably to gain some clarity. Then he noticed that the limbs were moving. They moved up and down in the same tempo as the breathing. Now his eyes widened and shook. It was then that he saw the body of the beast that stood six meters above him, just a stone's throw away. The torso was mostly in shades of dark green with narrow brown and black stripes that ran down vertically from its back to its belly. The animal was perfectly camouflaged for the foliage that hung around it. Studying the creature more, he could see its long tail stretching back and thumping against the trunks of the trees. When he saw its head, he had to resign his disbelief, it was dinosaur. At least it had all the appearances of dinosaurs he had seen in books and in movies. Of the size of a miniature car, the head was thick and long to its snout. The rows of teeth, like serrated knives, were exposed and seeped with saliva and rain water as it panted in large steamy breaths. He was close enough he could smell the breath of decaying flesh and rotten egg. On the sides of its head, its eyes were a midnight black. They seemed to suck in all the light around them. He was close enough to see his own reflection peering up into them, as if he were falling into them. They were searching.

Suddenly, the massive beast cocked its head in his general direction. He was sure it had seen him move or caught his scent. He felt his legs brace for movement. The beast would not even need to take a step to reach him. He looked over his shoulder and saw a thick patch of trees. Then, he ran.

Just as quickly as it had come, the vision dissolved away. The familiar path returned to view, now a distance away. He could feel the cold ground soaking into his kneecaps. The visual intrusion had left him in a kneeling position several meters off the path in a bed of wet leaves and twigs. These intrusions were breaking forth into his waking mind now. He could not even tell if they were memories anymore. Dinosaurs in the eyes of a man, how could that be? Was his mind now randomly constructing these pseudo-memories of dinosaurs and shadow people? That prospect brought a renewed urgency into his limbs. If allowed to go uncorrected, there was no knowing where this could devolve into.

He braced himself on a nearby tree and rose to his feet. With a few quick steps, he was back on the Sage Walk, taking to running once more. All the while wishing that Chris were here with him, even if he would be damned to admit that Chris was right.

Time passes strangely when an affliction takes hold, he mused looking at the clock near the entrance of the psychology building. Though only a few minutes had ticked away since he last checked his watch, the journey to the building felt as if time had doubled. With each step he took, he had felt the heavy pressure of the flashbacks pulling on his mind. Like a sleep long-denied, the lurking intrusions had grappled onto his thoughts and were trying to wrestle and pull him from control. At any moment, if he did not pull back, the heaviness would take him under the surface of consciousness.

At the main entrance to the building, thick drops of sweat started to pour down his face. The entire upper hemisphere of his head was burning up in a feverish heat along with a constricting headache. In the pulling struggle between alertness and unconsciousness, it was as if all his synapses were trying to fire at once, making his brain overheat in an unsustainable level of processing. He could not hazard a guess as to how long he could keep this up.

He rushed into the main entrance in a flurry across the atrium. Not chancing to wait on an elevator, he dashed up the stairs. As he climbed the flights, the heaviness began to pull him down with greater force with each elevated step. Several times the pull was so intense that his foot slipped off the next step. In the moment of peril, images flashed across his eyes before he could regain control and catch his balance. He pushed forward with all his might until he arrived at the landing to the floor of his laboratory.

Stepping out of the stairwell, the hallway was dark and empty. It looked like It had been days since it had last heard footsteps. He proceeded down the long hall, his steps echoing loudly at the other end in front of him. In the dimness, he quickly noticed that his lab door was set ajar by a body's width. He drew closer with caution. From the crack, a cold draft of air pushed back against his face. The contrast of cold on his fevered head should have felt relieving. Instead, the cold met his face with a million stings and prickles upon his cheeks.

He grabbed the edge of the door. It was so icy-cold that he let go instantly like a child touching a red-hot burner on a stove. A coldness slithered around his feet. He looked down to find that a dense vaporous fog was rolling out into the hallway from inside his lab.

Wide-eyed, he entered.

Inside, he found a dimly lit room. Shadows danced on the walls from the chaotic symphony of red and blue blinking lights from the equipment. As he moved deeper into the lab, a shiver overtook him almost instantly. An extreme chill had taken hold over the space. He searched for the cause and found an icy film was jutting out from the area of the Mindsai machine. Little ice icicles had formed all around it. Some were nearly a hand's length long hanging from the nearby tables. It did not take long to identify what happened, there seemed to have been some sort of coolant leak from the Mindsai. He looked over the machine more and noticed dark voids on the side of the Mindsai that he did not recognize. After a few blinks of processing these black spots, his rapid heartbeat almost stopped. His eyes widened as the realization of the mangled-nature of the machine became clear.

The Mindsai looked as if some sort of wild animal had punctured its long fangs into the precious piece of equipment. Nearly a half-dozen holes dotted the metal frame. A white mist of coolant was still leaking out in many places, freezing anything that it came into contact. A mist was also coming out of his own mouth as his breathing grew heavier and strained in the icy air.

He hurried over to the terminal on the machine. He rapidly tapped on the 'Home' button hoping for a response. After a short delay, the screen flashed bright white. He felt his eyes instantly constrict to the point of pain as the light was too great a contrast for the dark room. The home screen had come up. *At least some systems were still working*, he thought with relief. He navigated to the operating status menus. The menu icons gave off a ghosting effect in between the successive user interface menus creating after images that took time to catch up. The extreme chill of the room was slowing everything down, but it was better than the Mindsai melting down.

The status menu slowly popped up with a report that was not terrible. *Barely functional.* The Mindsai had one major coolant leak but was still being supplied via auxiliary lines. The recording drives had all been damaged, or disconnected, and memory was only at eighty-six point seven percent. However, the quantum processors were all still intact and in the green.

He sighed, letting out a huge cloud of mist that floated and whirled in the air. His head was throbbing and on fire, making it hard to sort out his thoughts. The constricting band around his head had surely tightened up a couple of notches. Any further and his head might just pop from the pressure.

After a few minutes of strained thought, he pulled up the parameters for the previous experiment. Since the experiment had been interrupted, perhaps going through it to completion would break the intruding loops that had been haunting him. With a few inputs, the Mindsai was ready to go using its automated AI functions.

The Mindsai was not in optimal shape, but there was enough untouched to make an attempt to correct his mind. He stepped over to the reclining couch. Its surface was covered in a light sparkling frost that would not look out of place in an ice palace. He brushed off what frost he could and took a seat. The leather was stiff and crinkled loudly as he tried his best to get into a comfortable position. He laid back and shrugged uncontrollably as the cold headrest kissed the back of his neck in an icy embrace. Once settled, he brought down the SEER goggles from their hanging position above him. They were cold to touch but had not been brushed with frost due to their elevated positioning. The headset seated itself in place on his head. The prickly probes were barely noticeable on his scalp that had been numbed from the cold. With headset positioned in place, he awaited in the darkness for the Mindsai to initiate the experiment, one that he would have to remember to mark down in his notes as 'Study 1b.'

Sweat began pooling under the SEER cap and meandered down the ridge of his nose, but the familiar hum of the Mindsai engaging never came. There were just the images flashing before him. Unlike the ones that came before, these images felt different. Instead of the limited purview of sensory experiences, little ideas and phrases percolated to the forefront of his mind, an inner dialogue not of his own. Was the Mindsai now able to access the thoughts associated with memories? With so many competing things in his mind, it hurt to try and determine that possibility. The only measure of comfort he could find was to not offer any mental resistance and allow the images and thoughts to come forth.

He cut to a scene of a man chopping wood on the edge of an old forest. The man was standing next to a pile of logs. The man would glance back at the forest as he grabbed another log and then turn to his business of splitting them on a large stump with a crude, rusty axe. When he was not directly looking, Bash could see, at the periphery of the man's vision, tall shadows. They appeared ape-like but contorted and creeping along the dark forest floor. They waited and whispered to one another at the forest's edge. The man's head jerked back to the forest and nothing moved.

Hunted.

The scene quickly changed. He could feel the warmth of the fuzzy blankets pulled in close around him. Tiny hands held them back at his nose as he peeked above them. Across the room of scattered plastic toys, his sight was fixed on the closet. The doors were white and slatted, and in between the slats, a pair of dull red eyes stared at him, unblinking. The door began to creak open.

Childhood monsters.

Before him was a staircase made of large rectangular shapes, like those he saw in Elizabethan homes in old paintings. A delicate hand held out a candlestick holder. Its dancing light reflected off the smooth varnish of the wood banister that was inlaid with delicate designs of flowers and curling vines. The light of the candle created an amber pool of light that stretched so far into the tall room and then dropped off into silky darkness. Suddenly, a glowing orb shot down from the ceiling. It streaked down with a tail of blue light to the top of the stair. In a blink, a semi-translucent figure appeared in the shape of a young woman. The figure's ivory face was plain but carved with a stony expression of sadness. She wore a long white nightgown that slowly disappeared into a void where her feet should have been. She seemed to float down each step. The old wooden stairs creaked with her invisible footfalls. Nearing the bottom of the stair, her head turned towards him. Her cold eyes locked with his own. Despite the silence, he could feel her sorrow screaming in his head.

Ghost.

He was in a vehicle alone, driving down a deserted highway. Out in front of him, the landscape was barren like a desert. He could see for many kilometers as the road stretched out and met the purple horizon. It was twilight, and the moon had just begun to rise with a field of stars as the truck descended into a deep bowl in the terrain. He could now hear the radio chattering off about some baseball game being played somewhere far away from here. The play caller was announcing Mantle's hit to left field when everything became static. He reached for the metal dial to try and find a better signal. The vertical red line swiped across the frequencies but there was no signal to be found. He looked back to see he was still on the road and that's when he noticed another light had emerged just below the moon.

At first, he thought it to be a shooting star but noticed that it was rising up, not falling down to Earth. Continuing to watch it, the light grew bigger, coming closer. When it arrived, it stopped within twenty-five meters above his truck going down the highway. Now, he could see that the light was a donut-shaped orb rotating on a horizontal axis. It was about ten times the size of his truck and gave off an icy-blue glow from its surface without any sign of light fixtures. Staring at the floating vessel, the engine abruptly sputtered out. The truck continued to roll on its course until it reached the bottom of the desert bowl. Above, the vessel continued to hover silently with no change in movement or structure. The driver in the truck leaned forward onto the warm metal dash and squinted into the lights. Along the vessel's sides, he noticed an opening that striped its mid-section. The opening looked like a continuous window that was fixed in position between the rotating top and bottom hemispheres. It was in this opening that he saw movement. Heads on slender torsos bobbed and turned side-to-side. At first the entities looked like tiny grey creatures with black eyes, but as Bash focused longer, the visage shifted in a hazy shimmer to reveal beings that were tall and beautiful, having a striking resemblance to Phosos. Then, like a flash, a bright light engulfed the truck and everything went white.

Alien encounter.

Some measure of time had passed but the white light did not subside. If it was not for the lack of pain in his eyes, he might have thought himself to have succumbed to blindness. What he was seeing appeared to be a projection within his mind from the Mindsai. All was a pure white void with no structures, walls, or sense of direction. There were no smells, sounds, tastes, or things to feel. The prospect of being trapped and alone in his mind with only his thoughts began to frighten him. It was hard to say what would happen to the mind when the brain is detached from all sensory experience. Stronger people could barely last a few hours with total sensory deprivation. Such a state of consciousness, a brain detached from the physical world, would drive a person mad.

In his racing thoughts, a welcomed movement emerged before him. They were nothing but blurry squiggles at first, like floaters in the wake of a camera's flash, translucent against the whiteness. Slowly, their contrast became more and more defined and he could see that they formed a single, small geometric shape—a circle.

The circle appeared to lack any sort of depth. Its flat, two-dimensional shape rose and fell in smooth motions. The circle's outline grew darker in color but its insides were exposed as an empty white space. These edges vibrated and, with an expansion, the circle transformed into a spherical object. He could only see its smooth surface that swirled about in various shades of cloudy smoke. The sphere shook again and changed its form into a more complex shape that was difficult to perceive. The black object appeared donut-shaped, but the shape was not constant. It pulsed and shifted in size. At one moment it was the size of a golf ball and, out of nothingness, it grew to the size of a beach ball. His mind had great difficulty keeping up with the movements, but it seemed that the pulsing was how his mind was interpreting the object's transformation over time in a higher dimension. The object's outer surface seemed to fold in upon itself such that the outer surface became the inside and the inside the outer. The shape changed again. This time it became even more nebulous and incomprehensible. The object was like a shadow which lacked any discernable form. It twisted and bent on itself, its surface shimmering with a strange electric pulse.

A series of disjointed ideas rushed to his mind again. Each idea translated crudely using his thoughts.

Orbs. Spheres. Circles.

The intrusive ideas turned into phrases at which were first were merely disjointed sounds but eventually the idea cleared in his mind as if the smoke were clearing from a window.

I am what I am. A complex descent to lower plane.

The nebulous shape in front of him continued to undulate on itself. Its dynamic shape made his mind feel uneasy and confused. He felt like some two-dimensional being seeing a sphere for the first time; his three-dimensionally-trained mind was struggling to make sense of an object of a higher state. He thought of the orbs and shadows that had appeared to him in memories. He instinctively felt a connection to them, knowing that behind their simple geometric representation, an entity with agency far more complex existed.

He stared at the pulsations. Rhythmic bolts of light signaled out and were quickly consumed by the surrounding murky surface that continued to change form.

More thoughts popped into his mind and he realized he was not alone in his thoughts. Some foreign entity was speaking to him. There was a common signal being woven across the memories intruding upon him. *Who or what could it be?* As this thought crystalized, a series of sounds repeated over and over in his mind. Unfamiliar sounds, not of his own inner voice, or any others he had ever known.

Zo-Zo...Zo-Zo...Zo-Zo.

The object began growing in size. He could not move or turn away as the undefined surface expanded towards him. Helpless, he starred into the cloudy void watching as glimmers of light flickered deep into the bottomless expanse. Just before the darkness engulfed him, he thought his mind had put together a face in the flashes of light. It looked like his own.

The light from the fireplace lapped at his face. In the haze of returned consciousness, it did not take long for him to recognize his location. He was back in his study. Not the one at home but the one he often escaped to in his head to think. There certainly was plenty to think on now.

It gave him comfort to finally be in familiar surroundings. Here, the shelves were full of books that never gathered dust. The fireplace gave off a welcoming light, and a crackle that helped his mind process. Next to him, his lampstand was filled with precious trinkets from his past. The only thing that never brought him a smile was the long black drape that hung on the wall in front of him. It had always seemed out of place in this space that he had created. He could never figure out how it got there or from what corner of life that he had seen it. The drape's tattered ends flapped from an unseen draft. Their movement revealing a glimpse of a space that was not solid but empty.

He leaned forward in the chair, bracing his hand on the wood armrest which creaked under the added pressure. Cocking his head, there seemed to be some sort of corridor that laid beyond. It was filled with shadows that seemed to have immunity to the firelight.

He leaned back. He was content to remain in the warming light of his refuge. He had been curious enough as of late.

The light in the room changed. All at once, it seemed to be retreating from his walls all around him. He looked at the fire and saw that its flames were not reaching as high over the logs that never seemed to get consumed. It was dying down into the red ambers.

A draft of air swept past his ears, and he heard his name.

"Bassssh." It came, like a distant whisper. Then again, "Bassssh, come closer."

It was Emma's whispers.

The sounds of Emma, he knew, were not of her making, even as a memory. It was a cruel mimicry. The sense of safety quickly drained away as he could not even find repose in his own mind.

"Imposter, come out and face me!" he thought he said aloud but could have just as easily thought it.

Either way, the entity had received his message. From some unknown location, a door slammed. He turned to look for movement. His eyes searched over the multitude of dim corridors branching off in impossible directions from his study. Each one contained a countless number of doors, behind each was a memory of his life.

He waited after the slam and it was not long before he heard footsteps approaching. Their sound echoed through a number of corridors making it hard to discern from whence they came. The footsteps grew heavier as they approached closer and closer. Soon, he was able to recognize their positioning in an adjacent corridor. He turned to see what he had called forth. The muscles in his shoulders and hands seized up as he braced himself for the reveal.

All he could see was an empty passage. Though empty as it were, the lumbering thumps and creaking wooden floorboards bore evidence that something was coming. They progressed slowly past the many closed doors that lined the corridor. Until they stopped.

Out from the floor a tiny glowing blue orb jotted up and disappeared through a nearby door. Moments passed. The corridor was silent and dark. *Very dark*, he thought. He then realized that he could no longer see to the end of the hall. A black mist had settled in upon the middle of the passage, obscuring what lay behind it.

The shadowy mass swirled and began to change form. What emerged was a three-dimensional figure. Tall and slender, the shadowy figure was without a face. Its bodily features vacillated such that its form was in constant motion like a whirling smoke. It silently glided towards him like a tattered robe passing through a stone dungeon making shadows look like bright sources of light.

When the figure reached the edge of his study, he could see its flesh—if that's what it was—dark as ash and smoldering. It stood tall, on a pair of cloven hooves that bent the floorboards from an unguessable mass. What is the weight of smoke?

He shivered.

An icy chill had befallen the room. With it, the light seemed to have been dampened to a dim gloom. His eyes darted to the fireplace to see that the fire had diminished to only glowing embers.

He readied himself to move but where would he go? If there was something attached to his mind, there would be no place safe. So, he remained resolute and again called out to the figure.

"Who are you? And why are you here?"

In immediate reply, the figure's narrow oval head blurred into distorted shadowy forms—a long-beak, an oxen's head, a woman, and then back to its previous shape. Again, the face lacked any features except now, a pair of dull glowing, red eyes emerged amidst the shifting black surface.

A response came, disembodied and without moving lips. It was raspy, panning in and out of audibleness as if it was perpetually gasping for a last breath.

"You are lost in darkness, but let me be your guide."

This can't be real. This must be someone else's residual memory...a supernatural fantasy...or a movie, he thought.

The figure's eyes flared.

"It was our greatest deception to not exist. Letting you build your world on a bed of loose sand," it replied seeming in response to his inner dialogue.

He shook his head in disbelief. Even in his thoughts he remained exposed to this *shadow*. In his nakedness, he wanted to know who was intruding upon him. Again, he asked the question.

"Who are you? I command you to tell me your name!"

The forcefulness seemed to affect the figure as it slunk away to the side of the entryway as if trying to physically dodge the question. However, once it had repositioned, its entire form seemed to shake violently and then he was blinded by a growl that pounded within his head.

"ZO ZO!"

He sunk back into the wooden seat. He knew in the presence of this entity that his commands lacked any real power. His mind began to ache from a building pressure. Just before a new rush of flashes burst forth upon him…

Through watery eyes, he saw a person cutting their own arm with a box cutter knife. The blood seeped over the peachy skin, tracked by scars of past wounds. He winced in pain…

A child cowering in a corner, pajama pants seeped with wetness, trying to avoid the blows of a heavy-buckled belt. The hate was discomforting, the fear in the child's eyes was heartbreaking…

He was running. No, he was chasing a group of women with long beige cloaks. The white cloths that covered their heads were falling behind them in the panic. Other men were running around them too, clanking in dull silver armor. Their eyes wide with unbridled desire. They were the visage of ancient Roman legionnaires with crimson-red capes beating behind them in their pursuit. In his own hand, his dirt-encrusted nails clung tightly to a pitted sword blade. With each stride, he could hear his own layered armor clanking against his shoulders. He was within grasping distance of a fair-faced woman when a haggardly-looking man intersected his path. With outstretch hands, he forcefully pushed the long-bearded man aside. The wood staff he was walking with was unable to prevent his fall to the ground.

The image seemed to freeze in place for a moment before the next one started to come forward. He could see a glimpse of the man's face that was falling. It was dirty red from exposure to the desert surroundings. But it was the man's intense blue eyes that seared into his mind, they seemed almost accepting to the encounter. Their quiet resignation seemed almost familiar...

People were yelling and screaming. An ancient-looking building engulfed in fire. Men in multi-colored tunics were fleeing from the flames holding armfuls of fire-tinged scrolls. He looked out to an adjacent harbor, beyond, to see a clatter of sailing ships engaged in battle underneath an enormous stone lighthouse. The bellowing of the nearby flames drowned out the meeting of swords and their accompanying screams.

Then, he was back in his study. The shadow figure still standing before him. A pointy nose had jutted out from its face under eyes that were presently less fiery and more subdued.

The destruction, the killing, and immense sadness, it was clear that these events were ZoZo's doing, or of his general kind. He felt that to be true. He could also feel a sense of pride and laughter being imparted to him. Even just with a flicker of insight, the mixture of enjoyment and malice were unsettling.

He feigned a nod in recognition. He did not want to see more images like that. The pain. The suffering. It was *too* much.

ZoZo's eyes narrowed. He could feel that it was not convinced of his belief.

"Even with a true view of the foundations you stand, you deny it still."

ZoZo's form transformed down into the height of a small figure not much higher than his waist.

"Do not reject truth that a child knows without doubt," the little figure began, in the voice of a young girl. "Born in purity, a child *sees* beyond the earthly; for in their youthful state, children are not too far enough removed from the ether in which they came. Yet, the ethereal afterglow fades with innocence, covering the eyes to knowledge, secrets, and truth."

ZoZo returned to its tall and slender shape, now more solidified. The addition of a pair of small ears had appeared on either side of its head along with a rounded nose and the emergence of pupils the dark shade of indigo. These progressive changes did not go unnoticed. It was peculiar to him that ZoZo was becoming more palpable and almost disarming the more knowledge it disclosed to him. It was as if it was growing more comfortable in his presence and allowing him to see a truer form—at least as much as his mind could comprehend.

Appearance aside, ZoZo's revelations were difficult to process. There were so many thoughts floating about his mind that any level of intellectual discernment grew difficult. All he could do was wonder how these things could be true. Had his aged mind barricaded itself away from a world beyond human measurement?

His thoughts somehow turned to the myths of old. Passed down like a collective memory of historical events, mythic stories somehow arose to a grand level of importance. So much so, that they survived the fall of kingdoms and changes of language, to spread across great distances and cultures. There must have been something about the great myths that was so enduring over the long stretches of time. Where many myths faded after an age, others endured. Some kernel of truth had to keep them alive without complete rejection by the successive generations. Something not explicit, but rooted deep in the primitive mind like that of a child. In a place that is fluid and unstructured by the earthly world of people. Where everything—the monsters, the spirits, the supernatural—was and could be real.

He sensed ZoZo's presence in his thoughts again. It had a heaviness to it, like a shadow casting upon him. Not under his control, it moved within his mind. With each movement there was a heaviness that weighed down on some thought or memory. His temples began to squeeze inward from the heavy pressure. There was something being dredged up into his consciousness.

The image only flashed for a brief instant. All he could see were the long menacing teeth and those hollowed black eyes reflecting the image of a cowering man in tunic clothing. It was the dinosaur he had seen in the vision before.

"Dragon," ZoZo said. The word matched the movement of its mouth that had materialized—pale lips that drooped into an off-center grin. ZoZo's entire form now appeared solid. Its skin was olive and silky smooth. No longer intimidating, the eyes were a shade of bright purple. Their look was electric. He wondered what must be happening behind their focused gaze.

ZoZo hunkered down slightly next to the lampstand. The faint amber light from it gave ZoZo an enchanting look as he spoke.

"It is time I reveal my purpose with you. Are you ready for what rarified choice you have hither?

He did not need to show a response, ZoZo understood his thoughts before they were even clear to himself.

"Just like Phosos offers a provision of the body, I offer provision of the boundless mind—knowledge. Before was only but a taste of a bottomless reservoir of memory to fully quench your desire."

The idea intrigued him. Perhaps in his own tampering he had stumbled onto something greater. A greater plane of existence perhaps. Was that not the reason he had set out for in the first place, to find greater sources of knowledge?

Yet, another part of him believed it all to be too easy. So, much was being offered but what was being gained? This all could be some elaborate alien trick. Their technology was truly advanced, maybe this was all a projection in one of their systems that had infiltrated into his Mindsai machine. That seemed unlikely given that the Mindsai was walled off from any system in the outside world. It was a protocol that had to be taken to ensure no noise was introduced into the experiments.

ZoZo offered a rebuttal.

"We are no more alien than the sky you see every night. We are so familiar, for we are eternal; next to you, guiding since your lowly beginnings."

ZoZo walked past the chair to the black drapery hanging on the wall. He regarded it only briefly with a stroke of a finger before continuing.

"Who do you think brought man knowledge that was withheld? Knowledge to subdue nature and build earthly things. To reduce your toils and amplify your pleasures. Without us, man would still be frolicking in ferns. But nay, look what power man has wrought unto itself!"

He rose from his chair. He was starting to make sense of it all. Not so much with his thoughts, but things *felt* right. Like a feeling awakened for the first-time since he was young. Without limits or bounds, the impossible felt possible. There was only one last piece to be resolved in his mind.

"But why me?" he asked, taking a step towards the drapery.

A sly grin edged across ZoZo's face, strangely charming.

He took another step closer.

ZoZo replied, "Know, I can see a record of your whole existence. You are unique, the first to do something incredible. You built a bridge to memories that mortality had once made lost to you. For memory is eternal, leaving a lasting imprint that is untouched by the grinding of time. You have glimpsed just below the surface, but the well is deep. There is much for you to fathom yet still. So, the question remains…at the end of your bridge, will you take the plunge into the deep?"

The proposal was enticing. In the quiet, he considered it as ZoZo's eyes eagerly examined him. In some ways, he felt he did not have much of a choice, or if he had, a part of him wanted there to be none. This was it, everything he had always wanted: total access memory to the collective experiences of unfathomable generations of people. His mind could barely grasp what that kind of power must be like. He would no longer be subservient to mankind's meager existence that had reached an evolutionary dead end. Here was his chance to arise to a higher plane, one that beings like Phosos must inhabit. At the very worse, he could use the power to examine the veracity of Phosos's claims. If false, he could be the only one that could bring the news to the world.

For some reason, an image of Emma's face appeared in his mind, then her whole body came into full view. She was reclining on a couch reading a book in a library. He had just met her there to tell her of a desk rejection of his first big manuscript. He had been devastated. The reviewers were especially vicious, even questioning why he was in the field doing research. But Emma, with a delicate grace, listened to his woes. When he had finished detailing his plight, she nodding her head and placed her soft hands on his own. Then with her words, she started rebuilding the foundation of his toppled castle. "You know you can do whatever you set your mind to Bash, there are no bounds to what you can accomplish. I will always be supportive of that. But remember dear, 'success is counted sweetest by those who never succeed.' " That was all he needed to hear.

Standing now, before a strange being in his study, he knew there never really was a choice. He had made it years ago.

"What do I need to do?"

ZoZo smiled with a slight bow of the head and then turned and grabbed the drapery to pull it back. The figure held back the heavy black cloth revealing a passage had been veiled behind it. Like a mirror reflecting upon itself, the corridor looked like it went on forever. The little light that remained from the study receded into a starry darkness.

"You need only step beyond the veil," ZoZo said instructively.

He stepped through and, with one step over the threshold, he felt himself free falling in darkness. An immense pressure, invisible to him, crushed down upon him. It was heavier than he thought any part of him could ever withstand; much heavier than going back into the memories of others in time before. At any second, he was sure he would blackout. However, to his disappointment, he remained fully aware. He was traveling at a great speed. The rush downward eventually began to slow. His whole body felt like it was being crushed down into a single grain of sand, like the first one to fall to the bottom of an hour glass. A grain all alone in a barren landscape.

The heaviness lifted. A faint aroma began to wash over his senses like a spring breeze. The floral smell was so fresh, so new...

11

Beyond the Veil
x months A.R.D.

On the other side of the veil, the darkness slowly receded into an unfamiliar place. In the gloom, he could discern a lush landscape shrouded by a pale blue light coming from an unseen source. There was no moon to be found in the night sky, just an innumerable cluster of stars that surrounded him like a cave full of shimmering crystals. There was enough light that he could see a path winding before him. It was headed on a downward slope, only interrupted by the dark silhouettes of twigs and branches reaching across it.

Looking around him, he was surrounded by colossal trees and ferns with flower blooms that were bursting with a wheel of color, perceptible even in the low light. Any one of the flowering plants would have been a cherished prize for Emma's garden. The plants explained the smells that were hitting him in waves. The earthy scents were a mix of freshly fallen rain, abundant new growth, and floral perfume. Together, the intensity of petrichor was overwhelming.

He observed his surroundings for a bit to gain some bearings in the strange place. It was too dark to see what laid around him beyond the path. The stony path was covered in tiny white rocks that had a white gleam, reflecting what limited light there was.

Stranger still, he had no idea whose eyes he was looking out from, but whoever it was, they decided to take the path. He would have made the same decision as it was the only route that he could see forward without stumbling through the overgrowth in the dark.

Walking, a humid breeze broke across his face. It felt pleasant and electric in the night air. Everything else was still and quiet. There were no signs of life other than the softly swaying vegetation, which was now progressively becoming more barren and harrowed as he descended down the path.

When he reached the foot of the hill, the path leveled itself out into a grey plane. It began to lead away from the overgrowth out into a rocky terrain. Small stone outcroppings began to appear to each side of him. First, the size of a melon, then a desk, then bigger than he. Looking ahead, he could only see the outlines of other large boulders and the glowing rocks of the path. The path was straightening now and, in about fifty meters, it seemed to stretch out into a dark void. On either side of it, the path ahead looked as if it were suspended in air.

Stopping, he had a chance to study the path. It seemed the person he was experiencing was trying to figure out if they should proceed any further. Suddenly, a figure in white silently darted out from behind a boulder onto the path. The figure stopped at the center and turned his way. It was a woman! Draped from head to bare feet in a translucent shroud, the woman looked directly at him. Her long hair flipped at her naked form under the shroud. With a smile and a gesture of her right hand, flipping her fingers towards herself, the woman beckoned him…to come closer.

Emma? he thought immediately. The thought burst into his mind with a such a strength and clarity. He squinted his eyes. Through the translucence, the figure was unmistakably her. But that was not possible, was it? She had the same brown hair that fell across her porcelain skin. The same ruby-red lips. Her flickering eyes.

His heart swelled in his chest.

She puckered her face for a kiss and took flight down the path.

Without a single thought, he was giving chase.

The sight of Emma blurred with every jarring step he took. He did not want to lose sight of her, but it was hard for him to keep pace. She seemed to effortlessly glide along the path. Every movement was graceful and alluring. She reached the darkness he had noticed before and seemed to float across it. Still approaching with haste, he could now see that the void was a great chasm that went down on either side of the path that bisected it.

The sounds of his footfalls echoed out like thunder as he came to a stop at the edge of the cliff. He gazed downward. Its depths were immeasurable and its darkness was absolute. A misstep here would be into an oblivion, forever falling.

When he raised his head, he saw that Emma had reached the other side. He could see now that there was some sort of stone structure that spanned the chasm. She turned just long enough to give him a flash of a smile and then disappeared into a fissure within a rock face on the other side. A white afterglow remained, marking where she had gone.

He proceeded across the narrow stone bridge. It was barely wide enough to walk with feet side-by-side, so he stepped with one foot at a time. The silence returned like an incoming tide as he slowly progressed. The sounds of his scuffling feet seemed to get swallowed up by the emptiness below.

Above him, a light lit his way, marking the material from the darkness. The source of the light was now in full view over his right shoulder as he edged further and further out over the expanse. The moon was enormous, larger than any supermoon he had witnessed before in his life. It seemed to take up a quarter of the sky as it hung low and moved as he glanced at it in between careful steps. It was so close; he could see that it had no craters. Its surface was pure and unblemished, reflecting a silvery light mixed with an iridescent prism of color.

Reaching the bridge's midway point, the stillness was interrupted by an arid gust. The air hit him flatly in the face. His footing became unsteady and he would have toppled over the edge if he had not extended his arms at the last second to maintain himself. As the wind tapered off along the chasm, he caught a whiff of desert air. He imagined it was blowing in from some far-off place beyond this tropical sanctuary. Out of place here, it did not belong and would continue on its way.

The second half of the bridge was easier going, once he got into a rhythm. When he reached the other side, he sighed heavily. Looking back, the white, moon-lit path was the only vivid feature he could see. It jumped the chasm and cut through the barren landscape beyond, going up the rise into a darker line of large trees. Everything else was subdued by a gloom of bluish-grey light.

Turning back, he stared into the fissure. It was narrow at first at the entrance but going back, it widened into a small hollow in the rock. A faint light was coming from within, pooling in circles of white on the obsidian walls. It was enough to see a way back...

He squeezed his body through the small opening. The rough stone scraped across the skin of his back and stomach down to the ankles of his legs. He then realized for the first time that he was completely naked. The thought of being exposed to this unfamiliar place the whole time made him cringe. He was unable to see in the tight space, but winced knowing that the tiny edges of stone were rubbing raw across his entire body.

Once through the gap, he brushed himself off the black rock dust. Looking down, he saw white and red scrape lines running in parallel across an otherwise unblemished body. It looked perfect, and not his own. *Whose eyes was he looking through?* he wondered.

He continued on a sandy pathway that narrowly cut through the rock. Nestled between the dark walls, the path wound and slithered beneath rocky outcroppings. He often had to turn his body sideways to pass through. But with each step, the light grew in intensity. He could hear a shuffling noise ahead.

When he turned a sharp corner, he entered into a larger cavity the size of his main lab space. There, Emma was waiting for him. She stood upon a bed of green leaves that had been piled there. She was likely some sort of ZoZo trick, he thought, but it was a beautiful one that he could not help but look past and forget. He could nearly fall into her eyes as they welcomed him.

She stood behind a pedestal of the same glossy-black rock that lined the walls. Upon its smooth top sat an old oil lamp. It was made of simple red clay that was rounded in the body and tapered to an arm that held a single yellow flame. It danced in fluid, slow waves. But it was not the main source of light in the room. Emma's skin seemed to give off its own white luminance that filled the chamber. She looked so perfect, so happy. He could almost feel her glow wrapping itself around him. She spoke to him in a voice just as soothing:

"Come closer, there is much for you to know, to see."

She stretched out a hand towards the pedestal.

"I cannot choose this for you, it must be your will…a bite."

He looked back at the pedestal and saw that she had placed a single blood-red fruit next to the lamp. It was small and looked something like a pomegranate. Beads of moisture ran down the smooth flesh of its sides that shimmered a ruby glow in the lamp light.

He had to hold back a laugh. This was his choice. The one that ZoZo had alluded to him. It was a strange sort of theatrics that the entity had orchestrated. Perhaps it thought that using Emma's visage made it easy for him. This was not untrue. He felt comfortable in her presence. If it were to be anyone, it had to be her. She had known for so long, even painfully so, his desire to unlock the secret knowledge in the recesses of his memory. It was fitting that she would offer him the key.

He picked up the red fruit. Its squishy flesh gave way in between his thumb and fingers. He brought it up to his mouth. The smell was fresh and full of energy that he could feel the prickles of electricity on his unseen lips. Taking one last look at Emma, he closed his eyes and took a bite.

The taste was sickeningly sweet. He could feel a surge of energy rush through his body and into his head. It was like drinking caffeinated coffee for the first time in the morning, but many orders of magnitude greater. The sudden onset of alertness was overwhelming, but continued to build.

He opened his eyes. He saw the area where he had bit into the fruit. The inner flesh was beige and folded in lobes like that of a human brain. Startled, he let it splash to the floor below.

He raised his eyes and saw that Emma was gone. In her place, stood a woman. She was perfect. The same woman he had seen in his vision of the two weird trees before. Though now, her face seemed to have lost some of its glow and luster. Her face was filled with concern and weariness as if the weight of the world rested on her tiny brow.

A thunderclap came from a distance outside the cave. Its echo reverberated loudly throughout the chamber. Bits of black rock fell from the ceiling knocking out the flame of the lamp. Everything was cast into a darkness.

Unlike lightening, the thunder was quickly followed by a light. It was nearly blinding and growing stronger from behind him at the opening of the cave. In the next moments, an iridescence pierced through and completely enveloped him until there was nothing more to see.

Bash felt himself detached in a sort of feverish dream. His mind was burning and floating. Outwardly, he was without any senses but what he could see. And what he saw was a dark void. There was no Earth, no stars, or any other celestial objects. It was just him and a cloud of iridescent light. The cloud appeared large but he could not tell since there was nothing for it to be measured against. From it, a medley of colors passed across his face, each one triggering a different feeling...of love...of peace...of wonder. When the colors left his face, he was only left with the lonesome feeling of fear.

Within the cloud of light were many beacons of light surrounding a much larger, iridescent light. Innumerable, the smaller lights seemed to attend to-and-fro at the whims of the light at the cloud's core. His sight grew more acute and he saw that the smaller lights were in fact white orbs. Within them, were faces, at least, that's how they appeared to be translated into his mind. Though each one was unique, the faces had the appearance of beautiful beings. Their features were like those cut from a precious diamond, perfectly shaped and formed. Their mouths were all open wide as if they were singing forth a joyous chorus that he had not the ears to hear.

He scanned the multitude in awe.

Near the top of the cloud, a particular orb caught his attention. He almost instantaneously recognized it as Phosos. It was nearly identical to the alien that had landed in that town square. He would say *nearly identical* because now, in this time, Phosos seemed to glow brighter and was somehow, more perfect and joyous.

Phosos's head turned downward. He looked around and saw that the rest of the collective of lights had also turned their attention to the void below.

He did the same.

There was a period of waiting until a variegated light projected from the cloud downward into the empty space. It split the darkness, and in a flash, a world appeared, spinning out of it. The light revealed a barren planet covered in watery deep of still midnight blue.

Once the new world had turned a complete revolution, another light came down upon it. From the waters, a lighter blue atmosphere projected outward from the surface.

With another revolution, the foundations of the world rose up from the dark waters. A large landmass emerged that formed a supercontinent covering nearly a quarter of the world's surface. As the waters ran down from the landscape, green sprouts of vegetation began to spring forth from the dampened black soil.

Though far above the planet, he could see as far down as his mind desired. It was like being able to squint to infinity. Up close, he was overtaken with the splendor of the freshness of the new world.

Another revolution came and the cloud projected light into every direction. When the light ceased, the sky was filled with the remnants of the light source in colors of whites, reds, blues, and yellows. They lit up the black void of space as stars, planets, and the moons.

The world below completed another cycle and life appeared in the seas and in the sky. Fish and other strange sea monsters began to team at the surface of the waters. Above, feathery birds and creatures large with leathery wings took flight to seize their place in their atmospheric home.

On its sixth revolution, life sprung forth upon the land. Beasts of every size and shape began to step on the untouched surface. Some were taller than the trees with long necks and tails while others were humble creatures that burrowed into the ground.

Finally, a singular beam of light focused narrowly on a dusty piece of ground underneath two towering trees. The trees looked very similar to the ones he had seen before. The spot was within a lush area of land surrounded by rivers and a sea to the south. He focused his eyes and saw that a man had been formed from the ground where that beam of light had struck. Next to him, lay a woman. She was of remarkable beauty with dark hair and a pleasing womanly form. When she opened her eyes, a familiarity washed over him. It had been her that he had seen under the trees and in the cave. In their nakedness, he observed that these humans were flawless in all their features, similar to the orbed beings watching from above. Their smooth skin even seemed to radiate the light of their creation in a warm glow. Unlike the orbed beings above, these two humans were distinctly of the world in which they had been created. Their flesh was solid and full of new life like all that surrounded them.

He wanted to study the figures longer but the world began to spin too quickly for him to keep up his view. When it eventually slowed, there was nothing but inactivity on the world below and in the cloud above.

Several rotations of the world went by until he noticed a discordance begin to take hold in the cloud of light hovering above. Phosos and a small host of other orbs had ceased their singing and began to rise towards the top of the cloud. They followed a singular blue orb that seemed to outshine the rest as a shimmering jewel that was growing brighter and brighter as it ascended. The brilliance of the leading orb was too bright to see a face and he dared not stare at it for more than a few moments at a time. Even looking at it briefly made him feel unsettled and cold.

The faction of orbs rose and rose until they were about to elevate themselves above the cloud and the world below. But, before they could reach the great heights, a great rumble came within the cloud. In the quaking of the cloud, the orbs who had made their ascent were expelled downward to the earth in trails of fire and sparkling dust. As they fell, their glow diminished and they were scattered into the low places of the world below.

The world then began to spin faster than it had before. The light and dark cycles began to pass before him in what was like minutes. He could feel time progressing more quickly as he desperately tried to fix his sight on the happenings below—the world was but a blur.

The blurring would continue for a time and then begin to slow for a short period. It was then that he could catch a glimpse at the state of the world. During the second inter-blur period—as he coined it—he saw that the two humans from before had increased in number to around a dozen people positioned just to the east of the lush landscape they had been in before.

In the third inter-blur period, the numbers had shot up to over 1,000 people and he could see them spreading out across the face of the giant continent…and with them so went blue orbs.

In the fourth inter-blur period, the numbers had increased to hundreds of thousands. City centers had formed in some places as the people had begun to concentrate together. With their hands and minds, they had crafted wonderous buildings in a golden age of technological innovation that he had never seen. Primitive flying machines filled the sky, lighting it up with their fire-fueled mechanisms. Down in their temples, the people worshiped Phosos and his kindred as light bringers of knowledge. In their streets, decadence was manifest in lavish displays of reckless abandon where the carcasses of great beasts were paraded, food was aplenty, and all manner of thirsty desires were filled without shame.

In the fifth period, the population of people was too many to estimate but covered the supercontinent like a horde of locusts. The once great cities were now but remnants and stilted mockeries of their former glorious works. Many had darkened from their once great light as some had been ravaged by war and self-destruction.

Instantly, Bash was overwhelmed by a sense of encroaching darkness falling as a heavy veil over humanity. The orbs were obscuring all memories of the past and any proof to the preceding ages. Those trying to keep a history of their people somehow became snuffed out. Without memory of their origins, the people were left docile to their own desires of the present and were easily corrupted. In the vacuum created by the darkness of obscured memory, it seemed that wherever the orbs of Phosos had gone, only destruction and degradation were left behind.

In the sixth period, the world was cloaked by cloud and rain. All looked drowned in water.

In the seventh period, the world came back into view with a changed face. A great upheaval had rifted apart the supercontinent into sperate, smaller landmasses. Sheets of ice stretched from the northern and southern poles and the atmosphere now seemed less dense and blue. His eyes searched far and wide for traces of the multitudes from before. But before the spinning began again, he could only find a small family clan in this transformed world.

In the inter-blur periods that followed, the number of people began to increase once more. They slowly spread across the new landscapes. As time went on though, he saw that the bodies of successive generations of people seemed to diminish from the original form. The glow that had marked their ancestors was all but gone after a half-dozen inter-blur periods. What persisted were bodies that had become dull and marked by imperfections and deformations. Many experiencing the times would perhaps not notice the slow appearance of freckles on the checks, rougher skin, or a lopsided eye. However, an observer not bound by time could see that humanity was not evolving, but becoming more degraded as the years went forward. The copies upon copies of the original form were now becoming divergent mimicries of their pure source.

Phosos and the orbs of his kind only seemed to bolster this process along. Over the flickers of history Bash observed, their presence was only associated with corruptions of the human spirit. They were not alien to this world at all; their deceit had been leading humanity astray since the beginning—obscuring and erasing memory and filling in the void with their own twisted truths. Without a comprehensive picture that covered the expanse of time, no person could put together the pieces. Their deceit was well-hidden, always at the edge of mortal memory.

As the revelation washed over him, a panic of alarm started to ring out in his mind. Phosos was not a provider, Phosos was a perverter! A diabolic force that degraded and twisted all that it and its kind came into contact with. And their first step would be to warp and hide documented history. They had already infiltrated the historical simulations; it would only be a matter of time before all accounts would be distorted or lost. This sparked an urgency within him. He knew he had to get back. He had to warn the world that he had left behind in the future.

The years flew by faster and the continents drifted themselves into the familiar shapes that he recognized of the Earth he knew. There was little doubt that it had been Earth the whole time. He had known that without seeing it. He felt a deep connection with its form and features. The features that he had come from. It was home.

He could now see North America drifting to its place alone between two vast oceans. It was covered in old forests and fertile green plains, untouched yet by humanity. As he grew closer to contemporary modernity, the continent he called home saw the arrival of man. The trees made way for small pockets of camping villages, then larger towns, and then to the world he knew, where megacities had stretched their urban tentacles deep into the once green and brown countryside.

As the landscape grew more familiar, he felt himself slowly falling downward towards the earth. The blue mountains of Virginia came into view first, then the scattered fields, and then at last, he could see the ivory spire of Hightower University perched upon its hilltop. He found himself floating above Hugenberg Hall and then, with a sudden lead heaviness, he fell through the roof.

He was back in his lab. His body felt cold and achy as if he had been laying down too long. His head on the other hand was still throbbing in pain and felt like it was on fire.

He looked around.

The lab was dark and flickering with lights. The whole space seemed somehow less real than the vivid images he had just experienced, not as vivid or colorful. To his side, the SEER goggles dangled uselessly next to the reclining couch. On the floor was a scattering of wires and sensors.

The throbbing in his head was starting to intensify.

He grabbed a nearby scarf from a chair and put it around his head. It was frigidly-cold from the room and served to keep some of the pain at bay.

He tried to think of what to do. He had to tell someone of his ground-breaking experience. He had to tell everyone the truth. Phosos was a lie. A deception.

He pulled himself up and took a few steps towards the door. On the third step, a blinding whip of pain cracked across his forehead. The throbbing almost brought him to the floor.

He scrambled to his feet and over to a desk. He saw a phone and pressed the emergency line out, putting it on the speaker.

As he waited for the dialer to connect, he grabbed a pen and paper to jot down some notes in case he fell unconscious before help could arrive. The pen was freezing and his hand shook as he wrote the words in uneven lines across the paper:

> Experiment was a success. I went into the Mindsai and all at once, a spreading of activation went through all my memories—and others—and every past moment became the present, which lost its meaning with the unbounding associations.

After a few lines, a jolting pressure struck deep into his head and he dropped the pen. As he leaned over to pick it up, a disembodied laughter echoed throughout the laboratory behind him. It was unmistakably the entity from before.

ZoZo spoke in a hissing voice that was almost taunting in its tone, "Here we are. A cascade of choices has put me here to halt your progress, and my work is almost finished."

Images flashed in Bash's mind of a bull-headed stone statue in a museum-like storeroom. In one of its hands, the statue held a bronze dagger with a red crystal pommel. Then there was a group of boys dressed in turn of the twenty-first century clothing gathered around the red crystal at the foot of the statue. The crystal pommel lay broken in a pile of white dust. One of the boys picked up a snake-shaped amulet from the pile of dust. It was golden with a New Eden tree in its center. Finally, he saw the snake amulet being placed in his basement archive room by one of the boys many years before he arrived to Hightower University.

The images faded and he saw his hand still reaching for the pen.

"Memory is a precious thing, so many treasures of wisdom. Without it, you are lost to repeat your mistakes and left to your own devices—devices we like to turn. But this device of your making is not meant for human minds; access to such knowledge is not desirable; you must forget. So, we will pull the veil down once more over these memories, just as we have done before," ZoZo said, as another image flooded into Bash's mind.

He saw a rocky outcropping at the edge of a great desert chasm. A man wearing a funny-looking hat clung desperately to the side of the cliff. On his face was an expression of pure terror at something that was approaching him. Above him, Bash could see an area had been excavated from the rock. The ribs of a massive fossilized skeleton had been uncovered that he knew, somehow, belonged to a carnivorous dinosaur. And, lodged within its ribs, was a rounded humanoid skull.

Bash began to feel the same terror as the man in the vision. The world that he knew was starting to unravel. His only thoughts were of how many others had seen this knowledge only to be covered up by dark forces and what other revelations have these beings hidden from humanity's collective memory?

The image quickly faded, and he was back in the laboratory again. ZoZo spoke no more but the silence was just as discomforting.

Cursing himself for the unnecessary detail he had written already, he picked the pen off the floor and tried to scribble the important points:

> Attention, my journeys through memory have revealed
> many things. Beware the offers of New Eden. The history
> he speaks is false and will obscure our memories. I have seen
> that Phosos is not alien. Phosos is a de—

Before he could finish the sentence, a heaviness overwhelmed his mind. The weight of it took hold of him and all he could hear was a croaking laughter as all went dark…

The picture on the mantle looked unfamiliar. A faint sense of recognition seemed to suggest that it could be of himself, but in that moment, he had difficulty projecting what he looked like in comparison. That seemed silly. Surely there was some image locked away in his mind—a picture, a mirror, a reflection on water—but such an image of himself eluded him. For the moment, he had forgotten. Maybe that was not so strange, he reasoned, a lot had been on his mind at late. How often does one truly study their face in the mirror, after all?

He whirled around in the wooden seat to find a mirror or reflective device. None could be found in the room he found himself in.

The room seemed strange as well. It was a kind of study lit only by a dying fire. It must be a dream because the corridors jetting off from the room and above him were configured into impossible directions. At least it was no architecture that he had ever seen before. Maybe he had forgotten that too.

A humming noise brought his gaze back to the fireplace. Next to it, a beam of light was filtering in from a dark passageway. A tattered dark cloth lay discarded at the foot of the passage.

The beam of light intrigued him, so he got up and stepped closer. As he neared, he could see little flashes of images, like old film, carried along the beam of light. The images were of people, places, and things. Perhaps some were of him. He had not a clue, they all seemed unfamiliar. He traced the beam to where it split down a corridor filled with closed doors. The light traveled into the distance until it seemed to fade into nothingness. Far off, he could hear the fast movement of air growing louder as it seemed to be approaching his position. Then, the doors in the distance flew open on their hinges. They progressively opened themselves one-by-one down the hall, closer and closer. As they did so, he heard the giant whoosh of pulling air filling in the newly open space. In synchrony, a branch of light split off from the main beam and was sucked down the newly opened doorways. It did not take long until every doorway was open and receiving its own feed from the beam of light.

He heard the same happening in the other corridors all around him. In their unseen places, doors were crashing open and being filled by the strange beam of images. He did not know what was happening but a looming dread knotted inside him. He paced the floor frantically trying to figure out what was going on, where he was, and *who* he was, but his thoughts were completely scattered. He found it hard to grasp at even the simplest of thoughts about what to do or what he had done in the past...

An image flashed before him of a little girl riding a bike...then another of a man crossing a city street...one more of a dried-up river bank...

The memories were crowding out his own thoughts. Instead of just images, bits of facts and knowledge began to filter in. The little girl on the bike was named Lilah and it was her sixth birthday. The busy city street was the crossing of King Street and Columbus street in Old Town Alexandria outside of Washington, D.C. How did he know these things? He just did.

He took a seat back in the chair at the center of the study. The sudden rush of insight was too much, too fast for him to stand. He could hear them coming down the corridors, all the memories. Each one had a voice that began to chatter incessantly in his head, chatting not with one another, but in their own slices of time. Their numbers grew until, eventually, there was but a cacophony of disparate thoughts and voices.

So much knowledge, so fast. The memories were coming through in waves, now larger and more frequent as a storm tide. Each one brought in the strange debris of another life. As the waters receded, they slowly eroded the pieces of who Bash was, though he could only feel it. He desperately tried to put up a barrier to keep the new memories out. He had to focus on the thoughts that were his...anything. With all his effort he concentrated on his identity, starting with his name.

"My name, my name is...my name is Bash, that's right," he said to himself. "I'm Seb-astion Si...Si...Silva." With a name, the rest came easier. "I am a cyber psychologist at Hightower

University, office number six-nineteen. I have a wife, her name is..."

He drew a blank. He could not remember. He could see her lovely porcelain face and brown hair but could not think of the name. Shortly, even her precious face was blurred by that of a small black dog catching a frisbee. His name was Reggie. His body began to shake at the thought of losing himself and the one he loved.

On an impulse, he took flight from the chair and darted down the nearest corridor. He ran along the passage as fast as he could go. Overhead, the white glow of the beam pulsed, providing the passageway with a dim source of light. He outstretched his hands, as he ran, and crossed them over his head back-and-forth in a chopping motion. It was his feeble attempt to disrupt the beam from pumping in new memories. However, the beam passed right through his hands unabated.

When the light of the study was only a flicker in the distance down the hall, he looked for a door to pass through. It did not matter which. He needed a memory to remember himself and he knew that memories resided behind the doors. He passed through the first one on his right, but it just led into another corridor of open doors being fed by the same beam of light—memories of others and not his own.

He turned again, taking the third open door on his left. It led to a corridor where three-quarters of the doors in view were already open and receiving the beam. Soon the junctions would all disappear and there would be no place to go. He had to outrun the beam and find some door to enter so that it might jog his memory.

He pushed forward to get ahead of the beam that was slowly progressing down the hall ahead. Placing all his mental effort on moving forward he caught up to the beam. As he passed it, a door burst open on his right side. He felt a whoosh of air pull him from the center of the hall towards the newly open door. He spared one glance to see that once the beam had entered, an entire new corridor of doors had been brought into existence to handle the influx of its information in addition to the solitary memory that had been there before.

He kept running, escaping the inflow of the open door. Now, he was surrounded by closed doors rushing past on his left and right. Behind him, he could still hear the whooshing sounds of more doors flying open with the beam. Once he had passed about fifty doors down from the beam of light, he grabbed the door handle of the nearest one to his right. He pushed it open with all his might. It opened with the glow of artificial light.

Just before he stepped across the threshold, he glanced down the hall ahead. He saw a sturdy, burgundy door with peeling paint. It was nestled in a termination point at the end of the hall. His heart immediately leapt in his chest. He felt a deep emotional connection to that door. In turn, his mind scoured what was left of himself to find a reason why, but to his distress, he could not remember one. He stepped through the opening, feeling a sense of imminent loss.

On the other side, he stepped out into a large room. In front of him was a stage with a banner of a bearded man dressed in purple tights with a funny, wide-brimmed hat. On one side, it was adorned by a large bird's feather. The character's face was smirking while holding a long, needle-pointed sword.

A cavalier, the thought came to him.

He was in a gymnasium. One he recognized from long ago. Big picture windows lined the top of the walls letting in sunlight that beamed into irregular shapes on the worn wood floor. The walls were covered in an ugly greenish-beige tile that went up to the ceiling. Above, large bulbous halogen lights dangled from the metal rafters. They always reminded him of rocket engines when they fired up in bursts of sparks.

Another memory was coming through. There was a day where one of the ultraviolet filters had fallen off the lights and caused burns on the kids who had gym class before him. He remembered feeling scared that a manmade light source could do so much harm.

Yes, the memories were coming back in rapid succession now. He was in his elementary gym. He could not be more than eight years old, probably in the second grade. Bashy they had called him. On this day, he was wandering the halls on a bathroom break. He had gone into the gym to see what it was like when it had been emptied of the dozens of cafeteria tables and not used for gym class. He felt so small in that empty space. As he gawked, a shadow wavered in a corner that led out a pair of double metal doors. Curious, he followed it out into the hall. When he got there, he could find no trace of it. He had spent long enough in the gym anyways so it was time to head to the bathroom before his teacher...Mrs....Mrs. Underly started looking for him.

Down the hall, the walls were decorated with murals of fairy-book stories. In the kindergarten classroom section, he saw Humpty Dumpty caught precariously in mid-fall. In the first-grade section, there were three pink pigs huddled nervously behind the brick walls of a house as a menacing-looking wolf puffed white streaks of curling air their way. Finally, just as he reached the bathroom opening near the second-grade section, there was a large Mother Goose watching caringly from one side of the door as her clutch of goslings caught up from the bottom of a grass hill on the other side.

Before entering, he looked around. It was mid-afternoon so the halls were empty. Off in the distance he only heard the faint sound of scooting shoes shuffling around into a classroom. He remembered he typically did not like to use the bathroom at school because it was often dirty. Boys seemed to have a difficult time aiming themselves at the trough that was embedded on the floor. The feeling of sticky sneakers while peeing was uncomfortable. His mom had just purchased a pair of white ones that lit up with red lights in the heel as he walked so he did not want to dirty them up. But today he had drunk too much apple juice and could not delay until home.

Before he went in, he heard the pitter patter of water from directly across the hall. He turned to see that it was coming from washing station next to an open mechanical room. Semi-circular, the water station looked like a green metal basin about the height of a five-year-old. In the middle of the basin, a metal tube came up and fanned out into a circular petal filled with small holes where the water sprinkled out. It was used for washing your hands and operated by metal pedals on the floor. It was strange that the water was on and no one was at the station.

He walked across the hall slowly.

Closer, he could see that the pedals were not depressed. He could find no reason why it had come on. He pushed down his foot and the water continued running and then let off the pressure. The water ceased sprinkling for a few seconds before coming on again. Then it stopped. Then it started. Then it stopped once more. The cycle of pulses made the sprinkles shower down in little waved patterns before they hit the bottom of the tub.

He stepped back from the station as he his heart rate elevated. That's when he saw a small, shadowy figure slide back into the mechanical room next to the water station.

He looked around again, but there was no one in the hall. Everything was quiet.

Turning back to the water station, it had fallen silent.

Looking for an explanation, he poked his head into the mechanical room. Inside, it was dark and smelled of water mixed with burnt dust. Somewhere in the back, a machine was making a rattling sound against a wall. His eyes scanned over the twisting pipes and air ducts; passed by the dirty mops and yellow buckets; ducked underneath the dust-encrusted window pane; but stopped when they saw a pair of yellow eyes staring right back at him. The shadowy thing was coiled like a snake around a large vertical steam pipe. It stared at him with curious yellow flickers, making him feel like he should explore further, to approach.

Before he could act, a group of voices came from down the hall. In quick response, the shadowy snake seemed to dissolve into the shadows of the room. He listened. The voices were not of children, but he could not pick out a single voice. They all seemed to blend together incoherently. As they grew louder, the scene started to dissolve away before his eyes. Soon the memory had faded and he was back to where he had begun.

A portrait of a man was before him. Now, he could recognize it as himself and the place around him. He was in his mental study with all the items he held dear. The sailboat, the sand, the globe, they were all here.

For a brief moment in his study, he thought he heard the voice of his graduate student, Aliyah: "Goodbye Professor Silva." The voice slipped away too quickly to verify if he had heard it or it was some wishful thought. Perhaps *here* was still in the Mindsai. She might be mere centimeters from his face, calling to him. *But how could he answer from in here?*

There was a way, it involved connecting another set of something to the machine. *What was it? Had that knowledge already slipped away too?*

He looked above him at a corridor filled with a ribbon of white light. He stared blankly at it. It was memorizing and eerily beautiful in its pulsations.

"I think I…forgot something…now what was it…what did I…forget? It must be something important…what a strange feeling this is…" he mumbled as if in a daze.

Flashes of memory sprung over him in quick succession. Like a flashbulb just before it burns itself out the memories were intense and faded away. He saw friends from his childhood playing in the dirt…darkness…his mother and father hugging on Valentine's Day…darkness…Emma in a see-through white gown on their wedding night…darkness…his colleague Chris helping him move into the cottage he had just bought…all faded away.

He was breathing frantically and turning around in all directions. Everything was beginning to become detached and disconnected. There was no grip of himself to hold onto. It was all going to become lost or pushed aside in his mind. Room had to be made for all the *other* memories.

The objects in the study began to disappear in clouds of dust. He looked at his table and saw them, the sailboat, the sand, the globe, they faded away into nothingness one-by-one. In the frenzy, he did not even remember what they represented. As the study became increasingly bare, he fell to the ground crying. The tears outpoured more than they had since…since…since his wife…

"What was her name? Emily?

No.

Eliana.

No.

Emery.

No. WHAT WAS IT!?

EMMA! YES! THAT WAS IT!"

He hit the floor with a closed fist, yelling to an empty room.

"Don't take these away from me," he cried. "Please, I don't need to know about everything else, not if it costs me who I am."

He paused and tried to muster up one final defense against the tidal wave of memories he had felt in the back of his mind. The pressure was building and soon the levy would break…

"I won't forget! Damn it! I won't! I'm married to Emma Colette Silva, who married me, Dr. Sebastian Silva, in the month of…June at…at…Salem…Harvest…Church."

As he spoke, he could see an image of Emma in his mind. She was smiling at him; the way she did when she was making a tiny request. He felt a smile curl on his face. Her ruby-red lips smirked to one side and squished together the soft skin of her cheeks. Her eyes shimmering for a response.

It was the shimmers in her eyes that were the first to dull. Soon, the regions of her eyes grew dark, then her face, and then…then the rest of her quickly slipped away into the husk of a murky-grey shadow. The figure featureless and unrecognizable.

"No," he sobbed. The fleeting look had vanished and there was no image of her to draw back up. Only a silhouette remained—a shade of what was.

"Nooo…please don't take her face away from me."

No one heard him, yet the sound of voices started to pour over him from all the corridors surrounding him. The wave felt like an icy draft with a multitude of people talking, yelling, moaning, all at once in *his* head?

"Am I a he? Or a she? I cannot remember that. Or tell?" There was no way to confirm.

"My head…there are so many voices. Who am I? Who have I lost? What was the name…I can't recall anymore…but my name…is something…something with an 'Sa' sound I believe, right? Yes."

An immense heaviness could be felt as the beams of light projected from every corridor onto Bash's head. The amalgamated number of memories ate through his consciousness like worms burrowing into a new home. Bash did not remember who he was any longer, because he was everyone and no one. The entirety of human memory had been placed into his mind.

On the floor beneath Bash, the black veil was the only object remaining in what was once a study. The veil had gradually melded into the floor and spread out like a creeping sludge. It did not take long before the blackness had covered the entire space. And when it did, the weight of all the memories drew Bash down into it, that bottomless abyss. There, so many thoughts, not his own, coursed through Bash's mind. Yet, there was only one fragment of a thought that remained that gave him any sense of familiar recognition, but with all his knowledge, he could not identify why and where it had come:

The brain has corridors surpassing
Material place.

Epilogue
Two months A.R.D.

"Ouch!"

"Don't be a child, Gabe. Have you seen my eye?" Aliyah traced the tender line of flesh extending from her eye socket to her right temple for him. Her finger bumped up and down over the stiches like a train clattering over its winding tracks. Two weeks had passed, and the wound still felt sticky and tender.

The nurse attending to Gabe, a leathery-faced lady advanced in her career, gave him a stern look as she continued her task of cleaning and redressing his wound. A rank smell floated up from the wound, breaking down all the resistance she could muster not to look from her seat on his bedside.

A stream of yellow-green pus seeped out of Gabe's stitching. The once round puncture wound had been transformed into a blotchy ridge of pinched skin and blotted-purple flesh.

Her eyes averted away and grappled Gabe's other hand. It was warm and soft.

"After everything, my hand is what scares you?" he said, wincing as the nurse continued her work. His face was still the kind one she had grown to adore, but appeared more tempered now than before. He had been through a lot, they both had. This tiny sterile-white room at the university hospital had been their home since the 'the accident.' That, at least, was what they had told the hospital staff and the authorities. Their cover story had been told that they had been walking along the trail on the northern ridge of the Woodlot when it gave way, sending them tumbling down into a locust thicket. The thorns had scratched them up terribly and one lodged itself into Gabe's hand. The story was plausible and there really was not any further questions. People really didn't seem to have time or care to probe much deeper after Revelation Day.

For that first week at the hospital, Gabe had been barely conscious from the infection that festered in his hand. She had resolved to stay by his side in the small room with no windows of any kind. She had requested it that way, she needed time to grapple with her thoughts without distractions of the outside world.

"All done here," the nurse piped up after wrapping the last stretch of beige bandages that matched her hair. She squinted at Gabe squarely over her dark oval glasses. The checkered wrinkles around her eyes and cheeks flared outward. "You're quite lucky, you know. If this happened a few months ago, we might have lost you to infection. Our old antibiotics wouldn't have been effective to treat this. You should count your stars that The Hands of Provision have provided new medicines to combat what ours could not."

"Thank you," Gabe replied.

The nurse nodded and then gathered her supplies back onto the clear-plastic cart. She got up gingerly and began to push herself out towards the door. Before leaving, however, she turned to speak over her shoulder.

"The doctor should be in to discharge you. If you need anything, just press the call button." The cart and her then squeaked out of the room.

Aliyah exhaled in a sigh of relief. It was nice to be alone with Gabe once more.

"Oh, and by the way..." The nurse had popped her head back into the room. "I know you haven't kept track of the news given your lack of telewindow in the room, but once you're discharged, you'll both need to obtain your unity mark. You're in luck since we have a processing station in Ward 1A. Just don't forget before you leave."

"Thank you, we'll be sure to check it out," Aliyah replied. Though she, or Gabe, had no intention of getting any mark. Everything associated with that symbol seemed sinister.

"Okay, I'll be out of your hair now," said the nurse. They waited together listening to the squeaky cart trailing off down the corridor.

"Aliyah…" Gabe squeezed her hand to grab her attention. "When are we going to talk about the letter?"

"Now, if you'd like," she said, patting his arm with her other hand.

In her sweater pocket, she turned over the parchment with her fingers. The paper was smooth and tightly folded. It had arrived a week ago in the physical mail. She didn't need to remove it to know what it said though. She had read it over hundreds of times while Gabe had rested. The letter was in her father's handwriting, short and cryptic:

> Aliyah, rely on your teachings—Psalms 81:10 and Exodus 14:22—and yourself. Our exodus leads us away from home to Montana. Carry on my sprout, our parting should be so short. Love, mom and dad.

She did not understand exactly, why her father was not more direct. The biblical passages he referenced were known well to her, they spoke of God's provision and guidance. She could only believe that he was encouraging her to keep her faith and to come find them, somewhere in Montana. Her heart had yearned to seek her family out, but she had to ensure that Gabe was all right. He was alone since he had not notified his family of his admittance to the hospital. They had taken the symbol of unity. He knew if they came, they would implore him to take it upon himself as well— perhaps, with their best intentions, even against his will. In his fragile state he did not want to risk it.

Gabe waited for her response. His eyes were so patient and understanding. They told her that he would be accepting of any decision that she chose.

"I think we should both go," she spoke affirmatively.

"To Montana?"

"Yes."

"I'll go," he responded, without a moment's hesitation.

"Well, that was easy."

"After everything that has happened, I suspect most things will seem that way," he said. His thumb lightly stroked the top of her hand. "But before we get going, I need you to find me a bag of Skittles."

She laughed. "That's all you need?"

"I think so."

She kissed him on his forehead and headed to the door.

"Regular, right?"

"Yeah! I don't want any of those sour varieties."

"Okay, be right back!"

Aliyah exited Gabe's room and headed down the corridor to find the candy machines. On either side of her, the patient rooms connected to each other like rows of ice cubes. The walls of the rooms were set at varying levels of transparency depending on the preferences of those within and, next to each door, a screen displayed the name of the occupant. She read them silently as she walked, *Aldo Pace…Shondra Tice…Tim Rose…Sabastian Silva.*

Aliyah stopped flat on her feet. Peering through the transparent wall, she saw her mentor, Dr. Silva, laying in a bed with his eyes closed. Crowding behind him, an assortment of machines shot their tendrils of tubes and wires into the bed. She went in.

Drawing near, Dr. Silva appeared to be sleeping. His eyes were shut lightly and he breathed in steady intervals. His face had a sort of surprised look on it judging by the way his lips hung agape. The rest of him was tucked tightly under the sterile hospital sheets which had an odor of commercial washing to them. Aliyah looked him up and down and could not discern any ailment that might have befallen him. Only three tiny parallel scratches on his right temple seemed out of place.

"Why are you here?" she whispered aloud.

"That's a good question," an accented voice answered from behind her.

Startled, she turned to see two brilliant blue eyes gazing back at her. The eyes were attached to an olive-faced man standing in the doorway. A youthful twenty-something man, he wore a white lab coat that fell down above his knees. The name 'Dr. Mordechai' was embroidered in dull blue script lettering above the left breast pocket which was stuffed, rather sloppily, with a golden handkerchief.

"Hello there, I saw you on the camera. Do you know Dr. Silva?" he asked with a disarming grin as he approached closer.

"Yes, he's my graduate adviser," Aliyah replied.

"I see…the staff couldn't find any relatives to notify. I'm glad he has someone to visit him though, I don't think there has been many. That open letter on his nightstand is the only evidence of any visitation. I think a colleague came by to read it to him."

The doctor gestured to the table next to Dr. Silva's bed. An ivory piece of trifolded parchment was perched near an edge.

"You're free to read it if you like. It was left open," he added.

"Thanks. What happened to him?" she asked.

"I can't tell you much, for not much is known. I was told that they found him, in his lab, attached to some sort of memory machine. You know the one?"

"I do, but I only just started this year," she replied.

"Right. When they found him, he was unconscious, repeating his name over and over before babbling incoherently, and then…he went totally unresponsive. The EMTs thought he had a massive stroke when they brought him in. He's been in this condition for two weeks now. They've run numerous tests and cannot seem to figure out what's wrong or why he continues to be in a coma. The scans show that his brain is awash with activity, especially in the hippocampus regions, but his prefrontal cortex presents itself as a person who would have advanced Alzheimer's disease. It's baffling really," he said, rubbing his thick mat of black hair.

"Do you have any idea what could have happened?" he asked.

"No, like I said, I just joined the lab a few months ago and I'm not totally sure what that machine could have done to him. I do hope he got what he was searching for."

The doctor gave her a raised eyebrow and crossed his arms.

"Well...from the looks of him, perhaps it would have been best if he would have forgotten to remember the knowledge he sought. He concentrated that power of knowledge to become a king, but a king of one makes for a very lonely kingdom."

Aliyah stood wordless. Not understanding the doctor's meaning.

"Well, all right. If you don't have anything I can add to his chart, I'll leave you two alone. It was nice meeting you..."

"Aliyah," she responded.

"Aliyah. Have a good day." Turning on heel, he left.

Aliyah looked over at her mentor. The expression of surprise was still frozen on his face. Two leads ran down from one of the machines attached themselves to the sides of his forehead, monitoring his brain activity. They reminded her of the Mindsai, the machine that put him into that bed. *To be hooked up by more machines*, she thought.

She wondered if Dr. Silva's Mindsai could access his mind and bridge the gap for communication or, at least, to see his own memories of what befell him. *No*, she thought. *It is better to leave well enough alone.*

Her eyes came upon the note once more. Tilting her head, she padded over to the nightstand and leaned over it to begin reading softly to herself:

> Bash, my old friend. I wish we could have had one last sparring match before I left. The institution of New Eden leaves little fight for the academic pursuits. So, I think I might head westward. I could live like those stories I so loved as a boy like *Hatchet* and *Robinson Crusoe*. Some good

old self-reliance and providing from my own hands—not the shiny hands of our new alien overlords. Let's just hope they have not got taste for the human-sort. Nothing is worse than a truth we learn too late.

I'm going to Montana. I heard there is a former Army major (a chaplain of all people!) out there who started his own resistance group, The Wayward Sons and Daughters. I guess if my academic work was never revolutionary maybe I could try being one myself. I'm sure they will find a use for an old, shriveled brain like me.

Always your friend,
Christopher

Aliyah felt wetness in her eyes as she drew back towards the door. It was time to go.

"Goodbye, Professor Silva," she cried out in parting and then headed back down the hall to Gabe's room.

Gabe held a loose smile as they came pass the intake desk to leave the hospital. He was still sulking about the lack of Skittles for the road. She bared him no serious concern, he would get over it soon. She just wanted to find the exit but the hospital was a labyrinthine fusion of interconnected corridors and rooms. She decided to go up to the desk to ask for direction.

"Excuse me," she asked the middle-aged man standing at the desk. He had grey hair with black streaks and was reviewing something on a tablet. "Where is the main entrance?"

He didn't reply. He just pointed upwards at the digital directory hanging above the intake desk. A blinking red light indicated where they were on the map. They just needed to turn one more corner and they would be at the front doors.

As she was about to thank him, she stopped. The name on his lab coat read 'Dr. Mordechai.'

"Are you the only Dr. Mordechai that works at this hospital?"

"As far as I know, why?" he answered, combing a finger through his swept-back hair that curled around behind his ear.

"Oh, I was just wondering, thank you."

He gave her a puzzled look and got back to tapping on his tablet. She shook her head and sighed. *Can the world be this strange?* she thought, staring down an adjacent corridor. A small boy was walking towards her with his mother. His hair was red and seemed to be around eight-years-old. He was wearing a shirt depicting a dinosaur with a meteor shooting down from above. Below the dinosaur's feet were two words written in big block letters 'Never Forget.' She also noticed that the boy was cupping his palm with his other hand as if he were examining it with great curiosity. As they drew near, she could plainly see what had him so enthralled. On the palm of his right hand, a Unity Tree mark had just been made. Her eyes glanced back at the directory. The mother and child had just exited the corridor to Ward 1A. Aliyah grabbed Gabe's arm; it was time to go.

Out in the parking lot, they both climbed into Aliyah's vehicle. It was a small grey subcompact over a decade old that had just started to show signs of its age—a quarter-sized patch of rust had begun to take hold over the front-left wheel well. The rest of its body was marred by small fender dents and white scrapes on the doors. These were the tiny scars that marked the memory of the happy little accidents over her driving career. Each mark, its own valuable lesson.

Gabe choose to sit in the back as he wanted to rest a little for the long drive ahead. After helping him in, she took her seat up front and pushed the start button. The car ignited in a flurry of lights and the sound of an old-fashioned combustion engine starting up. The electric engine was so quiet it was hard to tell if it was engaged otherwise. Then an unprompted voice came through the dashboard. It had the tone of a British woman and though she had known it for years, it now seemed unfamiliar and creepy.

"Good evening, Aliyah! Where can I take you?" the automated drive assistant said.

"No thank you, I would like to drive tonight without assistance," she replied, disabling the system.

"All right, let's hope these sons and daughters are not too wayward for us to find in the big skies of Montana," she said allowed pushing on the accelerator to leave.

Out on the road, the air was a crystal blue and a full sun shone down on the little grey car barreling down the highway. She glanced up at the rear-view mirror. Gabe had already slumped over asleep against his window.

Her eyes refocused closer and looked at herself in the mirror. The wound around her eye was darkening and she could tell that the stitches were beginning to loosen. In time, the wound would heal, but there would be a scar. Her own unique mark. It would be an enduring memory of the past pain she had endured, good to be misremembered but not completely forgotten—a future reservoir of strength and resilience. Because she was not the same girl that started graduate school months ago, and she had no desire to turn back. For the present was a welcomed interruption to the past.

The car bumped up onto a bridge that spanned the dividing line between Virginia and West Virginia. In the westward sky, the unveiled setting sun filled her face with glorious red light. Like she had felt before, a warmth hugged her face, and she imagined how much bigger things would look in the treeless Great Plains of the West.

© SHANA RAMSOOK

ABOUT THE AUTHOR

Nathaniel J. Ratcliff was born in the small town of Chillicothe, Ohio in the winter of 1986. He began his writing career in high school by writing poetry for local library anthologies. From 2005 to 2009, he attended Miami University (of Ohio) and majored in psychology and political science before pursuing a Ph.D. in social psychology at The Pennsylvania State University, graduating in 2016. To date, his psychological research has yielded several peer-reviewed journal articles covering topics of memory, social power, leadership, and organizational behavior. Currently, Nathaniel works as a research psychologist, or data storyteller, at the University of Virginia in the United States. He resides in Springfield, Virginia with his wife, Shana, who is finishing her Ph.D. in psychology.

Notes